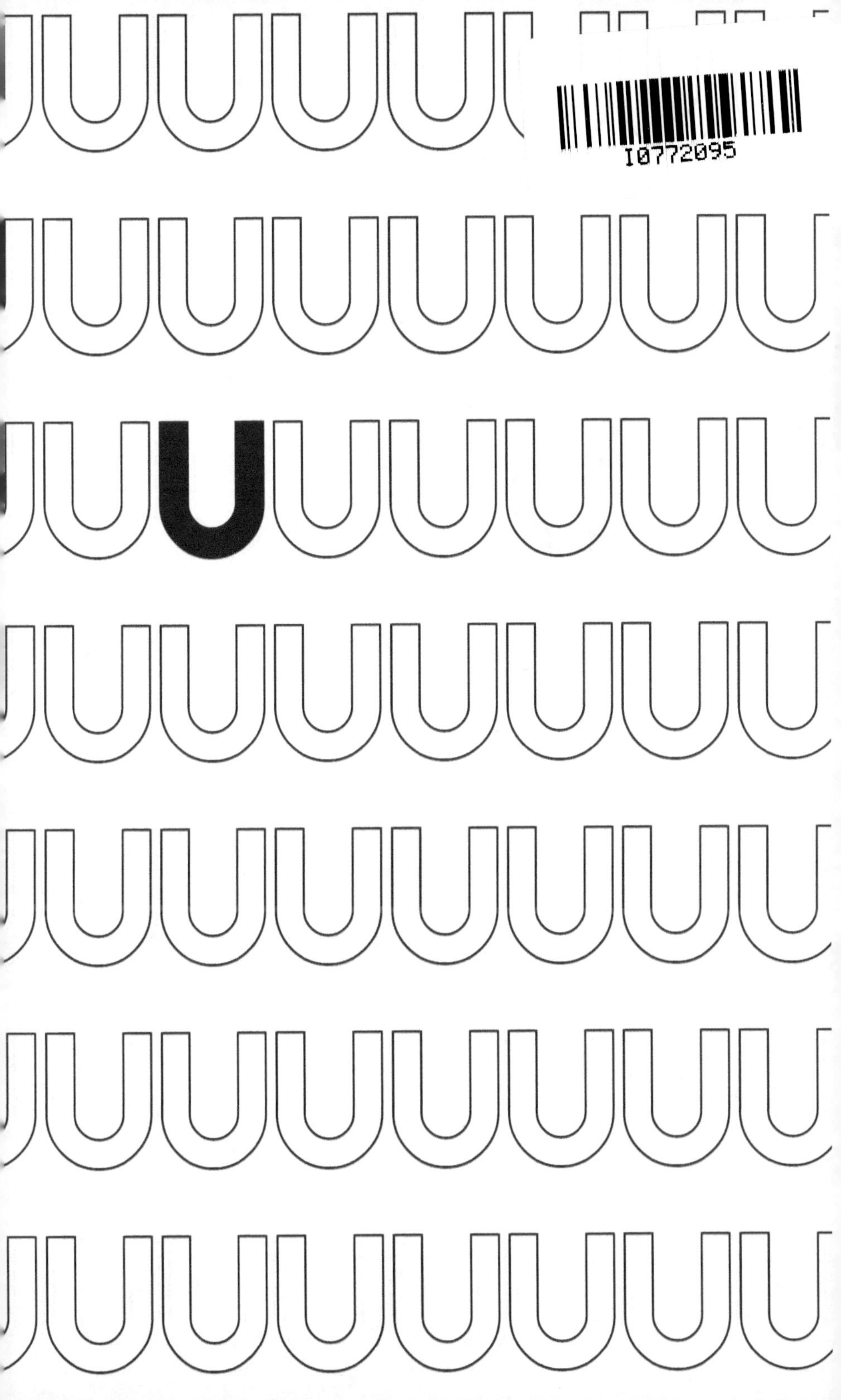

I0772095

About the Author

Carl Wilhoyte is from and of Ohio, the only state to ever actually exist. He admires dead malls, genuine American weirdness, and old forests (especially in late fall). He is also a speculative and literary fiction writer, and as a child of the internet, obsessed with the liminal border between reality and unreality. He was the editor-in-chief of *Zero Balance* and has been published in *Bourbon Penn*, *Abomination Magazine*, *Street Fight Radio*, and *District Sentinel*.

Bluesky: @carlwilhoyte.bsky.social

Website: carlwilhoyte.com

Cover art by John Michael Berry
Logo font by Muhammad Ariq Syauqi

Published by Zero Balance Media LLC
Copyright © 2024 Carl Wilhoyte

All rights reserved.

ISBN: 979-8-9911702-0-8

ULTIMART

CARL WILHOYTE

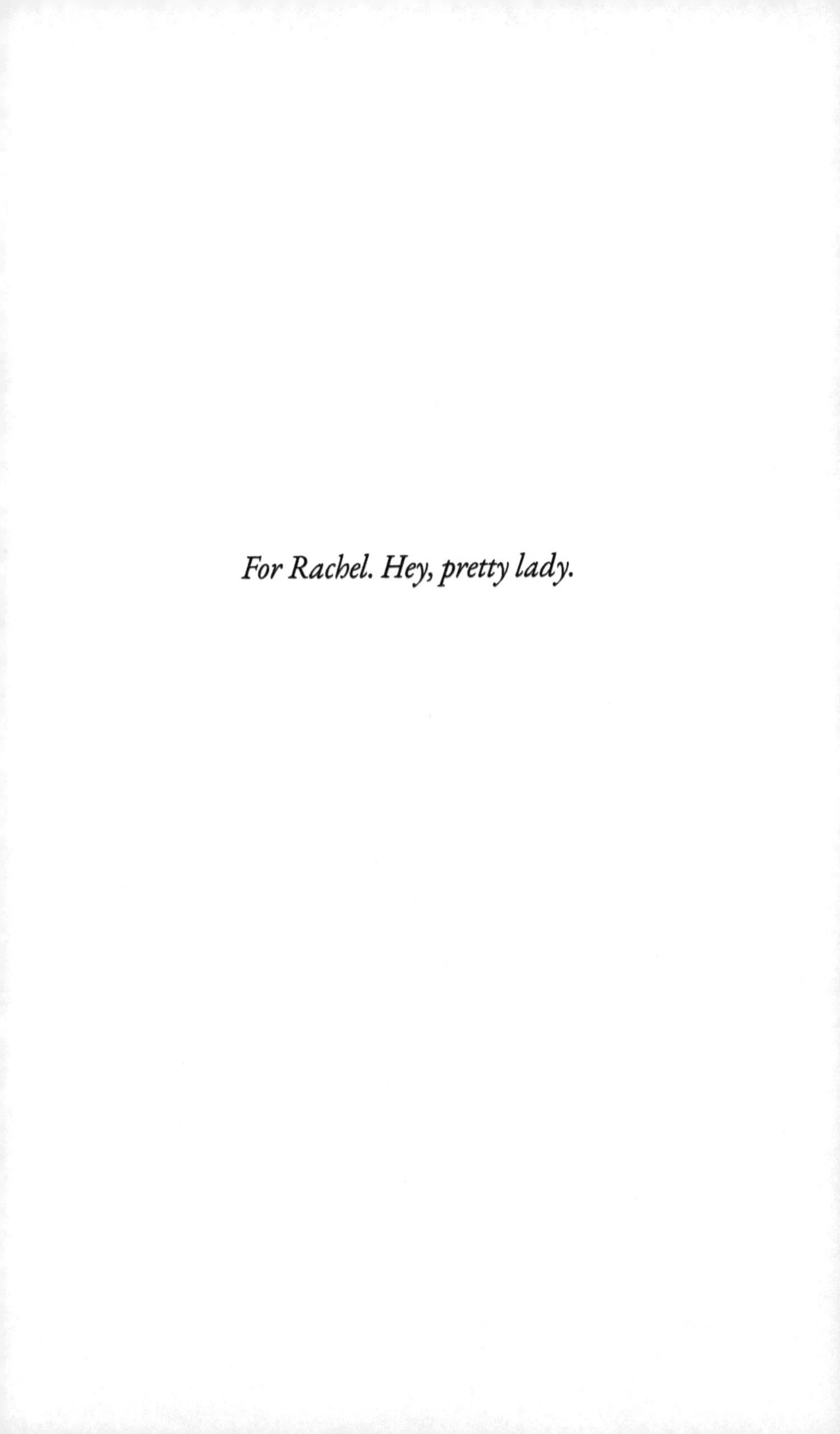

For Rachel. Hey, pretty lady.

1 ~ *home*

The digital sun rises in a television sky.

It passes an artificial cloud, then behind the Ultimart logo advertised on the series of billboards across from my unit. It's a channel that doesn't change very much, a TV in the background that you rarely notice. From where I'm standing, the sky looks immaculate, perfect, but when you zoom in and look closely, you can see the flawed pixels, smudges, scanlines.

My cloud is programmed like many others, but this cloud was meant for me, it moves at this exact moment with effortless ease. Some computer server in a closet determines where the clouds go, how much the breeze blows, the color of the sun. It is the cloud Ultimart wants me to see: light and happy without a care in the world, puttering along as if it were a real, tangible thing. It is more real than real, painstakingly randomized for maximum aesthetic value. Designed to be noticed for a moment and then immediately ignored. The cloud is a pretty image without the possibility of storms, anger or disappointment, hinting at a seemingly infinite blue expanse sloping above us. Above me, above all of us, rises the Dome and its shocking brilliance in that television sky.

Beyond it, there might as well be nothing. To me, this is the only sky I've ever known.

Bathed in fluorescent, imitation sunlight, my paint brush lovingly colors the nearly translucent leaf with a swift practiced stroke, smoothly coating it green in a single motion from stem to tip, allowing the light red veins in the plastic frond to almost glow. I inspect the plant. Satisfied, I move to the next leaf, finishing it with the same careful efficiency. There is a faint but pleasant chemical odor. Normally, the air smells like nothing.

Black Friday smells like blood and burning tar.

Even the toxic stink is welcome and even though it's just a day away, its reek billows over the Dome to announce itself. It is coming and I am trying not to think about it. That's why I'm up here: hiding, thinking.

I stroke the fresh petal, rub the plastic between my thumb and forefinger, explore the thing as if I have never seen or touched it before. I am fascinated by the green, lose myself in the tiny drawn veins, rather than living in the Dome, with all these things and people bouncing off of each other like the plastic stones on the beaches, the colored water that makes it that shiny blue. If I had to place itself in the lifecycle of say, a plastic plant, I would be at the moment it is about to be thrown away.

Not really sure when I woke up this morning or even if I went to bed. The nights, four hours long, are controlled by the electronic sun rising and falling so quickly. I dream of things in the opaque fog reaching out to me, or the black oil dripping from my eyes, pooling in my cupped hands like a little oil spill.

The sidewalk looks so very far away down the side of my building. I feel dizzy, a gnawing in my gut. It's worse these days, as bad as it's ever been. Something terrible is happening inside me. Small walking dots, people milling about, criss-crossing the courtyard.

An opaque smoke rises from the cracks in the walls. It lies to you. It ties the strings around my wrists and I feel the pulling and tugging as you lurch forward through what I call my life. Not just the fog, but a dark, infinite energy wave emanating in hot pulses from everything I touch or see.

I drop my plant.

That dark energy remains, written into the letters of UCorp's name everywhere I see. UCorp runs Ultimart, who runs the Dome, who runs us all. The real power is the smiling face, the polite "we're sorry, that's not possible" performed by a computer voice, that life you see and want so deeply just a fingertip length out of reach, the four hour night. The panic.

Yet there is that wonderfully slow, hot coiling growing tighter and tighter down in my guts. I feel on the edge of something beautiful maybe. The Ultimart Logo, the stupid smirking face and it breaks into pieces and layers and something awful is behind that smiling.

My phone beeps with a UNet reminder.

I promised Dad I would visit him soon, and the notification reminds me to pick him up a gift. It even suggests I get him a Vorto Box, and I'm not even quite sure what that is.

I imagine myself looking down at the top of my own head, and then the top of another head, like putting two mirrors together. All the way down to the spiraling landfill of myself. In reality, there are no dumps in the Dome. Everything is recycled automatically by the underground machines, and because it's good for the environment, it's good for me.

The plant I dropped is rolled over on its side. The foam dirt has spilled. I replace the foam, straighten the petals, place it back in its spot on the shelf.

I store my supplies in the hidden box, and walk to the roof elevator.

A TV on the far wall of the tube scans me, knows I have a son, and plays an ad for Joob, and a 3D green-vomit neon can spins and flashes and no one knows what it's for, but I know Axel will still want it. My head splits in two and Joob is a blotchy mess of shapes.

Violent red blood flushes into my cheeks and I want to smash the thing into shards, but I find the button, press it ever so gently. I carefully enter the maintenance code to bypass the ride fee. I learned if you press the 3, 6, and 9 buttons and the emergency release, the elevator thinks you're part of a fire suppression team and you can ride for free. The elevator groans like a robotic corpse, hovers for a moment over nothingness, then descends.

The cracked plastic window shows me the skyline as it zips downwards. My family lives in a vertical block, concrete boxes of apartments a hundred stories high. Clear mesh screens are pulled between the chrome handrails, to avoid pitching over into the hundred meter drop. Those better off, fitter, happier, have clear plastic that doesn't smudge. Stretching down into the dark, the canyon between the buildings curves away pleasantly, like a smiling axe handle. A rank smell of old plastic and garbage. There is always a low buzzing cacophony of noise: TVs inside cramped apartments, people screaming at nothing, power lines humming, cars whooshing by.

I wear the nothingness of this place like my disposable paper clothes. These stacked units look like cartoons of homes, a shabby attempt to make us feel like we're living somewhere with green astroturf and a big backyard and the big sun lightbulb hovering over us.

I reach the ground.

The doors open to the courtyard, strewn with trash, populated by a few late night partiers sleeping it off, hunched bodies clutching plastic vomit buckets. They wear garish neon clothes meant to glow in UV light. Graffiti covers nearly every flat surface on the ground floors. Motion ads cover every other inch, ads for nutrient bars, attractive ladies drinking fashionable alcohol, silver cars zooming across open plains, a campaign ad for Blu, one for Red, Black Friday sales, sexy pills. I even saw one of my ads once, for a vacation hotel at Lush Island Resorts. In the middle of the courtyard, an artist put a giant chrome skull about the size of an SUV. Near a rancid metal dumpster, a woman in a peach colored jumpsuit holds the hair back of her inebriated friend as she hurls up orange guck into a drain.

The light's too bright, the air's thick like water. I think I haven't slept longer than an hour in days, but I'm not sure, time gets fuzzy. You just float a few feet off the ground, and I've just been running on Koffee and handfuls of pills. My skin is too tight.

A red smoke grenade is popped and tossed against a rough spraypainted explosion on the wall. It's not Security, just some DJ who's party isn't quite over yet. Skinny men with gas masks, hunched over, skitter about jumping from light poles, vaulting over barricades, whooping and hollering like ferals. They have grimy faces, shadow people with stars for eyes.

The sickly neon sun burns down on us all.

They ignore me, I'm no fun. The woman in the peach jumpsuit is on fire, her friend vomiting flame, but neither are running or screaming, just hugging her arms close to her chest, lava pouring out of her mouth. Sulfur stink gushes into me. The streets turn sideways into choking cramped muscles flexing and gleaming while I stumble forwards. I am jerked along by metal strings along that golden road to the door that opens when I approach, as if it was meant for me alone.

~~~~

The Number works like a gun pressed up against your head. Yes, you are free to pursue all the opportunities in the world to make your mark. Yet that Number will still be there, bloody red, pulsating in the dark, a raw heart of your home, growing slowly like cancer. They tell you it's just a handy guide for making sound financial decisions.

You wouldn't tell this from the debt settlement commercials. Normally, a woman is packing her suitcase, kisses her husband goodbye, and then we see her in a yellow hard hat pulling a lever of
~~~~

some kind in a metal hallway. She gives up the thumbs up, as if to say "everything's going to be okay." It's not. It never is.

Last year my neighbor Herb Conway, who lives down the line, was hauled screaming out of his house by a squad of Security officers. I wasn't sleeping very well so I came down from the roof. They pepper sprayed him until his eyes bled and left him handcuffed to the railing. I knew better than to get involved. There are semi-popular videos of vigilantes barricading themselves in their homes, and the commentary is always "Brave mother / father defends home from Security". Notice how those sympathetic headlines don't mention the fact why that brave mother is being pummeled by Security.

They restrained Herb and his two boys. For the kids, they got garish plastic masks with cartoon faces on them. One's a fireman, the other's a soldier. He got a plain blue hood and kicked in the back of the knee to get down. They regularly do this in the middle of the night, to catch them sleeping.

Most people go quietly, assume their fate. Herb went loudly until a foot practically crushed his nose in. I watched the whole thing.

The next morning there was the stain in front of his door: a smeary mess leading off into the Dome.

I found out what happened to him. I don't want to think about it right now.

I go around the back to my rear door, placing my finger on the bright blue panel, unlocking it. When my wife Raylene and I rented the house, the tour video told me it only detects living skin, so if a thief cut off your hand, it wouldn't work.

Thank you for the reassurance.

Inside is my home, a series of small, cramped square rooms with beige carpeting and rattling air conditioning. A warm, stale smell like from a soggy pair of shoes. The apartment is a standard model H unit we rent from the local consortium. There's always someplace worse to live, and Raylene, Axel and I have carved out this little piece of our own. When we applied to license our son, part of the requirements was a model H, the suburban vertical unit.

I need to do a quick check of our Number. It's not like just a bank account balance, but rather a combination of metrics. Credit score, social media traction, purchasing power, etcetera all rolled into one. Too much into debt, too few UNet followers, not enough purchases made the right way, and it dips. It's good to be green, mellow to be yellow, and better dead than red.

I pull up the app and a symbol like a speed dial appears. We're right in the lower quarter of yellow, which is where something like 75% of all people are right now. So good to be part of the club. We've managed to stay above water by borrowing when we need to, paying back the minimums, and keeping our heads down.

Going red is the fast-track to having your child be reassigned to a family with a "better situation".

If they're lucky, they may, just may, get sponsored by a family in the Sprawl and they can limp on working off their sponsorship answering phone calls in a cube farm. You hear about other things that can happen to kids. I don't want to think about it and no one knows the truth. Maybe it's just rumors, but I doubt it. Whatever happens to Axel, you and Raylene "go downstairs" like a toilet flush. Like Herb. I think about him every now and then.

There's an entire industry dedicated to managing red liners' suffering, handling their affairs before they get shipped down by buying all of their property and accounts for pennies. The official story is always one of miraculous, last-minute economic recovery, but the rumor is that it's a constant stream heading down.

Most people when forced with red line bankruptcy make a mature, informed decision based upon a logical assessment of their options and just kill themselves.

Raylene's on our bed still knocked out. I slip through the living room, enter our bedroom, sit on the edge of the bed and just think.

Her alarm goes off. It works with her sleeping pills and the tone jolts her right awake. She sees me on the edge, not sleeping, and knows where I've been. I feel ashamed for some reason, like I'm having an affair with my dream world.

"Hey you," she says warmly.

"Hey."

She doesn't say anything else, just wraps her arms around me and grips me tight. I clutch her hand, kiss it, feel her small heat behind me. I get up for the shower.

"May I join you?" she says, playfully biting her lip.

I really want her to, but it's too expensive. Blue water shower prices have been gradually rising and we're already too close to the red for the month.

I give her a tight, apologetic smile. "Sorry, I have to get going."

She's disappointed. "Oh, that's okay." But it's not okay. "I know you're in a rush, but can you drop Axel off at Training this morning?

"I don't know. There's some big stupid meeting this morning and I really need to be on time."

"I'll get him ready?" she says, bargaining.

Axel is like many children all across the Dome; a turbulent force of nature. Trying to get him to focus on anything longer than a commercial break takes drastic measures.

"Fine, I can take him," I say.

She slowly blinks her eyes and breathes out, like I've lifted an enormous weight from her shoulders. I love her, love her weird smile, the way she points to the sky and lets out a fart, like she's announcing its arrival. When we were first together, she was my Amazonian Warrior woman. We were both young and furious and unstoppable. Not so much now.

"Do you think it would be funny if I just started rotting in bed?" She rubs her midsection and giggles.

I jump on top of her on the bed and she squeals in delight.

"Only if you, like, really let yourself go. Scorched earth. You could start this whole new trend. We could do a UNet stream of you slowly starving to death. People watching you scroll on your phone, watching you watching other streams."

"I like that. We could take bets on which of my teeth would fall out first."

The moment grows quiet as we lay together on the bed. There's an ocean of time between us.

"I love you," I whisper.

And then it's gone. Her eyes go blank, her face slack as some unseen darkness washes over her. I can't control it and I am powerless to do anything now. Her moods just needs to run their course. She buries her face in my neck and I hold her close.

"I know you just want to help," she whispers.

"Because I love you."

"I know."

"What... what the hell am I supposed to say to that?" I get up and sit on the corner of the bed.

"I don't know. Remember you're taking Axel to Training, if you still can."

"Sure. Whatever."

I don't have time for a shower, so I just wipe myself down. Disposable towelettes that slightly sting my skin and leave me smelling like furniture polish.

Normally, I'd take a seven minute shower, my phone informing me our account has been billed. Our shower drain is broken and always stays open, so I can piss there to save the six dollars on the toilet flush.

On the vending rack in the closet, a new set of disposable clothes is ready. I break them out of the plastic. Blue button down shirt and beige khakis. Brown plastic shoes. The shirt and pants have a texture like paper towels; a thin, rough fabric that disintegrates into shreds after a few days. I toss yesterday's duds down into the recycler.

Now dressed, I step out into the house and a wall of noise smashes back into me, noise from the TV, appliances, music turned all the way up, and voices all screaming at full volume. Raylene is shouting to Axel to please get up off the floor. Axel squirms and twists, so badly I first think he is having a seizure and screams "rah rah rah" over and over, so loud his small neck might burst open. This miniature war happens in the living room, and I wander through to the fridge, casually scrolling through the screens for breakfast. Nothing looks good, but I swipe and select 3 Xmas Chows, which appear with a thunk. I order 2 Koffees, one for me, one for Raylene. I buy 30 seconds of hydro heat in the microwave, pop in the boxes and breakfast is ready.

I give Axel his daily Rodoral in his drink and he grabs my arm. He's transfixed on the 3D TV once I let him go. His strength is sometimes inhuman, leaving a red handprint on my bicep. A dose of Slurora will be coming soon as he eats to balance him out. A little too much or one or the other and he's feral.

Axel watches colored explosions, sugary characters throwing knives at each other, guns shooting rainbows. He mildly shakes as the Slurora hits him and then he finally grows quiet. A little smile creeps across his face. I mute every screen and it's finally quiet. Raylene gently rubs my arm as I sit and I weakly smile at her. Her own chemicals are finding their equilibrium.

Both her arms are covered in colorful tattoos, from shoulder to wrist, something she's very proud of. They're tastefully done, and I love their angry beauty. I twist the cap off my bottle of Koffee and down the entire thing in a single gulp, feeling the warm rush fill me.

Raylene touches up her tan with the mini spray gun. She's a fashion therapist, helping people make better fashion decisions and cope with their wardrobe choices. We orbit each other like twin suns. We thought nothing could hurt us. I don't know what happened. Maybe nothing happened.

These two people are alien creatures to me now. A slow white fog creeps in my periphery. I push it away.

We eat in silence. Axel then yells that he needs his Big Boys changed, and Raylene takes him to his room to get cleaned up. When he comes back, Raylene gives him his dose of Requiet and gives him an ice cream pouch, which he greedily sucks. Axel stares at his lap as he sucks, his Rodoral and Requiet and Slurora mixing and bouncing off each other like electrons.

"Maybe we should cut him back a little," I say, watching his eyes flick over nothing.

"Yeah, maybe you're right," she says, not looking at me.

She throws the TV remote on the couch, and starts to gather her things to leave for the day. One last check in the mirror. She kisses Axel on the cheek. Axel stops, places his pouch down very slowly, as if having to document every step in his brain.

Axel moves his hand up and down mechanically, like he's eating invisible food. I want my son to grow up like those kids you see in the ads for the drugs we give him: happy, smiling, playing soccer, running on a beach somewhere, landing the big deal. He doesn't run anymore. We go to the beach sometimes and look at the freshly dyed water.

<div align="center">~~~~</div>

Ten minutes later, Axel and I arrive at the station and wait. The Training Success Line is a network of skylines that transport kids to and from their daily sessions. Axel starts to get fidgety and starts making that soft "rah rah rah" noise again. I don't have my phone with me, so I can't show him anything. Thankfully, there are Short Laffs playing on the station columns, little one-liner jokes scientifically designed to brighten our day. I don't laugh, but it's nice to have something to just look at.

With a horrid metallic groan, the Training Line, painted an awful mustard yellow, screams to a halt on the platform. A handful of other parents are there, looking as drained and exhausted as I do. On the side of the Training Line, there's a screen near our faces. Driver Dan, the mascot for the Line, flies out from his netherworld and greets Axel. The image is programmed to look the child right in the eyes with his own creepy, unblinking stare.

"How is our happy camper today?!"

"He's good," I say, my voice as dry as air conditioning.

The face slowly turns up to me, its grotesque gaping smile plastered across its cheeks. It drops down to Axel like a predator.

"That's good to hear! Hello there, AXEL SCAGGS." The name comes out in robotic efficiency. "Welcome aboard, Trainees!"

The doors swoosh open and a blast of chilly air hits us. I push Axel inside with the twenty or so other kids, on his spot with the smiley face, hook his Kid-Stop up to the railing, and take a moment to give him a hug. He doesn't hug back. The driver's digital face on a nearby screen politely scolds me to leave. I pay Axel's fare. The doors cut us apart.

Training is a period of my life I don't really remember. I used to be on some of the same meds as Axel, and Training feels like a smeary blur. They mainly watch videos and take simple tests. I think Training makes sure they can do things like use touchscreens, understand pictographs, and understand the general rules of the Dome. They learn about Bargainville. That's where you go when you hit the red too badly. Downstairs. It's one of the "Opportunity Centers" located down there. Typically, you only attend Training until you're 13, then it's assignment to a Chik-N-Lil or something basic like that. If you can afford Executive Training, then you get taught other things, I think, like how to write and read text, a pretty rare skill in the Dome. My dad splurged on me.

Most interfaces have pictures or one or two buttons for convenience, or use a voice prompt. There's no official stats, but something like 85% of Ultimart can't decipher text, having to depend on pictographs and simple one word instructions. I'm a rare commodity.

Stop. Go. Eat. Don't. Sleep. Here. Buy.

Axel tested out of any Executive Training at an early age. I was a rare case, I actually learned how to read text as part of my Marketing training during my 13's. I kept up with it far beyond what I needed for the various jobs I had. Not sure why I bothered, but it felt good to know something everyone else didn't. It felt like I had a secret.

Outside the bus, I wave to Axel, his head tilted back. He weakly tries to wave, but instead just wipes his hand down the window. The skyline carriage pulls up and away and he disappears into the distance around a bend through a rat's nest of wires and steel beams.

A sudden tightness grips me like a fist in my chest, slow, colorful streaks like stains in a gun barrel. There are nothing but insects behind walls. Giant gears cranking undead life. The entire platform rising and falling with the weight of my breath, oxygen in and out, expelling poison gas outwards to be recycled by that same invisible, violent engine.

The Machine.

I run at full speed towards Brand Street and pass through tunnels packed with neon colors and lights flashing, filled with ever-changing odors. One stretch: lemon-pine, the next: honeysuckle. Surfaces here appear spotless, clean, and new, unlike my pockmarked skin, crisscrossed with worry lines, old craters of picked pimples, flecked with troublesome moles, beneath the sparse patches of brown hair I desperately cling to. Even as I run, I continually compare myself to each passerby. A tall, well-to-do statue with a sculpted chin, with thick arms and legs, his massive weight almost denting the walkway. A tanned, white-haired shark practically screaming into an earpiece.

Brand Street comes into view as I exit the platform tunnels outside the edge of my stacked house block. I stare at the sky wordlessly for several minutes.

A car door opens and I snap towards it.

A neighbor of mine, Axton, is getting into his new car in a nearby parking spot. The vehicle is a Bolero: a burnt orange candy-burst hue shining like a newborn metal insect. All cars are actually electric, but you can buy one with a special engine like this one that roars and growls like an old gasoline model. Gasoline is made of dinosaur bones crushed under enormous pressure for millennia. I learned that on UNet. The Bolero is a self-driver, even the ability to kill oneself in a traffic accident has been erased. Most just throw themselves off a roof or commit suicide by Security. They go into a taco joint and just start shooting, Security shows up and mows them down. If they're lucky, they get a weekly spot on Blood Bath, a streaming show about workplace murders.

I reach out to touch the smooth, sensual curve of the car's hip. Axton is about to step in, but see me admiring his beauty. Inside the car are two men I don't know, one is asleep in the backseat behind the driver's seat. I'm too jacked up to sleep now, the Koffee and panic firing through me like hot needles. Just like the inevitability of mass murder, complex algorithms cause the cars to change lanes, speed up or slow down, so everyone gets to work on time. The shooter feels pulled towards a certain destiny, fired along like they themselves are a bullet, powerless to stop the sudden impact and screams of blood.

"Bolero. Complete primo. I know," Axton says. His voice sounds like oil.

"How much was she?" The question is almost automatic.

"Not cheap. But they got this new auto-repay flex plan. Makes it sooooo easy."

"Auto-replay flex plan," I repeat. The words arouse me.

From the crack in the open window, I am immersed in the intoxicating odor of New Car.

"No doubt. It has a drop transmission, doublewide calipers, a big, fat fusion delocator, and the most executive warranty."

"That sounds awesome." I have no idea what any of those things are. I just like the jargon and how it flows.

"You know what? I think this primo baby wants to take us to the next level."

I let out a little noise. "Oh, man. I wouldn't bother. These types of relationships are so high maintenance." Axton is scrolling through his phone, looking at an endless stream of hairstyles for his UNet avatar. He nods in agreement.

The growing population of men engaged in serious, long term commitments to their cars is more common than it used to be. Axton presses a button and the car wakes, rising slightly on its suspension. A satisfying hum emanates from the hood, like when Raylene moans when she's near orgasm.

"We're trying things out right now. Testing the waters. Unfortunately, I have to bug out. These two gentlemen are actually 3Drive customers. Dropping them off on the way in. Happy to give you a 3Drive if you have an account."

I really want to be inside Summer. But I shouldn't.

"Nah, I got my own lady back in the garage."

He smiles, nods. "Sure you do," he says, in such a way that you don't quite know if he's laughing at you or not.

"Catch you later. Peace," he says, waving two fingers. "Hey Summer, take us to work, baby."

"Whatever you say, big boy." Summer has a deep, husky female voice. The window slowly closes and Summer disappears into the smooth flowing lanes of other gorgeous cars.

~~~~

I hide my lease in an unauthorized spot barely big enough for it. I slip into the alley tucked away between two buildings near my own. It's in one of those types of spots you have to hunt for, saves
~~~~

me on renting a parking spot. I whip the blue tarp off, salvaged from a nearby construction project, and reveal the dented doors, busted headlight, scratched windshield. It looks like a squished hamburger box with square corners and stains. A 12 month lease from Car Town, one of the few shitboxes left that fit my price range.

I cram myself in and voiceprint. The shitty biometric reader takes forever to read my palm print on the wheel. I wonder why does it even bother; no one would steal this thing, they wouldn't even set it on fire for fun. My current remaining mileage pops up, and it burns an angry red negative. I'm way over for the month and I need to glitch out the odometer again. I discovered by accident that if you reset the radio streams at the same time as attempting a system firmware update, it'll get confused and crash the onboard network connection. For some reason, it'll forget the last 200 miles or so on the clock. When I figured this out, I waited several days and there was no adjustment, no angry call from Car Town IT, so there you go.

I mash the radio stream button while the progress bar jitters and shakes on the dashboard. There's a high-pitched whine, a screech, and the entire car goes dead. While it reboots, I wait staring at the blank odometer screen. It takes what feels like a year to start back up, but when it does, the odometer hasn't changed. I try it again. Same result. My heart pounds and there's that cold metal feeling in my stomach again. They must've patched it. I grip the wheel so hard it groans, the plastic straining underneath. I stop, my mind going blank. They just patched it, that's all. Bound to happen sooner or later.

Nothing will happen. Nothing will happen. You're fine. Everything will be okay. Just go to work. Just go.

I press the power button and the car starts up with some effort, the batteries crackling and a hot stink blowing in my face from the vents. I choose "Work" from the list of destinations and sit back. My calves ache from the weird angle I need to sit at. There's not enough room to turn, so the car's wheels turn 90 degrees to the right and skillfully slips sideways out of the impossibly small parking spot.

The voices from the radio all mix together in a soup. The hypnotic hum of traffic is like a river, slipping through the maze of underpasses, each car a tiny universe hovering inches from each other, just about to touch. The tiny microcosm of chit-chat on the radio isolates me in the plastic womb of the car, enveloped in the comforting emptiness. I listen to my podcast about homework strategies the Son could be using. It's a spirited conversation and I vote for a private tutor in the viewer poll at the end. It'd be nice to see a new face on the show.

Ten minutes go by as the car silently cuts through the automated traffic. I lay back in a cottony half-dream doze. Someone like Axton wants his hands on the wheel, even though it's impossible for him to direct the driving system unless it's an emergency.

A billboard has a woman tossing her hair back on a beach, an ice cold drink dripping water onto her heaving breasts. A rich man tucks a successful fist underneath his chin, advertising a luxury watch wrapped around his enclosed fingers. Their eyes are too clear, hair too slick and perfect, and they stare at each other with that crystalline sense of purpose that I do not have. I would dive into that water at a moment's notice, hating every second, but happy to be free of the now and the tomorrow.

My son smears his drugged hand against the window. My wife's hip as she sleeps in bed. The silence now in the car rises above me like a tidal wave, but it doesn't crash down, just rising and rising forever. I swallow it down.

2 ~ *work*

I walk up from the parking garage and check in at the front security
desk. Infinite Solutions has a gleefully paranoid attendance policy,
so you need a biometric check-in at the start of every shift. They
scan your fingerprint so no one sneaks in and steals all of the
incredibly important advertising we're pumping out in here. The
whole thing is theater: the guard stands, the cameras, the check-in.
I don't really see the point.

I've been at Infinite Solutions for the last six years as a Junior
Advertising Executive. The building is a glass box molded in
concrete, black steel, and cold fluorescent lighting. Honestly, I
don't really remember how I got the job at Infinite Solutions. It
just kind of happened. I think I was referred to the job by a temp
agency and they just forgot about me. So I stayed.

The box I occupy for 72 hours a week is smashed up against a
multitude of other high-art cubes, intersected by sloping carways
and circular support columns, a confusing mess of people, work,

business, colliding and crushing against each other. Light shafts filter through the carways and platforms above, pools in yellow squares, lines, dotted patterns from chain-link fences and the concrete noise buffers. Billboards shift ads outside its windows, changing images, faces to new opportunities, new wants, new excitements right beyond the glass walls outside your touch.

They promise escape. They promise everything.

Outside, cars silently shoot by like bullets, violently carrying other people to other boxes, like me, to boxes in boxes, the building lobby to the elevator, each a smaller one than the last, until I'm walking out of the elevator onto our floor, then to my cube.

If our building wasn't populated by adults, you'd think that you were inside a playground on a cartoon show. The walls are stark white, naked in their emptiness, with colorful photographs of people giving each other the thumbs up, high-fives, winning the Big Account, nailing That Sale. Everyone is smiling. Everyone is happy. On the Path to the Good Times. Hanging In There. Motivated. Engaged. Primed for Action. Animal Instincts. The frames are small screens which change images every thirty seconds, so you get a continual Cycle of Success.

Part of me would greatly like to morph into one of those smiling maniacs, assume that shape with those clothes and good hair.

I'm slowly losing my hair at odd intervals, and Raylene kindly assures me that I'm not, but I am. I run my hand obsessively across my scalp, feeling for thin spots. Looking for missing pieces of me that slipped away in the night, in the shower. I started collecting my hair in a little baggie until Raylene found it and made me throw it out. She's not someone that has secrets.

My plastic shoes squish on the sickly bright green carpet, with globular patches of dark green at irregular intervals like urine stains. All the conference tables and counters are curved white shapes, sloping in circles and droplets around corners to create an overall sense of "playfulness". Bright primary color coat surfaces with a glossy sheen.

Everyone at work is a walking skeleton, pounding on their keyboards and clicking mice with furious urgency. No one talks, but the tiny plastic sounds and that tapping sound of touchscreens is like a chorus, an ocean of work. People move mechanically but purposefully, getting over the four hour nights by adding supplements to their Koffee, chemical concoctions of a variety of stimulants and necessary energy vitamins. People pour it into giant thermal mugs with bending straws, but I prefer the patch because I'm not a huge fan of the metallic taste. A man with a giant blonde wig uses an eye syringe to inject himself right in his tear duct outside the pay toilet, while the older woman in the floral print dress sticks with an inhaler mask, sucking down huge gasps of aerosol.

Black Friday has added extra glass into our blood. The office is a maelstrom of activity.

Our desks are arranged in honeycomb fashion, so I'm always facing 5 other employees to promote Workful Interactions and Sense of Community. Mostly I get to watch them slowly age while I age reflected on my screen. I thumbprint in and my day starts.

The computer, a shiny, grey box that sometimes smells like burning hair, clicks on, humming low. Our logo appears on the screen.

"Good Morning, Corwin," it says in a dusky female voice. "Hello.".

A comforting smiley face fades into view on the screen. I stare for a good thirty seconds, unblinking.

There needs to be a better word for boring, but at least we can bring music, which I almost can never listen to because the brunette, sweatered lady behind me always listens to that obnoxious show on her headset. I can see the tiny video screen out of my periphery. Every five seconds or so, she cackles out loud. Which after nine or ten hours, boils my blood.

She's watching a show in her video headset, a set of glasses that displays UNet content in a never ending stream of garbage. The glasses overlay information about the Dome, or whatever you're looking at in real time. Most people just use the facial recognition software to search for nude pictures of people they're having lunch with.

She's watching one of those shows where they've scientifically engineered the exact art and subtle science of public humiliation. They call it Donkey Punch. For example, they get a woman who's eager to get pregnant and end up putting a fake, misshapen fetus in her, only to reveal it was latex all along. My coworker cackles with delight.

Or they trick a Chik-N-Lil worker into thinking he's won the Lottery. He yells and screams at all the other co-workers that have wronged him in the past, then to reveal he doesn't have a single extra cent afterwards. Hilarious.

Or the random nobody slowly being crushed like he's in a trash compactor, constantly worrying about his sickly father, trying to understand how to be a decent father himself, a husband who can't figure out how to love his wife, and who is repulsed and nauseated by the world that surrounds him. Someone with no way out, who will probably end up throwing himself off the roof, with the camera crew discovering his hysterically pathetic "garden". They discover his obsession with the Wife, which is good for a snicker.

This show goes on for thirty-seven years. There's no punchline.

My screen comes up. My work queue appears and I start. The purpose of the Junior Advertising Executive is to fix AI generated images for personalized UNet ads. Too many fingers, mishappen faces, mouths like horrors, fucked up text, that sort of thing. They're called "units".

Vast server farms analyze web traffic, spending habits, biometrics, movement patterns, health records, gaze timings, phone call transcripts, and even solid waste samples to create hyper-targeted ads for an individual's UNet account. Your fecal matter has peanuts in it? It gauges how many peanuts are in your shit and then lets you know it's time to buy more. The new image appears on my screen, and I drag over targeted digital images and place them in pre-selected spots. I take away extra heads. I add smiley faces, warnings, and other explanatory icons. I click the happy face indicating I'm done. I will do this thousands of times today.

Also at the end of the day the highest performer gets a star sticker for their employee account page. Lowest performer gets a permanent pay reduction. Three days as lowest and you get canned.

You can't even put the image in the wrong place or add something that's not supposed to be there, not at my level. The system somehow knows you left something wrong in. The screen will flash an angry red, let off an annoying beep inside your headphones, and you have to start all the way over from the beginning.

Across from me, a new employee motions to me. I pull down my headphones and look up. I'll make up the time later. I don't even know his name and I don't ask. He looks like he came out of the pod too early. He's hairless from head to toe, and wears a white button-up shirt that makes him look transparent.

"I don't get it," he says.

"What's to get?"

"Okay, so... if our job is to fix things that are wrong, but the screen tells you if you missed something. Why doesn't it just fix itself?"

"So you're making the compelling argument that you shouldn't have a job."

I seem to have stumped him. If he quits, it's more work for me but one less person to play against.

"Listen, you're confused and my advice is to simply be confused. It doesn't matter. Just don't be last for the day."

He nods. "What's your strategy?"

"I don't gotta be the best. I just have to be faster than you."

"You'd think we'd want to help each other out," he says, a little hurt.

"You'd think you'd want to stop yapping and get going. I've already done three during this conversation."

Answering with any sincerity means no job, no house, nothing but a blood red Number and the Machine. The poor guy doesn't get it yet, but he will. If he doesn't, tough. He looks at me with a confused twist in his face and sits back down.

I'm in the fog now. I work. I make good pace.

~~~~

After lunch, there's an announcement over the loudspeaker for a mandatory team meeting.

"WE WILL BE DISCUSSING YOUR HOPES AND DREAMS. PLEASE BE IN THE CONFERENCE ROOM AT SIXTEEN HUNDRED FOR A GROUP HUDDLE. HAVE A SPARKLING DAY, WINNERS!"

I love the fact they call us a team when we would easily knife each other in the gut for easy units or a few hours of PTO or a measly medical voucher. They did toy around with the idea of a talent show or perhaps a fight night, but I'm not holding out for either. I would love to see these people beat the living piss out of their friends. Maybe the older man with pinched eyes and sweaty ears takes on the entire customer service department in a marathon bloodbath.

I contemplate faking an uncomfortably large nosebleed by bashing my head into the corner of my desk. It's the human equivalent of gnawing your leg off.

It's the day before Black Friday and so many subsidiaries depend on Black Friday being more successful than the last, since every year the sales projections are set higher and higher and you'd
~~~~

better make that goal or else. "Positive reinforcement," it's called, and not "sheer terror."

Then there's the riots. You need to lock yourself in your home, stay quiet, and hope it doesn't spread beyond the Ultimarts. Keep your head down.

I purchase a 7 minute break and I use the time to make a phone call to Raylene, trying to calm her down. She's freaking out about her meeting later today and she's locked herself in the bathroom. I don't really know what's happening on the other side of this phone. I try to calm her down by telling her lame jokes, which seems to work.

"I gotta go, honey. I love you," I say it like a sales pitch.

"I love you, too," she says in a near whisper.

She hangs up the phone. No sale.

~~~~

It's 16:00. The conference room of Infinite Solutions resembles a movie theater with stadium seating fitting 500, every person in the company. I'm early because I hurried and slammed out some units as quickly as I could so I could come into the meeting room and watch the TV clouds outside. I'm so tired, so utterly exhausted, and I rub my forehead with the heel of my hand. The floor looks like it's a mile away. The pattern becomes a fractal with shapes and point melding and flowing into each other. There is something in there clawing its way out to me.

The pre-meeting music begins, blasting cheap techno from tinny-sounding speakers and flashing to pump us up, to energize
~~~~

and motivate us. I snap my head up. Everyone's cracked eyed and exhausted, fueled by the new batch of Koffee. I didn't hear anyone come in.

I saved a seat next to me for Jerry. If it was possible to have friends in this place, I would consider him my one and only. He lets out a little wave and plops down.

"I see how you look at me," he says, deadpan. He downs the rest of his Koffee.

"Sorry. I see you've been doing squats. I have to admit, I have a fetish for pudgy tech guys with pasty bald spots." I look around. "It's my curse."

He chuckles. "We should just run away together."

"Yet we are tragically heterosexual."

"It's the modern age. It's all the same. We wouldn't need money, the power of our irony would shield us from the brutal truth of this awful, awful world." He says it with perfect sarcastic sincerity, mimicking the pomposity of someone who learned everything they know from TV.

"We could open up an organic, fair-trade, vegan BBQ chain that caters only to progressive, open-minded, proud single mothers," I wave my hand, painting the scene for him.

"One can dream."

"So what's new in tech support?" I stir my bottle of Koffee, engrossed in the swirl.

"I really don't want to talk shop."

"Why not?" I say it like I'm consoling a small child.

"Because it puts me into a murderous rage. And you, how are the wife and kids? Are you regular? Are your bowels top notch, old sport?"

"Nope."

This amuses him to no end.

"Careful about that 'shooting up the place stuff,' I say, "They'll haul you in for an Eval. Last thing you want."

"Oh come on, we're just joking. Anyway it's easier to get a gun these days than a cheeseburger," he says, laughing.

You'd think he was just exaggerating. He wasn't. The Galleria has several Quik-Gun vending machines that only asks you if you're really angry by making you select an emoji for your mood. The official marketing is that they're for the protection of businesses, due to the rise in mass shootings because guns are available in vending machines. Funny thing, people about to shoot up an office aren't angry, far from it actually. I've seen their eyes in videos and Security mugshots afterwards: calm and placid as a mannequin. They go blank and robotic.

"You alright?"

"Doing FINE," I proclaim.

He looks at the bottom of his bottle, poking at it with his stirrer, like there was some answer down there.

The unspoken truth hangs over everyone wandering in: Black Friday is tomorrow.

"Black Friday, am I right or am I right?" Jerry says, reading my mind.

"Black. Friday."

Just its name brings up images of last year's carnage, the gleefully assembled UNet montages of shoppers pummeling each other, ongoing coverage of the franchise wars between Ultimart stores, and the Splat Cam. This year feels different somehow, more pressurized and enraged. The screws have been tightened even more.

The overhead lights dim and the television sky outside vanishes. Jerry and I, at the same time, groan to ourselves. He sinks in his chair, slouching so far he practically slides onto the floor in a puddle.

"That's the kind of spirit I like to see! Okay, team, you ready?!"

Deathly silent. Some shuffling noises, a cough. Middling claps.

"I saaaaaaaaid, are you ready?!"

More techno plays. Colored lights wave to and fro in hypnotic patterns.

Our Creative Director, Blake Pierce, enters and claps for himself, waving to everyone. He waves his gangly arms like a puppet. He's wearing a slightly shiny suit that absorbs and reflects light at the same time. His grin resembles dull razor blades. People awkwardly clap, and Jerry goes absolutely nuts, screaming and yelling, so much that Holly is momentarily taken aback by it. I refuse to clap or cheer.

Blake's smile returns to its stiff position. It's actually kind of amazing he can hold that pattern and talk.

No one else makes a sound.

Imagine standing on a stage where every single person in the room absolutely hates you. I wish my eyes could shoot caustic plasma and burn two clean holes through his head. The last few weeks I have been powered by pure spite with a splash of exhaustion tossed in like a dessert.

Yesterday, my son Axel demanded that I assemble his MurderFort and I begrudgingly accepted. I was too tired to say no, and I did the mental math that the argument wouldn't be worth it. I picked up one of the plastic tent poles and bent it in my hands to a shallow U shape, the tension of pole bending and flexing, just about to snap. There are many people in this room bending like that.

Pierce shouts at us, "How is everybody doing?! I can't hear you!" He's playing to a stadium audience that doesn't exist.

Our silence is our protest. We shout "FUCK YOU" with our minds.

Even through the blinding lights, he gets the message and signals to the meeting DJ with a slit-throat gesture to cut the music.

More ugly silence. A smattering of yes's ooze up. Jerry lets out one final yelp and sits down.

"This is amazing," he mutters to me.

"Fucking blow my brains out in the break room."

"Alright, team. I hope you're as pumped as I am. Today we're going to talk about... your dreams." Blake has this habit of speaking to us in that sing-songy voice that is supposed to sound energetic, hopeful, and friendly, but really just ends up sounding like he thinks we're babies. He uses his hands a lot.

"Your dreams are like bubbles. Delicate, just floating in the air like... crystal butterflies. Each of us has dreams. Rainbow dreams. Puppy dog dreams. Starlight fantasies that come to us when we sleep, like when we find that special someone. I want you to take out your workpads and take a few minutes to think about your dreams. Those of you with text skills, jot them down and submit. Try to keep language units... simple. For those of you at E level or below, which is probably most of you, you can just browse the pictures and select the one that fits your dream the most. Look, prioritize, synthesize your action items."

He smiles weakly, his eyes burning like coals.

I pick the third picture in the stock Dream Library and submit it. It was a shirtless man, muscled chest glistening, his teeth pearly white. Jerry is trying not to explode laughing.

"He's very handsome," I say, in mock defense.

"I know, right?"

Blake looks at his workpad. "Looks like we have a few stragglers. Please note, this is fully voluntary. However, we do appreciate your participation. We're a team!"

A few moments later everyone seems to be done.

"All right, thank you everybody! Awesome sauce!" he says, putting away the pad. "Now, the World-Class Service booklets will automatically open to the video titled 'Black Friday Safety Extravaganza'."

It's a five minute video on how to rebuild your face if someone breaks it. Thankfully, it ends.

"Tomorrow is the big day," he says. He wiggles his hands like he's going to tickle us. "Tomorrow. Is. Black. Friday. Our clients are so jacked right now. They've been cheerleading us on and they are just so... excited to hear what we can give them tomorrow. They are stoked. We've been pushing our core micro-markets thanks to you folks, collaborating with MA on delivery channels and price

EAP's, getting directions and metamarkets to their best in the last three years. I am so proud of every single person in this room right now. We've all sacrificed a lot in the last month."

I look around and see bewildered faces. None of this makes any sense to us. I glance around again at the folded arms and hard stares. There is real hatred here, barely contained, and if he says sacrifice one more time, they may sacrifice him off the roof. More likely they'll just wait out the meeting.

You want to know who sacrificed? One woman here was so stressed out and overworked she started throwing up blood at her desk. She has a name: Angela, and she's sitting a few rows down from us. I can see the back of her straight hair and her head is tipped a bit down, like she's looking at the floor.

This happened a few weeks ago when the new quotas were announced. She started getting stomach cramps, took some antacids, and went back to work. It got worse. When she started bleeding from her mouth, she didn't notice it at first because she was focused on meeting her micro-market goals. She didn't have a time off voucher and no one could donate one. Pierce said absolutely not, and did that thing where managers tell you to fuck off with a smile, that it's out of their hands, and that this situation is actually her responsibility. And by "her responsibility," he actually means "her fault."

She used to be loud, brash, sometimes obnoxious, but she was a woman people liked and respected. She's very quiet now. They broke her. I wonder what day that happened to me.

The next day she was back at her desk, which Infinite Solutions cleaned but didn't bother to replace.

"I couldn't have done it without each and every one... of you." He points to us, and in his fantasy world, in his own little Dome, we lavish our undying love onto him.

During his moment, the side door opens next to the stage. A blonde woman enters unexpectedly. She might be executive management, definitely not one of us. The sharp, hard Teutonic-brand face gives her away. She leans against the wall, annoyed at being here, her hands stuffed into a dark colored coat.

She's probably from another division, maybe she's Memetic Analysis, those wise and all-knowing sorcerers. They come around every now and then to give us a tune-up, and MA always sends one person, never a team. Their agent always has a dark aura about them.

Blake notices her, genuinely surprised, and motions her to come up to the stage. Uninterested, she doesn't budge.

"One moment, folks."

He goes to her and whispers to her. We can't hear them, but from my angle, I can see both of them. Her mouth is a tiny silent "no", polite but annoyed. He begs her, trying to be charming. "No" again, this time with a look that says she's going to violently chew off his balls in front of us.

"Okay, then. Maybe not. Moving on!" Blake says, smiling.

There are now 501 people in this room who want to murder him. That is a woman who knows she's in control here. I swallow dry air.

"Everyone knows we've been moving into the product space. Make our own markets. It's open season on ideas, let's get some winners."

Fuck me, this again. Come up with ideas so he can initially deny them, then claim them as his own when MA vets them as possibilities. That's why she's here. He wants to impress her and by extension MA.

"Shoot me some product ideas for our clients. Let's workshop them. Crowdsource your ideas, people. We are all our own best critics."

A few people raise their hands and ramble. Nicotine-laced toilet paper called Buttz, an energy drink that "tastes like hot sex", a gym that exercises your self-esteem, fashion shock therapy, and an app based around traffic patterns that only pays out in a currency called Car Coins which can then be traded for gems or power amulets which can then be traded for coupons at an online store. The coupons? To purchase Car Coins. The concept is so convoluted Blake may actually go for it.

"Good, good. Those are all just great, just great. I don't know why people say you're not creative. You just proved all of them dead wrong. Let's open up a question to the floor. What is the greatest invention of all time? Go!"

I raise my hand. Several others do as well. Blake hovers his pointed finger over the crowd and settles on me.

"Yes, the gentleman in the very nice and probably expensive wig."

I pause for a moment.

"Nothing?"

"The common cold," I say.

He shakes his head, smugly chuckling at me. "Sorry, that's not an invention, either."

"Yes, it is. And it's brilliant."

Now he wants to prove me wrong, punish me for embarrassing him.

"Alright... why? Share with us."

Without really thinking, I just start talking.

"The common cold is actually over two hundred types of different viruses that can infect you. The term 'the common cold' is one of the best marketing devices in history. 'The common cold.' Sounds ordinary, harmless, not a big deal. It spreads like a, like a meme, and the more people share it with each other, the more popular it becomes. You can't really die from it, there's no cure and you can only treat it. Repeat customers. It's not artificial, so you can't be blamed for creating or spreading it. You catch it, like you catch a break or a fly ball in an outfield. You can patent and sell billions of dollars of merchandise to attack the symptoms, but never the disease itself. Remember there's no cure. It mutates every year and in fact, treating the disease only makes it stronger. The only thing all these cold remedies really do is filter out viruses with a resistance to the remedy. Billions of dollars on salves and pills and suppositories and syrups and all these other products. Consumers are literally willing to shove their money up their ass to stave off a few days of discomfort. The best part of it is, the real cure is just staying in bed. Drinking fluids. Rest. Anyone here able to spend a day in bed? Anyone?! Can anyone in this room take one day off? It's the perfect invention because the only cure is something you're not allowed to do and you can't do even if you were allowed. The units never stop. You can't stop."

My heart pulses hard in my chest and my hands are shaking. My throat is sandpaper. There are eyes on me from everywhere, and I suddenly feel hot and flushed. "I mean... um... that's why I think the common cold is a good invention."

Blake smiles. I can feel Jerry's unabashed joy at my little outburst. His mouth hangs open, silently laughing.

"Well... there you have it. Good answer. Thank you for... sharing. Everyone, tomorrow's the big day. Let's make today the best day it can be. This day is about you. Thank you for your attention and your attendance. Meeting adjourned. Let's get those unit numbers up, we are behind. Go get 'em!" Blake says, taking a bow.

People stand up wearily and wander out. No one is eager to get back, me most of all. I stay seated for a minute, collecting myself. A few faces look at me on the way out, mostly with bemused scowls, a chuckle to themselves, as if to say "That idiot is done for". They don't want to get caught in the crossfire. Down by the stage, the blonde woman is locked on me, staring from underneath her brow, a strange smile carved across her face.

<center>~~~~</center>

An alarm bell appears on my desktop with Blake's face next to it. He's buzzing me over the instant messaging system. The icons show an arrow pointing to the image of an office.

In his square tomb, he huddles behind his desk, pretending to type out something when I enter. I know for a fact he can't read text very well, and communicates mainly through pictographs. He can't read because he doesn't have to. Something like 85% of the demographic topside has almost total comprehension failure for text. I've pretended to be an E level to avoid scrutiny. Simple instructions are okay, like where to take a dump or pick up a hamburger, but anything more complex than that and the shopper just shuts down.

Pierce lets out a satisfied puff of air as he pretends to finish. I never noticed before how shiny his face is.

"Corwin, are you happy here?"

"Sure."

"That's not what I asked. Are you happy here?"

That's exactly what he asked, but I play along. "What are you asking exactly?"

Blake employs his tight-lipped smile when he's most angry.

"I'm asking about your dreams."

"Yes, this is my life's dream," I say flatly.

He nods. "That's good. That's good to hear."

A speech is coming on.

"I want every associate of this firm to feel like they can say anything to me if they need to. I have an open door policy. What really drives this firm, this business…"

Is ideas.

"Is ideas. Creative thoughts. People like you. The machine doesn't work without lubricant. You know where that came from? They used to have cars that ran on dinosaur blood. Imagine that. Someone saw this stuff coming out of the ground or out of a dinosaur and had the idea to run a car on that. It built the modern world. It built the Dome. Those are ideas with a capital I. And what you said in there..."

Embarrassed you.

"Impressed me. I see nothing but potential for you. You're smart, capable, outgoing."

No, I'm not.

"You actually remind me of myself when I was your age. You've never been top of the board, have you? That's okay. I think it's because you're not motivated enough, challenged enough."

I go cold. I don't like where this is going.

"What you said back there was interesting. Interesting ideas."

That means he didn't like it. A gigantic, toothy grin slides across his face like a knife cut.

"So what I want to do is actually give you a very special project. Since you have this keen perspective on our trusted clients, I simply want you to go down to the Doorbuster Sale at the Main Street Ultimart and buy Joob. You spent the better part of this fiscal year making copy and working your ass off on this. Go there and get me some 'on the ground' market research. I want the 'on the street' view of the product we're helping to sell. Consider it an opportunity to get the feel and the smell of the sale. It's an experience, something you can't get out of a report."

I am filing a report of the effects of prickly sweat on my back.

"Sure."

"We'll need an in-store receipt."

"Do I get to keep the Joob?"

He thinks for a second, nodding his head from side to side. "Sure! Why not? Give it to, uh, your kid."

Blake stands, indicating we're done here. His smile is the worst part, he knows he's probably saying goodbye for the last time.

"Corwin, all you have to say is 'thank you.'" He extends his hand, and I shake with my clammy meat.

"Thank you," I say, my voice distant and small.

"We're done here."

~~~~

In the second half of the day, Infinite Solutions holds an active shooter drill, and we hide under our desks. The guy across from me, whose name I still can't remember, wheezes loudly. I acknowledge his existence. He rambles. He wasn't in last place, surprisingly.

"You see, it's not just about the body count. Anyone can go out and shoot a bunch of people. It's about showmanship. It's about creating something that can strike with the zeitgeist. Like that guy that used the fart-thrower. That really connected with people," he says, out of breath.

One guy, Earl Stoker Wates, used a methane-based flamethrower powered by his own stored farts. People thought it was terrible, just terrible, but they also thought it was "kinda funny." He burned 7 people to death in an elevator.

I saw the elevator video online, one of those videos you know you shouldn't watch but can't stop clicking on it. I don't know why. There was a blackened claw of a mother, failing to shield her daughter from the flames, slowly scraped down the chrome finish of the elevator wall.
~~~~

In that moment, I disconnected from the human race. I tried to feel something for that mother, that child, but I just couldn't. They were pixels, the idea of a mother and child. They might as well have been slabs of pork oven-roasted to golden perfection, ready for a plastic tray, waxy wrapping paper, and a child's toy included.

Last year, there was a gap of about 26 days when a mass shooting didn't happen and a task force was implemented to find out why one hadn't happened. $150 million later and they realized that there was a critical expanded magazine shortage. After a deafening outrage, XXXtreme Gunz, while condemning any "pointless tragedies" that may occur from the purchase, usage, or lack of usage of these devices, stressed the necessity for defense against such atrocities by offering coupons for discounted "personal protection hardware". Splat Cam praised the coupons as a "sensible and heartfelt gesture to the public" in a video statement soon after.

The victim's families are often a mixed bag. About half of them, eager for an interview, will drag reporters pretending to sympathize through the child's room. It's always a tragedy, everything is a tragedy, unavoidable and eternal.

Raylene asked me to buy us a gun. I said no. I got a replica one for Axel.

"Why not? There's all sorts of sickos out there," she said, hands on her hips.

"You're right," I replied.

I watched another video where a trader at some sort of financial firm, armed and ready, trips and accidentally shoots a nearby woman in the left lung. He fires again and shoots another co-worker in the spine, paralyzing him. He's really bad at this. The gunman pumps five rounds into his boss and a woman named Marsha Goodman throws a cup of hot Koffee right in his face. The other employees took turns beating him with their chairs while he screamed.

People play the lotto where you can guess on where the next one is going to happen, how many bodies there will be, how many wounded, the mixture of male vs female, adults versus teens, teens versus adults. Stocks are always up when blood gets splattered on a wall.

Tomorrow is Black Friday. I can see it in my mind, far off like an approaching superstorm in a disaster movie.

I don't sleep.

3 ~ *shopping*

I slip out an hour before dawn. I give Raylene a small kiss on the back of her head, she moves slightly, still asleep. I peek inside Axel's room before I leave, and he's snoring quietly, a puddle of drool forming on his pillow. I pull down the security shields on the windows and doors, and lock up from the outside. I briefly thought about us making a break for it, but where would we go? I checked to see if I could just buy this stupid thing online, but I realized I'd need a record proving I got it on site. Not enough time to fake it. I breathe light and fast.

Far away, the Main Street Ultimart waits.

~~~~

I'm several blocks away, making my way through an Adway towards the main promenade. There's bodies knocking into each other in the tunnel, blanketed with a grim silence as all eyes locked
~~~~

on the eight sets of doors out front and the neon sign stating "Opening Soon." The quiet is the worst.

People grit their teeth, check their safety pads. A wizened man standing next to a vending machine puts a mouthguard in to protect his crooked yellow teeth.

A crowd of thousands has gathered in the parking lot for the Main Street Ultimart, the largest shopping center in the Dome. 7 floors of shopping stretching out over an entire district, with the capacity for almost 50,000 shoppers at once.

Beside me, a frantic woman is digging for something in her purse. She pulls out a collapsible nightstick, flicks it outwards and it extends with a sharp plastic snap. She collapses it back into her palm. Her son, not much older than Axel, wears colorful kid-sized riot gear. It's bright blue and red, most likely made up like a favorite superhero. I didn't even bring anything. No guns allowed, but anything you can carry with you is fair game. The young boy in his toy armor looks at me with blank, dead eyes, a sideways smile on his face. His mother notices me with suspicion. Kids often go missing on Black Friday more than anyone wants to acknowledge.

"Think it's a good idea to have your kid here?"

"What the hell do you know?"

"My son's about his age. It's dangerous."

"Everything is dangerous. Everything kills you," she says, like it's supposed to be on a t-shirt.

"At least it's a nice day out," I say.

Everyone else is watching us tiny people crawl like snails through the square, flat roofed building, music blaring like air raid sirens, all pumping like blood through organic tubes. We stand on our own stage in front of the whole Dome, eager to play our parts. They are watching.

It's a nice day out, I repeat to myself over and over. The weather is a consistent channel, shining like a smile, and the sun a giant bulb lighting our way to better and happier days. It's happening soon. Everything will be okay tomorrow, just you wait and see. The television sky is above, we're done below. Some days it is slightly cloudy to break up the light, or simulated rainstorms like last week to add drama to the nighttime darkness. Time slips out of my clammy hands, always escaping.

Today, Ultimart wants the sun to be warm, inviting, inoffensive, for people to spend, to wage the war of daily life, climbing over themselves to be the first in line, to grab the last.

I suddenly realize I have no idea what Joob is. Joob is your all, your reason for being. It wants nothing but the best for you. Joob cares for you. Everything except Joob is a lie, and you know it. Accept Joob into your heart. It knows best. Joob will cleanse you of your sins.

Joob loves you and you love it.

Soon the fog horn will go off, and the doors will open, and this will begin. Soon.

The crowd is filled with surplus people like myself. Not like Her, the giant wondrous female face beaming from the side of a glass-eyed building across the freeway. The woman is the Wife, the lovely creature inhabiting the home on my favorite show, titled Life. In a brief, free view of the show, she drinks from a dripping cold glass of lemonade, smiles at everyone, at me, and goes back to doing the laundry by hand (which no one does, but only her, showing her domestic authenticity).

Her plain but attractive face is over 30 meters tall, each window a tiny pixel, some brunette, some blue. Her plainness, her medium build with small hands, smart glasses perched on the end of Her nose, that's Her beauty. An unpretentious realness. Look at the way She folds Her Son's pants, making sure the fold is on the seam of the jeans. She nudges a hair behind her ear, then holds Her hand up to her nose, then sneezes. I laugh. She was someone who could wake up with me in the morning, help me walk Dad to the bathroom when he used to be able to, eat Jamboree-style pancakes, and then go with me to the garage, waving to me as I got in my very own car. After I came home, we would watch TV (it didn't matter which show) and She would hold my hand in Hers in the dark of the apartment, bathed in the light of digital faces, smiling and confident of a bright future, filling us in turn with their glory. I immediately feel the burn of my guilt, holding my wife's arm, dreaming of what Her hair would look like spread over a pillow. I look away.

We now return to our regularly scheduled programming, coverage of Black Friday all around the Dome. The TV show of your life.

We're moving.

The crowd flows through a narrow corridor. The walls are lined with Smart Mirrors, which are regular mirrors, showing your pockmarks, receding hairline, your slight paunch hanging over your belt, the cheap disposable clothes you're wearing, your exhaustion, your secret dread, all the special things that make you

You. They're on both sides, so your reflection gets doubled into infinity.

I don't like looking at pictures of myself. I get lost in them, wondering who is this bizarre creature in them, that odd face I know is my own. The Smart Mirror then lays over an immensely cruel image, showing you who you can become: fitter, happier, more productive, whiter teeth, clearer skin, confidence in your stride, surrounded by those who love you, so far away from death you don't even know the word. I see myself mutated into a mannequin of perfection and immortality, the man the Dome wants me to be, wants me to strive endlessly to be. Kill yourself for this.

And inside the Ultimart is everything I would ever need to be that.

The mass of people is swelling in size, some have been here for weeks. Typically, there's several factions of consumers here, color-coordinated like paramilitary groups. They stake out primo territory around mid year, raffling off seats and holding strategy meetings in impromptu shanty towns when UCorp approved temporary permits. You get tons of friend requests and spam messages the weeks before. A man in a hot pink tuxedo matching top hat shouts at me to sign up that they'll guarantee me a spot at the front of the line. The few first rows of people are destined to run smack dab into Security's clubs or get trampled by the wild, panicking herd behind them. I politely wave him off as I take the escalator down to the Ultimart parking lot, oozing down with the crowd.

Main Street is a mix of carnival, religious sermon, and tailgate party all mashed into one. Partiers are packed tight like hot dogs wrapped in brightly colored disposable clothes. Some are wearing costumes, dressing up like their favorite Brand Names, like Sasha Hot in orange knee-high boots or Dread Lock with his vinyl trench coat. I'm just wearing whatever came out of the Closet this morning, relatively light and inexpensive plastics, and I pass by the roasting stench of fried dough and street meat as I look for a cheap spot to hide and wait.

An hour passes. The sun has nearly crept over the horizon, just behind the Ultimart sign, a small bright glow encompasses it. The army of shoppers wait impatiently, now quiet, with only the sound of the heavy breathing under clattering plastic armor. There's no countdown or clock poised to strike, and Ultimart often changes up the time by a few minutes, so that shoppers are suddenly thrust into the fray as soon as the doors are kicked down.

The sign light turns on as the sun finally rises behind it.

An ear-shattering airhorn splits across the sky. The deep bass of the sound hits me in the chest, and a visible wave passes through the crowd. A vast electric buzzing, like a mechanical tornado, rises as hundreds of security gates behind the closed doors rise across the Dome, signaling the start of the Xmas shopping season.

But the doors haven't opened yet. 50,000 people hold their breath, clutch their weapons, and finally, it becomes clear to me. I see through the moment. To be thrust so close to your fellow human being, with nothing to lose and everything to gain, is exhilarating. This is why they come, for the chance to feel alive. You may get your head cracked in, but the pain from the broken bones centers you, and in that moment of power, bearing down on your enemy, you feel in control of the universe. There is terror and excitement within my guts and everything feels like it is on fire. I breathe deeply, in and out, my eyes focus on the doors.

We wait.

Seconds pass. Minutes.

Wait.

Watch.

The stale air hangs.

I am coiled like a spring.

The doors fire open outwards with such force, several shoppers are tossed backwards several meters, landing in the crowd like couch cushions. A control tactic to clear the front entrances.

This is the moment where the curtain is drawn back. Any other morning you would wake, dress yourself, eat, climb in your car, drive to work, work, come home. Today you are a warrior and this is battle. The crowd surges forward, screams like thunderous waves rising from a violent ocean of people.

The moment suspended in time like glass. Roaring in my ears. This single second has been carefully and painstakingly orchestrated and refined to be the most exciting, pivotal moment of the year. It's like a gunshot in a crowded room. The immense collective effort all over the Dome for this one sudden shock.

Every person in this crowd, including myself, has been following an invisible line to get here. The masses of people swell forwards in lurching waves. A crush.

The cheers and jubilate cries of the faithful have been rewarded. God isn't dead, he was just laid off. There's no room in the Dome for gods or goddesses anymore. The only thing that deserves our eternal worship is the Machine, the Dome, and Ultimart. But they'll never tell you that, and that's the point. Nothing is forbidden or against the rules, and formally, there are no rules. No laws.

Everyone is free, remember. Free to live, free to die, free to kill. Move.

People are being trampled underneath. I can't see them, but I can hear their screams. I see a face, their hand up, broken fingers. I can't stop. Stop and you're dead.

That's the power they have: making you think you made a decision in the first place about if you would be the trampler or the tramplee. The grand magic trick of modern life that you, little old You, could one day be One of Them. That you would be the one stepping over the bodies.

I try to help the screaming face up but the mass is pushing forwards, the shouts and screams rising upwards, the cattle realizing they're in the abattoir. I glance down to see the bloody face staring up at me, eyes unblinking and cold. Even if I wanted us to get out of here, there's no way I could push against the tide of flesh and designer coats to go back. I could perhaps scramble to the top of a light post and wait it up.

Just look closer. Look here. See how it moves. How it all works together. The flow of it. I scramble and am pushed about. Don't fall. Don't ever stop.

A person clicks a link for a pink-colored cat picture, then 3 seconds later checks their email, deletes an email for steak, but gazes at an ad for a new jacket long enough to determine "interest".

Their webcam captures their eye movement on the page. Their keystrokes and gestures are logged. How often they masturbate. How many funny comics they read. How many times they typed or said the word "love" or "hate". All fed into the Machine. All collected, collated, archived, regurgitated. All to get us massed and fat and pushed into the sluice gate.

All this raw, pulsing data is then cross referenced and counter-cross referenced against every other link and television show and movie and video game they've ever played and through an immensely complicated, time-tested series of tables and algorithms, which for all intents and purposes appears to be magic, they are targeted for a 50% off a Pussy Pussy t-shirt if they've watched 11.9% of this season's episodes within 60 seconds of their availability. Or a DrumModder if their music trends meet a certain BPM and they like to flail around while listening. Or heat-sensitive condoms if they've stopped jacking it 22% less and started calling a man named Ripper Tomtom twice a week and speaking on the phone for 12 minutes on average, then spent an average of 185 minutes at his place every Thursday, which is both of your days off, and you mainly enjoy watching pony porn and ice cream. If you want to get married and have a child.

It works because it's invisible.

It works because people like it.

I admire its purity. I can hate and still respect. The cold, raw, unapologetic efficiency of its deadness, yet how effortless and natural the system feels to an observer. How alive it looks. The illusion is completely flawless, from this Ultimart to the television sky. An advertisement for itself. This is the best of all possible worlds and there is no other. There's no orders or jackbooted thugs demanding you buy something or for your vote. Which soda do I prefer, Red or Blue? Who are you voting for in November?

You don't get the luxury of thought. Work sleep work sleep work sleep death.

There's no tyrannical despot spouting jingoistic slogans, but rather a smiling, pleasantly attractive woman or man enjoying the product and a pleasant, inoffensive pitchline. You feel good when you buy something nice for yourself.

I'm almost at the doors.

That sensual need locks into some hidden desire, either real or created, that the Machine recognizes and provides to us. We need this mass of flesh clawing at each other, it releases some darkness in us to inflict upon others.

Everything about you is codified and metric-ed and analyzed and tabulated, fed into the gaping maw of the Machine, whose stomach is never empty. Days like Black Friday fill you up. I am unsure if I have ever made a genuine decision on my own, and after a while, that fear just fades into the background like wallpaper or the paintings at the dentist office, to be replaced by blood as I scramble forwards, pushing and shoving the other bodies aside.

You can't unplug from it. You get your food, your bottled water, your clothes, your job, all your knowledge comes from their instructional videos, their training classes when you are young, from birth to the recycling vats. The Dome is your ecosystem, inside and outside of you.

Ultimart cares about U, the slogan reads above me as I pass under the arch.

The river of people surges me inside the doors and a multicolor light show greets us as shoppers plow over each other, kicking and scrambling, tumbling over and over into a great pile. People are spilling in like water. Security, decked out in black riot gear, assaults the crowd to push them further inside. Shoppers smashing children into walls and trampling each other's faces is normal, ordinary, expected, and glorious.

A mountain of asses in tight plastic pants collapse over each other as I duck to the right, just out of the way of a runaway scooter, and slip through the swarm of arms and legs, mashed with perfume and body sprays and designer condoms. Cries of joy and pain as hands grab boxes, shoppers curling up with their packages, tears running down their faces. I feel electricity all throughout me and I am plugged directly into this circuit.

I spot one of our consumer plants, a shopper hired to make sure good internet-worthy fights happen over the chosen toy that that firm is trying to push. A GyroJet, some sort of urine-powered bathroom chopper, I think, I'm not sure. I don't have the time to check. The Children's Toy Department is a jungle of snarling faces, animal screeches as the shelves are emptied and tipped over. The music is so loud, pounding, blast-beats and joyous voices. I step over a bloody smear heading around a corner and I decide not it's better not to know sometimes.

I can't find the Joob display. The crowd has metastasized throughout the store.

Seconds feel like minutes and hours and decades. The floors are coated in a non-slip material, prepared from the experience of years of collected blood and vomit. I move quickly through the forest of people towards the Joob section, which has its own set of aisles, dodging and avoiding debris, limbs. The fire suppression system puts out a small blaze in an alcove leading into the displays, the acrid stink of burning plastic chokes me. After a few hundred meters and witnessing three murders, I see the familiar orange, yellow, and green colors. The soft, friendly shapes of the word Joob.

I see a can has been knocked to the ground, stuck between an overturned shopping cart and a stuffed jackalope. I reach for it, and there's a smear across my vision as a fist slams in my solar plexus, doubling me like a closed book. That goddamn woman from outside, complete with Officer Baby, cracks me over the shoulder blades with her baton, and while I'm sucking in hot pain, her brat gives me a sharp kick right in the ankle.

A security officer, a real one, bashes the woman right in the chops with his shield. Her son goes into full attack mode, and for a moment, it looked like the security officer was actually fighting an action figure version of himself. The officer picks the boy over his head and chucks him like a sack 3 meters into a Xmas tree display. I can barely hear the kid wailing over the roaring.

A dark composite faceguard looms over me. He picks up the loose can of Joob and puts it in my hand.

"Finders keepers," he says, smirking. His voice is low and mechanical. After a moment, I take it.

The Ultimart is in complete pandemonium. I make sure to keep my can tucked into my armpit. The cashier's lines are properly barricaded at least, and I scamper into the nearest available unit, which has been converted into a mini field hospital and self-scan checkout lane. Security controls the flow of shoppers with taser guns and shields, forcing them into a caged line that separates them from each other in small segregated boxes. The checkout line is an automated walkway that jerks forward for the next shopper. Happy music is piped in through the ceiling over the gladiatorial mayhem behind me.

I get a $37 bandage for a cut on my forehead and combined with the $199 Joob, I finally check out. Outside there are bodies lying on the ground, groaning and reaching for me, and I step over them. I can't help them. The parking lot is mostly empty now and I scamper across it trying to stay out of sight. Across the Dome, smoke from secondary fires rises in thick, black fingers.

Far enough away from the sirens and the small breakout fires, I collapse against the wall of a Chik-N-Lil joint. I twist open the top of the Joob can and let the contents flop into my hand. It's a green jelly mass with orange nubs that squishes when you touch it. That's it. I squeeze it. I pass it between my hands. I even throw it against the wall, and it slinks down to the ground, then reforms itself.

I just stare at it for a long time.

My car is parked under an overpass under piles of cardboard and oozing recycling bags. As I pull them off, my hands and forearms are nearly coated in the stinking juices. But as I smear sanitizer over them, my hands won't stop shaking and I feel like I'm going to vomit. The image of the kid in riot gear getting tossed into the tree display sends me into a laughing fit until I'm crying, and then I'm crying for real. I get in my car and sit for a second, catching my breath and waiting for my heart to stop exploding. My hand punches into my palm with a hard, meaty thwack. The adrenaline wears off a little and I calm down. I'm careful to not make too much noise.

I flip through my phone and UNet is already hedging their bets on the total death count at the end of the day. There are hundreds of thousands of posts and photos of fights and dead bodies, snarky jokes, and some bland pleasantries to "stay safe out there".

My can of Joob lays sideways on the seat. I pick it up and turn it over in my hand.

A loud crunch comes from the car's roof. Suddenly, in every window, there's a dirty angry face. They all wield plastic pipes and chains, rocking the car back and forth. Some of them film it, holding their phones in front of their grimacing teeth. My passenger window splinters into a spiderweb pattern. I slam the on button, wait ungodly seconds for the battery to warm up, slamming the wheel impotently. The car starts up and I mash the emergency power pedal, spilling the bodies backwards off my hood behind me. I cackle and holler, slamming my fist into the ceiling in triumph.

<p style="text-align:center">~~~~</p>

It takes me most of the morning to get home, navigating the roving consumer gangs, avoiding Security patrols out for fun, and I ingress into my block tower. I pass the houses stacked on top of each other, containing their own Xmas presents and terrified huddled people clinging to each other for safety and warmth. Bloodied wanderers in their cars filled to the brim with products. I head home instead with my own prize, cuddling it against my chest like an infant. I slowly climb the flights of stairs because the elevator is on fire.

The siren wails at midday to let everyone know all the fun is over for this year. As soon as I unlock the door, Raylene hugs me by the neck and looks me right in the eyes. I hold up my can of Joob.

"You always know what to get me," she playfully chokes out.

She chuckles, tears smearing her mascara. She cries black drops and hugs me again, refusing to let go. I'm okay with that. We have so few of these small, fragile moments.

"Where's Axel?" I whisper.

Raylene wipes her cheek, creating a smear like a cartoon swoosh. "In his room," she says, touching the side of my face.

"Okay," I say. She moves her hand away, smiling. She sits on the couch, her head in her hands. She looks up at me and I have to escape.

Axel is watching cartoons in his room, his face slack and empty despite the bright flashes of light from what he's watching. He's enjoying Hypno, which blasts a continual pattern of light and color to place your child in a relaxing trance. I'm just happy to see him, alive and watching TV like a normal kid.

"Hey buddy. What are you up to?"

He doesn't say anything at first. He lifts his finger weakly and points at the TV.

"Yeah, I can see that. You all ready for sleepy time soon?"

He nods.

Axel will get ground up in the thresher that is this place soon enough, probably go into Sales. He'll fit in just fine when he realizes you never had a choice to begin, and that all the noise about opportunity and destiny was just that: static on the TV drowning out the absolute crushing truth. I don't know how to tell him this, and maybe that's what happened to my dad. The man was just too polite to tell me I wasn't special.

Like me, my son isn't special, but he's mine, and I'd like to shield him from the world as much as I can. I'd like him to never learn about days like today and that Santa isn't real. I tuck Axel in, spray his sleeping meds under his nose so he doesn't thrash. His face turns into a doll's. I wonder what he dreams about.

I splurge and take a medium length shower to get the dirt and grime off of me. As the water hits me, something inside me breaks. I can't breathe and the shower is three times too small. I get out as soon as I can and catch a stranger's face in the mirror.

In the bedroom, Raylene lays with me, holding me close, as if her gripping me close will push away all that happened today. Her soft breath is warm and slightly wet on my shoulder. She holds me close and she tries to hide the fact she's been crying as well. I'm in that wavering moment before sleep, so exhausted I can't focus except on how tired I am. Her hand moves down towards my stomach, rubbing it in long, slow circles. Her long, black hair is in my face but I don't particularly care. She smells like peaches, a delicate and smooth odor that I've always enjoyed.

"It's okay. I'm just glad you're safe," she says in a little voice.

"Am I?" I say.

"What happened?"

"I had to go. I didn't have a choice. Something happened at work and Pierce ordered me to go."

"Fuck that guy. Why didn't you tell me?"

"I knew you would just worry."

"Not knowing is worse. You can't do that to us."

"I'm sorry."

I sit up. I think of my neighbor Herb Conway, the guy who lived downstairs who got hauled away. His muffled shouting under his blue hood. He tried to get a few bids on a Brand Name in, but his wife got smacked with several staggering HealthLine bills for dialysis. Her kidneys basically shut down, something to do with heavy metal poisoning. They tried to make payments, but couldn't and she was forced off. She later died in a botched back-alley surgery. He was part of a big automatic layoff at his algae distillery. I looked him right in the face. Herb's eyes were soft and empty before they threw the hood over him. I don't remember his kids' names.

"Something is happening to me and I don't know what."

"Talk to me."

"It's nothing, I'm just tired. Been a long day. I keep thinking about Herb."

"That's not going to happen to us. You're overreacting." She doesn't look at me, but she knows I'm right.

"I'm sure Herb thought the same thing."

I found out later through some digging that their franchise license was purchased by a private investor who did who knows what with the kids. They were old enough, around 13 or so, to sign their own contracts to save their dad from being thrown into the

Machine. I'm sure they thought they were doing him a favor. What would I do to save Raylene and Axel? I think I already answered that today.

I just wish I could catch my breath, sit down. All I do is think about the Number. I imagine the grinding metal below. Pressure pushes at me from all sides, like I'm deep underwater in the cold and dark.

The Machine moves and changes when it wants to, and there's no one really controlling it. You can easily be crushed in a compacted wall section, sliced to bits in a rotating duct fan, dissolved in a vat of boiling chemicals. One wrong step and it's a long fall into nothing. They never find you.

Herb had a few contacts, got a lighter reassignment and a new contract due to some backchannel negotiations. Who knows what he had to pull to make that happen. The boys went to the Wildcat, an executive gentleman's establishment in the Blue District, and he spent nearly every dollar he had to buy them out before it was too late. It officially doesn't exist. In a final humiliation, he had to buy them as his own "personal assistants", a common euphemism, not his children. System loses track of him after that. I don't think he ended up well, but I hope he did.

I rub my face.

"Do you want to talk?" she asks from the other side of the room.

"I think I'm just going to watch TV or something."

"Okay. I need to do some stuff before bed. Try to sleep tonight, okay?"

"I love you."

"I love you, too. I'm glad you're safe."

She goes to her work setup. She starts editing photos of herself at Black Friday, posting photos of fashion tips to cover your BF injuries, and how best to show off your haul. I can hear her crying from the other room. Sometimes you just have to keep moving.

4 ~ *show me*

Opening Credits

My show is on.

My show is always on.

Life is a show that should not exist. It sounds painfully dull and uninteresting. The pitch of the show is "a normal family". The livestream is 24 hours a day, 7 days a week if they're awake or sleeping or eating or taking a shower or anything at all. They're aware they're on a TV show, it's not like Creepshow or Voyeurz where the stars are hapless suckers. The Family knows they are on display and are just themselves all the time. They melt into the show's plastic. Right now, the Family is three: the Husband (or Dad), the Wife (or Mom), and the Son (sometimes Kid). They're never given names and they always call each other by their role in the Family. But that's okay, because they don't need names. Young people who watch say Mom and Dad and Kid, while adults like myself say Wife, Husband, and Son.

You think it would be the least interesting show in the Dome. It's not. It's the most popular program the Dome has ever put on.

276, if you were wondering. That's how many were killed yesterday. But you never hear about their stories on the news, only the happy faces clutching their products. Right now, I'm watching a woman with a gaping head wound hold up a white box and scream with pleasure. The annual ritual of bathing in other's blood is over for the year, and we are now in full sprint to Xmas, that most sacred day of remembering what matters most.

It's morning. Saturday. I purchased a day off. Treasure it. Drink in every second. Tomorrow is Workday, the first day of the week, and the cycle starts over for another year.

I clutch a blanket around myself on the couch, feeling myself sink deeper, enveloped by the softness. I grab the remote and switch the channel to Life, the edited episodic format. I decided to not watch it right away.

"Axel and I are heading out. Do you need anything?" Raylene has Axel on his Kid-Stop. He walks towards the TV, gently holding onto his cord. Raylene gives it a gentle tug and he bounces back to her.

"Nope," I say.

"Alright, honey. Get some rest, alright?"

You are absolutely right, dear. I have earned it. I deserve exactly what I get.

"Bye, Dad," Axel says, waving as he leaves.

"Bye, kiddo."

I weakly return the wave. They leave and I unmute. The ads around the frame of the TV shrink back to their smallest size, considering I've paid the premium package for Life.

There's three channels for Life: the episodes, the livestream, and the talk show. The episodic app (or the "E") where the show is edited down into 1 hour chunks 2 times a week, the livestream ("Live") where the Family is shown in real time, or the talk show ("Talk" or "the News") with celebrity guests and discussions about the show.

E is running ads, so I flip. Suckers is on, and there's an old man just finding out his entire life savings is gone, the hosts barely holding back their laughter.

I flip.

Woman washing a car. Licks her lips sensually.

Flip.

Pre-Dome documentary about jackals surrounding a striped animal called a "zebra." I wince. I hate pre-dome docs with animals in them. Disgusting. Too much dirt and germs.

Flip.

Another commercial. Super absorbent towels or something.

Flip.

Science fiction. Alien getting shot in the face. Green blood. I think it's The Reckoning.

Flip.

Zombies shuffle down a hospital hallway. A child screams in a corner.

Flip.

Re-election ad for Red. New look, same taste.

Flip.

A show about franchises living in each other's houses for a week. A man punches a wall while his wife shits on a dining room table. Probably a Town show.

Most of the Dome's reality shows and livestreams are filmed in the Town, just like Life. The Town is an enclosed city of about 500 TV production studios that make up most of the Dome's 10000 channels. It's domed over, just like we are, a small microcosm of the pre-Dome world, built to historical specifications and aesthetics. For example, there's no highways or billboards. Houses aren't stacked, but separated by yards with real grass. No neon tubing, no static and noise. There's office buildings and factories and stores ripped from the past. But you can't go there. It's hidden behind a dome of its own, and if you get high enough, like on the roof where my garden is, you can barely make out the dark grey metal hemisphere poking up above the cityscape. Most people confuse it with the Sprawl, which sits directly in the middle of the Dome across the bay. Regular people can't go in and out of the Town as they wish. They're in TV land.

Flip.

I start my episode.

~~~~

Act 1

The Wife, a woman in her early thirties with a slender frame, is seated at her bedroom vanity. She is brushing her chestnut-colored
~~~~

hair with firm, confident strokes. She looks at herself in the mirror, a face I know every centimeter of. A closeup on her eye reveals a small wrinkle that's been developing since last season, which she tugs and plays with, trying to smooth it out. She sighs quietly and smiles. The march of time goes on and she is turning a bit older, but not old at heart, and we can see from her brave face that this is a moment of acceptance.

There's a special kind of quiet in the House today, where you can reflect and remember all the good things that make up your life. Yes, you're getting older, but that time is filled with beautiful memories. Like when the Son got picked for the baseball team or last year's BBQ when you and the Husband danced.

Baseball is only played in the Town. Dome Sportz, like Blitz and Throwdown are less pastoral, so to speak. Baseball appears to be a sport where not much happens, most of the time players stand around. Normally, they show flashbacks like they do now. The Wife begins to fold laundry and the camera moves to a picture of the Son in his dark red and white uniform. Emblazoned on the front is a type of flying animal called a cardinal.

The Son is on one knee, leaning on a thick wooden stick in his hand, and he smiles, as if the uniform fills him completely with joy.

"He looks very sharp," the Wife often says.

The moment of that picture is a moment of triumph, of validation, emphasizing the fact that yes, she is getting older, but not old. Her time is meaningful and bright.

I pause, grab an orange soda from the vendi-fridge. It tastes like orange and after I drink it, I still feel thirsty.

The Son comes home, shutting the door behind him too loudly, and runs into the house. He's no longer playing baseball, as that season is over. He plays football now, which is a game I've tried to understand the rules to but completely fail. He kicks off his big spiky shoes and throws his dirty helmet a little too close to the new carpet.

"Mom, I'm home!"

"I'm upstairs, dear!"

The Son pops into the bedroom, trying to scare his mom, and she chuckles.

"How was school today? Help me fold laundry and tell me all about it."

The most amusing thing about Life is how unrealistic the Son acts. He actually goes over and helps her. He doesn't demand anything in return. He donates his time to her. No Dome kid would ever do that.

He tells him about what he did that day and how he's having a minor argument with Sally, an actress in his second period geography class. They show the "class", a brightly lit room with rows of desks. There's no AutoTrainer or even a screen in the room. The elderly teacher is named Ms. Cortwood; a plump, cheerful woman with curly grey hair and glasses about a kilometer thick. I actually find her charming, but most people think she's obnoxious and slows down the story. She's important, though. She provides valuable exposition about things happening in the school and provides fun pre-Dome trivia for us.

To do this, sometimes she wheels in an old pre-Dome TV on some sort of metal cart. School is such a bizarre concept when you think about it. First of all, there's no admission fees, unless you go to a place called "college", but I don't know much about that. It's a little confusing. The Husband and Wife went before they had the Son, but they don't talk about it much, except when an old "college buddy" drops by for a short episode arc. A lot of this world is baffling.

The Son continues. "Well, in geography class, Ms. Cortwood talked about the Founding Fathers and how they bought the New World from the savages."

"The savages huh? Were those the people who lived in huts?" The Wife says.

"Yeah, it's a good thing they bought them."

She folds a pair of blue jeans. "Mmm-hmm. What else did you learn today?"

"We did some math and that was kind of boring."

"Math is important, son. How else would the Founding Fathers know how much to pay those people for their huts?"

He cocks his head to the side, thinking.

"I guess you're right. Eww, these are your undies." He pinches the white bloomers between his thumb and forefinger, holding his nose like they're radioactive. It's cute. I sink into the couch a bit more.

"Do you have any homework?"

He sheepishly rubs the back of his head. "No..."

She's not buying it. She sets down her half-folded blouse in her lap and patiently waits for him to "spill the beans" as she often says.

"Alright mister, spill it."

"All the beans?"

"All of them."

I smile.

"Alright..." He tells her about his problems in Chemistry class and how this one kid, Chris Turkins, an insufferable little fuckhead, keeps picking on him. The initial conflict for the B Plot has just been established.

A poll comes up on screen and I vote on my phone that the Son will probably fight Chris at some point. 37% agree with me. I scroll posts about the show for a bit.

. A montage of chores and the Son doing his homework. Mom helps. Dad comes home later and sets down his briefcase. He passes the Son on his way out, but since the Son already explained the B Plot to the Wife, it doesn't need to be repeated. The Husband is square-jawed, confident, and has a smooth haircut. He's almost always in a suit, an old pre-Dome one made of fabric. He is very clean.

He closes the door behind him and fixes himself a small alcoholic beverage from the bar. The Wife comes down and rubs his back as he takes a sip.

"Make me one of those, cowboy."

"Sure thing, pilgrim," he says this in a slow, looping drawl.

They take their drinks out to the patio, right next to their garden. Real vegetables growing out of dirt, something that always makes me slightly gag. Dirt is worms and rat shit and dead things rotting and they're just going to sit right by it. I have to look away for a moment.

They enjoy the setting sun, purple and red clouds pulse from the horizon like waves. I imagine the air is warm and smells like freshly polished furniture. Their day is coming to an end, and in this beauty is the right time to introduce the A Plot. The sunset, the playful banter, drinks on the patio set us up for something calm and tranquil, yet slightly boring. The Husband stares into his drink with a worried look on his face.

"What's wrong, dear? I don't see any storm clouds out here."

It rains in the Town. Drinkable water just falls from the sky filled with bacteria and viruses that can turn your guts to jelly. Outside the Dome, people, if you can call them that, just catch diseases from the air. Right from the air they breathe. How could you live like that? My skin is a bit clammy. I sanitize my hands.

The alcohol rub stings, but also feels good. A metallic, clean odor that burns my nostrils.

Dad finishes his drink. "I just don't know about this promotion. I know I'm right for it, I know I'm not valued correctly. I worked hard for it. I put in the most hours, have the best presentations. I did everything right."

"Then you're going to get it."

"It's Marshall again. You know, the vice president's nephew. He's going to sabotage me, I know it."

"Why do you say that?"

"Because he doesn't want to work for it. He's lazy, he's dumb as a brick and acts like the world owes him this job."

He finishes his drink. "I mean, the kid just plays games all day and whines that he's not getting what he deserves."

"Sounds like a winner there."

"He'd do just fine in China."

She laughs. I don't quite get it. They never really explain what "China" is.

"People who work hard and play by the rules win the game. You know this. I know this. Losers like Marshall just want to take what other people earned," Dad says.

"Like you said, he doesn't play by the rules."

~~~~

First Commercial Break

Life goes to commercials. Or at least the episode does. The livestream has no direct commercial breaks. Instead, subtle advertising is presented on screen. What cereal they are eating for a delicious breakfast. Their brand of TV. Their styles. The Wife's fashion choices are heavily debated topics online. Ads can appear in the frame of the TV, or if you're watching on your phone, a popup in the corner. Nothing too distracting, and certainly not as smooth as the transition here from the actual episode to the location of the ad, like they're happening in the same place. It's quite masterful how you almost don't realize you're watching an ad. You just find yourself in the middle of it.

The ad now playing primarily focuses on small phrases and ephaptic emotions to remind your audience that these products are a solution, not an extension of their problems. Make the viewer realize they should feel like part of an exclusive and secret club. Upon swiping their card at the register, or clicking the Buy button online, they will pass through the doors of cosmic mystery,
~~~~

whispered from the lips of the sages, and the grand mystery of the galaxies will be revealed to them, but only if they purchase a stylish handbag with a silly cartoon dog on it. He is comically grumpy, thereby making your discontent palatable, expressed via something else. A small release.

Since my phone is connected to my TV, a Xmas 3D ad plays, projecting a miniature version of Santa's sleigh onto my coffee table. The TV, playing along with this little game, has the faces of young children pressed up against the screen, like a store window, watching the display below. Santa's 8 tiny reindeer patiently clop their hooves on my coffee table, with Rudolph's nose burning a bright red. Santa climbs down out of the sleigh, plopping his magical bag on the ground. He asks me if I've been a good boy or not this year.

"I am not well, Santa."

"You've probably been a good boy this year! HO HO HO!" He laughs, shaking his little potbelly and beard. "Remember, Xmas is right around the corner!"

A slow, high pitched whining noise rings in my ears.

The camera moves past the children's gaping maws on my TV, out to the window in Life the show. Green trees waft in the fresh wind in an open-air private park, where family franchises eat and socialize under the Dome's warm sun. A young girl, about Axel's age, with light blonde hair and a red-checkered dress, chases a butterfly projected from her phone.

"E-fluenza can affect anyone at anytime, young or old," the disembodied female voice says, "If you experience feelings of restlessness, irritability, mood swings, or generalized unhappiness when using your personal computer, mobile device or tablet, you may have the symptoms of E-fluenza. And we can help."

An elderly man, bald, wearing thin-rimmed glasses and a white coat, appears with a clipboard tucked underneath his arm. He gives me a caring smile, from someone who is patient and understanding, who wants to help. All medications are actually Machine-made and provided by automatic HealthLine stations around the Dome. I spend a lot of my time talking to computer screens for Axel's meds. If you see a doctor, it means you are about to die and they need to assess your Brand Appeal for buyout. They're a type of therapeutic device: a human face to human tragedy.

Last year, there was an epidemic of e-fluenza at Infinite Solutions. A Junior Advertising Executive Supervisor brand-named Tamalla Marcel complained that her skin felt itchy and her eyes hurt. So much that it was agonizing for her to work. At first, we just thought she just wanted attention, or it was mold, and that the air recycler was on the fritz again. But, no. It was working fine. She said it felt like bugs underneath her skin, swarms of insects crawling over her muscles, behind her eyes, everywhere. Soon, two of her neighbors started complaining of the same condition. IS brought in some air quality guys, who found nothing, just like I thought they would. This was some stupid prank, I thought, they just want some likes online. Tamalla posted about it endlessly, streamed her treatments, blotchy skin, scratch marks.

No, it was more complicated than that. Tamalla and the other afflicted employees paid their air quality inspection fees without complaint, so it wasn't some sort of scam. You know, like someone walking into traffic in hopes of a big fat settlement or a lucrative interview. The next week, 4 more people. By the end of that week, 8. Then over twenty. It was growing exponentially. People's arms and legs would be red and sore from all the scratching and rubbing. We had to be quarantined and sleep at the office for several days.

Finally, the office declared a medical emergency and brought HealthLine in to assess. Infinite Solutions is owned by Panorama Group, who are themselves owned by Altamere Conglomerate, who is, at the top, owned by UCorp. Their medical drones didn't find anything, not one microbe or bacteria that would cause something like this to happen to this many employees. They did find a nasty case of d-tex from someone in Sales, but a strong dose of ofloxacin and doxycycline took care of that.

After a month of this circus, IS announced they had found a "miracle cure" for the mystery disease and began to distribute the medication for a nominal fee to the employees. Thankfully, no one had died, although about ten people had permanent scars from scratching so much. When I was given my dose, I put the pill in my mouth and hid it underneath my tongue. Later on, I spit it into a trash can.

I had a theory that I wanted to test.

Right before we were about to be cleared, we were scanned by a HealthLine drone for any traces of the disease, but also to verify everyone had taken their medication. Everyone was cleared, including me.

I didn't take any medication during the quarantine and those drones do not make mistakes like that. Especially when a valuable subsidiary company is at risk.

The truth was simple, laughable even: there was no illness and there was no medication. There was probably not even any actual toxic exposure (or least none more than normal). Tamalla got the whole thing into her head that she was sick. She was so convincing to her coworkers that they genuinely thought they were ill as well. The cause? Tamalla had overheard a conversation about an unknown itchy infection that may have been the cause of death for an elderly Ultimart greeter. When she looked at the picture of the dead woman, she resembled Tamalla's aunt who recently passed away.

That's not where it got strange, but what is even more surreal is that I found out from Jerry. He said he was asked to assist the effort and actually had to sign a NDA about it. We were drinking beers on my balcony when, after seven cans, he finally just told me.

"Okay, listen up. There was a mixture of totally fake fucking medicine that caused genuine side effects, like headaches or the shits. It didn't cure anything. It was just the clincher to make everyone believe. But there was a large percentage of people who received the placebo that didn't cause side effects, yet also felt those side effects even though their medication was completely inert. Franklin from row 3 barely made it to the discount toilet because he thought he was going to shit himself."

He leaned in close, his head bobbing a little bit.

"Now, this is where it gets fucked up. HealthLine told these people that their fake medicine could become potentially addictive. It was 'unlikely', as they put it, but 'possible.' After their pills ran out, they started getting actual withdrawal symptoms from stuff they could never have been addicted to in the first place." He plopped back in his chair.

He called it the "Nocebo Effect."

~~~~

Act 2

The Wife is speaking with a neighbor, Mrs. Jones, about how the Son is struggling with some subjects in school.

"He's having a bit of trouble with history."

"Have you thought about a tutor?"

It's important to note the Son is not particularly brilliant at anything. Life makes an effort to showcase his averageness. He is not an especially skilled athlete or intellectual savant. He will most likely follow in his father's footsteps in the same industry: selling personal and property insurance. The Son prefers checkers to chess, which Dad dutifully tries to teach him. The episode of him learning how to play chess (and failing) is one of my personal favorites. Dad informs him that not being good at everything is okay as long as you try.

I keep switching back and forth between the Livestream channel and the episode, back and forth. I break time in two. I pause. I unpause. I pause both and switch between. Both women frozen in time. Both the same but not. I switch to the webcam on my TV and I watch myself watching myself. I turn on picture-in-a-picture and see a third me hovering in the corner. Behind this new me is an infinite row of my slack face stretching back to infinity.
~~~~

Back to the edited episode. The Son is in History class, and they're describing the Dome War when UCorp fought the crumbling government for control of the Dome itself. The face of the CEO of the company, his rugged war face covered with grime, is projected onto a hanging screen. He's sitting behind a metal container with several other Security officers, they're all smiling and clanking their Chik-N-Lil cups together. It's a famous picture.

Ms. Cortwood clicks through more images, her soft voice describing the hostile takeover of the Dome by UCorp from the corrupt, dying government, Security sealing off the armory from military troops, its consolidation of Dome security, and the renovation of the Administrative Tower. And of course, the sealing of the Dome, that grand image of the enormous steel and concrete freight tunnels being sealed to all but the automated freight trains. The workers are tiny black splotches against the immense grey machinery. You're told the world is savage and frightening outside. I think about the bloody face underneath my feet yesterday. I sip my Koffee.

I turn off the TV.

I turn it back on.

I turn it off. I'm still on the TV and I'm looking at the back of my own head and the front at the same time. I'm looking at my living room from underneath the floor. There's no reason for this. I don't know what's happening. I don't understand. I don't know what to do.

There's just the shrieking white wall and the dead black screen tearing me apart with hot metal fingers down my throat. My walls are screens and I see myself from all angles. The top of my bald spot. Me as a child crying. Making love to Raylene for the first time. Birth. Sleeping. Eating. Showering. Dying.

I turn the TV back on. I'm inside.

~~~~

Second Commsercial Break

The scene subtly goes to commercial again, just sliding off center to something new and fresh. It's not Saturday, it's Wednesday. I'm a kid again, that blurry smudge of time before you emerge from the meds and you're already an adult.

"Corwin, it's your turn for Show and Tell. Please come to the front of the room," Ms. Cortwood asks, not looking up from her planner.

I'm in Ms. Cortwood's class. Ten years old, wearing my favorite Dome Devils shirts and blue sweatpants. I'm nervous, terrified that I'll wet myself like I did last week. Ms. Cortwood made me mop it up with a baby wipe. No one laughed, that was the worst. Everyone just watched me clean it up in an ugly silence.

"Um..."

"Hurry up."

Slowly, I trudge up the front of the room. This isn't Training, there are happy faces from Life, not vicious, darkened faces of the other children in those Training classes ready to drink blood. They smell weakness and devour the soft parts of you. In Training, I would often dread the first five minutes before classes started, waiting for some snarky comment about my hair, or something
~~~~

thrown at the back of my head. You stupid, dumb, weak pussy. Everybody hates you because you're a loser. Loser. You smell like shit, you fucker. That's a dumb name, you shithead. The hard metal against your shoulder when someone shoves you. The taste of blood in your mouth. I grow older on the show.

I snap a few times, try to stab a kid in the leg with a pen. I don't break the skin and I keep thinking about it if I had. Would I have put it through his neck?

I stand at the front of the class, manage a weak smile, and I speak. My voice is my own with my mid-thirties deepness. Jonas Cramlin, a vile little mutant, chuckles to his friend, March, when I start to speak. I glare at him for a moment. I clear my throat.

"Um... hello, everyone. For Show and Tell today, I'd like to show you something really cool."

I pull out a gun.

~~~~

Act 3

I'm still in the show. After school, I'm crying on the soft brown couch and the Wife is rubbing my back, whispering words I can't understand. The episode ends and the Son has learned the value of history. So have I.

I wake up and Raylene is there, her small arms cradling me. Axel is on the floor, playing a video game on her phone. Her eyes are red and raw and I know she's scared.
~~~~

She touches my hand and tells me everything is going to be okay. I don't say anything but I kiss her softly and she makes a small noise. Roll credits.

5 ~ retirement

Morning. Toilet flushes have gone up again. I see it's now $6.25 this time on our homepad. I pee in the shower, and then receive a warning that shows a No symbol next to a man happily urinating. It's a warning.

The faucet costs have also gone up, so in protest I just use a baby wipe and some hand sanitizer. My hands smell like floor cleaner. Raylene is fast asleep, her half-tanned leg sticking awkwardly to the side. She'll be up soon, I think. Saturday is when she tries to flush out most of the meds that keep her "energized" during the week, cleaning herself out pounding nutrient shakes and clear water. I should make up for scaring her on Friday, but I have no idea how. She'll just say it's okay or that I'll owe her big time, and give me one of those irresistible smiles. I hope she does, I like it when she smiles that way at me. I like her leg sticking out from the bed.

I don't hear Axel, so I assume he's still out cold. Should be a few hours left on his sleeping pill. I carefully sneak into his room, check his restraints. He's all good.

After choosing two Jamboree pancakes, I indulge myself on some syrup from the machine, and throw away my dishes. The news is standard stuff, markets are up, somebody died, scandal, makeup tips, robot dog tricks. Most of it is dominated by Black Friday. I glimpse a few shots of the Main Street Ultimart, and look for myself, but it's just a seething mass of arms and legs pretzeled together. People truly coming together to celebrate the holidays. That bloodied face in there somewhere, still looking up at me.

I need to get out of here. Every angle looks wrong. I grit my teeth, looking out the window.

I want to go visit Dad. Yesterday made things clearer than normal for me.

After Dad retired, he got lucky when an old Training buddy recognized him at the Chik-N-Lil plant while researching a role. This Training buddy found out Dad was "retiring", the polite way of saying he was useless to them. When you pass a certain age, your joints go bad, you're "out of warranty" is what people say. You don't have a lot of options and Mom was gone at that point.

After a few meetings and a passing conversation with me, he took a second career at the Hollywood Executive Retirement Village playing Sy Gorman. He rents the Brand Name, you see. The real Sy Gorman passed away a few years ago during a charity marathon when the man's heart practically exploded in his chest during the first quarter kilometer. There were several high profile bets that he would self-destruct and made several gamblers quite rich, and I mean actually rich. Millions. A few went to the Sprawl from that little debacle, fat as hogs and brimming with cash. The name became a hot commodity.

Sy Gorman was technically married to Evangeline Tanner, part of the cast of a reality show titled Drunk Tank, noxious garbage where intoxicated people would fight each other with increasingly bizarre circumstances, like smashing gigantic light tubes over each other's heads, or ramming each other with cars, fighting robots with steel halberds. It was a freak show and Sy Gorman was always the butt of everyone's jokes. In a rogues gallery of morons and neurosis, he was actually the most sane of all of them, the most well-adjusted. Almost normal, whatever that means. That's what got me the most. It's that my dad wanted to pretend to be a man pretending to be a cuckold and an idiot. The real Sy Gorman was smarter than people knew. He turned his modest salary from the show into a small media empire. Even got the rights to his own Brand Name, which is no small feat, and sailed off into the sunset to the Sprawl licensing his name to people like my Dad.

Holding my phone in my hand, I briefly consider calling him. I decide against it, as I know he'll just want to talk about nothing for 10 minutes, make some excuse, and vanish out of my life. I really need to talk to him. I text Raylene that I'll be gone for a bit, and to do something fun with Axel. I take the elevator downstairs, hop in the car, and drive out to meet him.

~~~~
~~~~

The retirement village is much more upscale than the typical setup, which is a filing cabinet filled with dying people. The Hollywood Retirement Village resembles a pre-Dome palatial estate, or at least the front does. The Dome loves Hollywood. It's one of the few historical pre-Dome eras religiously studied by UCorp. People come here to be entertained by their favorite celebs in variety shows, knock off reality TV, pornos, everything.

Past the front facade, foam made to resemble classical granite sharply changes to grey concrete. I enter the vast foyer with its high vaulted ceilings and enormous crystal chandelier. The bored receptionist registers me with my thumbprint, accepts my admission fee with a swipe of my UNet card. I mistake another Sy Gorman for Dad near the escalator.

I wander for a bit, recognizing Yale Deeds, The Fat Fart, and Kitty Kat before I find Dad's room. His door is cracked open, a common practice. He's reclined in a high backed chair, tablet in hand, intently tapping. His tongue is tucked in the corner of his mouth. The concentration is unworldly. It's one of those games where you have to collect fruit or gems or something, and apparently he's doing rather well. I clear my throat. He looks up, then back down, and when he realizes it's me, sits up straighter in his chair. I caught him being childish.

"Hey kiddo. Wasn't expecting you! Why didn't you call first?"

"I wanted it to be a surprise."

"Hold on, I'm almost at the Omega level."

I smile politely as I enter. He's just finished with a performance, I can tell because he's still in costume. Sy Gorman has been under the laser too many times, so his skin looks like wax paper wrapped around a plastic rock. Dad is just old. He's wearing a blue jogging jacket with small yellow shorts. His arms and legs are veiny, pale, and clammy, almost like linoleum filled with blood and wizened meat. That wig doesn't suit him, the long stringy brown hair that belongs to a middle aged mom, stretched back with a pair of oversized red sunglasses. When he came home from the Chik-N-Lil plant, he used to rub my face against his 10 o'clock shadow, scraping me. He smelled like ammonia and sweat most days. He was a perpetually exhausted man worn down to a nub at the end. I wonder if he's happy or if it's just another show.

I pull up the chair from his makeup counter and sit. "I've heard that level's pretty tough."

"It's a bitch. Spent a fortune trying to get here," he says, tapping.

"Worth every penny."

"Oh hush. It's my hobby, I'll spend every last cent I have on it if I want to. I don't even bug you about it on your phone."

"Okay."

He glares under his brow at me. "Fine, I'll put it away. What's up?" He tosses the pad to a nearby couch.

"I almost died yesterday. How's it going?"

"Now he's interested. Now he cares. He calls me once every couple months. I get emailed a photo of my grandson at the holidays. What did I do to deserve such blessings?"

"Hey, good talk. Good to see you. Guess I'll be going." I start to get up.

"Sit down, sit down. Fine. Sorry. You, uh, talked to your mother any?"

"Not for a while. She's doing her own thing, I guess."

"Woman couldn't hack it, fine. I don't need her dragging me down."

"I'm not even sure where she is exactly. Does that bother you any?"

"She's a grown gal. And she's not my problem anymore. You know women, they just wander off."

"Uh huh."

I tap my pant legs with my fingers, waiting for the moment to pass. I didn't come to talk about Mom.

He grunts. "How's the work? You still in customer service?"

"No, I moved to Infinite Solutions like six years ago. Junior Ad Executive."

"Sounds like fun," he says sarcastically.

"Loads. Did I mention I almost died yesterday?"

"You were always drawing when you were a kid. I remember when we got you that drawing game and you spent hours on that. I was surprised you didn't become an artist or something like that."

"It just didn't work out that way. Maybe because you told me there wasn't any money in it." Conversations about how I should take up something reputable. Like now, where I'm helping to sell ads for pre-teen asshole bleaching.

"Yeah, if you're some jerk who just wants to sit around and doodle. I'm glad you didn't do that. You know what I saw on the TV the other day? Some lazy bums down at Transportation wanted management to cut back to a ten hour day. Ten hour day. Might as well throw in a bed and some sleepy time tea if they want to take a nap. Next thing you know, they'll be asking for a whole extra day off. I say fire the whole lot of them. Just get rid of them."

"Yeah, they should totally do that."

He picks up his phone, scrolls through his feed.

"Sorry, I gotta keep tabs on my feed. You can keep talking if you want."

"Maybe they should go to a ten hour day."

"No way. Kills jobs."

I know better than to try and have this argument. Just let him run out of gas. It's cathartic for him. He likes to play the martyr.

"Dad, stop. I don't care about that stuff."

"You should care. These people are trying to kill our way of life. They want to kill jobs."

"Maybe they should." Fuck. I should not have said that. I bury my face in my hands, waiting for the deluge of slogans and talking points. He goes off about how the Dome was founded on the principles of the free market, of fair competition, the invisible hand, the nobility of job creators.

"Which sounds nice and good plastered on a t-shirt."

"I'm sorry you feel that way. You're wrong, but I'm sorry you feel that way. The Dome proves you're wrong. We're the greatest economy in the world because of that."

"It doesn't feel so great to me, Dad. Listen, I didn't come here to fight. "

He rolls his eyes, sighing. "You have a funny way of showing that. You always seem to start these little chats."

"You complain I don't call, but you complain when I talk to you about anything that you don't like. Pick one."

"Can't we just talk about... you know..."

"Stuff that doesn't matter?" I mutter, looking away.

"I was going to say your family. Wife and kids. Go."

"They're fine. Axel's on new meds. He's better, I guess?"

"That's good. Maybe he'll calm down a bit. How's Raylene? How's fashion therapy working for her?"

"She seems to like it. Money's tight." Tight is not the correct term. The knife edge of near-panic that has seeped into my cells.

"I know the feeling. Keep working hard. Things will turn around for you. Maybe you should start going to Mammon again."

They took me to Mammon for most of my youth. The church that says positive thinking makes you rich. Be wealthy in faith, they say. Consumers waste away praying for Mammon to bless them. I gave it up as soon as I left the house.

"Keep working hard? Like I'm not working my ass off already? Are you not listening to me or something? I was at Main Street yesterday because my boss ordered me to."

"Calm down. Why not go? What could it hurt?"

"Because I don't think that's a good idea. It's not for me."

"I go every week. I might even teach a class as Tanner. I got a few contacts there. Before your mother left, she used to worry about you. Now she doesn't worry about anything. Just going around, doing whatever she wants. I hope she's having a good goddamn time." The old wound is still there, right under his tightly packed skin.

"Thanks, but no thanks."

"Are you happy? Is whatever you're doing working out for you?"

"I don't even know what that word means, Dad. I have literally no idea."

"Isn't that your actual job though?"

"What do you think I do for a living exactly?"

"Settle down."

"No, I will not settle down. 'Are you happy?' 'Are you happy?' What kind of question is that?!"

"Do not talk that way to me. Maybe if you went to Mammon you wouldn't have this problem. You need to get your markets right, son."

"Like you? Pretending to be someone who pretends to be someone else."

"Thanks. At least it's an honest job. I'm older, but I'm still working. I'm not some sad greeter at an Ultimart or shucking Chik-N-Lil anymore." He shakes his head in disbelief. "You think just because you're young that you have all the answers. You think you're so smart. So clever. You want something that's not 'from a t-shirt' as you put it, fine. Here you go. There's going to come a day when mocking everything isn't going to be enough. This attitude is not helping you. You know I love you..." He throws his hands up.

I don't say anything, too angry that he might be right. I like my anger. It's something that's mine. I own it.

We sit in silence for a few minutes. He goes back to his game, angrily tapping. I make up an excuse that I need to meet Raylene somewhere to do something. I give him a rigid hug goodbye. I feel his bones. He's gangly, fragile, like a quick shove would snap him in two.

Down the hall, I look back to see the door to his room is still cracked open. I hide behind the corner on a corridor's turn, peering into his room. I spy him taking off his wig, showing his grey and spotted pate. He instantly ages twenty years. He picks up a hairbrush and grooms the wig with swift, sharp strokes, then stops, holding it in his hand, inspecting it.

~~~~

I sat alone in the empty, dark cafeteria. Surrounded by vending machines and plastic chairs and the emptiness. I don't even really know why. Maybe it was the fact I might be looking at my own future self, angrily playing games while my son withers into dust. Feeling like a trapped animal and having accepted it long ago. After a while, I stopped caring, and that was somehow worse. These are the times you're supposed to cry and feel all those big emotions. But there's nothing. A long stretch of lightless cafeteria, cheap plastic chairs and that lemon polish smell.

"Hey there, killer. Smile!" a voice says.

There's a phone camera flash from the dark, sharp like a burst of static.

Out from the blackness, a woman emerges, laughing softly to herself. The room grows hotter, tighter. It's the blonde woman from Infinite Solutions, the MA agent that humiliated Pierce. She holds her phone up to her eye, covering most of her face. She checks the photo. I can tell it's her, even in the murk. That same predator vibe, that jagged-toothed smile, a sharp face, small nose, impossibly pale eyes. Wearing a different coat, though. When she
~~~~

speaks, her voice is acid, like burnt wire or a saw cutting through bone. Something you hear before a bullet enters your forehead.

"I call it 'Sad Man in Repose'. I imagine if I squiggled some lines and put a picture frame around it, I could sell you for millions. Would you like that? Being sold for millions?" She puts her phone away and steps into the circle of my light.

"I know you. You were at Infinite Solutions, weren't you?"

"I was. It was... educational. I learned a lot about myself. I became a better person. I work for MA, are you familiar with our work?" She smiles tiny little knives. She's walking around me, circling me like a drain.

Memetic Analysis is a labyrinth of bizarre fetishes and borderline psychotics, the esoteric occult priesthood of Marketing. Their temple, the MA Department, is a blank white cube. No logos, no billboards, no face. Like soothsayers in designer clothes and unfathomable technology, they predict the future and report directly to Executive. They're the Chosen Ones. You don't just casually meet someone from MA, you experience their world at an uncomfortable closeness, like dancing around the barrel of a loaded gun.

I spin around, trying to keep track of her. "What are you doing here? Are you following me?"

"Maybe. But then again, not everything is about you.""

I don't really know what she means by that.

"What are you doing here?" I ask.

"What are you doing here?"

"Visiting my dad. He works here as an actor."

She nods. "I'm visiting my Nana. She still acts like she's people."

"People like you don't have a Nana."

"People like you don't normally have clever things to say. Speaking of which, why did you say that to Pierce? In front of everyone. I like to play with my food too but that was different. It hurt my feelings."

"You don't strike me as a person with feelings to hurt."

Her face closes, tightens like a fist. "Pretend then. Use your imagination like you did in that meeting. I ask again, why did you go off on Pierce? I hate repeating myself, by the way."

I shrug. "I was just angry and tired. Plus that guy is a human disease."

"Did you feel good about it? Do you feel vindicated?" She hisses the word vindicated like it's a curse.

"No."

"Liar and I know you're good at it. Lying, I mean. That wasn't just angry, tired drone talk. You would've just said a new phone that predicts hair loss or just nothing. What you said took thought. You thought about that for a long time. The final sweetener about Angela Trell was... poetic. Dug that knife right in."

"Who are you? I know you work for MA."

"Coyote Voyd."

"Nice brand name. Must've been pricey. I'm Cor-"

"I know exactly who you are, Corwin Scaggs. Junior Advertising Executive for six years. Married. One kid, Training Class Eight. A survivor. Most people get burned to a crisp at that job. Very high churn. Six years? That's rare. Are you rare?"

"Everyone is unique and special in their own way," I say. Coyote makes a disgusted laughing sound.

This conversation is going nowhere. "Is there something I can help you with?"

She looks at me for a long, uncomfortable time. She spins a chair around and sits on it backwards.

"Would you like to fuck me?"

It wasn't a proposition, more curious if anything. She lets out a sick little laugh, like the idea itself was ridiculous.

"No," I mutter. I can't meet her eyes.

"I forgive you. Look at me. You'd do me right on this table, with your Dad in the next room, and then go home to Raylene with my stink all over you."

"You know, for someone who picks trends, you really whiffed on that one." I glance to the door, trying to think of an excuse to leave. To go anywhere else. Her perfume is a cloud around me. Almost choking.

"I know you wouldn't really go through with it. You're a good boy. Loyal. Plus you're kind of a pussy."

"You're just trying to get a rise out of me."

"And I know it's working." That look again. She cracks her index finger knuckle with her thumb. Dead silence. There's a dripping faucet somewhere in the room. It echoes, cavernous in the empty room.

"I wonder what would make you snap. I mean, totally lose control. Not like in a boring shoot-up-your-cubicle type way, but something... special. More productive. When you have nothing left to lose, you know what it makes you?"

"What?" I barely croak it out.

"Free."

Her phone makes an electronic chirp.

"Say hi to Dad for me. Could you do one last thing for me? Could you have yourself a great day?"

She slides her chair away, scraping it against the linoleum floor with a gruesome screech. She answers the call without saying hello, listening. One last look at me up and down. Like a specter, she vanishes back into the dark. The tiny lit rectangle then vanishes around a corner.

I wait about two eternities before getting up myself, my legs shaky and weak, head weighing about the same as a block of concrete.

Shouts from the hallway. Some applause. A woman with hair like a mop says something about a "command performance". I leave the cafeteria to people filling the hallways, all looking down the way towards something. My dad is being wheeled out of his room on a gurney. I grab the nearest EMT and bark questions at him.

Massive stroke. He emphasizes the word "massive" by making a basketball shaped size with his hands, like he's impressed with how big it was.

6 ~ *health*

"We're going to the hospital, Dad. You're going to be fine," I mutter.

Dad is still alive. He weaves and bobs his head around, confused, mumbling words to himself in that slurred speech that comes out like a soup made of vowels. They found him in a crumpled mess on the floor, pants filled with piss, screaming at the ceiling that he had been "stolen".

A hospital's a great place if you have a bottomless bank account, you can practically live forever. Modern medicine can grow you a new heart or a hand if you lose it in a speedboating accident, a new face if you are splashed with acid. What they can't do is a coupon day.

The ambulance ride costs $16,000 and lasts approximately 8 minutes, or about $33 a second. A traffic light costs $990. I know this because I can see the financial screen in the ambulance quickly tallying his charges as we zip through traffic. A majority of the cars automatically pull to the side of the road, except for premium drivers, who pay for the ability to keep zipping along.

The EMT dabs my Dad's head with a sterile cloth, which costs $45 for a one time use item. When the ambulance pulls into the Val-U Emergency Health Center, Dad already owes the place a small fortune. I don't even know which hospital we're going to, and they already own everything that he has ever built in his life. Every cent is theirs before we even pull up to the curb or step in the door.

While my dad is dying, I have to electronically sign more forms than I've ever read in my life. The text is infinitesimal and there's literally thousands of pages. The screen flashes and beeps a hateful red to tell me to hurry up. Dad's heart rate is pinballing, so I scan them as quickly as possible. I guess it's pretty standard stuff: no liability incurred if Dad is misdiagnosed, injured, intentionally or accidentally killed by staff, doctors, or other patients, and there may be supplemental fees for HealthLine Service if he is discharged.

The EMT jokes and tries to keep Dad calm, who smiles through the oxygen mask in a delirious haze. He has no idea what's going on, but laughs because he should. His eyes roll back in his head and turn into white ping pong balls. His back arches like a frown. I finish signing the last form with my thumbprint and hand the pad to a nearby outstretched hand.

Hospitals stink of chemicals and slow death, and this isn't even the worst one. If this had happened in Bargainville, they would have carved up his organs fresh out of his still-living chest for sale.

After a few moments, the EMT tells me to go inside to the lobby and "chill out". He gives me a cheerful thumbs up and I weakly return it. The driver swings open the doors, yawns and scratches his bald head. They grab Dad by the armpits and yank him out of the ambulance like a piece of raw meat, slamming him onto a gurney. The EMT takes a photo of Dad, chuckling to himself. They leave and take him inside, his fragile head knocking around as they hop the curb. The doors slam shut.

Outside, it's quiet. A vent fan pumps a light breeze through the parking lot. Cars whizz by on the highway. A nearby speaker plays some gentle piano music, some water sound effects like there's a creek nearby, then an announcement welcoming you. The way they make it sound, you'd think they would be a rollercoaster shaped like a large intestine like at Forest Glen Executive Hospital. The trees have convincing birds bobbing up and down. Several customers, actors I assume, wander about the front door, talking to each other about the great care they've received, how reasonable and affordable the payment plans are. They have TV hair and clothes, that upper middle class confident gait that says "I'm okay, you're okay."

I brush past a couple loudly agreeing that the Dome has either great or the greatest healthcare system in the world. I open the door and a security camera audibly whirs in my direction, greeting me with its one black eye.

After showing my ID at the Security check-in, I pay my admission fee at the booth. I'm pointed in the direction of an escalator, which I take a full story down to the waiting area. I can't believe what I'm seeing.

And it's not just the sick. There are people with injuries that should have killed them. A stringy, pale twig around the same age as me holds his own hand in his lap, a red-soaked t-shirt wrapped around his stump. He's flying high on a handful of orange pills. An enormous nude woman with a gaping hole in her back sits with her equally naked child hand in hand watching a cartoon about a green owl that solves mysteries. The pockmarked child of undetermined gender is eating a butter popsicle. The women's open sore is about the size of a pink and glistening volleyball.

I take a moment. Several moments. I jump when a little girl wearing a complicated neck brace touches my arm.

"'Scuse me, mister."

The desk. Get to the customer service desk. I step over a stretched body lying on top of a child's sleeping bag, soaking in pools of fluids. A pair of ancient men wait wordlessly, one with his head on the other's shoulder. They look like skeletons in love. I carefully push aside their homemade IV, and the cogent one politely lets me pass, nodding. Acid burns and flayed limbs and ponds of bloody vomit. A galaxy of gunshot wounds. The lights crackle overhead. A robotic janitor mops a corner, but he's mostly just smearing around swirls of smelly brown liquid.

I wait in a cracked blue chair as far from everyone as I can.

~~~~

Hours pass and Raylene and Axel show up. I collapse into her. I'm so tired, so raw and empty that all I can do is let her hold me.
~~~~

Her hair smells clean and fresh, and I can tell she wanted to look nice for me.

Raylene and I wait, wait, wait in the waiting room. Axel is snoozing on a chair next to me, his thin arms roped around mine.

Raylene has her hand in mine, her head on my shoulder. Like when we were first married, waiting for Axel to come out of the incubator. I am composed entirely of cold metal. I have no idea how any of us are going to pay for this, Dad's savings are not going to be enough. He sank all of his money into his persona. My head is filled with pulsing hot lights that sting and burn. The hammer of the gun rises up, ready to fire at us.

I check the HealthLine app for an update on Dad. The image shown is an indistinct blob, the blood clot, happily driving a car traveling down the red road of my dad's vein. The "driver", the mass of coagulated cells killing my father, gets all confused and crashes in a goofy puff of smoke, clogging the "street". A big red frowny face appears with a thumbs down.

A loud siren squawks on and off, indicating a shift change.

Dad has no savings, no insurance, no assets to speak of. I push the nurse for info and he's partially being kept alive by the HealthLine, an incredibly expensive service that keeps his life support machines functioning. Don't pay your bill? They turn it off. You never know who "they" are, and there's a theory that not even they know who they even are. I imagine a bank of computer monitors with tired, drained people like myself staring into a wall of black and white numbers. As soon as a blocky number drops below a certain range, they type in a meaningless set of their own numbers. Somewhere else, a life ends and no one is even the wiser.

~~~~

The HealthLine app on my phone beeps, we can go see Dad now. The health center is a layered maze of corridors and hallways with blind turns that often double back on themselves. Signs are faded or nonexistent. There's almost no windows on the grime-covered walls. We pass a wandering patient tightly gripping the molding, steadying herself. She knocks into an occupied wheelchair. We pass rooms filled with the dead and dying.

This is actually a decent place, too. Unlicensed clinics, like the ones you see on Thrust, are basically butcher shops for bad cosmetic hackjobs and risky operations.

We follow the app and find Dad's room. Axel doesn't want to go inside, his chest rising and falling like a pump. Raylene wants to stay with Axel, so I go in alone into the darkened room. The frail patient sharing the room with Dad is actually more like a percentage of a woman. She only has one limb remaining and a portion of her torso, but she's flying high on Delox, smiling and humming as I enter. She waves her remaining hand. Above her, there is a cheerful poster with a doctor giving the looker a thumbs up. It's so big it stretches from the top of the bed to the ceiling.

Dad is barely visible behind two dozen tubes and pipes running into him. He looks like a fleshy pincushion, each IV causing an awful, splotchy bruise on his arm. He's curled, a little on his side, his legs tucked up underneath him. He gently touches the wall over and over.

"Hey, Dad. It's Corwin. Ray and Axel are here, too."
~~~~

He doesn't respond. I don't know if he heard me or not.

A voice behind me. It's the kind of voice you hear from a cartoon dog who smokes too much.

"Right now, he's so doped up he couldn't tell you the color of the ceiling."

The doctor is about my Dad's age, but rail-thin, a slightly crooked nose, with a short shock of white hair, looking over his glasses at me. He's wearing a white coat, so he's an actual doctor or a very convincing actor. They hire those sometimes to go into rooms like this and give terrible news to people like me, get me to sign documents transferring money, organs, etc. This guy looks like the real thing because he's not smiling like the poster behind him. Plus his breath smells like a bar's floor. He methodically taps through a medical chart on his pad. Swipe. Swipe. He rubs the screen with the cuff of his shirt.

"Hi, Doctor... whatever your name is."

"That color is technically called 'Pearl'. And you should be doing a backflip right now. There's only two people in this room. They're about to transfer him to the economy suites."

"Is that better?"

"Ten to a shelf, maybe out in Overflow. There's no infection control. So I'd say... no?"

"Are you drunk?"

He takes off his glasses and looks at me like a disappointed pet owner.

"No, I'm Doctor Silver. Listen buddy, I was on for thirty six straight hours dealing with a drexia outbreak near the Rockney exchange overpass. I was in the middle of a libation when I was called back in. Him over there? Resting comfortably in that bed, when he came in, they were ready to throw him out on the street. I got him that luxurious, palatial spot next to Miss Stumps over there. So climb down out of my ass and say 'you're welcome'."

"Miss Stumps? That's not funny."

"Wrong, it is. Her name actually is Miss Lyla Stumps. So objectively, scientifically, it is funny."

Miss Stumps rolls her head in our direction.

"I did it!" she says with a smile that's all teeth and drugs.

"Go back to sleep, sweetie," he says to the woman. "So, if you're concerned about my ability to take care of that man over there, I recommend as his doctor that you go get fucked."

"Fine. What's... what's the prognosis?"

"He. is. dying," he says matter-of-factly, crossing his arms.

All of the air escapes me. I am weightless. Dad coughs a dry puff of breath, his hand scraping the wall again.

"How long does he have?"

"That depends on how long that HealthLine stays on. It's regulating several of his automatic functions. Like his blood sugar production, heart rate and breathing. He is alive because of that machine."

"How much is it per day?"

"There is a family of zeros involved."

"How soon till the first payment?"

"He's already tried to make it and it bounced. He's racking up overdraw fees now. So are you going to step in or is someone else?"

"I don't have a lot of credit. I have even less liquid money right now. I couldn't even pay you with cash. All my paper cash expires at the end of this week. I can't."

"Can't or won't? Sorry, that came out wrong. I don't judge, but I need to know because this machine can save lives and there's only six in this building. And that's number six."

"Are you asking me if I'm willing to let my dad die?"

He coughs slightly.

"No, I am not. I am merely stating a situation as clearly as I can. Listen, let's go for a walk."

He takes me by the shoulder, a non-threatening paternal gesture. He's playing the Good Doctor in our little bit of theater. He takes me down the hall, chatting about his favorite sports team and how they rig their stats. His favorite bets are the ones he knows are wrong, just to be excited when they fail to fail. At a blank metal door, he scans his doctor's card and takes me into a space resembling a parking garage. He taps in some commands on a panel and half the lights flicker on. Concrete and beds. Coughing and moaning like an ocean wave crashing on the shore. There's no cars, only gurneys and stretchers filled with people.

He vapes in the silence.

"Where are we? Who are all these people?" I mutter.

"This little slice of heavenly hell is called Overflow. Charming, isn't it? Everyone who works here knows about it, no one wants to talk about it. If you think that zoo out front was a waiting room, you're wrong. That's more of a, uh, marketing experiment to see how people react in a compressed stress environment. All that paperwork? No point. To keep your mind busy while we rack up your bill. We know everything about your medical history as soon as you're thumb-scanned. You think the term Overflow means the space. No, it's the people. They're surplus."

"What do you mean?"

"You're smart. You know exactly what I mean. Some of them may get better and just get up and walk away. They'll escape the debt somehow and be fine. But the vast majority of them don't. Both of my moms died in a place like this. They were surplus."

"Yeah, life sucks."

He takes another puff of his vape and puts it away. "No, don't dismiss this. This isn't some existential bullshit thought experiment. These are real numbers."

I blink several times. More moans, suffering.

"Deep down there in some computer bank, there is an actual risk algorithm that determines if you are profitable enough to keep alive. My moms had no interest in reproduction. They grew me. Like I said, I'm okay with that. The point is no babies, no consumers. But not too many babies. Too much strain."

"I don't believe you. An algorithm? Come on. Also, what strain? Strain on what?"

He waved his hands around.

"Everything. That soda you wanted so badly and so cheaply. It has costs you can't even see. Just like how I can't see how slowly I'm murdering myself with these." He holds up a fresh vape cartridge. "Plus it helps the whole ironic doctor image. Part of that brand. Doctors aren't supposed to smoke this crap, but I do. Wet lung and everything. That means I'm edgy, possibly even a little rebellious. Customers are willing to try new things. But not too much, keep it in moderation. That's how I survived in this business as long as I have. I'm not a threat. I'm a flavor, just like low tar or menthol."

The smell from his vape is disgusting, like a burning pile of garbage.

"There used to be actual cigarettes made from tobacco. Grown in real dirt. They were the perfect product. They killed slowly, they were addictive, and sexy for some reason. I'd like to try the real thing sometime. Die for real."

"I always thought the best invention was the common cold."

Leaning back on the wall, he takes a puff, exhales, thinks.

"I know what you're getting at. That's clever, I like that."

"Thank you?" I say.

"You're very welcome. What I'm talking about you will never see on any medical database or financial report or stockholder statement. You'll never see it anywhere. It's buried so deep, so integral to how it works, this is just one of many, many..." The doctor bobbles his head from side to side, struggling. "Erosions of the surface."

"Sure. Whatever. Are you saying you're not going to help my dad? Every second I have to listen costs us money."

"I didn't say that."

"Then what are you saying?"

"You're not dumb, but no offense, you're little people. You can't see the Big Picture. The Big Con as someone told me once. Your dad is surplus, trust me. You think even if you came up with the money they wouldn't find a way to off him?."

"Bullshit. If that was even remotely true, there would be burning cars in the streets. Everyone in Bargainville will hang Management from the Tower for that. Prove it. Show some evidence."

"Proof? Are you on pills?" he exclaims, "Maybe I know because sensible, upstanding consumers like yourself won't believe people like me. Look at me, do I look respectable to you? Do I look like I should be advertising anything? Sorry to burst your ego, but I tell this to almost every person I meet, and I'm not in a security cell. If I was a genuine threat, this place would be surrounded with goons, ready to bash me against a curb. To the Company, it's not checkers, it's chess. Prediction and reaction."

He puts away the vape again.

"This has been a fun experience, but I need to figure stuff out." I turn to leave.

"I've seen how much your dad owes. He can maybe make one or two weekly payments before they shut that machine off. Maybe. And then he will die. As in dead. No more Dad."

"Thank you, doctor. It's been so much fun."

"It doesn't have to be that way."

I sigh. I stop.

"Why's that?"

A cloud of vape stink approaches me from behind.

"Because I have a secret. Do something for me, I do something for you."

"Nope."

"I haven't even asked you yet."

"Don't care. I'm done here."

I throw my hands up in surrender and walk back to the hospital. My phone rings. It's from a number I don't recognize. I answer.

"Hello, Corwin. This is Coyote Voyd. We met right before your dad's head imploded. What are you wearing, sexy?"

My blood runs solid in my veins. "I'm in the middle of something right now. What do you want?"

"I want to have some fun. I have some delicious info about Doctor Sterling Silver you may want to know."

"How did you...?"

"Consider it a second round of interviews. You passed the first one, by the way. Be a bad boy with this info and we'll talk again real soon."

She hangs up and a few seconds later I receive an email.

~~~~

Dr. Silver slumps on the floor against a vending machine, face smeared with chocolate, reeking of booze like he'd been soaking in it for good measure. He looks like a pathetic, lost child. His head wobbles downwards and a croak comes out.

"I can't get up."

"What are you doing?" I ask.

"Your Dad's stable for right now. Breathing and such. Guess what I did today?"

"Drank until you puked?"
~~~~

"Nope, already did that." He points a shaky finger towards a biohazard bin. "Can you check that for my lung? Looks like a burnt steak."

"We need to talk. You and me. Right now."

"Listen, I'm sorry that I am less than professional right now. I'm having a moment. And I'm off duty for right now." The doctor grabs his collar, shakes it out.

"Let's have a moment."

"Spill it. We're practically friends at this point."

I grab him and smash him against the vending machine. He laughs, like it's an amusement park ride. The metallic clang echoes. We are totally alone. There's not a single conscious person expensive enough to hear us.

"You said my dad didn't have to be this way. Start talking."

"You look so dumb when you're angry," he says laughing.

"A little birdy told me that you've been siphoning off meds and selling them. It's mostly pills for cancer pain management. Assume you're selling this under the table, maybe having some yourself. But considering the amount you've been moving..."

"Bullshit," he says, but the word has extra syllables slurred into it.

I tighten my grip around his tie. "How would you like to face down a Commerce Board and tell them all about it? I could send them a quick little text."

"Fine, tell the Commerce Board of the hospital. Tell Security. I'll put my hand on a stack of the Ways and Means and throw myself before their mercy, which they won't have, because if they really cared, I won't even make it to a hearing. I'll fall into traffic or

I'll overdose, which I probably would at some point anyway. My name will be a blip in the company newsletter, which no one reads anyway. I'm really scared, my man."

"I'm serious." I hold up my phone with the inventory transfer report right on the screen.

He snorts. "Wait, you think I'm stealing them? Fuck you. I buy with my medical license and resell wherever I can. To real patients who can't cut the cost. Hospital gets thirty percent and leaves me to deal with the buyers. Real nasty crowd. I can't count how many times I've had a gun pointed at me. It's very memorable."

I stop, loosen my grip. "This doesn't bother you that I know this?"

"So what? I make more money for them than I cost. I'm a bargain. Yes, I fudge the numbers but it's more expensive to hire a goon squad to rough me up. As long as I don't sell too much or get too sloppy, they don't care. Industrial feuds are expensive as hell. You know what the fine is for murder? It costs a fortune for someone like me."

He stands up the best he can, slinks over to a couch, and falls over it. He lays on his back. "You said you had a unique day today. I had a day like that once."

I'm too dazed. I'm living in a white fog now. "What?"

"There was a mother and daughter in that room right over there. The daughter had stomach cancer, which makes eating solid food impossible. The pain, you see? She was fed through a tube right in her stomach with a soft syringe. Before she became totally unresponsive, I used to inject Chik-N-Lil dinners into her. Even though she couldn't taste anymore, she said she liked the Shrimp

Cocktail. That is, I used to. Cost is too high. Hospital won't give her any more credit. Food stops and it's an unavoidable tragedy and the hospital is of course very sorry and they did everything they could. Etcetera etcetera. Pretty standard. By the way this just happened while you were checking your email. For the last six days, her mother was forced to watch her daughter starve to death right in front of her. No insurance. No credit. A C level employee at a restaurant."

"Why did she watch?" I ask, my voice barely above a whisper.

"She actually had to. She had to visit the hospital twice a day to thumbprint the machine to keep her daughter actually alive. Due to her exclusivity contract with this place, she couldn't move her to another competitor. She brought liquified food and tried to inject it, but it wasn't the right kind. DRM. I searched everywhere I could for extra. Business keeps it locked up tight. Eventually Mom just stopped coming. I guess it was too much. HealthLine did nothing and her little body was sold off for organs and didn't fetch that much. That girl loved to draw the sun. Her mother sang to her while she starved. That's why I'm fucking drunk right now."

"What was her name?"

"Jodi Thornton."

"What happened to her mother?"

"I don't know. I don't want to know. I don't want to know anything anymore."

Surplus.

"Doctor Silver, you're going to get up and you're going to help me."

"Help you with what?"

~~~~

I locate the little girl wearing the VR headset I noticed when they brought Dad in. I don't know which brand she uses, but it's expensive. She can't be more than eight or nine, but after a quick search I learn she's a top sponsored player. She sits with another girl the same age, probably a sister or visiting friend. They're a duo: Kira and Toppy. I hover in the doorway, not sure how to introduce myself without sounding like a pervert.

I turn back into the room. There's a monitor for the non-player child to watch. They're playing Legend of Heroes, a free-to-play title where, if you're dedicated, you can spend thousands of dollars a day on items, characters, quests, all sorts of stuff. A sandbox playground for theft and fraud, making it perfect. Your most valuable currency in a game like this is your ability to scam and get away with it.

Kira's face is slack, motionless and she gestures wildly. Her haptic gloves dance in the air with the skill of a surgeon. Not unlike the one who left an angry red surgery scar in her back, wrapped in a red-stained bandage. Every so often, Toppy checks her phone and whispers something to the player. Kira nods back, absorbing the information. A team, like a pit fighter and a coach slapping her on the back to get back out there.

She's in the Depths of Rathbane, a particularly advanced PvP zone. You fight other players for control points and mana springs. The rush is that you bet real money on the matches, some put down tens of thousands of dollars. Beating someone could
~~~~

potentially be sending them to the Machine. It's quite literally the power of life and death. I tap her friends on the shoulder and she whips her head around, staring at me with red-rimmed eyes.

And then it shows up on the screen. An animated pulsating mass of black leaves blossoms in front of me. A gold border surrounds the item box, indicating its very special value. The idea, grinding like a set of rusted metal gears, crunches and strains until the flaking iron cracks open and the wheels begin to turn. It whirrs around and around in my head, fast and hot and perfect like a diamond wheel. I know how to save Dad. I can do it.

~~~~

My phone is in my hand. Go back in, stupid, spend what little time you have left with that stranger you call Dad. Text Raylene and tell her you'll be home soon. Patch things up with a nice dinner, a backrub. Play some video games with Axel and let him win. Make this as nice a day as it can be.

I'm not exactly quite sure why I called her, but I did.

"You pass, killer. You're hired," Coyote whispers.

"What are you up to? Where is this going?"

"Enjoying myself with a little trifle right now. Why do you ask?"

"I need to talk to you about something. An idea. And I wanted to thank you, I guess."

"I just said I was enjoying myself already. And plus, men like you always just want 'to talk.' They always just want to 'thank me.'"
~~~~

My face feels flush. "It's not like that."

'What do you need, Corwin? This is the part where you ask."

"I need help."

"I thought you had all the smart answers, mister smarty-man."

"I need an assist on an investment plan. Please."

I hear silence. She's trying to make up her mind. She chuckles, pleased I'm groveling. "I like this. I like you asking with sugar on top." Coyote waits an eternity before speaking. "Sure. I'll meet you at the health center in... an hour? Sound good?"

"Fine."

I text Raylene and tell her I'm staying until later to get the results of a test. She replies with a thumbs up.

<div align="center">~~~~</div>

Coyote meets me in the hallway outside Dad's room. I can hear her high heels clacking on the tile, drawing closer. She sits in the chair next to me, putting her arm around me, pretending to cry.

"We all think we got things figured out until a new variable is added. You had a decent chance of throwing yourself off your cute little garden rooftop until today. You've probably thought about it at great length," she says, taking a sip of her Koffee.

I had.

"How did you know about my garden? I never post about that."

"I work for MA, stupid."

"I don't know much about it. But that's just anonymous metadata. We use it at IS all the time. Targeted ads."

"It's anonymous when you get it because you have to buy it. Raw data is useless to a shitshop like IS. But not to us. We get it raw. You like it raw?"

"Cute."

"You often look at pre-Dome images of trees and plants an average of forty-two percent longer than your actual porn. Plus the amount and cluster of purchases of Real-Life Plantz, combined with their type, size, variety. That's why you see more images of plants in billboards when you walk by them. Why the internet provides you with a steady stream of nature vistas, waterfalls, pre-Dome animated screens about twenty percent more than the average person. It's also digitally inserted into the background of a lot of your favorite shows. It's not hard to figure out. You like plants. You like how they don't ask anything of you. That they represent something real that you can never truly have."

"How astute of you. You get that from the manual?"

"Hey jokester, you wanna see something really funny?"

She shows me the picture on her phone. My limp dick hanging lazily out of my pants in a bathroom stall. I say nothing.

"We see everything. I mean, I can take it off my local device, but it's still in the cloud. Imagine, all those dicks and titties and alleyway fucking just floating around out there forever. Even after that person is dead, I can still look at their clit or shaved balls whenever I feel like it. Especially if you're famous and dead. People know you're corpse jelly and still jerk off thinking about you."

No smile. No look of disgust. Nothing. Don't give her anything.

"I said I need your help," I say through clenched teeth.

"Nothing adorable to add? You all done?"

"My dad, who is not dead yet, needs a HealthLine. They don't have one here. I need to move him out of this place, get him to my place."

"You're using the word 'need' a lot. I don't need you, you know. I like you. You have potential. Sell me."

"You're right, you don't need me. You want me to work for you or whatever. He isn't dead, but he is dying. He needs a HealthLine and I can't get it here for much longer. You want me for something? Do this and I'm in."

She gives me a small, almost imperceptible smile. "Even if I didn't know your exact Number, I know you don't have the money. No one does, they're not supposed to."

"What do you know about 'alternate' HealthLine sources?"

"There are no legitimate third party HealthLine vendors. Are you asking me to... to violate UCorp and Val-U HealthLine policy?" She puts her hand to her chest, mockingly shocked. "Well, I never!"

"Be creative."

"There we go. That's more fun. That's the game I want to play. Come sit down next to Mommy." She pats the cracked plastic of the seat.

I cautiously sit down.

"What do you think, I have a coupon in my purse or something?" she says, tapping out something on her phone.

"You seem to like me. I don't know why. Figured you'd find it amusing to watch me squirm and beg. Plus I already said I'm in if you do this."

"If you think I need a fumbling fuck in the back of a car, think again. I dress like this because it makes idiots like you turn to mush. I don't need your help. I just think you have real potential. Consider this your audition."

"What, no teenage insecurity hiding in there? No daddy issues?"

"Do I look insecure?" Her voice is made of steel. She's a vicious creature by her own design. She enjoys me and terrifies me to death, but she's the only help I can get right now.

"I have an idea. It's worth a hell of a lot more than what I'm asking. Consider this an investment opportunity." I show her the plan.

She lets out a sick little laugh. "You want a lot of money, no strings attached, no contract."

"Correct."

"You got some brass balls, Corwin. You are just full of surprises."

"Everyone underestimates me."

"I'm just curious to see if it'll work."

"Yes or no. Do we have a deal?"

"This is walking around money. It's not the amount. Maybe I'll buy a nice couture t-shirt with your dick pic on it."

She pleasantly smiles and moves closer to me. I think she's about to kiss me when she viciously grabs my balls with her left hand in an iron grip. Imagine your testicles crushed under a thousand leagues of pitch-black seawater. A rusted garbage compactor crushing all future generations of tiny, swimming Scaggs. I grab her wrist and she squeezes even harder.

"There we go. There we go. Shh shh shhhh..." she whispers as I writhe. "We have a deal. No handshakes, no contracts. I felt this is more... accurate of our relationship now."

After about a million seconds, she lets go, flexes her black glove. I slump over, trying to catch my breath with a wet, hacking cough. She taps on her phone.

"Done. I'll be in touch."

~~~~

I find Dr. Silver vomiting into a chemical toilet. I buy him some fresh bottled water and get him a cool compress for his head. We go to his office, a tiny cube with an empty desk. The whole room is the size of a storage closet. His head lays on his desk and I lean in close, trying not to talk too loudly.

"So how does this work? You play online poker or something?" he asks the floor.

"What you do is, you sponsor a player in Legend of Heroes. You don't play it yourself. You have a job and a wife and kid, whatever. They do nothing but play the game all day long. They don't bathe or shave. They have jars of piss all around them and survive on stims and only logout to crash. They live and die for this game. It has a body count."

He lifts his head a bit. "There's a theory that it has a low level hypnotic wave spliced in between frames." His forehead drops back to the cool surface.

"Irrelevant. If it does, fine, whatever. I want my player to be addicted to it. Back when we did copy for them, we had to play and
~~~~

spend some money on it. Be familiar with your client's product. There's an item in the game called 'Black Lettuce.' It has no use in the game, but it was supposed to be in every drop variety, white, green, yellow, orange and the purple ultra-rare."

"You said it was black."

"It is black. Never mind. The point is that it never drops in anything except purple."

"Is this just some nerd crap or is there a point?"

"Rare equals valuable. It looks rare, but actually isn't in certain circumstances. I'll have to go into a lot of lore to catch you as to why, but most importantly, it's unintentional. In this certain area of the game, if you wear certain gear, there's a still unpatched glitch that causes Black Lettuce to drop more often. That's what it's called: 'Black Lettuce'. If a player stays alive and farms for it in a certain way, there's another bug that makes it drop a lot."

He's reeling. "Stop stop stop. This is making my head hurt."

"Fine. You contract them with a NDA to not to tell anyone about the exploit. Maybe you don't even tell them about the exploit. Say you're going for a shadow achievement. Plus if they get caught, they get IP banned. They'll kill themselves if they get IP banned."

"So it has no use in the game. It's junk. Why would anyone want it?"

"Because it's rare and people will buy it. Who cares 'why'? Sell it for in-game credits, buy other items with it. Sell those items on a cryptocurrency site. Take that cryptocurrency and resell to a clearing house exchange. Buy stock. Then sell stock for money. No one thinks about this because it's too many steps and it's not a gigantic payout. Here's the thing: I don't need a huge payout, just enough. We're going to pump and dump this stupid thing as much as possible before it crashes the in-game economy." I point towards the general direction of Dad.

"HealthLine is thousands a day. Thousands," he says, rubbing the bridge of his nose.

"That's doable. People get caught when they get too greedy. All I need to do is pay the minimum for a couple weeks until I figure something better out."

"This is a bad idea. Plus, why the hell do you need me for this?"

"You know the ins and outs of the HealthLine. Where the cracks are. I'll take care of the money."

"You know what's going to happen if you get caught doing this? What do you think is going to happen to your wife or your son if you get hauled away? They'll slap so many fines on you, you'll be pulling midnight in Bargainville for the rest of your life."

"Once I get it set up, I'll, I don't know, scrounge together some second hand parts and move him home. Then you can duplicate Dad's specific program and route the HealthLine to whatever address I put him at."

"Route the HealthLine. You mean pirate it. Steal it."

"If I walked out with one of those machines under my arm, yeah. We're just cloning access to the program. We're not stealing anything. And if we were, so what?"

"We?" He points to himself.

"You're in trouble just by listening to me. Violation of terms of service to participate in a discussion of a violation. What? Why would you show me that parking garage? Why tell me about that girl? You wanna save that man's life? This is how we do it."

He waves his hand. "Alright, enough." He rubs his chin, thinking hard.

A crash team runs by, and I clench, expecting Security to kick down the door and throw me in a cell. But no one comes. No one out there's listening, maybe they never were.

I find the two girls and offer them a contract that same day. They agree.

They don't even ask why.

7 ~ neon

It's 18 o'clock, my shift is over. Cars on the main highway slice the air silently like sniper bullets. Concrete ribbons rise above and curve through the dimming night, their dark smiles grinning at me in the dusk.

Silver gave me the address where I could possibly find what I needed. A heart and BP monitor, a liver regulator to fight sepsis, and a dialysis machine.

I walk several blocks as the day dies.

The night does not immediately happen like a light switch turning on and off, and more of a gradual dimming of the lights. Dusk is programmed for around 45 minutes, and designed to bathe everything in a sensual glow. The artificial sun dips towards the sight horizon and angry red or orange pixelated clouds swarm around the blob. Four hours later, the cycle begins again. 4 hour-nights are theorized to be the minimal amount of sleep time necessary to avoid permanent neurological damage, lowered from 5 hours of night about 10 years ago. Management protested that the extra hour disrupted their workflows, and a variety of logistics would have to be recalibrated, but they begrudgingly accepted when coffee brands were updated with new stimulants, leading to a 14% increase in worker activity. There were an acceptable amount of psychotic breakdowns. A real shame, of course, but acceptable. They were "so promising" if what you hear. Taken before their time. Silver's theory about the intentionality of it grows a little bit in my mind.

A Security officer, barely old enough to start thinking about girls, looks up from his phone as I pass him. I can tell from the sound effects that he's playing Taxman, one of those brain-liquifying horror shows where the purpose is to click a thing as much as possible, then you get some stars, which you can then turn into coins, and it exhausts me just to think about it. I've been doing enough of that lately, I'd like to not look at a screen for a moment.

He puts the game away.

"Can I help you with something, sir?" Sir. It's a word surrounded by condescension, smugness. It's a word that actually means "asshole."

Violence beams off this kid like radiation. He enjoys his job: the ritual of putting on the uniform, the crude sense of power coursing through his puckered skin, wearing the disturbingly black and blue uniform, the weird hat, his oversized flashlight, pepper spray, the shiny gold badge pinned to his chest. The gun attached to his hip.

The uniform barely contains his rage; a primal, base color. Pasty and clammy, brimmed to the gills with a combination of aggression enhancers, digital murder, greasy porn vids, fried Chik-N-Lil, and caffeine.

An odor like a stale workout sock hovers around him. He most likely hasn't slept in days, just spending nights online, escaping his vacuous pain with another round of Fuck Gun, another quality title from the company you can trust. I can't tell if he's perfect or a tragedy.

He repeats his question.

"No, I don't think so."

"Where's your car, sir?"

"Felt like walking tonight. It's so nice out."

He lets out a snort, half-laugh, half-mucus. He's leaned up against a railing, high above a darkened lot. I look around. We're alone.

"ID."

I fish it out and hand it to him. He keeps looking at it like it's going to speak up for me.

I must have flipped a switch in him because he immediately goes through the entire security protocol, asking me where I work, where I live, running my card. This whole process feels designed to waste my time, make him feel important, show me how small I am. I've never seen a Security Officer ever stop a crime, or help someone, or made me feel any more secure. Also, there is over $10,000 in cash taped to my lower back. I look around again. Empty street in both directions.

"So one more time, why are you walking, sir?"

"I don't know. I just wanted to."

He shrugs his shoulders. "I don't get it."

"Okay."

"Watch the lip, sir. You're fine. The final total for this interaction will be auto-mat-ically de-duct-ed from your account, sir. Have yourself a nice night."

He hands me back my ID.

~~~~

The address I arrive at has been closed for some time. It has that rank desperation all around it. The former sign has a big black line through it, obscuring the name. It used to be a tropical-themed store, one of those kitsch shops that are perpetually going out of business, emblazoning jagged neon letters on their windows. After this place closed, they just dumped all the crap in a big pile out back and threw acid on it.

A molten hillock of plastic palm trees, boogie boards, piranha-shaped clocks, cheap neon T-shirts, animatronic hermit crabs, shot glasses, foam pool noodles, car chargers, Swine Pearl lunchboxes, fuzzy keychains, hot pink sandals, beer coolers, spiritual enhancement pills, the stuff of dreams and landfills.

Raylene climbed the kitsch hill and I puttered around the base of it. About a hundred other boys were busy smashing light tubes against the ground and eventually each other.

I find a little half globe filled with blue water, the same toilet bowl blue as the River, with a replica of the Dome, when shaken, a white tornado of foam snow would erupt and terrorize the nested Dome, then settle like a soft hand, covering the North and South in giant pearly rocks.
~~~~

The parking lot is desolate like an asphalt desert. Harsh sodium vapor lights create yellow pools in the murk. The blackness is ribbed with the bones of former car tracks, now removed, leaving looping cuts in the surface, like a slasher victim.

Tattered bits of foil rattle past my leg. This building's lot is also in a strange wind trap, possibly a convergence under one of the circulators. A mini-cyclone tosses the detritus about in random patterns. I'd like to think that all this chaos was working towards an act of meaning, this pathetic store closing, my father dying, and that it was just the ecosystem of the Dome sorting itself out. An invisible hand pushing us all ruthlessly along. Like how the first molecules congealed themselves into self-replicating proteins. But those processes had rules and guidelines and the benefit of endless time. We're those molecules, rebounding off of each other, trying to find electrons to trade like tourist trinkets, like a gigantic organic stock market, where everyone is assigned a price and can be bought and sold at discount. The ecosystem of the economy, the amoebic animal devouring anything succulent in its path, spreading its wings to new markets, new flesh. Always growing. Always hungry. Blind, hateful, and indifferent.

I walk closer to the store. The aisles are blank, void of their contents, leaving behind the unnerving perspective of row after row of empty shelves. I feel lightheaded.

"Welcome to Tropical Delights. Can I help you find anything tonight?"

A young woman is standing behind me. I turn around, slightly startled. She's wearing a rumpled blue vest, a pair of ratty jeans, with a sweater covered in rainbow-colored gems in the shape of an

Xmas tree. She looks scavenged. Her hair is a confusing color, both sassy red and sky blue at the same time. She must think the store is still open. She smiles courageously and then lets out a rough, wet cough into her wrist.

"Excuse me." Her name tag says Destiny.

I motion to her tag. "That's a very nice brand name."

She blushes slightly.

"It's actually not a brand name, but thanks. Were you looking for anything in particular today?" She doesn't really look me in the eyes, more off to the side.

"Can I speak to your, um, manager? I have an item for curbside."

"Sure, one moment. Follow me"

We walk behind the wall into the alleyway.

On the side of the store, there's a service corridor; a faded cardboard display with a beach scene welcomes me to the new Tropical Delights. Beyond that, hidden in a mix of shadows and barrel fires, some folding tables covered with a dirty blue tarp. Someone has taken a grease pen and drawn waves on the tarp, simple little w's, like a child would. The tables are covered with cheap off-brand tablets, toys with misspelled labels, a pile of metal bolts, doll heads, some expired paper cash wrapped in packs of $10,000, squirt guns, protected by malformed action figures.

Beyond the tables, I'm led to a staircase heading to a service tunnel underground. It's a place you find a dead body at the bottom of. I follow her down the metal stairs, our footsteps echoing. At the bottom, she politely knocks on a rusted door. A slat of metal slides open, revealing a set of bloodshot eyes and pounding, deadened bass.

"This gentleman has an item for pickup."

"What's the item?" The voice is thick and icy.

"Um…"

"H Care," I say.

He sniffs, wipes his nose, then looks me up and down. He disappears. There's scraping sounds on the other side of the door, then it opens. The music is almost deafening now. Destiny waves me in, like she's the hostess at an expensive restaurant.

A fridge-sized man, dyed blonde hair and covered in tattoos. He looks like he spends most of his day on that stool next to the door. A shotgun is lazily propped up against the wall. He yawns and sits back down, slams the door shut with a massive arm.

The basement isn't any larger than a two car garage. It's swelteringly hot, probably a maintenance tunnel that leads further down into the auto-distribution machinery underneath the old store.

A high-pitched, feverish drum-and-bass scorcher pounds in my ears. Greasy furniture, nondescript boxes, and a table covered with pill dispensers. In the corner, I see the pearl white containers, emblazoned with the blood red crosses.

"Those are probably it," I say, pointing to the boxes.

"Not yet" A mask of a foul-smelling monkey screams up to mine and I jump back. The mask comes off and I'm face-to-face with Titan Brass. He's a clammy, sweaty skeleton with a mop of tangled dreadlocks, pitch-black teeth, and orange, reptile eyes.

Titan cackles and tosses the mask away on a fart-soaked couch. Barely standing, he fights against gravity and sleep.

"So so so. The Good Doctor sends little old you to pick this up all by yourself? Huh? Naughty naughty."

"He knows where I am. Anything happens to me, if I don't get what I want, those-" I point to the table of pills. "Vanish."

"Relax, man. Shotgun's just for uninvited guests," The bouncer says, flipping through a magazine.

"Yeah, mister man. Mister Doctor Man. Mister Man About Town. You want pills?"

"Those three boxes and that's it. Agreed upon amount was ten thousand. Hey Door Guy, lift up my shirt. There's ten grand, unexpired, strapped to my back."

He sighs. "My name's Gregory."

"Sorry, Greg. I just don't want to reach into my shirt and scare you two."

"Only my mom calls me Greg." He gets up off his stool like he's never walked before. He untucks my shirt with a sharp tug and carefully removes the tape. He does so almost delicately.

"Thanks for not ripping that off."

"You're welcome. Ugh, it's all wet."

"Sorry. Been taped there for most of the day."

"Gross. It's okay, don't be nervous. Titan's just antsy."

Titan Brass is sitting upside down on one of the couches, gawking at me, his dreads spilling out onto the floor. "Hey Mister Man, if you want us to fix you up, we can fix. You. Up. We can put a little face on your dick, give you some big titties, a moving tail, the works. We got our own chop shop and everything." He opens his mouth and sticks out both of his tongues, wiggling them at me.

"Just the equipment, that's all."

"Give him the shit," Titan cackles.

I look at Gregory and he motions to the boxes. I walk over, and with eyes in the back of my head, inspect them. BP monitor has some wear and tear. Dialysis needs a new power cord, and most annoyingly, the liver regulator needs an adapter.

"All good?"

"For the most part, it's what I need. I'll need a few boxes and a cart to hide these in."

"No worries. We'll get you some smelly ones so no dumb Sec sticks his fat nose in it. Saw one shuffling around outside. Think he's gone now."

"That'll do. Can we hurry this up? I'm on a tight schedule."

"Time waits for no man, Mister Man," Titan says, showing me his black teeth. As I'm packing up, Gregory is working on a penrose model kit, a lovely pink one. It looks perverse in this dungeon.

"Oh, you garden?"

"Good for color down here," he waves his brush around the room.

"You having problems with petal drooping?"

"Actually, yeah. The silk ones keep practically disintegrating."

"You should use Type B, not A. Preserves color tone and doesn't weigh it down too much. Switch to polyester."

He nods a thank you, turning the penrose in his hand. Titan is staring at his naked toes.

At the register, I pretend to buy something from Destiny. I pick up a plastic plant: a purple hyacinth. I turn it over in my hand, inspected the molding around the stems, checking the curls for cracks. It's a decent but flawed find and has potential.

"Would you be interested in our Premiere Club?"

"What's that?" I immediately regret asking.

This must be the first time someone has asked, because she brings up a printed card and rattles off a sales pitch.

"All purchases made by UCard will have transaction fees waived for the first five percent. If you spend more than fifty dollars on a single purchase, you can earn points."

"That sounds very nice, but no thank you."

"I like you," she says this in a matter-of-fact way.

"I appreciate that."

"Do you like me?"

I smile and slowly walk away, not trying to appear like I'm running. Gregory sits back in the creaking chair, belches, and calls for Destiny.

"Thanks for shopping at Tropical Delights. Come again," she says, her voice distant and ghostly. She wanders over.

An empty store, surrounded by the ghosts of its former luster, and just like all the things I want to experience, so fragile, distant, just out of my reach. Dad's life fits conveniently into 3 boxes on a hand dolly, my new plant resting on top. I call for a Drive and it shows up a moment later. The driver, a sullen woman with a permanent smoker's lip, even helps me load the boxes in.

As we drive, my mind wanders. Once on TV, the Memory Channel aired a special called "The Architecture of Loss" in which several building companies were competing to create the saddest building possible, or one that evoked an intense feeling of loss, so shoppers could go and stare, safely unloading their collective sense of grief. The buildings they erected were things like abandoned orphanages, toxic oil spills with realistic dolphins, an empty billboard over a dumpster. I don't remember who won. They obviously did not see Destiny twirling her hair aimlessly, scratching her neck with chipped fingernails. They did not see the faded palm tree display. All gift-wrapped up with the ever-present possibility of grim, ugly violence.

We drive away quickly from the skeleton box and all its ghost voices.

~~~~

Dr. Silver discharges Dad quietly and we move him into my house in the back of the Drive I ordered. The storage closet is now a miniature hospital. Silver splits apart some wires, elegantly solders the connection to fit the HealthLine adapter into the hardware.

Silver hooks Dad up without tripping any of the sensors for his respiratory and heart monitors. Axel finds the entire setup fascinating, he thinks it's a video game. Raylene says little, rubbing my back as I enter the room with Dad in my arms. He weighs so little, like a paper and wire man draped over my arms. The connection is solid, so the machines keep operating. For now.

Every second is a stolen moment of life for him, the Black Lettuce transactions running automatically, the billing handling through the grey market resellers. He's on autopilot for now.
~~~~

Dad's heartbeat flutters on the black screen. My heart, my own fleshy, pumping blood organ, feels black or grey, some color of dead static. I smooth out his blanket on the bed, reattached all his tubes and lines, place the electrodes on his sagging pectoral, the thin metal sensors to monitor his brain activity on his clammy forehead.

The human brain weighs about 1-2 kilograms and has approximately 100 billion neural connections. How many of them are used to remember a commercial jingle? Your TV schedule? Your favorite laxative yogurt? Your pet's birthdays? The first time you had a dirty thought? The moment you first remembered?

I attach the last sensor to his temple to track these things.

My first memory of him, one of those blurry smears in the back of my head, is him walking through the living room at our first apartment. I must have been around 5 or 6, if people even have ages like that anymore, and I was staring at a block toy assembling itself, trying to figure out its eventual shape.

He was digging through the couch cushion, those spindly legs awkwardly splayed out, and he fished out the remote for the TV. He had an argument with Mom about what to watch. Then I was probably on Proxol, Halitonin, and Metabrax, so most of my childhood is smeared across my memory. Like a poorly edited commercial of frightening, confusing moments.

Mom should be here to witness every second. Every labored breath. Every drip from his saline bag into his vein, every electron passing through his body keeping him alive. I need to go see her. I've been in panic mode for days and I forgot to even call her. I don't even know the last time I slept.

She's no more at fault than those hospital vultures. Silver's insane explanation doesn't seem so insane when you see it up close like this. The machinations of a maniacal device designed from the ground up to squeeze you into oblivion. To lock you away while your organs slowly shut down one by one, like that pathetic strip mall, every store closing its gates.

The heat kicks on.

I check the time and it's late, or it's early, one of those strange hours when it's no longer evening. The deep dark of our short nights, with each night revealing a new way to suffer, survive, and live again. I stay with him until morning happens.

The world has shrunk to the size of my father's closet room, the four walls lined with cardboard boxes and exercise equipment. The borders of the known universe. A box within a dome. Smaller and smaller until we're each inside our own heads, staring at each other.

His gallbladder has almost shut down, that storefront nearly shuttered, his liver is barely functioning anymore, and his skin turns a sickly banana color.

His breath sounds plastic.

His eyes aren't so much open as they are present and accounted for. An inventory of my father's failing body, the clammy, mishandled wreck that no one would accept on trade.

I stare into my future.

His feet have started to turn black, mainly due to the lack of circulation. His whole body is now a gigantic traffic jam. Everyone has places to go, except they don't know where exactly. Life revolts against him, the complex machinery of the body which he fueled with pastries, vat-grown meats, a galaxy of complex chemicals, television.

My father.

His middle name is Ernest. Borson Ernest Scaggs, the last wonder of the world. Watch his organs fail right before your eyes. Watch his raspy breath tell you mystical secrets. The body is such a poorly designed thing. The people downloading themselves online may have the right idea, just live as electrons in a sea of porn and murder until the heat death of the universe. Dad didn't want that, he didn't understand the way it worked, and it was too expensive. Funny. I almost don't remember a time when he wasn't dying of something.

There was the first cancer he got: from an irradiated bean burrito.

The second cancer he got: a contagious one, caught from an errant cough in an elevator.

The third cancer: a rogue television meme.

The fourth cancer: self-tanning foglets. He turned bright orange, like a carrot, and it nearly murdered him.

No one dies of cancer anymore, even habitual smokers who enjoy huffing car batteries. No one dies of anything they can afford. But he's not dying of cancer this time. There is no name for the disease I'm dying from. No name for the chaos filling up our lives. No name for the freedom to be told what to die off. Some people have fashionable suicides, they're big events that draw a huge crowd. A TV special. A movie of the week. Some ironic buttons surface months later.

Mitsy Bit It.

Dead Dorner Does Domes.

A skull with a pink bow on it.

My dad's life has not been a star-studded extravaganza. His death won't bring in the numbers. No courageous final speech before he dies in his loved ones arms. No attractive headwrap or goofy, self-deprecating hat. People dying of cancer on TV always grow more glamorous when they die, even when they're not actors. They get to give long, poetic monologues about what they've missed in their lives, then tearfully reuniting with an ex-wife or ex-son or their focus-grouped dog. He's not any of these things, but he deserves to live.

They never show the raw fear clawing at you. His eyes dart as I insert a comically large catheter into his genitals. My dad's arms flail at the ceiling and screams that he can't hear his phone call. The room is filled with silence and sounds. The tinny metallic sound of his phone turned way down. I turn up the painkiller and he drifts off, his head rolling to the side. I inject the nutrient supplement into his IV, just like Dr. Silver taught me.

Other than his main vitals, there's a long procession of numbers slowly dipping down. I have no idea what they mean, except that lower is bad sometimes. His health icon shows a slightly frowny face. The sun clicks on and a fiery line of light blinks from under the blinds. The great machine, the one watching his heart rate, talks. The goddamn thing talks.

Perk up! Today is another great day! Why don't you go enjoy a Quik-Fast Break Link breakfast? New from Dometastic Snacks!

"Shut up."

The gods punished Prometheus.

This is new.

"Excuse me?"

He stole fire from the gods. Took their arcane knowledge for man's benefit.

"What."

Enraged, the gods lashed him to a rock in the underworld and every day, a vulture would tear out his liver.

"I guess he got what you would call a raw deal."

Ask yourself, are you the vulture or the god who chained him?

A giant, black winged bird is on my father's body, its beak filled with bloody chunks of him. I blink and it's gone.

I think I just fell asleep for a second. A micro-nap.

His breathing has changed to a raspy drawl, wet and crunchy. His failing liver has caused fluid to fill up in his lungs and if I don't drain it once a day, he will drown himself from the inside out. But his meter shows it was drained almost an hour ago.

This is different.

"Monitor, what's happening to him?"

"Hi there! Let me check on that for you!" Its cheerfulness is clawing. The monitor makes a few bleeps and bloops.

"It looks like the customer's blood is getting a little dirty! His liver is leaking bile into his bloodstream. That's gross! This is pretty serious, so you better get a move on to a hospital!"

His breathing chokes, and for a pregnant moment, stops. The voice continues, a little sound in the infinite space between my father and I. His whole body shakes and he starts breathing again.

"I can't do that. Is he going to die?"

"I'm sorry, but I can't tell you that!" The voice is smiling at me through the screen.

"Why not?"

"I'm sorry, but I can't tell you that!"

I scream at the top of my lungs. I'm shaking so much I can't press the stupid mute button on the machine.

Raylene knocks on the door. I open it and she's tugging her robe shut. She doesn't have her face on.

"What's going on?"

"Dad. He's..."

She sighs, her face a desert of exhaustion. "What can I do?"

"Just... I don't know. I don't know."

She stays with me in the room and we sit on the floor together. Dad stirs in his sleep. We say nothing, because there is nothing to say anymore. Words don't help.

"He was always nice to me," she finally says. "I hope everything turns out okay for him. "

She leaves and gets something from the vendi-fridge. An ad plays while she waits. A few moments later the door slides shut. I slide shut. The future slides shut. Dad sleeps. The heartbeat monitor sleeps. I don't.

<div align="center">~~~~</div>

The Black Lettuce transactions, the grey market intermediaries, the payouts, work well enough, barely just enough money to be under the radar of the game publisher, too convoluted for anyone but the most dedicated TechSec to care. The HealthLine account we cloned is being paid for like clockwork. Nobody cares as long as the bill gets paid.

Weeks pass. My numbers at work are excellent. I am focused in a way few people are. I come home from work and check on Dad. I talk to him constantly.

"How's he doing?" Raylene asks.

"He's improving a little bit. He can look at me."

I go into the closet. I've set up his tablet so he can watch stuff and scroll if he wants to. Stepping into a pocket universe, and except for the soft beep of the man's health monitor, the room is dead quiet. The walls grow when I enter. Dad is a fleshy pool plugged with clear tubes and hoses, lays in a small trundle bed, breathing and living still.

The main monitor shows a neutral face, rather than a happy face (indicating all is well) or a red frowny face. Dad regained consciousness yesterday, and I've been trying to spend as much time with him as I can.

"Theeeeeeere are too many cloudsssssssss," Dad says, his large, wet eyes not seeing anything in particular. His words are long and slurred.

"Hey, Dad. How are you feeling?"

"There'ssssssss too many. Way too many. I need to help."

I touch the man's rough, tiny hand, and it was hard to believe that hand ever held anything at all. Dr Silver says Dad's organs are slowly shutting down after the stroke. They were expired, out of warranty. The defective veins and clots in his brain would soon burst, shutting him off. Silver explained that the only thing I needed to do was make sure Dad felt okay and to watch the monitor to see if the smiley face turned from a pleasant yellow circle to fiery red.

"Then again, he could turn it all around with enough time. Strokes are funny like that. Next week he could be sitting up, complaining about the food. We just need to wait and see," Silver says over the phone.

Before this happened, I used to sit with him and watch TV and we would sometimes bicker about which show we wanted to watch. Dad would always let me choose, no matter how worn out or sick he felt. We would watch cartoons together and he would pretend to be as excited as I was.

"Do you need to go, Dad? Or did you already?"

"I need to go."

His face is pained. I lift up Dad and slide the cold bedpan underneath him. Dad grunts for a few moments while I try to avoid breathing in the smell.

"Bombssss away," Dad says, panting a bit. He tries to laugh, but it comes out a wet gasp.

I wipe my father's shit away with a damp disposable and carry the waste to the bathroom. Thankfully, the toilet hasn't been flushed yet, saving me $6 on a double flush. I use some sanitizing wipes to clean him head to foot. I replace his diaper. Those glassy eyes watering and wavering back and forth like they want to ask me a question but can't. There's shame behind his hazy look. Worthlessness. I take it in for him. That's what I can do. I can bear that helplessness for him. I can carry him. I can't do much, but I can do this.

He places his impossibly light hand on my arm. The man is so light, a paper bag filled with bones and air. I just want him to be safe and at home, not surrounded by strangers and antiseptic stink. He is here, and for right now, he is alive.

"Thankssss," he whispers in a soft, ghostly voice. His eyes wander off.

Axel whines at me that Dad smells weird. Raylene thinks I got a Black Friday bonus or something, she's not asking many questions. She and my Dad were fast friends when we met; she saw his humor and kindness in ways I never did. She knows there's nowhere else for him to go but here and didn't put up much of a fuss. I keep the details vague.

Dad coughs a bit, spits up, and I wipe it away. I give the old man a contact patch to help him, and I recap his weekly shows as he falls asleep. After a few minutes, his chest rises and falls like a smooth hill made of skin. I tuck him in. I close my eyes.

~~~~

The spotlights turn on slowly one by one, lines of hot lights hang from the ceiling like miniature suns, and I'm the center of their galaxy, a billion suns floating around me.

The room slowly rotates around me. I am on a studio set with no audience watching. I am watching a show happen, on a stage that resembles an Ultimart store. The fluorescent lights are unholy, evil. I pick up a product, a surprisingly heavy canister sold by a cartoon ape, a label reading "Deth Deth Deth" and sold for a price whose number I don't understand.
~~~~

All the shoppers are grey, their ashen faces on the verge of crumbling. Inside, I can tell they are made of insects and wires. Machine life. They are all sad but can't tell me why. They mumble, fall to pieces, tape themselves up with bandages, tape, nails, labels, price tags, neon clothes. I try to talk to them in a language they don't understand, and all I know is that the words aren't mine. They're words I found somewhere in the dark outside the store, words that were given to me. Powerful, primordial words and thoughts dredged up from the bottom of the chlorinated river. From a real river. No, there are no real rivers. There's nothing outside the television sky. Why would I ever think there would be? The real is not real.

I just scream at them, right in their faces, and they don't know how to speak to me. I'm an alien visitor, but they have to tolerate me. I don't know why. I am a planet of dangerous ideas. I am a mental disease.

I am on the set for many, many seasons. The actors, the grey shoppers, can't get rid of me because they can't stop thinking about me. My language infects them. Ideas grow like ghost plants out of their heads. The show, now my show, can't be canceled, just renewed and rebooted with different but same actors, playing the same parts, consuming the ashes of the last cast in ice cream cones, cigarettes, breathing them in through the stagnant air. People post photos and clips of me, they're all anyone talks about. There's a light haze on the store floors, like a weak smoke clinging to tiles, products, people. The sad actors keep going through their motions again, night after night, the same show in reruns, death after death, piled up like stacks of expired paper money. I shovel their ashes into dunes and their black-eyed children make ash-castles. It's the same show with different actors every time, played on every channel, stopping every eight minutes for a word from our sponsors, and I'm eating the scenery with bloody hands, rattling them awake in their little cages, or when they're spinning on their giant metal wheels. They watch other shows on their own show, and there's another show on top of that. I separate from my body. Two mirrors facing each other. For the first time, I notice tiny strings binding them at the wrists, the ankles, around their eyes, keeping them open. They think they're moving on their own, but they're not. I learn their language and ask them about the strings.

We are free to make our own strings!

I show them the strings. They look right at them. Right at them.

So? Don't make trouble, they say. This is how it's always been.

Yes, one person can't cut all of them.

Stop bothering us.

You'll have to leave the store, sir. You're being a nuisance.

Think of the children.

A violent cut to commercial. All of us, waiting to die, just killing time. Killing ourselves. Killing my dad.

Years pass. I continue trying to shout at them in the diaper aisle, when they check out at the registers, when they're deciding which lubricant to purchase, what flavor of gum best represents their modern lifestyle choices, if they should splurge.

Eventually, I crumple into a pile in the music section. Over the loudspeakers, I can hear my dad's labored breathing over and over.

I slow, breathe, and pick up a discount headset, ready to direct my episode of the show.

No one argues. They humor me to get me to stop making such a fuss.

The actors assume first positions. They glare at me, their eyes made of television static. I'm directing the show to a packed live studio audience, made of cardboard, laugh tracks, bits of data, dead air, a patchwork of demographic, some stragglers just wanting out of the rain. Everyone has just been watching each other. Laughing at them. Weeping ash. I'm so nervous I shake almost uncontrollably, but I manage a pained smile.

I begin.

"Hello, welcome to this week's episode of Killing Time. everyone, I'm sorry to tell you that this will be our final episode."

I expected a sad aww from the actors. I'm standing in front of a red velvet curtain, lustrous and new like a fresh baby. I signal to the control room and the curtain pulls back, revealing my father's hospital bed, the vulture hovering over the metal rail, hungrily tearing out his liver over and over for them. He doesn't scream, but giggles like it tickles him. Some happy clapping, as if their favorite character just appeared on screen.

I failed. I wasn't in their heads enough.

I meant to show them how horrible it was, but they liked it. They laughed and pointed. There's boredom in the crowd after a while.

Look at the big bird, Mommy!

Oh, this is too much.

Did you want to get food after this?

Maybe, I don't know what I'm in the mood for.

You have something in your eye, dear.

My dad's last coughing breath, amplified through the loudspeakers, fills their ears, the site of his twisted body evaporating in front of them in perfect 4K resolution, in a Real 4-D, UltiMax experience. My last attempt, shouting and screaming at them, comes to the sound of thunderous applause and cheerful laughter.

My credits roll.

His credits roll.

The vulture gulps down the last bit of liver. I can see it regrow. It anxiously awaits the new meat and screeches in mechanical beeps, loud and sharp, one after another.

8 ~ *i tried and i failed*

The beeps come from the monitor. I don't know what time it is, early. I might be late for work. Axel and Raylene are moving around outside. Raylene turns the TV up and I can hear the blare of cartoons. The monitor continues to beep.

The icon on the monitor has turned a bright red. A sickly face, tongue out like it's eaten something gross. The system would automatically notify Silver if it was legit. I frantically call him.

The phone makes a shearing, sharp sound as Silver changes it to a secure line. The video feed comes up and I can see his tired expression, his unshaven face. He wipes sleep out of his eye. I must have woken him during one of his naps. He doesn't really sleep, he says, he just coasts from nap to nap.

He asks some basic info about the situation and taps into the HealthLine feed and I tell him as much as I can.

His face tells me everything I need to know.

Dad is going to die and there is nothing I can do about it. That feeling is coiled within me like a frozen metal wire wrapped around my heart.

"Do anything. Do anything you can," I beg. I beg. I beg and cry.

"Corwin..." He shakes his head a little, and his eyes say I can't.

"Why not?"

"Because I'm not all-powerful," Silver says. It's not dismissive or sarcastic. He's just so very tired.

"I know you have something that can help him. You just won't because we can't pay for it."

A dead pause. We lock eyes.

"That's not fair and you know it. I took serious risks to help you and your dad. What we're doing, I could lose my license for this. I'm doing this because you-"

"You don't care!"

"You're just saying that because you're angry. I get it, Corwin."

"Whatever."

"You think I'm some computer voice on a machine? I see what's happening to your dad every day. Every day. Every single goddamn day I have to tell a nice guy like you that there's nothing I can do. Earlier today! Earlier today I had to-"

"What about him right now?!"

The monitor beeps. A giant red "X" flashes for a second and the entire apparatus shuts down for a second, then restarts. Neither one of us looks up.

He sees something on his phone. "Oh shit. You shouldn't have called. I think, uh..."

"They found out? Are we in trouble?"

"Yes and no. They know something but not what. Listen, I can stall them. It's going to take them a few shifts to run through the account logs. I need to scrub as much as possible. Your dad has a few hours of inflammatory left, which should help. Corwin, I'm sorry. I need you to know that I'm sorry. I tried."

"What's going to happen to him?"

"I really need to go. I'll stop by later."

"Promise me?"

"Yes, Corwin. I promise."

I wait. Neither Raylene or Axel knock on the door. They probably think I'm at work, who has left 10 automatic messages on my phone. I ignore them. I'm probably fired. Or not. Whatever. I don't care anymore.

It's late in the day. Dr. Silver finally arrives. By the time he arrives, I'm fuming. I'm volcanic. I pace. He slides open the door to the closet. He immediately goes to work, doesn't even bother to say hello to me.

"Where have you been?"

"Corwin, I shouldn't even be here."

"Tell me what's going on." My voice is brittle.

"Nothing good. His liver is finally shutting down. It's going to drop all of its unfiltered fatty acids into his bloodstream. He's going to feel very euphoric for about the next hour or so due to the influx of glucose, then he'll start to have embolic seizures or possibly another stroke."

"Then what?"

"Then I figure out how we hide all of this. I'll do what I can."

"So what do we do?"

He stares me right in the face.

"Nothing."

The closet grows even smaller. The monitor beeps.

"Nothing?"

"We make him as comfortable as possible. I've unlocked the pain meds so you can add them to the drip as much as he needs. Don't add more than four icons worth. Listen to me, if you add more than four, he'll die in minutes. Do you understand? Not more than four."

"This can't be happening."

"It is happening. It's all part of their plan."

"Don't start with that."

"Here's the truth Corwin, even if he was a trillionaire, if he had infinite money, there's nothing we can do. It's happening. Even if I could rip out a liver from some J Class and slap it in him, it's just too late. I know you're angry at me but I've risked everything on people like your dad. And what you did to help him was... extraordinary." He stumbles, grabs the rail of the bed. I reach for him and he waves me off.

He gathers himself. "I'm sorry, I... just...."

"I'm just so scared right now."

"I know. It's okay," he says, looking at me with red, ragged eyes.

He grabs my shoulder, looking a decade older than when he arrived. A grey, ashen face tied. He touches my father's fragile hand, looks at him breathing for a very long time, gathers his things, and then goes to leave.

"Remember, not more than four. Please don't call me ever again."

I should say thank you, but I don't. I don't know why.

I see him leave, shutting the door to my dad's life behind him. Raylene sleeps on the couch, probably taking something to avoid all of this. I'm jealous. I'm tempted to dip into her stash just to numb everything. Axel is thankfully distracted, entranced by some game and doesn't hear a thing.

I kneel down by Dad's bed and try to hold his hand, but I can't. That knotted, tired fist grips the blanket with an impossible strength.

"I'm sorry, Dad. I'm sorry I..." The words don't come, lost in a crimson swirl in my head.

He grunts a reply, lost in his pain.

I tried. Those are the words I can't say out loud. My mouth forms them, but nothing but air emerges. The monitor's red face deepens to a dark crimson hue. Numbers climb and drop. Minutes pass, maybe an hour.

It's close now. I can sense it like a growing shadow. A dark wave.

I hate these machines. I hate their smarmy, programmed sympathy. Underneath, it's just cold plastic, loveless metal and circuitry. No one even uses the word death, there's always a buzzword floating on their tongues.

His coupons expired.

Warranty ran out.

Had his last sale.

Went out of business.

No, he's dying. There's no cute ironic way to say it. He is dying. These machines try to slap a smiling emoticon on this horrible moment, make it pretend that it's not happening.

I tried and I failed.

After about fifteen minutes, I add another painkiller unit. He's up to three. His eyes dart around the room, to me, to the red monitor, the slow drip-drip of the IV, to all the silence surrounding him. I tuck the blankets underneath him tighter, for no reason other than I need something to do with my hands.

Time aches along, throbbing seconds one by one.

It's been about two hours since Silver left. Dad's breathing is backfiring and stalling, his hand flexing open and closed. This man, my dad. All those moments he lived and loved are almost gone. Almost lost.

When I was younger, he used to play Danger Disc with me. It's a video game. I was way better than him at it, and I absolutely murdered him, but he just wanted to spend time with me. I tried to show him how to play, and he listened intently, watching my hands as I Double-Dodged and backhanded the disc into his goal time after time. He tousled my hair afterwards, which I hated.

He and Mom, before she left, always got me the newest game systems. No matter what, every console cycle. I made a big deal, and was very specific about what I wanted for Xmas. If they screwed up, or couldn't afford what I wanted, I threw a fit. A childish, stupid fit and right now I wish I could say I'm sorry. I can see my son now, spending dollars I didn't have for their acceptance. Yet always afraid of a secret hatred of me. How much of a disappointment I'll be.

The pain meds kick in, and he raises his hand into the air, grasping at something invisible.

I feel like I should be crying. People in these situations should cry, but I don't know how to cry for him. I just don't know how. A vast ocean of nothingness flows through me. I am outside myself, looking down like a security camera at the room. My sagging body by the bed, my dad in the grip of the machines barely keeping him alive.

From the look of the monitor, it's not much longer. I figure out how to turn the volume down on the alarms. I don't know what to do except wait and watch and be there in this room with him.

Borson Scaggs is dying. I am watching him die.

I continue to watch him die.

My phone receives another message. I check it. Work wants me in for an executive review tomorrow. Before it felt empowering to tell them to get lost, but I don't feel anything anymore.

Except one thing. Like the Black Lettuce idea, a sudden urge compels every cell in my body.

I want the Dome to know Borson Scaggs was alive. That he was my dad, and maybe not a perfect dad, but that he was mine and he tried to love me the best he could. We all succeed and fail the same way as our fathers, and I wanted to be forgiven for all my stupid mistakes, all the pointless insults I threw at him, how good I felt when I broke down his will. He tried to love me the best he could and I couldn't see it. I was selfish and stupid. He deserves better than this. He deserves to be alive.

An oily voice inside me tells me to shut up, be a man, stop crying, stop whining, lock every door to yourself, take what's yours, burn it all, what does it matter.

What do you have left to lose?

Something inside my mind becomes untethered, like a creature waking up from a long, unwelcome sleep. It's ravenous and enraged, eager to devour. It doesn't have a voice, but rather a single powerful urge. Maybe it's always been there, growing like a tumor.

The monitor breaks the mute. They must have finally cut the HealthLine. The machines shut down and all that remains is the static fuzz of the now-dark screen. The only thing left is the vitals console, not connected to the HealthLine. His heartbeat is low, very low.

It's starting. My dad starts to tremble a little, those small seizures Silver mentioned earlier. I stare at my phone, the message, my dad, the phone again.

The Dome deserves to know he was alive. I want to show them, whether they want it or not. I could tell a long, sad story about his life, him playing games with me, his bad jokes, his tacky sneakers, the fanny pack, his off-tone singing, stained teeth, but it wouldn't be the same. I need to show them. I need them to see.

I start recording with my phone. I have a little trouble holding it steady. I'm terrified, nervous, and my gut churns like I'm about to vomit. I start the camera on his face. I try to think of something to say. Nothing. I just video him.

His rattled, shallow breath. His clawed hand lowering now. The space is silent except for his gurgling. His chest rises and falls in tiny waves. I want something pure. Some stripped and ugly and real staring them in the face. I want to remember this so I can revisit this moment as long as I live. His wonderful, shriveled arms, his hairy earlobes, his awkward haircut. His head wobbles from side to side, as if he is trying to shake something off.

His yellowed teeth shine, slick and plastic in the dimming light. He closes his eyes and places his hands to his chest. The euphoria Silver mentioned. I'd like to think Dad was remembering me showing him how to use the game controller. How he would get mad at me for sneaking in movies for grown-ups. How we would sit out on the balcony of the old house and count the stars in the electronic night sky. How he would try to get me to play esports, pretended to be interested in what I liked, and I rejected him for it. I threw him away. I resented his tackiness. His unpretentious wanting. I loved him and hated him.

I keep filming his face.

Another seizure hits him and his face goes slack, his eyes go white and disappear up into his head. his hands and arms start to shake stronger than before.

He is dying and there's nothing I can do.

Nothing.

Nothing but watch.

His name is Borson Ernest Scaggs, and he is my dad and I love him and I am watching him die.

Gasps of stale air, and I want to look away but I can't. Wet strands of saliva cross his mouth like spiderwebs. The sun is rising and spills through the outside window, sneaking in, a bright beam of light cuts through the dark of the closet. It slices him in two and he raises his hand and it glows in the light. Dust motes waft in the beam. He's reaching for something in the light. The vital monitor is still up, running on the house's power, showing numbers rising and falling, like a stock market crash. His other hand grips the railing, fumbles, then my wrist outside the phone's frame, stronger than I expect. It almost hurts, but I keep recording. I can feel his weak pulse against my skin. I almost recoil, but instead let me hold onto me.

I feel his hand tighten a bit.

My dad recoils a bit, stiffens his back like a miniature bridge, his head tilts towards the sun. A strange guttural sound comes out of him. I can smell his stale sweat, feel the roughness of his fingertips on my wrist. The vital monitor starts to alarm loudly. A flashing square pulsates next to some numbers and the colored lines begin to flatten like a horizon. I watch.

He falls back into bed and looks as if he's daydreaming. His pupils swell to giant black dots and he lets out a ghostly cough. His hand falls to his side, his grip on my wrist loosens. His body starts to gently shake and tremble, his eyes roll back into his head. His pink tongue peaks out of his mouth. He falls back.

He dies.

The screens go quiet, the 4 colored lines pulled straight and taut like drawn with a pen. The horizon. Flat and endless and silent. A straight road to nowhere. The camera catches about ten seconds of my soft, painful sobbing, and my heaves crash like waves against the beachhead. I stop the recording and drop the phone in my lap, the face a silent black rectangle.

9 ~ *the cost of living*

I unplug the HealthLine machines one at a time, pack and hide them away, and try not to look at Dad's body. Finally I have to. He's smaller somehow, shrunken into a stick figure with paper skin and doll hands. I look as long as I can take it, then cover him with the sheet. I think that's what you're supposed to do. You see dead bodies online all the time, but it's always after the fact. There's some grim power about them.

Time passes. I don't know how long.

In the living room, Axel is on the couch, mindlessly flipping channels. Noise, cartoons, gaudy women slapping each other, the middle of a bad movie, a laughing audience, gunfire, a neon-soaked concert. Raylene is in the kitchen, ordering a snack from the fridge. She looks so tired. She presses a few buttons, waits for her energy bar to arrive, and leaves the kitchen.

"Dad died." My voice is hoarse and I don't know what else to say.

"When? Like... just now?" She takes a bite of her bar. Not dismissively, but in shock. She's on autopilot.

"A bit ago."

"Oh God, Corwin. I'm so sorry."

Axel glances over from the couch. He looks confused.

"What's up?"

"Papa died. He passed away, buddy."

"Wait, he's here right? Is there a dead body in the closet?" She shakes her head, unable to understand.

"Honey, it's okay. I'll... call someone or something."

Raylene rubs her face, her forehead, all while chewing her energy bar. Seconds later, she's packing.

"Can I see it?" Axel asks me. He's just curious.

"No."

"Why not?"

Raylene shoves some things into her day bag. "We're going to Maxi's place. Come over if you want, okay?"

I'm numb, everything is very far away. "I think I may have to sign stuff, I don't know. Go ahead without me, okay?"

"Alright, alright. Axel, get your toys. We're going to Maxi's and then pizza."

"He won't let me see Papa."

"No arguing, come on."

I don't notice when they leave. I don't know who to call exactly. I dial Information and they connect me to Maintenance, who then connects me to someone I don't remember. About an hour later, two stone-faced men in white hazmat suits arrive and take my father away in a plastic bag. I just have to stand there while they move his body, not sure what to do with myself. A few minutes later, I get an email with a receipt.

~~~~

Whatever is gnawing inside me has no color or shape. It's like an inverse black hole; instead of devouring light, it expels it with violent purpose. It grows. It shifts. It looks out at me with disgust.

I try the online UMed Therapist, but it suggests I should go get some fresh air and a snack, and that I may be suffering from economic deficiency with some bonus symptoms. I'll need to upgrade the software to find out. Normally, I wouldn't, but I upgrade to a Platinum Health package and the diagnosis is that I need to purchase a Religion Pack to get through this troubling time in my life.

There are no gods, just a colorful buffet of religious iconography left over from before the Dome, before the creation of the known world. We use it in ads all the time, a subtle halo around the protagonist, images of clouds and skies emphasizing freedom, rolling green hills, etcetera and so forth. Ultimart loves iconography, its merch: statues, flameless candles, amulets, incense plugins, hummels, holy bottled water, crosses, gold stars, glow-in-the-dark posters. Most people, when they start Religion, they buy a package deal: the whole dramatic narrative, sins and virtues, whatever their fancy. It's good business, a unifying market, that sometimes springs into cult, which Security is quick to quietly extinguish. Storefront churches rise and fall like the artificial sun.
~~~~

The crunchy people, the health addicts, they're the True Believers. The spiritualist affect, with greasy dreadlocks, flowy clothes and sandals, subtly scolding me for living in a house with a television or a phone.

"I don't watch television. I don't scroll. It pollutes the pure mind," they say on their livestreams.

"You have to have a home birth. Modern medicine is a curse. Go natural."

"I'm trying to spend with my conscience."

I tell them I spend money on environmentally sound, green-labeled, recyclable products officially endorsed by the Dome Conservation Society that minimize waste. I drink only natural bottled water, the kind with the rain image on the label.

I'm doing my part. I'm being one with the universe. I order a Spirit Sphere.

The Spirit Sphere is supposed to realign my energy centers for maximum happiness efficiency. It makes a weird humming noise and changes colors, and the kids like it because they think it's a video game. Supposedly, it picks up emotional vibrations, which it interprets as color changes. Actually, it's just a temperature-sensitive gauge. Technically, if you're angry, your body puts off more heat. I check my guide to find out how I feel today.

"Honey, it says I feel resplendent."

"Are you okay?"

I don't answer.

"Is there anything I can do for you?"

She looks at me with a sadness I haven't seen from her before.

The Spirit Sphere says I'm still resplendent with an Alpha Moon rising in my fourth energy quadrant. Infinite Solutions calls and asks me how I'm feeling, just to check in, keep tabs.

"I'm feeling resplendent with an Alpha Moon rising."

"Which energy quadrant?" The lady on the line must be a True Believer. She never says her name, just that she's "Infinite Solutions", as if she were the physical embodiment.

"Fourth."

"Oh... that's good."

"Something is very wrong with me."

"Feel better!"

"No."

"Have a good day!"

I take the elevator down to the ground floor and throw the Spirit Sphere as hard as I can against the wall. Its electronic guts and shattered temperature sensitive skin lay strewn across the alleyway. The pieces are an angry mauve, indicating "enraged malaise."

Laying on my side in the living room, TV on mute, I look at pictures of sunsets and watch happy faces with happy products wandering to happy places.

~~~~

I'm referred to a memorial service provider called Peaceful Dreamz. I meet the manager in a stuffy back office. Raylene refused to come, said the place made her feel dead already.
~~~~

"Rascal T. Crow, but you can call me T-Bird. Everyone does." The man in the cowboy hat in front of me has an aw-shucks, guffaw air that's slightly clownish, exaggerated. I can see why it'd be hard not to like him, but right now, I find it cloying and obnoxious.

"Okay."

He waves his hand across the showroom.

"So what brings you into my fine establishment today?"

"My dad, Borson, recently died about-"

"Whoa whoa whoa..." Rascal put his hands out, his mouth pursed. He shakes his head paternally, like I'm a child who's done something foolish but understandable. He puts his fists on his hips and looks at me from underneath a set of bushy eyebrows. "First time at the rodeo, right?"

"At the what?"

"Listen, I like you. I met you for two minutes and I already like you. Think of this as planning a big party for a guest of honor who's not there. That's all. First of all, we at Peaceful Dreamz are truly sorry for your loss. But you're in luck. His organs would have only fetched approximately seventy-six thousand dollars after we factor in age, weight, personal brand value, minus the complete loss of the liver and brain, of course. Honestly, you should find comfort in the fact that he was rejected from organ markets because his sale price would have been, well, embarrassing for you and your family."

"Thanks."

He takes me on a tour of the showroom and explains the LikeLife system.

"We're thinking about the environment. You know, going green. You know before they used to actually bury bodies in dirt. Filthy dirt. Such a waste. But strange times breed strange limes, so to speak. We respectfully cremate the, uh, remains."

Small statues of nude children with wings are everywhere.

"You're probably a little down right now. That's alright, partner, that's normal. Hell, we all get down in the dumps every now and then. We're not here to make everyone feel sad. We're here to make 'em feel glad! Your pa, what'd he do for a living?"

"He was a Chik-N-Lil inspector then a professional impersonator," I say.

The guy doesn't skip a beat. "Hell of a good trade. I eat the stuff myself all the time. He made good food for good people."

"Not his entire life. After that, he was a look-a-like for Sy Gorman when he got ill and..."

"Yeah... the point is we have a lot of options for you."

He explains the galaxy of possibilities. Borson's remains, like his kneecaps or gristle, could be turned into a small decorative gem for me to wear. An urn with his own clothes made up like a doll.

"Sporting man? What about an Action Kasket unit here? We got kayaking, tennis, rock climbing. The whole shebang."

"Not really."

"Have you thought about a theme? Like a vault? Maybe a sexy VIP ceremony with some lovely ladies? If he was more of a channel surfer, we could always put him in the Grim Sleeper. Spend the rest of the afterlife in the utmost comfort."

"No."

He shows me the flower arrangement in the shape of Dad, including realistic looking eyes and teeth for his mouth. He could be made into a standing, plasticine ornament with a waxy face, eyes open. A pineapple shaped coffin.

"If you're looking for convenience, we could always do drive through."

"I'd like everything as normal default as possible."

"Alrighty there. Man of modesty. We do have 'default' package if you're not looking for excitement. So, did you want to try anything out for yourself? Take it for a test spin? Never hurts to think ahead!"

Roscoe tries to talk me into the laser show and the animatronic choir, and I settle for the Bubble Shower for the younger kids. Borson had enough religious UNet friends and clients that we don't have to hire many fillers, so we talk shop and numbers. At the end, I'm presented with an invoice with no number, but I have to assume it's enough to buy a decent car. I sign everything in front of me without thinking.

We shake hands and I leave.

I take a wrong turn and end up in the employee's section. The LikeLife assembly area. A harsh fluorescent-lit workshop filled with mannequins designed to look like the departed. Two dozen metal tables with a variety of mannequins in various states of construction.

Roscoe claps me on the shoulder from behind. A black ocean boils within me and I turn around.

"Sorry, I just got lost." I sway on my feet and tears start.

Roscoe's demeanor has changed. The knee-slapping yokel routine has evaporated. A small shouldered, weary man stands in front of me. He gives me a tissue from nearby. I thank him.

"You said you were there when he died, didn't you?" he says.

"Yeah, I was."

"It's something, isn't it? You see someone dead online or on TV and it's just like, 'well there you go'. Up close, really real, it's an awakening. All those memories, all those moments he had, just gone. The light just sort of turns off in their eyes like a switch. Everything he was "

"Yeah. Exactly like that."

"My own dad was like that. He spent his entire life making other people feel better about dying." Roscoe rubs his chin, thinking. "'Spent his entire life.' That's such a strange turn of phrase, don't you think? How do you spend a life? Like a dollar? Like in a vending machine? You know, life is a vending machine and we spend most of it figuring out what we want to buy. And then at the end, we often never buy anything at all."

He shifts on his feet. The air circulator kicks on.

"This whole redneck bullshit I gave you in there is just training that we all got. I'm not even sure what a 'rodeo' is, either. Something with animals from the old days outside, I think." He stops, staring off into the dark warehouse. "At the very end, my dad was crying and begging. That man I'd seen my entire life acting like he was Lord of All Creation and everything was just annoying him, you'd think he would give all of us up for one more day of air. It was the saddest thing I've ever seen, him yelling at doctors, throwing money at anyone who would listen, offer him all sorts of magic crap to 'help.' Oh, and they took every penny."

I look right at him, feeling words rise up out of me. "I don't even think my dad really even knew he was alive. This was before he started to go. Sometimes I get that way, too. Like I'm watching my own life on TV and it's not a very interesting show, but I keep watching because..."

"There's nothing else on. But that's life, isn't it? You already signed, so I already got your money. It's not about trying to scam you. You're gonna get everything you paid for. You look like you need someone talking to you straight for once."

"Do you do this to everyone who comes in? Put on a big show and then rip the curtain back to make them feel better?"

"No. Most people are just happy with the pageantry of it. The coffin and the LikeLife help them say goodbye. All this, it's not for your dad, it's for you."

"Everything feels like a copy of a copy of something that never existed in the first place."

Roscoe sighs in agreement. "The only thing I can promise you is one, your dad will have a quality memorial service. And two: it does get better. Maybe not better, but... you don't believe me, but one day you'll wake up and it just won't hurt as much. You'll look back on this one day and be shocked at how much it doesn't hurt."

"I want it to hurt. I want it to stay real."

"You don't get much say in that. At some point, you might even resent the fact it doesn't hurt."

I take out my phone and show him the video of Dad. He watches it in silence. I can hear my own recorded sobs from the front of my phone.

His face is grim and grey. "Why?"

"I want everyone to see it."

"But why?" he says, shrugging his small shoulders.

"Because they need to."

~~~~

The children's show was called LOOK and that's what it was about: looking your best, avoiding the gaze of others in the wrong way. How to prevent embarrassment, worthlessness, fear, doubt, the slow, inevitable onslaught of time and age. How to prevent sagging skin. How to prevent spots. How to keep your youthful, 7 year old glow for as long as possible. Hang onto it with a death rictus grip. Ignore the slow ticking clock. Be a glowing orb of light for others to worship. Take their love and eat it. Choke on it. How to wax your unsightly nipple hair. Bleach your anus. Remove. Pluck. Tweeze. Shave. Change. Don't change. Stay hermetically sealed inside the plastic wrapping. If you open it, it will go down in value. Just like how a car loses 1/3rd of its value as soon as you step inside it. Drive it one kilometer and it's worthless. Stay a beautiful, loving, caring individual capable of strong decisions and look fantastic doing it. Now you can sunbathe and sauna without people noticing your scars.

Everything is going to be okay.

Everything is not going to be okay.
~~~~

Right after the commercial break, the host of the show, Tippy, took a scouring knife, one used to scraps dead cells from the bottoms of your feet, turned to his audience, a group of doughy-eyed eight year beauty contestants, and shoved the sharp point of the blade into his jugular, and with a happy laugh, carved a second smile into his throat. The six foot spray of blood coated a handful of beauties in a fine, even mist, like spray tan. Tippy was quickly shuffled away, the moment over.

Tippy supposedly left a video, but no one could find it. No one knows what happened to it. Very few people are interested in the depression and black thoughts of others, unless it has some special weirdness attached to it. There were thousands of videos of people offing themselves in creative spectacles, and the novelty of death wears off faster than one thinks if it's not dressed up. The image of a body falling off the roof of their building isn't enough, they need to throw themselves into traffic, then the cars need to pile up and explode into a fireball. It needs to be either spectacular or intimate, something unique and impossible to fake.

The news on Tippy's "accident" exploded online after it happened, the same day Dad died. Full video segments were immediately slapped up. I'm thinking about Tippy more and more, the views, the shock, that contagious darkness metastasizing like cancer, a plague of knowing.

~~~~

Mom won't pick up her phone, won't return voicemails, video voicemails, pings, alerts, or notifications. I've never seen someone
~~~~

so dedicated to not communicating with people. I finally stop waiting.

Outside the tram station, the air today smells strongly of cinnamon, the DayScent, and it almost makes me gag. Cinnamon days are the worst. Air should smell like nothing. When the DayScent first clicks on, it's overpowering and settles over the day, with only a few refreshers needed. The best days are the ones that smell like fresh-baked bread, or cut grass. "Cut grass" is an abstract idea for most people, since there is no actual grass in the Dome. Grass is a non-toxic, soft plastic weaved into a yard's perforated lining. It just looks and feels like real grass, but the smell is what makes it special. A living thing.

Death has its own smell. Cold and metallic. Iodine and lemon. Warm breath and baby powder to prevent bedsores.

I wander around looking for her. A crowd of streamers, now thinning, hangs around the front of the studio. Interest in Tippy is now waning, less than a week after the tragedy happened. I duck around them and see a gigantic plastic child's head in a nearby playground. The eyes are wide and white, with blue pupils the size of a dinner plate. Its constant grin shows a grid of painted teeth. On the perimeter, there is a sign warning that the playground is merely for show and is not safe for kids. The mulch, a carpet of used cardboard, is undisturbed.

A blue glow in the dark inside the head.

"Hey, Corwin. In here." His mom's voice is surprisingly cheerful. I guess she has to be, considering what she does.

I enter the ear, shudder at the slight cold inside. I haven't seen her in quite some time. She's gone silver. She shakes her vape, trying to get every drop, then gives up. She pops out the cartridge which plinks against the inside of the head. I weakly say hello and lean against his side of the head. Immediately, we begin drawing territorial lines, a truce, a vast wasteland between us.

"How's work going?" she says. Her first question.

"It's... tolerable."

"You still temp to hire?" she says.

I laugh, and she doesn't appreciate it. "No, not for a while. Except for a few people. At least I get paid. There are some interns who've been working there for years."

"You have a good job. You should be happy for yourself. You got a wife, a kid. What do I got?" She turns her head to the side, blowing smoke away from me.

"Mm-hmm. I thought you quit."

"There's nothing wrong with some vices. I have two small pods after a shift."

"There's a rumor those give you cancer."

"Everything gives you cancer."

"Sure, I don't know. How are you? Isn't that what people say?"

"Oh, I'm fine. This place is a mess, let me tell you. I'd show you around, but it would be too much for you probably. Lot of blood." Mom smiles, a pained, tight-lipped smile. A splash of blood can do that to you, and she does nothing but wipe up tragedy. Mop over someone's last bad mistake. Paint over their regret. Clean away their sins. The endless rooms she's been in, piecing together that violence, despair, and then being asked to wipe it all away.

"Work has been, ooph, hefty lately. People aren't like they used to be. If I cared about Tippy, I guess I'd call it a waste?" She lets out a sick little giggle. "After I'm done here, we should go to this little bistro I found, they the best all-natural hamsteaks I have ever-"

"Dad died."

She hears me, pauses for a second, but continues on. "The best hamsteaks ever. Your father liked to go to this place when he was feeling blue. By the way, who are you voting for? Red, probably? Or Blue?" She starts to breathe heavily.

"The memorial service is going to be this Saturday. You should be there."

"It's very nice of you to invite me to your party, but I don't think I can make it. I'm very busy with things."

"Cancel them."

"If I cancel my fashion appointment, I'll lose my deposit."

"Cancel any plans you have and show up."

"Can't we just have a nice chat for once?"

"You need to be there."

She takes another drag. "I don't need to do anything I don't want to."

"You don't get a choice. If anything, you should be first in line to see what shape you left him in-"

"In what shape is that?"

"You know, when you two split, I never blamed anyone. You left: see ya later. We don't have a relationship: whatever. You duck my calls: fine. I came down here to tell that he died and there's a funeral."

"Fine, thank you."

"You're so welcome."

At that, she throws up her hands and walked out of the plastic head, making a disgusted noise. I wait for about ten minutes before realizing she pulled another vanishing act. Like a magician, her sleight of hand taking her car keys and her purse and making us disappear out of her life again. Their marriage had been nothing special, ended with the same lack of spectacle. No blowout fight, no crying. Neither one of them had ever talked about why they split. They simply refused to acknowledge the other. Even now, she didn't want to see her ex-husband crumble and decay like an old billboard, bleached white and faded by the artificial sun. Her job was to sweep up and polish tragedy, not watch helplessly as the father of her child slowly turned into demented skeleton jelly.

~~~~

The night before the memorial, I give Axel his sleep meds, and waited for Raylene to fall asleep herself. On my UNet page, various friends and co-workers are leaving status updates consoling me on our loss before posting again about what food they were eating and sharing funny videos of people falling down stairs. I check Dad's page, bots posting spam on his feed, begging him for crypto keys and warning him of viruses on his computer.

I very much want to see the lights that call themselves stars. I put on my shoes and leave the house. I take the elevator up to the roof, the ads slightly quieter in the elevator car at night, switching to scantily clad men and women selling their time, wanting to buy my company, or minutes of my voice.
~~~~

On the roof, in my rented garden, I adjust a few plants, some simple begonias. Many people don't know the flower is actually the ovary of a plant. Real flowers only exist as a mechanism for the union of sperm and egg, from other flowers or even from themselves. They grow wherever their seed falls, wildly, effortlessly, needing only the sun. These are flawless replicas, frozen in time, outside death. They watch me perfect them. Seal their image in plastic eternity. Show them to no one except myself. I stop painting a petal, drop the brush to the ground. A nearby air convection rustles through the leaves. The stars are bright and clear and so far away on the inside surface of the Dome. They look so real, so infinite, but also close, like I could reach out and pluck one from the sky. Outside the Dome, there must be nothing, an endless sea of blackness, and our place trapped inside.

I drop the begonia, hitting my foot. I wince at the slight, throbbing pain. My head is turned up, soaking in the calm. The stars, the dead images of burning gas billions of miles away, as if anything outside the Dome and my tiny pain is real. For a moment, I forget my mom's first name. It's Gelena.

~~~~

The Borson Scaggs Celebration of Life takes place at Miracle Hill, a rectangular room coated with TV screen, wall to wall, ceiling to grass floor, displaying a comforting knoll, a sunny day with clouds rolling by. Rows of white plastic benches line the space in two columns side by side, a corridor down the middle, and the guests slowly funnel into their assigned seating. Guests laugh,
~~~~

  Ultimart

compare brand names, clothing, worry about their hair, and do not think of mortality for a moment. The 3D glasses make the clouds really pop out, something Raylene desired so people wouldn't be bored. Many have already begun posting their outfits, taking selfies together. I wait in a dark maintenance corridor, bathed in red light, watching Axel fidget with his tie.

"What's going on?" Axel says.

"It'll be over soon. Just be patient."

"This place smells weird. I'm bored."

I scroll down through the eulogy on the complementary Spiro tablet. The eulogy is ready: mostly borrowed from prominent Management celebrations, which he purchased for a reasonable price. Borson's service is sponsored by Chik-N-Lil, and a representative at the door automatically emails everyone a coupon for attending. The rep smiles at everyone, says thank you to all takers. The Chik-N-Lil rep notices me, waves robotically from side to side, oscillating like a room fan.

Raylene sits, wearing a new black sheer outfit. She claimed the outfit's high cost was part of an overall "grieving brand strategy". It's an important phase for her, she said. Deliver a great speech, get some laughs, a pat on the shoulder. Raylene invited some Lower Management trainees, guys with jet black hair, smooth hands, holographic cards, and they mostly hang out together like clusters of cancer cells. They look so powerful, capable. Raylene helped a few of them with fashion counseling, helped them reach their inner brand. I didn't protest.

Mom is there. She's not crying or wailing at the heavens, but rather staring quietly down at her plain shoes. I cough. The woman is a living ghost and we meet eyes for a moment. In that second, a lifetime of memory hits her. She nearly doubles over.

It's time. I step up to the podium. My tablet lays in front of my hands and he presses play to begin the slideshow. Various pictures of Borson play behind me, cycling through his entire life. The U-Score on the speech is about an 8.7, meaning that it has a high percentage that people will be able to follow it without confusion. The pictures behind me were touched up quite well, with my father's blotchy skin smoothed out, his hard, wet eyes softened.

I start, and try to be chipper, but my voice is flat and colorless. "Hello. My name is Corwin Scaggs. Borson was my dad and what a man. We're gathered here today to celebrate his life." I make a pained smile, swallow and continue.

"Borson Scaggs was a man of many talents. He was special. Special in the way that few people are. One could say he was a brand without the name. He was born in the same year that the movie 'Triton' was released in theaters, and like that film, his life was an adventure. He spent his time enjoying the finest TV shows, his favorite being 'Management, Inc'. He enjoyed really good movies, and he always had a funny thing to say."

I show a screenshot of my dad's cleverness, some funny posts he made. A few chuckle. A tidal wave of nausea splashes inside my guts.

"Borson wasn't a frugal person, never saved a dime. He considered the act of not spending to be like stealing from everyone else. He would tell me that not shopping took money from someone else's family and taught me the value..." I pause for dramatic effect. "Of value. It wasn't until he passed that I realized everything that he taught me."

I think of the video, the machines snaking into him, the panic and dread. The high-pitched alarm whine of the brainwave monitor. Lessons he taught me indeed.

"He wasn't just a loyal associate. He enjoyed traveling to the north to such places as Opulence and Mammon Hills, and had actually once slept in the same bed as Starry Fox. Not at the same time, of course." A hearty laugh from the crowd. "Borson believed in the Dome. He believed in the value of value, and..." I stop. "Chik-N-Lil's fine products. Their savory and tasty meals were always a highlight of our weekend. I remember one time that we-."

A pair of teenage boys, seated in one of the back rows, cackle to themselves, cutting off my sentence. I continue. As I go on, I begin to see the crowd grow restless, politely laughing when they sense a joke. Kids get up and wander around the rows. Raylene herself pulls out her phone and scrolls her finger up and down, making sure to touch up her tear-stained mascara. Mom is quiet now, fixated on me. My heart pushes against my ribs, icy and metallic as if dunked in mercury.

"Borson liked only the best clothes, especially a real polyblend suit that he purchased from a store on one of his trips. It was gorgeous. Hand sewn. Fifty fifty polyurethane and... something. That suit made him look like Management, and to me, he was."

An audible yawn from the middle row. A low murmur flows through the crowd and half of them are on their phones. Snacks are devoured. I spy a pair of earbuds and a bobbing head.

I stop talking.

I remember Dad's hand reaching up to the light. The beep of the machines as they let him die. The helplessness. His final, raspy breath.

"And none of you care."

My heart furiously pumps blood. A hot wave covers me. My teeth grind.

"I wrote this stupid speech because I thought you idiots would like it. You know, it wasn't cheap to put this event together. Not cheap at all. A celebration of his life." I realize how ridiculous the words are. "Celebrating what life?"

Eyes start to hover up from their phones. Silence settles over them.

I speak again, but with that voice that keeps telling me to shut up. I speak without thinking.

"You want to really know what my dad taught me? It wasn't the value of value or whatever the fuck that means. I learned something else."

I stop myself before I say anything else.

"I'm sorry, I'm very sad right now and things are very confusing. I haven't been sleeping. Sorry."

I go back to the script, that bland pap that rolls out of my mouth like a toilet flushing. I just read, not focusing on what the words say, just trying to steamroll towards the end. Everyone is looking at me now, they're made of eyes all over their bodies. A crowd of livestreams broadcast at me, their clothes a walking billboard, hair and skin so unnaturally perfect, plucked and tweezed and painted up like dolls, each status update they make in itself a little ad for how amazing and perfect their lives are. My own dad's facsimile lying in his disposable box, like some action figure, Dad Man with lifelike death action. That's not even him, just some plastic approximation of what he should have looked like had he been able to buy everything they tried to sell him. A thin shell of skin, filled with shrieking fear of inadequacy. He always felt he was never good enough, that we never had the best toys or watched the best shows or lived in the best house. I loved him and now he's dead.

I reach the end of my eulogy, and I make sure to add the necessary endorsement.

"This celebration of life was brought to you by Chik-N-Lil. One hundred percent all natural. Please enjoy a Borson Scaggs Memorial Combo at the reception. Thank you for coming. Especially to the professional mourners for doing such a fine job."

I turn off my tablet and leave the podium. Soft angelic techno music plays as we slowly trudge to the reception. I have to wait outside the door and shake every single person's hand. I can't tell which ones are the real guests or which are the rentals, but I guess that's the point. Yet I try anyway. Soon, I realize all the professional mourners approach me, hand outstretched, their eyes childishly pink with tears, continually saying, "He looked so good. They did a great job."

In the reception hall, the line for food is long. Chik-N-Lil recently changed the formula for their additives, increasing physical dependence on their product by about 6.5%. "You've Love Us More Than Ever" is the slogan our company came up with.

Tabitha Charm, a woman resembling a pink fuzzy beach ball, hugs me close to her like a parasite. Her breath is hot and sticky.

"What are you going to do now, Corwin?" She's crying softly.

"I was going to order."

"No, you know what I mean. How is your family holding up?"

"They're doing incredible," I say.

"That's good to hear," she says, not listening.

Raylene and Axel are waiting at the table. Axel is complaining to Raylene about something, throwing things on the floor. She gives me a look that says she desperately wants me to come back to help. I nod.

"That was a lovely eulogy you gave," Tabitha says.

"Uh-huh. My dad died because no one would help him. He was killed by a computer."

"We're all here for you."

I let go of her and soon I'm at the front of the line.

"Welcome to Chik-N-Lil. What can I get for you?"

Caught off guard, I spin to the menu and glance around. I order a Chik-Nik and a medium soda.

Outside the chapel, I sit in the soft realistic grass, Axel sleeps against me and I gently stroke his hair. The air feels hot and stale and I start to sweat. My skin prickles.

I tell Raylene I need to go talk to the director and I hand her Axel.

Inside, I'm bathed again in the hum of the television walls, broadcasting a TV image of a TV image, an electronic version of an electronic sky. Digital clouds. Winds powered by fans. All natural odors, all custom made and ready to order. The casket has already been removed, the action figure of my dad is gone, too. I see an open door.

The backroom is dark, quiet with a low whistling sound of hissing AC. I'm walking through their prep area and I see the image of my Dad's LikeLife propped up against the workbench. His fake head is gone, resting on the tabletop on its side, looking at me. His left arm is slightly outstretched, as if to reach out for a final hug goodbye.

My phone vibrates. It's a sympathy e-card from Coyote. I open it. A lonely man on a beach, a lush jungle behind it. Tiny white boats and calm waves. It's been altered: dead fish and black oil slicks coat the sand.

THINKING OF YOU, it reads.

~~~~

I drop off Raylene and Axel and drive nowhere. I end up at the Church of Mammon, an incorporated offshoot of the GraceWay Shopping Center, which was itself a part of the Ecumenical Unitarian Corporation, a wholly owned subsidiary. Mom and Dad attended on a regular basis, always re-upped their subscription, and happily allowed 10% of their income to be siphoned off. Mom sort of stopped going after she and Dad split up. She stopped doing everything actually, just short of scrubbing blood and brains off of walls. Sponging off red splashes on bathroom tiles. Pouring seltzer water on gore-soaked carpets. You dab, never rub on a carpet. She's the woman to hose off the cross after the crucifixion, clean out the dirty burial rags from the tomb. She would cut down Judas from his tree and shovel his guts into a biohazard container.
~~~~

The cathedral towering above me is immaculate, polished, and golden; a beautiful structure so utterly alien from the other concrete boxes strewn around the Dome. I pay the modest entry fee and enter through the impressively large doors. The painted fresco towers above me, showing a crowd of worshippers laying down jewels and gold to a glowing Christ, his heart on fire, bestowing blessings for their tribute. A handful of other parishioners mill about. Some pray in earnest for better investments, health, a grandchild, a new car, a sign. An old woman deposits a paper dollar, a candle lights for one hour. She whispers a familiar mantra to herself, smiles, and walks past me, her ritual complete.

I sit in one of the hard pews. I needed to feel something larger than myself, maybe to fight against this idea burning itself into my mind. I'm not praying, that's too expensive or buying candle time, but to be around something that feels eternal and all-encompassing. It's not true in the sense of what I am experiencing is true, but at least it's something that pretends to have an answer. I see why people like it, why they keep coming back.

The elements of the Christ story don't necessarily work on their own, but together make for a compelling narrative of self-sacrifice. The Bible has a powerful central character, tense drama with Christ vs. the Romans, the Pharisees, his own dual nature as both God and Man, his rise to national power and the tragedy of his betrayal, only to miraculously rise from the dead and show up in a climactic moment of catharsis. You couldn't write a better series finale. You are in fact loved by someone unconditionally, an inoffensive, traditionally handsome man who exudes confidence and strength. For women, he's the ultimate husband and father figure. For men, the best bro. For children, a mixture of Santa and Dad. The strong jaw, those photogenic blue eyes. The carefully trimmed beard. Just don't step out of line.

It's no accident everyone gets their own golden mansion in Heaven.

I walk into the confession booth and shut the door behind me. I want to be in the dark, the quiet. The glow of the confession screen is comforting, a warm, pulsating heartbeat. I swipe my card to confess my sins. The moment is almost ruined when I can't get the screen to accept my card. I try it again. I thought God accepted you as you are, worn-out card and all. The face of Christ appears.

The calm male voice from the screen glitches out and assures me that all is well, and that I am loved by God no matter what I did. I am His child and He cares for me. The screen fades to black.

The cathedral is nearly empty when I exit. The last couple, hand in hand, is about to leave. The man deposits his soda can in the recycling bin and closes the door behind him. I find a seat and flip through the hymnal tablet. It's an interactive tablet with SmartClick guides for hymns and games for kids. You don't even have to sing, you just pop in some earbuds and listen along.

Up at the altar, underneath the sculpted abs of Christ, Coyote fixes her lipstick in her reflection in the ceremonial chalice.

"I got your note," I say. I see her smile in the reflection.

"I said I'd be in touch. And I figured you might want some company. Some spiritual guidance. Electronic transfer lacks the touch of the divine. Plus you said you wanted cash."

I'm in no mood. "That's rich."

"I'm sorry about your dad. Sucks the big one."

"Thank you."

"What you did with the HealthLine? Inspired. I couldn't be prouder."

"What can I do for you?"

"Wrong, Corwin. What can I do for you? That scam didn't really make a profit, but then again it was never supposed to. I just wanted to see what you'd do."

She looks upwards at the cross. "Christ is ripped. Makes you wonder why he didn't just flex those guns and tear those nails out."

"No one wants a flabby savior."

"Plus the whole death cult is essential to the story. He has to die, so he can somehow absorb all the sins of present and future generations. That's the price tag of eternity. Believe that he did this, and everything gets wiped clean. You could kill every person on the earth and accept Christ as your Savior, and you would be let into Heaven. You could drown a baby in your own piss."

"You a believer?"

She scoffs. "What do you think?"

"That I hate rhetorical questions."

She blinks, stares at me like I'm a space alien. I say nothing. Christ watches us both, his head turned down.

"Why save him? Why go through the effort?"

I can't believe the question. "Because he's my dad."

"And you are his only begotten son."

"It didn't matter." My voice wavers.

I sit down on the altar steps. Coyote hands me a bottle of Holy Water.

"What are you thinking right now?" she asks.

"That it's not just my dad." I'm searching for the words. Coyote rubs the back of my neck, her face close to mine. Her warm breath causes the hairs on my nape to stand straight up.

"What then?" she whispers.

"It's like there's this machine happening all around us. And not just the thing underneath us that makes all our shit. A machine fueled by people. You're just born and immediately there's this invisible set of gears that sucks a person in and chews them up. You're devoured. You can try and claw your way out and every now and then, just maybe, someone makes it. You try and read the rules for how to get out of the maze but the map doesn't make sense. The big lie is that you're just waiting to join that party if only. If only you worked hard enough or weren't so stupid. If you weren't so lazy. If you were prettier or stronger. That's why people shoot up their offices. That's why they go insane. Because it doesn't make any sense. Because it's a lie they can't accept anymore. If you can't have justice, why not revenge?"

She smiles with pride.

"And it's always been a lie. One big con, just like how I scammed that game. It's all rigged and maybe always was. There's no point playing by the rules, because the other side never bothered to care to learn them."

She mockingly touches my face. "Do you accept Jesus Christ into your heart and let him forgive you for all of your sins?"

The dark thing beats like a heart inside me.

"No," I hiss.

"Good. Now listen closely."

10 ~ break

It was as if the plan, this urge has been inside me for my entire life.
Born with me, grown like a weed through the concrete of my mind.
I knew of it, like a far off wave, but refused to accept it as part of
me. An illness to be treated. A foreign body. It chips away at my
fear. It feels warm and comforting. It's not an illness or an invader,
it's an imprisoned version of myself that I locked away and forgot.
I'm digging out.

At work, I become the paragon of excellence. I take no breaks,
no lunches. I don't even piss. I use a catheter that Dad didn't need.
Since I'm stopping for any reason, I have the highest productivity
of any employee at the company for a week straight. For my efforts,
I'm given a full lunch hour as long as I meet 3.0 PPX. I'm top of
the scoreboard and I don't particularly care.

I spend my hour luxuriously eating a sandwich, the last tuna-
flavored one out of the vendi-fridge. There's a block on the
machine for management only, but I power cycle the unit and

when it boots, I put in the IT code Jerry taught me to remove the block until the next restart.

The empty break room is a white cube with a blue, dingy couch. Pictures of clear skies and beaches and animals adorn the walls, all telling us to hang in there, keep up the good work, to be motivated. My sandwich is ready, stiff foam bread with some kind of mush in-between that smells something like packaging material. I mechanically eat, bite by bite from left to right, making sure that I cut a clean line through the sandwich. The taste is somewhere between drywall and chalk. Blake wanders into the break room, looks at the vendi-fridge, glances around for about 5 seconds, and then turns to me.

Leave. Just go. I still have 7 minutes left.

I'm halfway done with my sandwich, now a beige triangle.

"How's it going, Corwin?"

"Fine."

"PPX is decent for the day. That a good sandwich?"

"Not really, but I'm hungry." I take another bite.

He nods but doesn't leave. I'm not in the mood for how big he thinks the receptionist's breasts actually are.

"What's on it?"

"Not sure. Like tuna flavoring or something. Tastes like cardboard."

"You think you're funny?" He says, snorting.

"Yeah, I'm hilarious." I swallow a mouthful of tasteless matter.

"So you're a smart guy, Corwin?"

"No, I am dumb, Blake. I am not a smart man."

"That I believe. Being a smart guy is a good way to get your ass kicked around here."

"Not all the time." I finish the last bite of the sandwich and stare him right in the face.

He clears his throat, mutters "Alright then", and walks out of the break room.

The rest of the day I slam through units. I'm soon at the top of the leaderboard again for the day. All he has to do is walk over and ask to speak with me. Sign this little document and we'll take away your little life. Don't bother apologizing, he'll just fire you anyway.

Nothing happens. He never mentions the tense incident or even the fact I ate the last sandwich he likes out of the machine. I am not warned or written up. Somehow I changed the channel. This is all new programming.

That night I sleep soundly and deeply. I make passionate, desperate love to Raylene, who asks me what I'm on and if I'm okay. She rests her head against me and rubs her hand over my chest, not exactly disappointed, but certainly concerned.

"I'm worried about you, honey."

"I am perfectly fine," I say to the ceiling.

~~~~

The sandwich encounter taught me something new, a fatal flaw in his design: Blake is actually an enormous coward when pushed. He doesn't like confrontation that's not on his terms. Most middle management is too terrified to let anyone hate them for a
~~~~

millisecond, but not Blake. He doesn't care, as long as he's in control of the situation.

My job now is to make him not in control.

Due to my high PPX rating and unit counts, I'm given new privileges. More creative control, and by more, I mean minimal. Jerry slides me some extra accidental permissions. I start changing ads more and more, leaving in extra fingers or toes. I make the eyes slightly different colors. In the background of a corporate office building, I hide a gaping anus. The words "dead" and "corpse" and "nowhere" work their ways in by the highlighting of certain letters. If anyone notices, they're not saying anything. I have a suspicion no one notices ever. This stuff is designed to be non-stick mentally.

I eventually slip a QR code into the wood grain of a floor polish ad. The man rubbing the wood down with a nice terry cloth has fangs and behind him, a bloody raw steak rests on a silver plate. It's blurred. The QR code, if skewed back into the correct square shape, unmistakably links to a picture of a penis bisected in half like a snake's tongue.

Blake is now finding his desk occasionally rearranged ever so slightly, like an item missing or out of place just so. His computer screen is flipped upside down. His internet connection is malfunctioning. His mailbox becomes more and more full of pornographic spam. I never touch his lunch options again. His phone rings more than normal and there's no one on the other line. I find his Legend of Heroes character, which is a buxom Dark Elf Pentacaster and hire assassins to constantly hunt him down. The players I hired don't even charge anything. They just enjoy pissing him off. They constantly kill him. And I mean constantly.

Even if my days are numbered, might as well make them count. I'm very careful.

His girlfriend is not a secret to anyone but his wife. He leaves his phone unlocked, a tragic mistake, and I switch their contact names: the wife and the girlfriend. About an hour later, he walks out to make a call or something. After about ten minutes, Blake saunters back into his office, sits back in his chair, his face covered with sweat.

You can't imagine how much I would pay to have heard that conversation. I should ask Coyote for the audio.

But you'd never see it from my face. I was as calm as an azure sky from one of the posters in the break room. I am a model employee, the mold from which others should be made. My days are now filled with smiles. I even apologize to Blake about the sandwich and he says not to worry about it, that he'd forgotten all about it; which is a complete lie. It's burnt into his memory. I also have things burned into my memory.

~~~~

After work, Jerry and I sneak up to the Infinite Solutions roof. It's almost night, the TV sun sneaking behind the Central Tower. The Wife's face greets us as she turns down a bed for the Son. Jerry tosses me a Blutsauger Stout, and I take a long, long chug. The liquid is the consistency of drainage oil, just the way I like it. Anything that numbs is good. I may actually enjoy myself. Jerry kicks a paint bucket upside down and squats on top, letting out a guttural belch to the sunset. I sip, enjoy, look at the Wife.
~~~~

"Can I ask you a question?" Jerry says.

"No." We both chuckle, an inside joke.

"Who's the person you hate the most in the Dome and why is it Blake?" He takes a second long chug.

"Do I really need to explain that?" The Wife is tucking the Son in. Raylene doesn't tuck Axel in. We have to wait until he drops down, then snatch him up and quickly secure him in bed. He thrashes in his dreamless sleep.

"I work with him all the time. You just have to get used to him," Jerry says, deflecting.

"That's another way of saying he's a fucking asshole until you stop caring."

"Maybe. This whole undercover war you're waging against him. I don't get it. What's the point?"

"There is no point. That's the point."

"Okay. So you want to make him miserable. Fine. But I don't know what you're trying to get out of this. You have Raylene and Axel to worry about. Why are you trying to sabotage yourself? Someone is going to catch you."

"No they won't. I've done worse."

"Like what?" Jerry asks, cocking his head.

"I trust you and that's why I'm about to tell you this." I finish the remaining half of my beer is three big gulps. "I pirated the HealthLine for Dad before he died."

Jerry almost spits out his drink. "For real?"

"For real. I used a glitch in Legend of Heroes to farm this really rare item, and then I sold it on these third party sites."

"No way."

"Yes way," I say.

Jerry nods. He picks up another beer, offers me one. I wave him off.

He cracks it open, laughs a bit. "I'm really worried about you."

"Worried. Like in 'call Security' worried?"

"I hope not. Talk to me. What's going on?"

The roads are teeming with cars starting to drive home for rush hour. Every little person down there has their own version of a dad in a closet, or their own private war to fight. If I pass them on the street, I am an extra in their starring role. Millions of stories. Tragedies. Romances. Comedies. Tales of horror to chill your blood. My own story is unwritten.

I drop my can. "Maybe I'm losing my mind."

"Who isn't? But that's not really a surprise. Can anyone be right in this place?"

"I can't. Not anymore."

"Let's say you quit. Or if the Dome was gone tomorrow. UCorp out of business. Would you still be any less miserable? It would follow you wherever you go. You don't get to ragequit life."

"My dad was dying and there was nothing I could do about it."

"Bullshit. From what you tell me, you most certainly did something."

"All that and it didn't even work."

"This isn't about winning, Corwin. I know you and your dad had issues, but you were there for him when no one else was. That's not nothing."

"Corwin, you ever thought about leaving?

"What, like this job? All the fucking time."

"No, this." He gestures at the sky. "When was the last time you heard about someone leaving the Dome and coming back?"

"We get shipments in from the outside all the time. Other Domes. Trains and stuff."

"Yeah, freight does. But have you ever seen a person from the outside?" he says. The question hangs in the air.

"Probably nothing can live outside the Dome. All the governments fucked it up, I think."

"I know. I went to the same Training class. I've seen the same videos."

"What are you getting at? Where's this coming from?"

"How do you know anything's out there? Other Domes, I mean. Maybe there's nothing. Maybe the train just turns around and comes right back."

I hang my head.

"It's late. Thanks for the beer and the talk. I'll, uh, catch you later," I mutter.

"Peace," he says.

I'm halfway to the stairs when a sensation of enormity strikes me, like a sheet has been torn back from a hidden part of my mind. I stop dead in my tracks, gripping the metal handrail.

No one enters, no one leaves. The freight trains run in circles on programmed cycles, looping in and out, and the wheels keep turning until a cataclysmic shock derails them. In and out, day after day, an unending cycle until it breaks under the force of its own weight.

11 ~ xmas

To make a little extra money this season, I take a job as a Santa. Xmas decorations start sneaking in around after Dome Day in the summer. If Black Friday is foreplay, this is the hard plow, the main event. Xmas. The bus passes smears of neon reindeer and fake snow splashed across some post-apocalyptic version of Winter Wonderland. A hellish-red sodium vapor display shows Santa being flogged to his sacrificial execution at the cross for all of our sins and shopping needs. The Dollar Bill, a popup holiday strip club, advertises little women dressed as real, actual elves straight from Santa's sweatshop, some sort of demonic and ultimate humiliation.

For the kids, you see.

A fat man who climbs into your house, eats free food, and deposits gifts like droppings should not be eroticized. In fact, many fathers and actors have been shot dead by over-eager home defenders. Colorful trees peppered with electric lights, sprayed with toxic fake snow, and bulbous ornaments hung from each branch smacks of a psychedelic fever dream, like someone came up with the whole idea during a hard drug detox or a weekend Nuke binge, sweating and vomiting holiday cheer and gift-giving elves with hypertension. Eight reindeer, a magical snowman, gingerbread slaughterhouses, red and white candy canes like bandages streaked with blood. Across from the club, a diaper ad shows two men dressed in festive Santa suits changing the stained nappy of a squealing, pink infant in a manger. A "manger" is something farm animals used to eat out of Pre-Dome, and also a handy container for prophetic saviors.

Last night I sweated through a sugary, cheerful nightmare about spiders with elf heads and a banquet table filled with Santas with pitch black eyes. There was screaming, but I don't know where from. I squirm in my seat and the bus slows at an intersection. In a nearby display, the plastic, bulging eyes from a snowman nearly pop out of his skull, and the gingerbread house looks like murder has happened there. The children beating the display with metal candy canes have crazed smiles and harpy shrieks as they attempt to destroy the holiday.

Blinking lights and cookie smells bleed together with lemon and cinnamon, pumped up and infuse a sense of collective nausea. I grab a silver flask from a passed out Santa and down about half of it, the liquor tasting like drain cleaner.

It works, and when we arrive at the Main Street Ultimart, teeming with deranged children and their barely=-conscious parents, most zooming around on motorized carts. I feel the joy and warmth of the season as we're scanned, searched, and some are even given anxiety meds through a nasal spray. We're herded in by black-suited riot cops, and as soon as the children see us, a roaring wave of screams practically bowl us over. We're assigned our thrones and each presented with demands for toys. Spittle coats my cheek as I pat each on the back, some screaming in terror at my enormous beard.

A child dressed like a monkey, his nose running, stares at me blankly. A small phone attached to him squawks and his mother demands that I get him a Roller Zip and I say sure thing, kid.

"Have you been a good little boy?"

Silence.

"Can you understand me?"

Silence.

"Are you the Savior of the World?"

Silence.

"Know a cure for stroke-induced organ failure?"

Silence.

An elf, a bored looking woman in her thirties, drags the kid off my lap, and I'm happy for the lack of a damp spot. Only six more hours of this. He's presented back to his mom, who quickly returns to breast-feeding him.

Xmas normally involves the kid renegotiating the cost of their gifts into their own personal Number. Their debt limit has to be regularly re-established to ensure they're "pulling their weight". Chores and accomplishments, like not pissing on Santa's lap, can get you a few dollars off your Number. It's Training of a different kind, telling kids that you shouldn't give anything without expecting something in return. Training them to compete over everything. Making them model employees. Making them vicious at heart. A few of the less opulent children have strange requests. Things you don't want to hear.

I wish Mommy wouldn't drink her juice and get so angry at me.

Have you seen my Daddy?

I don't like my Trainer.

Is God real? Are you God? What's heaven like?

Can you build me a little sister? I'm lonely.

I want to grow up faster.

Is the North Pole outside the Dome? Do you take the big trains?

Can you make 'can sear' go away? Is that what it's called?

After a while, it gets numbing. You just see past their faces, their tears, their trembling lower lips. They want the fat, happy elf to simplify their lives. I'd like to tell them that the North Pole is where their dreams come true, and that there's a place where they can not be afraid all the time. But I can't lie to them. I just say "Only if you're a good little boy or girl." Then I realize that's worse. If they don't get what they want, like Mommy's tumor to shrink or their little brother to stop screaming in his sleep, they'll think it's their own fault.

The last kid on my shift wanders up. It's Axel. Raylene waves and smile at me, exhausted from her shopping. Her arms are loaded down and she's wavering on her feet. I deepen my voice,

"Ho ho ho! What's your name, little boy?"

"Axel Scaggs." He says it slowly, carefully.

"What would you like Santa to get you for Xmas?"

"A Picodon."

Confused, I look at Raylene. She holds up a bag, shaking it. I rub my fingers together, the wordless symbol for money. She nods, indicating she stayed on budget. I breathe a sigh of relief.

"What else?"

"My papa stopped working. He broke." Papa was his name for Borson.

"I'm sure your Mom and Dad tried to get him fixed."

"He broke and and and they couldn't fix him." He plays with his fingers. "He was hooked up to a bunch of things."

I immediately hear the soft beep of the HealthLine, the soft yellow smiley face turning Xmas red. Blood red.

"I'm sorry to hear that. What can Santa buy for you to make you feel better?"

"I dunno."

"Are you sure?"

"Maybe. You're magic, right?"

He's asking if I'm all-powerful. To a ten year old, I might as well be God on his Golden Throne. I dispense judgment on the wicked and reward the faithful. No one can withstand my Xmas might. Bow down before the power of Santa or be crushed by my jolly boots of doom.

"Can I get a magic raygun to help my daddy not be so sad?"

I stop.

Unconsciously, I'm speaking in my normal voice. "I'm sure he's just going through a rough patch right now. It's tougher for grownups than you think. He had to go through some... bad things. But you need to know he loves you very much."

"Oh, okay."

Back to the booming Santa voice. "Anything else for you, young man?"

"Can I also get a raygun that makes mommy stop talking to the person in her closet?"

Raylene takes a quick picture of us, her eyes damp. I'm not smiling, and Axel's looking off into the distance. A perfect Xmas moment. After posting it, she takes Axel's hand and leads him off my lap.

"See you at Xmas, Santa," she says, "Love you."

"Love you too," I reply, "Merry Xmas, ho ho ho." My voice is so quiet. They disappear into the crowd.

~~~~

At the end of my shift, the store is still teeming with bodies, like an infection of humanity spreading uncontrollably. The noise is a drone of voices and chirpy music. A migraine is spreading like a wildfire behind my eyes. I have 4 minutes left until I get to go home. A young girl with blonde hair sits on my lap and I can barely make her out. I give weak-hearted Ho Ho Hos, Merry Xmases, etc.

"I want to own my own advertising agency."

"Good for you. Be a job creator. All done?"

"But some jerk is running it." She stops, thinking hard. "We need to enact a bloodless coup in order to get it." She repeats the words slowly and carefully, like she's been coached.

I look up. Coyote is waiting by the velvet rope, giggling.

"I'll see what I can do." The girl starts to get up, but stops, turns, and before I can react, punches me right in the groin. The
~~~~

cup doesn't help and I nearly fall out of the chair. I reach out to grab her, but she runs to Coyote, who gives her a high five and transfers her some money. Coyote chuckles and sits down across my lap.

"Christ, did you have to have her do that?"

"I want a Stacy Malibu DreamHouse with the pink Rekker Convertible and a EZ Cook drug den set so I can cook up my own illegal Snake Oil." She chirps this in an obnoxious chipmunk voice. Snake Oil is a powerful stimulant that turns your teeth black and your brain into a sponge.

She grows serious. "I also want my own advertising firm."

"That's what the last little girl said."

"Then it won't be easy. We need all six board members to vote out Blake and replace him with you."

"Me as Santa? We going for the drooling toddler demographic?"

"Three are already on board. I'll give you the lowdown on the last three."

"That was fast."

"I was motivated by your description of this vast machine out there. You're so inspirational." She mockingly pats her heart.

"I doubt that. Can you get up?"

She slides off. I take off the hat and beard, a big no-no in the company guidelines. The bored elf woman shouts at me. She can't hear what we're saying, but she sees me from the corner of her eye. She's texting.

"Xmas spirit! Never break the illusion!" She starts to run over, but Coyote viciously grabs the girl by her ponytail and yanks her to the tile. She points one of her long sharpened fingernails right in front of the woman's shocked eyeball, the white as wide as a pool cue. The nail looks like it could cut glass. I realize I don't even know this poor woman's name.

Coyote cocks her head at the terrified figure under her. "Do you know who I am?"

"No!" It's more of a shriek than an answer.

"I'm Mrs. Claus and I am speaking to Santa," Coyote states in a tone the color of concrete, "Go back to the North Pole and tell them we're coming for all of them."

She lets go of the poor woman's hair. The elf scrambles off into the crowd, who momentarily stopped to gawk. Now that the fun's over, they go back to their phones.

I start walking to the dressing room. "Was that necessary?"

"Listen, fat man, get your shit together. Keep that woman and that brat out of the way. You gotta a lot of work to do. I'll send you the details all wrapped up with a bow. Merry Xmas."

~~~~

Xmas Eve. At home, I open the door to Raylene's closet. Suddenly, she's right there. Mommy talks to her closet, Axel said. He says a lot of things that don't really make sense at times. That was oddly specific, though.

"Did you need something?"

"No, just need to put this away." I hold up the Santa costume. It's not a disposable set and I want to save them.
~~~~

She looks annoyed. "Put them in the storage room. That's my stuff for work and you reek."

"Alright."

After I put them away, I check our holiday mail on my pad. Mostly junk, coupons, last minute deals you can't stand to miss.. I turn on Life and the Family is gathered around their tree, drinking warm cocoa with marshmallows in front of a real fire. My electronic fire to my left is cold and lifeless, but has the appearance of fire.

I text Coyote to say Merry Xmas and fuck you. I call Jerry and he doesn't pick up. Voicemail. He has his own life, but I need to talk to someone. I leave a bland message and trail off. I hang up. I call Mom. No answer.

~~~~

Xmas morning.

We place a small wakeup patch on Axel to get him moving. Two hours of sleep and I'm on my second cup of Koffee, and Raylene is barely conscious. Xmas morning is always a bleary-eyed affair and like a tornado, gifts are shredded, opened, briefly loved, and discarded. Mom sits in the recliner, tapping her legs with her hands, trying to enjoy herself but barely saying anything. I have the feeling she's scared of something. I down my Koffee and try to get Axel still to take pictures of him and his gifts. So many toys that make noise and sing and beep, mountains of round plastic corners and digital displays, toys made for violence.
~~~~

Axel's favorite gift is the Dome Riot Cop outfit we got for him. It comes with a jet black armor set and a foam baton so he can pretend to beat the rest of his toys to death, especially the overstuffed panda bear we got for him. The baton rises and falls on the cute, cuddly face over and over.

Raylene scrolls through her phone. She shows me adorably staged photos of her friend's Xmases and I smile, agreeing. Sit back and watch Axel violently assault the panda. On the TV, the Family is huddled together in their living room, all on the floor. The Son is unwrapping his last gift, a bright red fire truck, which he zooms across the floor. The Husband lays on his side, laughing. I unconsciously smile, too. The Wife picks a piece of tinsel off her sweater, right on top of her breast, and flicks it away. The moment is there and present, the Husband enjoying his Son's enjoyment, the Wife basking in the joy of the morning. There is love in that room, an effortless synergy of all the good things of the universe focused on that morning. There is family, good food, and love collected in distilled potency not so easily visible the rest of the year. Family and children realize they are wonderfully dependent on each other in their lives.

The Son plays joyfully, my son plays violently. There is no other way to live, it seems. We're watching our own lives like some sort of documentary, wondering how we should react, how many pictures to post, where we should sit to get the best angle on everything. To make us look the best. Raylene, frustrated but trying to stay happy, shouts playfully at Axel to sit still so she can get a good shot of him with his Machine Man playset, but he doesn't want to. The picture comes out all fuzzy and she sulks. The moment is ruined forever to our spongy memory, shot full of holes and constantly shifting like sand.

We have an early Xmas dinner from the vendi-fridge, and I splurge on a Nu-Ham with stuffing, mashed instant potatoes with real butter, puddles of Greenies, and cans of Blue for everyone. Raylene prefers Red, but she doesn't want to talk politics at the table.

Afterwards, Raylene takes Axel to the bathroom to clean him up. From the kitchen, Mom cautiously approaches me after insisting on doing the dishes, even though everything is disposable. The meticulously cleaned paper plates, the plastic forks and spoons, and even sit in a pile on the counter next to the fridge. The empty water bottles she paid for with her own money are emptied and saved as well. I wonder what the inside of her own home looks like.

She fidgets with her hands, her eyes darting everywhere.

"I want to see Borson's room."

"It's a storage room, Mom. There's just boxes in there."

"I know. I still want to see it."

"Why?"

"Because... because he was my husband before he was your father. And I loved him long before you."

I show her to the room and its door, and I solemnly open it to the warm stale air inside. The smell of cardboard and dust. She enters like she's walking into the darkness of a shrine, taking small steps, anxiously rubbing her Xmas sweater. My mother looks shrunken, hollow.

"So this is it."

"I told you, there's nothing here."

"There is." She pauses. "I never thanked you."

"For inviting you over today?"

"For trying to save his life. I'm sorry I didn't come. I didn't know what to do. I didn't want to... see him... like..."

She turns around, and the look on her face is frightening. It's not grief, it's complete, utter defeat. She didn't even look like this during the memorial, but I assumed she was propped up chemically.

"You didn't owe him anything. Why did you do this?" She waves her hand in the empty room.

I don't respond because I don't know. I don't have the words.

"Raylene said you did some strange stuff to help him. She didn't give me many details. Something about an online business? Why? What did he ever do for you?"

I'm taken aback. "Nothing. But that's not the point."

"Was it worth it?"

I think for a long time. "I don't know. All I know is I had to try. Even if it was pointless, I had to try."

"I don't want to be here anymore."

"Maybe he didn't, either. Maybe it was the smart move on his part."

We see her out, exchange the same empty pleasantries to stay in touch, to get together more often. We'll send pictures from today to Mom. I hug this woman goodbye and she feels like she's made out of toothpicks, all elbows and ribs. Her eyes are pale and grey like faded wallpaper. I tell her I love her. She pats my face.

The storage room is left empty as a reminder to me. Sometimes I open the door and I forget that he's not in there anymore, hoping that there is still hope. That I can still make it work. But there's nothing in there anymore. It was something I couldn't control no matter how hard I tried. That's my Xmas present to myself: that immeasurable failure. I have played by the rules long enough. I have done everything right, as least as the rules were explained to me. I have bought and sold and birthed a child and rented a house and made relationships with these people around me, worked the right job, said the right things, been a good boy. I saw other people who played by the same rules get decimated. None of it mattered. Dad still died. A big empty hole right in the center of my life. Our Number right on the edge. One more mistake and it's all over. There is a separate set of secret rules behind those, hidden behind the livestreams and billboards and TV shows, behind all the profile pictures of smiling faces, unwritten and unknown.

12 ~ *game time*

At work, I log into my computer and immediately I receive a popup window telling me I have been fired. No explanation, no excuse as to why. There's no overt animosity or mustache-twirling villainy. It's all cheerful, kind, encouraging words, or sent to you in an impersonal computer message. My smile right now is different.

My termination notice looks like an Xmas present on-screen. Animated snow falls in the background, the North Pole decorated with candy canes and snowmen, elves going about their own jobs. I click on the sparkling box. The bow uncurls and opens with fireworks, pizazz, and an audio message plays through my headphones.

"Congratulations! Due to unforeseen circumstances, you've been chosen to be released from your contract with Infinite Solutions! This may seem unfortunate, but be positive. Imagine all the opportunities that now lie ahead of you!"

Trust me. I am.

"Please gather all your registered personal belongings and vacate your desk as soon as possible. Security will make sure you find your way out safely and without incident. You've got to get out there and discover all those new chances for a better tomorrow! Once again, congratulations on your new life! Please immediately vacate the premises!"

I wasn't expecting this quite so soon, I'll have to move up my timeline by several weeks, but I'm not the only one being let go after the Xmas rush. Seven more employees are fired. Some cry at their desks. One even furiously storms to Pierce's office, where she's met by Security who politely turn her away with 150,000 volts from their tasers. I don't say or do anything. I calmly pack my things and place them in a cardboard box.

Down at the IT server room, I find Jerry hunched over one of the racks, swearing to himself holding a handful of plugs. I pat him on the shoulder and he spins around, surprised.

"Hey, what are you doing down here?"

I rub the back of my neck, as if I hadn't rehearsed this. "I just got let go."

"Are you shitting me? Like let go let go?"

"Yes, they fired me. Before I leave, I need a favor."

"Anything. What's up?"

I take a deep breath. "I need my raw time records."

He stands up. "Why?"

Because the flash drive I have will automatically access and install spyware tracking Pierce's emails and network usage. It's accessed from an undiscovered bug in the time record system. A gift from Coyote. My idea, her resources.

"I think I've been short timed, but I need proof for Arbitration," I say.

He thinks for a moment. I'm his friend. Why would I lie? "Makes sense. Follow me."

I lie because I need to. Jerry has a shocking amount of access and relatively little oversight, and I know he would never agree to something like this willingly. It's because he's a good person. I am not. In his office, a tiny room the size of a closet, he inserts the thumb drive and accesses the time card system. A few computer clicks is all it takes.

"Where do you see yourself in five years?" I ask him. It's a game we play, asking each other pointless interview questions.

He turns around. Behind him, the computer screen goes dark for a second as the malware on my flash drive is silently installed. It flashes back to the time card download window. In that one black second, he breaks over fifteen company policies and didn't even realize it. I just may have ruined his life if this doesn't work.

"Running a cult. I would look good with a shaved head," he says, rubbing the top of his head. "You?"

"Mopping up urine somewhere."

He turns around and takes the thumb drive out. "Here you go. I'm going to miss you here. Hit me up later for a beer or something, killer."

"Will do."

I don't.

<p style="text-align:center">~~~~</p>

The Promenade food court is practically deserted. Coyote has a green salad I know she won't touch, and I get a Koffee to take the edge off or to put an edge on, I haven't decided. This is all such an enormous risk. It's too easy to imagine myself screaming help to a neighbor, Raylene tearfully scrambling as Axel is ripped from her arms, tossed into an unmarked transport. I think about that beer with Jerry.

"Basically, you're shooting in the dark," Coyote says.

"What specifically can we offer an investor? IS is boring as fuck," I say, staring off into the distance.

"But it won't be with you in charge."

"That's a big 'if', mind you."

"I don't think you correctly understand how... influential my support can be in a decision like this. I'm one of their very best because I know how to leverage this. How to situate you."

I don't say anything.

"You don't believe me. After all this time, after I helped bankroll your video game thing, hooked you up with those med vendors. Etcetera etcetera etcetera."

"There's just a lot at stake. It's not just me." My attention wanders towards all the chairs, the tables, the warbling music.

"I know. That's why we're not going to get limp dick and fuck it up. Look at me when I am talking to you!"

She slaps her palm down on the tabletop hard, rattling her plate. A few diners turn our way, curious to see a fight. When one doesn't appear, they tuck back into their nubblings.

"What?" I say calmly.

"You mean, what happens to you, not us. Nothing happens to me. Blake will most likely file for a corporate conflict permit, which they may approve to thwart your little plan. If our idea works, it may set a bad precedent. They don't want the peasants thinking anyone can swipe a crown, even a small one. You'll have a 'retirement party.'" She makes a gun with her hand and points it directly at me. Her nails are like pearlescent claws. "Your wife bankrupts herself trying to make your Number payments. She and the brat go off-contract, get my drift? She gets ground up into the Machine and Axel becomes a plaything for Uncle Touchy."

I blink.

"MA is an enormous asset, but we can't do all the work for you. Only you can do this." She picks up her fork, as if she's about to eat for once, but she stops. "You shot that video of your dad. You refused to monetize it, for reasons you've never fully explained to me. You haven't even posted it. I don't think you understand the raw power of something like that."

"Have you ever had to watch someone you love die?"

"No, and I don't care about your paw-paw and your full diaper. We have a meeting with one of our last opportunities soon. Use that video. Get your war face on. It's game time."

~~~~

The PTS headquarters is a perfect concrete cube with no windows, edifices, or signs of any kind. It looks like a storage bunker or a power transformer. The interior of PTS is bathed in a sickly off-white light, its walls a flat light green paint, and the
~~~~

overpowering smell of pine floor polish on speckled floor tile. We're led by a receptionist bot who rolls silently across the floor. In the cubicle farm, about a hundred or so heads are covered by VR headsets, with the runner cables heading directly up into the ceiling. Hands furiously type on specialized keyboards in a cacophony of clicky-clacky noises; a hive. Tinny pop music is piped in through an ancient sound system, dusty speakers tucked into the high corners of the rooms, probably the first time they've turned it on this decade. The carpet we're crossing is orange and brown, with zigzagging shapes crossing into each other, making me dizzy to look at. The rooms feel upside down and backwards somehow, and I soon lose track of how to get out if we need to.

At the elevator, a grim-faced man in a flat grey suit sits at a green metal table robotically tapping on a desktop sized screen, moving yellow columns around, adjusting numbers, closing and opening white boxes, every few moments stopping completely until it resets. His whole head turns to me, rather than just his eyes. He looks me up and down and mutters hello. His voice is cold and distant.

His hands dart to and fro, clicking buttons, shuffling papers, answering phones, typing endlessly, gesturing wildly in the air to move fictional numbers from one screen to another.

The grim, quiet efficiency of an organism perfectly in motion. Screen with numbers, graphs, and shapes. The men wear nearly identical suits, the women wear pants suits or modest skirts, various shades of blue or grey. Everyone has grey eyes. Down another elevator we go, then up again. Hallways and lobbies. Now a new, long hallway with glass doors at the end, the walls lined with photos of what appears to be the same middle-aged man staring straight forwards, a small, pained smile on his thousand faces. It's not the same man, there are subtle differences in the cheekbones or nose, but squint and they are all clones. Each photo proudly proclaims the Employee of the Month. No year, no month listed.

We arrive at the office of Hubert Cumberlin, and we enter with the solemnity of a military conference. The doors automatically open. Cumberlin is in the middle of a phone call, but he's not talking at first. He holds up one finger, and gestures for us to sit. Several minutes pass. He answers the phone with a simple "yes" or "no" in a soft, smooth voice. He is a small man with perfect hands, and when he shakes mine, he's stinking of toxic cologne that reeks of paint thinner. His eyes look slightly vacant.

Cumberlin leans back in his chair, fingers weaved together on his desk, as if he is posing for a picture.

"So, you want to sell me a company you don't own?"

"Yet," Coyote says confidently.

"I look at the numbers, they're solid. There are many variables and risks. That's not the issue. The question is why should I trust the two of you? You have no track records running a firm of this size, MA normally does not involve itself in industrial actions of this nature."

"MA is not formally involved," Coyote quips, "I am here unofficially."

"Oh?" He raises an eyebrow.

I jump in. "One of the fringe benefits of Ms. Voyd here quarterbacking this thing is that after acquisition, we gain priority access to MA's data pipelines and analysis grids."

"This is not an acquisition at all. In fact, we don't have a term for what you're attempting. A hostile takeover is one thing. One company eats another, law of the jungle. This is a coup."

"Almost seventy-three percent of IS employees are in favor of a change. That will snowball based upon our execution and plan of attack," I say.

"It's primarily based around a guerilla advertising campaign targeted at half the corporate board. One failure, one 'no' and it all falls apart."

"We have contingencies."

He flips over a page without looking at it. "You have multiple industrial contractors on retainer. Are you expecting a full scale conflict? That gets messy and expensive. Account retirements come with hefty fines if not done properly. We do not want that."

I lean forward. "But like you said, you've seen the numbers. The potential. Yes, there is risk. A lot of risk. Which quite frankly, we are taking, not you."

"Our fingerprints would be all over this."

"Which is only a problem if we fail. And by then, we'll be long gone. No longer your contract responsibility. You have everything to gain, and little to lose."

"IS could retaliate once they discover we bankrolled you."

I chuckle. "You're PTS. PTS. Are you afraid of Infinite fucking Solutions? Of Blake Pierce? The guy is a meat sack. He has no idea what's coming. And when we win, you'll have been part of one of the greatest corporate takeovers in the history of the Dome. Drink it up, because it's fucking delicious."

Coyote keeps quiet. Cumberlin leans forward, his arm on the desk like he's modeling that expensive watch. I continue.

"You admire this plan, I can see it. You admire its audacity, but also its subtlety. This is a finely tuned machine designed to do one thing."

"I do admire its courage. And as for machines…"

He stands up like a lever being pulled. Hubert goes to a nearby monitor, an enormous curved screen, which he turns on. It hums and buzzes, then shows a series of numbers, his own personal stock ticker. He watches it, enraptured. "I'm in awe of it. Of this. It gives birth to everything we need and it only asks for more. More and more and more. Like a starved lover, it can never have enough. The Machine is pure. It has no ego and no fear, no mercy. It knows exactly what it is and doesn't care if you agree. It has no vanity. An engine with one perfect goal. I look at these numbers and watch them rise and fall, like the chest of some sleeping companion. You can give yourself completely over to it, and never for one second would it turn you away if you accept it for what it is."

"Sounds like you're in love," Coyote says. She runs her hand down the back of my hair. The tips of her nails pull across my scalp. I tense up.

Hubert continues. "I'd like to think so. It certainly feels like it. Sometimes it doesn't love me back, but that's just how it goes sometimes."

"All's fair in love and war."

"Wrong. Industrial war has rules."

I move my head away from Coyote's touch. "So what do you say? You're not rolling the dice. You're investing in people who understand that machine as well as you do. This is part of it. A malfunctioning part, an obsolete mechanism ready to be replaced. Sometimes the gears get stuck and you need to force them out."

"I like the cut of your jib. And these margins." He extends his hand. "Good to be working with you."

I shake it. His hand feels like dry rubber.

~~~~

The pieces are all assembled, the board is carefully set, all the cameras are running. Yet the players don't even know their scenes are coming up. Coyote and I are the directors of a live spectacular with its star, Blake Pierce, completely unaware that machinations are happening all around him. Every word he types, speaks into a phone is being cataloged and analyzed to understand his patterns.

Coyote is that dark whisper in my ear, telling you to slap the obnoxious waiter or ignore the screaming baby when you need to be somewhere else. She's teaching me to step over the bodies. The machine churns to life in kind, and we are its fuel.

I'm shaking the hand of Gregor Scott, one of our board members. He's been doing a tour of Infinite Solutions with one of the CSR's, meeting us afterward, so we all had to shave our various pits and faces. He's the exact opposite of someone you imagine working on the board of a dying company like this. His eyes crinkle when he smiles, and his laugh is infectious. He tends to ramble and burp in public. I like him.

"I've been looking at your stats specifically since the holiday. I'm impressed." He lets go of my hand.
~~~~

"What can I say? I'm a machine."

He grows quiet, looking down a bit.

"I heard about your dad. Sorry for your loss."

"How did you hear about that?"

Gregor cocks his head a bit at me, like I'm supposed to know. "The video."

"Video?"

"The one you posted of your dad. Real tragedy. Very sad. There's a lot of hits on it."

"I'm sorry, what?"

My dad's outstretched hand. The electronic ping in the dark. His last breath escaping like a ghost. There are things the video can't show: the antiseptic stink or awful waiting in the long stretches where nothing happens. The fear. The impossible emptiness of the room when Recycling carted away his remains. The cracking little sound of my mother's voice when I told her. And then after it all, the boiling, impotent rage.

I show Gregor a brave face. My stiff upper lip. My bootstraps firmly pulled.

"Anything I can do for you, let me know," he says.

"I will."

I don't know how he saw the video. I ask Coyote about it. She blows me a kiss and doesn't answer. I look online. There's millions of views.

~~~~
~~~~

Gregor Scott was chosen as our first target because of the fact he already knows who I am. Plain and simple. He's the easiest, most likely to listen. He's predisposed to engage with me. Coyote tells me this is called "contamination". Later, I'll contact Gregor with some inconspicuous question or, even better, a chance meeting in a place of mutual vulnerability. He will open up to me, or I will open up to him, depending on the order of events. Convincing a person that your idea is actually theirs is incredibly valuable, powerful. A mental virus infected a confused mind embattled by the stresses and warfare of everyday life. I don't think very many people truly analyze how much pressure they're put under. Like how you pass a janitor using a particular brand of cleaner, then you see an ad for that cleaner later on in the day, an ad subtly pops up online while you're scrolling, and then you receive a coupon for that cleaner in your email. Price is irrelevant. Cost is irrelevant. You are going to buy that cleaner because it seems like it was the only inevitable solution. And during every step of the way, there wasn't one single coincidence, not a drop of chance. Look at you, trying to make a decision between those two cleaners. Yes. The other, the one you really want, is more expensive and not as effective, but you don't care. You know the universe will not be perfect until you own this. To top it off, the woman in front of you, the perfect supermom with her neckerchief and bright-eyed baby, just picked one up herself, smiling at the bottle and placing it in her cart at Ultimart. You "decide" to buy it. All by yourself, because you are an informed consumer. All is well.

The replica of Dad's tombstone is made of a polycarbonate blend, his name hewn into the fiberglass in blocky, stoic letters. Borson Scaggs, loving father.

Gregor's Scott's wife died of pancreatic cancer several years ago. He hides that pain very well, or maybe he's one of the rare ones who actually gets over having a hole torn in your life like that. Did he personify her tumor? Did she give it a name? A face? Did it talk to her in her dreams?

Right on time, he visits her grave, which is conveniently only a row down from Borson's. There is no way he can miss me. I even bought the same funerary flowers as him, the "Rays of Light Spray". It's a corny arrangement of roses, gladioli, chrysanthemums, carnations, snapdragons, oriental lilies, and ferns made of a variety of plastics and felts. High quality stuff, he spared no expense. Our meeting again is no coincidence.

He passes right in front of me, his head turned down to his feet. He's wearing a bulky jacket even though the Dome's temperature is set to a calm 71 degrees today. They decided to make clouds move in front of the electric sun.

I cough and he glances up. I do my best to look surprised.

"Corwin..."

"Hello, Mister Scott."

He waves me off. "Call me Greg."

"Alright."

"Are you visiting someone?"

"Actually, I was here to see my dad. When we talked last, it reminded me that I hadn't been here in awhile."

"What a coincidence. Marjorie is right over there." He points vaguely behind him. "Where's the family? I'd like to say hello."

"They're not here today. I wanted to take some time for myself." I made sure to rub my eyes raw, and I lick my lips like I've been crying for a while.

"Are you alright, Corwin?"

"Yeah, I'm fine." I pretend to start crying. "No, I'm not."

"Talk to me. The best thing right now you can do is talk."

"I wouldn't want to bore you."

"They don't call it being on the 'Board' for nothing." He chuckles.

"Listen, I've always respected you. When we've talked, you've always had good advice for me. You got me out of the call center..." I say.

He sticks out his finger and pokes me in the chest. "You got yourself out of the call center. I just opened the door. Plus, the work you've been doing recently is... exceptional. Striking. There's real potential here."

"Thank you."

"I could even see you, I don't know, in a creative position. Have you ever thought about that? I know you got let go from IS, nothing I could do about that, mind you. A real shame. Automated."

This is going a lot faster and easier than I imagined. Dad's video really greased him up.

Out of nowhere, he asks: "What do you think of Blake Pierce?" Tell the truth. Don't worry, between you and me, I like you a lot more than I like him."

I'm not sure how to interpret this, but I pretend to think. "He's a man with predictable ideas. Sunsets and babies and pretty women."

"People like sunsets and babies. And pretty women for that matter."

"Not really. They like comfort and the familiar. But all that does is... remind them of what they have or think they have. It's boring. It's obvious."

He shrugs. "What would you do differently? Pitch me."

I hadn't actually planned to pitch anything. Our metrics stated that Scott would definitely try to divert an emotional connection and talk about work, but only in a very general sense. Small talk. We had planned two to three more follow-up contacts, even subliminal interference, to further infect him with the idea.

"Give me a product."

"Funerary flowers."

"Alright. You ever heard of the life urn?"

He shakes his head.

"Make an installation where your loved one is laid to rest in a garden in an urn that decomposes. Their body is broken down and then feeds a square meter of flowers, for example. Those flowers are then harvested and presented to the widow or widower. Or even better potted. It's like the person never passed away. The difference is, you make it public. Anyone can watch it happen. They can see the flower being born, blooming. With a certain amount of decorum, mind you."

"A grown plant? Like a real one? You know how expensive that would be?" He says, a little incredulously.

"You know how many people would flock to it? How many people would be fascinated? It would be all over social media. No one could stop talking about it."

"Or they might think it was a morbid display meant for cheap shock."

"Still, they would show up."

"Not all press is good press."

"Yes, it is. But more than that, it would be unforgettable. You could never repeat it. People who lie about being there and seeing the first flower bloom. Something as dull as plants growing would be headline news."

He nods and smiles at me. Like the death blossoms, I keep growing silently in his mind.

~~~~

By some cruel twist of fate, Tayla Cummings is on the board at Infinite Solutions. She's an influencer but not in the traditional grim, cloying sense. Over 10 million followers for shockingly basic content. She folds her reusable clothes, provides naturalistic makeup tips, shows off what she got at Ultimart that day, tells corny jokes, and sends happy birthday messages to supporters. Impossibly nice, completely genuinely a good person if there ever was one.

The party is being held at her condo in Bayview Terrace on the western coast of the bay, just overlooking the Sprawl across the blue, undrinkable water. It's a gated community, secured like a fortress. Fences are everywhere. Outside, a hand-combed
~~~~

beachfront rims the island with glittering white sand and cool water that would poison you if you drank it for any length of time. I found out she resides in a forty story glass box for the illustrious and well-to-do, a gigantic, reflective headstone populated with the vain and unnecessary. My stomach churns and I'm secretly sweating as the limo pulls up to the curb. A valet curtly takes our ticket and Security scans our passes again. We're let out and I'm immediately struck by the space and the air. There's no noise or grime. A cleaner bot scuttles past my feet, swiftly avoiding my ankles as it sucks up dust and occasional gum wrapper.

"Dust is primarily human skin. I wonder how many layers of me have shed over the years."

Coyote likes the idea and vapes while we wait for the elevator. "This party of yours? I lust for this idea. I have no idea how it's going to turn out."

"That's the plan. To have no plan. We set up the pieces and we improvise. Plan too much and there's too much that can go wrong."

"I don't like not knowing." She scowls as we get in the elevator and slowly ascend.

Private security scans our badges again. Coyote slowly breaths a cloud into one of the guard's faces, a woman the same shape as a wall. She doesn't flinch and finishes her scan. Coyote grabs my tie and drags me behind her like a lost child.

"Why do you think she's so popular? She's so ordinary. By the way, she's one of the few truly organic accounts. We don't boost her at all," Coyote asks.

I smooth out my tie. "It's very smart actually. She can be unattainable but still attractive. Pretty but not vain. There for them but she can walk away at any time. That makes men want her even more. She's not married yet, says she's 'looking for the right guy' and every guy thinks that could be him. It's the same reason the Wife is so popular. She's totally ordinary and safe."

"You like her, don't you?" Coyote smirks.

"Not really. I get why she does it, but she'll never be remembered. Maybe that's the point."

~~~~

Her penthouse condo is a stark difference to the cozy, homely surroundings of her videos. Most of the walls are white or grey, with countertops being a polished metal finish. Sconces and overhead lights are sharp white wattage. Her furniture is blood red and spotlessly clean, the mark of someone used to cleaning.

Everyone is on their phones, or taking photos of themselves, or chatting about what they're looking at. No one is actually talking to another person at the party, but no one is having a bad time.

"Let's mingle, start planting seeds," I say, buying Coyote a martini.

The people here think the party has started, but it really hasn't. In the atmosphere of the condo, a miniscule amount of a psychotropic substance is being introduced. Colorless, odorless, and a person who normally passes off the slightly copper taste in their mouth as just a bad mixed drink. It will start a heightened
~~~~

sense of awareness with a wave of euphoria, like having an extra strong cup of Koffee or a Zuum pill.

I get to mingling with the illustrious stars of the net. Coyote has briefly shown my stats of my own small popularity online, with the video of Dad slowly climbing in view counts and shares. Coyote and I have yet to talk about it. I dread the conversation.

I don't want to think about it.

The first person to bring it up is Xander, some sort of VR musician who plays the themes to video games in abstract light shows. It mostly just gives me a headache with the headset. He's wearing an outfit that makes him look like a schizophrenic neon traffic sign. His date, a pen-thin waif who only photosynthesizes, downs her fifth Molotov.

"Wait a minute, you're the Corwin Scaggs?"

"Uh, yeah?"

"How did you make that video so... I don't know, real?"

I blink, not sure how to answer. "Because it was real."

"Wow. It's something else. I mean, I'm real sorry your dad died but fuck.."

"Thanks." I sip my drink, which contains a counteragent to the gas.

"My own mom passed away in a jet ski accident two years ago. Bummer."

He laughs unexpectedly and his eyes are slightly dilated. I boldly take his drink and spit in it right in front of him, and he thinks it's the funniest thing. Coyote giggles and stirs the drink with a straw, which he downs in one gulp, still laughing. I gently push him against the wall to steady him.

Tayla Cummings in the flesh is all business. She looks permanently bored and angry; her tight, pinched face annoyed as phone after phone is shoved in her face for photos, status updates, brand engagement. This is a party of dead people.

The night is endlessly documented. Tayla snaps a grinning, cheerful selfie and posts it immediately. Blank-faced and serious. I check her feed as she stands next to me, surprised to see half of me on the left, staring right at the lens. I am slightly blurred out.

"Thank you for inviting us."

"I invited Coyote plus one. Are you plus one?"

"Hello, Tayla," Coyote says quietly behind me. She wanders to the bar, Tayla ignoring her.

"So you work for Infinite Solutions? I'm on their board of directors, you know."

"Yes, I know," I answer.

"Doing what?" she asks rather rudely.

"Junior advertising executive." I neglect to mention I got fired. She chuckles in disbelief.

"Are you her date or something? Where is she? I forgot my fucking contacts."

"Yes, I'm her date."

"Then why are you talking to me? Go talk to her."

"It's a party."

"Okay."

"I think it'll liven up."

She looks me up and down. "When? Did you bring another dying parent with you? I know who you are by the way."

"I take it you saw my video."

"It's weird and morbid. I don't like it."

"Yeah, I wasn't a fan either."

"Although, it was fascinating."

"For someone who revels in the ordinary, that's quite a compliment."

She smiles, rubs her arms. A glazed look comes over her eyes and her breath flutters for a second.

"What do you want out of life, Tayla? What's your big dream?" I ask, making sure to take another sip of my drink. The inoculate makes me feel slightly warm.

"My own TV show and brand line," she says.

"Of what?"

She starts to waver on her feet, and she starts licking her teeth with her tongue. "Me."

"Your home looks like a morgue. Did you know that?"

"I know. I think I'd like to film myself dying. Can you do that?"

"It's not terribly original. People film themselves dying all the time."

"I know, it's so ordinary. But it'd be ME though. Why was your dad so special?" She drinks more, ruffles her hair.

"He wasn't special. He was completely ordinary. Suffered just like the rest of us."

"What's wrong with the air in here?"

"You know why I hate you?"

"Hate me? I'm NICE. I'm a nice person!" She starts breathing rapidly. I glance around. It's starting.

"Are you, though? You claim to show the world as it is and you still lie. I told the truth."

Coyote grabs me by the jacket and pulls me backwards onto the couch. Tayla follows us and plops down next to us.

Coyote shoves the woman's head away and she slides off the slippery couch onto the tile. "If this doesn't work, you could always put a gun to her head. Hold an online poll to see if we should blow her brains out or not."

"No," I say.

Tayla twitches on the floor, her eyes wide as plates, and begins her journey through time and space. Soon her entire party begins to travel with her.

We wait.

~~~~

Near dawn, sleeping bodies lay like piles of laundry. Vomit is everywhere. Crude drawings are scrawled across the walls and nearly every window is broken. Some sort of mythic epic has been written at this party, a story told live for all her viewers to see. Tayla clutched Xander and they wept together, speaking on tongues, being one. It was a media event unlike any other.

Tayla is asleep against her vanity, her clothes torn, makeup smeared. Xander lies with her, curled up against her like a baby. I nudge her awake and she shakes her head violently around, spits out a bad taste in her mouth. Oddly enough, she looks overjoyed, orgasmic. Xander is dead asleep.

"What happened? What time is it?" Tayla's eyes are foggy.
~~~~

"Time to wake up."

"I'm awake. I feel... warm. Like I've just been born."

"That's good."

A tear rolls down her dirty face. "I... I've never felt this way before. I feel like I know everything about myself. And I love it. I was in love with the world." She holds her hands out, rough and scarred with battle. She crawls into the bathroom.

"I'm glad you enjoyed it."

"I did. Did you do this?"

"Yes."

"Are you an angel?"

I wait for a long time before answering. "No."

"Thank you thank you thank you..."

She grabs my hand and hungrily kisses it, crying joyously, her jubilant sobs echoing in the quiet cave of the bathroom.

~~~~

Lucy Talcum has a permanent suite at Memory Lane, an executive establishment that will take your memories, photographs, status updates, combine it with your responses to a questionnaire, and then lovingly recreate a single room for you from your own past. You can get your childhood bedroom, the first place you got laid, the birth (or death) of a child. Normally, skilled actors portray people, like your first kiss, but dead children are trickier. For all the things you can buy in the Dome, dead children are of little value to Memory Lane. They use robots mostly.
~~~~

If you're hard up for money, you can do the VR version, but it's not the same. You can't smell your old boyfriend's cologne, taste your Mom's homemade pie, rub a tear from that child's cheek. It's just a very immersive home movie. You need the smells and tastes of memory to make it feel real.

As for Lucy, she's an enigma. Never attended a single board event. Completely silent partner.

"I wonder what Lucy's hiding in there. Probably some sort of sex dungeon," Coyote says.

"You think everyone is hiding a sex dungeon."

"Because they are."

"I'm not."

"That storage room in your house is your dungeon. You keep going there for your own personal punishment."

"You don't know anything about that."

"I know enough."

"Don't talk about him."

"Is this how you killed him? With boredom?" She laughs.

"Stop." I pound an entire double to steady my nerves. My hands are shaking. Adrenaline.

"What are you going to do? Choke me or something? Be a good boy."

"Don't push me. I said stop."

"That's what I said when he started to choke me, officer. Please stop. Pwetty pwease with sugar on top."

Her laughter is demonic. The car slides through traffic like a silver drop of molten metal.

~~~~

At Memory Lane, we find Lucy's account manager, Dalia, and I hand her the cash transfer order. A shockingly low amount to betray a client's privacy. She hands me a uniform for the maintenance staff and a temp badge for the suites. I zip up the orange jumpsuit over my own clothes and enter the dark hallway. Coyote waits outside, arms crossed, awaiting judgment.

I walk down a dark mirrored passage, like the inside of a computer, with doors simply marked with numbers. The back entrance. Each suite has a small screen, and I randomly press one of them on. An obese man sits on a swing with a grown woman dressed as a little girl. They hold hands and chastely eat ice cream. Another monitor shows an Xmas dinner, a mother in tears as her animatronic children tear open gifts. Birthdays and backyard barbeques. Work parties. Sex parties. Hundreds of suites, cube after cube, each with their own small memory locked inside, the most intimate moments carefully reconstructed.

Room 0317 is occupied. Lucy has specifically blocked outside views. I open the door and walk in. If I need to escape, I can always quickly make up an excuse that I'm just lost.

The cube is a young girl's bedroom, bright pink and purples and pastels of every color, like being inside a birthday cake. Everything has ruffles and ribbons, and brand new toys litter the floor. They look arranged, presented to the viewer. No one has ever touched them with their original intent. Lucy Talcum is older than I imagined, in her 60's, and she is busy spoon-feeding mush to what looks like a malfunctioning robot. It's not a robot at all, but
~~~~

an actual child. Her head is too large and smooth, its eyes very close together. It's not a child, but rather a young woman. Her skin is a waxy grey color slick with a thin layer of oily sweat. A tube runs from underneath the child's nose to a nearby HealthLine. The pink sheet is tucked under a small, crooked arm. Lucy feeds the girl's mouth another spoonful.

"I don't have to feed her, since she gets it from a tube. But I like to," she says. Her voice is soft and low, and she doesn't look at me.

I panic. "I'm sorry, I'm in the wrong place. Sorry..."

She finally looks to me. "Corwin Scaggs. I've been expecting you to find me at some point. I just didn't expect it to be here."

"How did you-"

"You've been systematically working your way through the board of directors. Smith, Alpaca, and Horris went down at the first show of a paycheck. Gregor first, then Tayla, now me. Just because I don't sit on those endless phone calls does not mean I don't know what's going on at my company. Thought you would have more tact."

"Why?"

"Because you think I'm the big fish. That I need to be landed last. Proves the biggest point. If you can convince me to vote for you, then you are truly the Chosen One." She cleans the child's face with a cloth napkin.

"Blake Pierce has no vision for IS, no idea of what he's doing."

"That was the same when you first started probably. Why do something about it now? Why this moment?"

"Because I choose to."

"You could've done this at any time. You didn't have the will, though. Where did that come from?"

"You tell me, since you know so much."

"Blake Pierce is an awful human being. Petty, childish, entitled. Curls my teeth to just think about him. The worst of mankind always seems to be in charge, doesn't it? What makes you so different?"

"I disagree with the basis of that question. I'm not comparing myself to Blake. If he suddenly fell off a bridge or stepped in front of a car, let's just say I wouldn't cry. They'd just hire another empty suit. I'm not just better than Blake. Mold spores are better than him. All you have to do is attend one presentation and I'll show you why."

She raises an eyebrow. "I have to take care of my daughter here."

"One hour. That's it. Just one hour of your time. I can show you a different vision of what we can do. Something bold. New. And if I'm willing to go through all this just to talk to you, imagine what I can do when it matters." I pause. "With all due respect, why are you even on the board of this company?"

"The dividends from my stock options provide for her. I cause no problems and make no requests, so no one even thinks to vote me out. I participate as much as I need to. Has anyone even mentioned me?"

"No. We actually had to go looking for you. What's her name?"

"Only she tells me her real name." She feeds the young woman another bite. A weak hand starts to reach up, but Lucy gently but firmly pushes it back down. A small, loving gesture.

"Are you a parent, Corwin? Do you have a child?"

"Yes. I have a son. He's ten."

"Would you want him to grow up just like Daddy?"

"God, I hope not."

"But this world you want to create, would you want him to grow up in it?"

"He's not going to have much of a choice."

"When I found out my daughter was going to be permanently in my care, I wept. My wife couldn't understand why I would want to suffer. I couldn't stop crying."

"Why do this then?"

"Because I choose to."

<center>~~~~</center>

The audience is taking their seats on an empty floor of the Infinite Solution office building. 5 of the board members are there, including Gregor Scott and Tayla Cummings. Lucy Talcum is still a no-show, which terrifies me the most. She's the truest unknown variable.

Tayla, who last week kissed my hand in thanks, looks bored and disinterested. Gregor is trying to keep up a good face, but is worried for me. The other 3 board members, whom I've never even met before, show up. They say little and sit impatiently.

About sixty seconds before I decide to start, Lucy opens the door and sits next to Gregor. She sits and warmly grabs Gregor's hand.

I can feel Coyote's breath on my neck. She says nothing, but gently nuzzles my neck with her chin. A wet, slow kiss on my nape and she gently pushes me out.

I begin.

"You're sitting in a slightly warm room, eating bland food, enjoying mid-shelf wine I picked up at a Ultimart Neighborhood store. The room is boring, the presentation looks cheap and frankly disinteresting. You are doubting why you are here. You are sitting in the physical manifestation of what a man like Blake Pierce has done for you. He's a man who has committed the greatest sin in this business: he has no ideas and doesn't care. This company is modestly successful and has virtually no brand awareness. Worst of all, it's dull. The company is called Infinite Solutions, yet there's only one solution: make it like everyone else. Here's an example of what he picked to be the best ad the company put together last year..."

I click the first image up. A smiling man, with his beige jacket over his shoulder, walking down a beach towards a sunset. He looks back over his other shoulder at us, as if to say everything is going to be okay.

"This says nothing. It says less than nothing. What are they selling? I have no idea. Maybe cigarettes? A vacation hotel? Erection medication? It's so abstract and so removed from the thing. All it's showing me is a vague idea... of what exactly? Dome doesn't need more ads or brands. We need something more. And not just something like performance or guerilla advertising. We need something real."

I click to the next image. It's the video of Dad, paused at its first frame. His outstretched, withered hand, the soft sunbeam covering his arm, making it glow. I play the video. The beep of the monitor, his labored breathing almost knocks me over. It misses the smell, that chemical ammonia stink.

Their eyes search me for an answer.

"Why is this important? Not because this is my dad, but because it can't be faked. It can't be repeated. You can watch the video again, but you can't recapture it. Even if you did the most accurate recreation of it, down to the atomic level, it wouldn't be the same. Here he is alive..."

I pause.

"Here he dies," I say, moving the video forward. The beeping has stopped.

"Alive. Dead. Alive. Dead." I move the video back and forth, murdering my father over and over again. Obliterating him.

"Everything he ever was. Everything he loved, hated, feared, dreamed. Gone forever in that split second. He was my dad, and I was his son and I loved him. I have a son of my own and I wonder if he'll be with me at the end. I filmed him because... I wanted to show the world that behind this ordinary, unremarkable man was something else. Something invisible and real. I have this very specific memory of him. We were at some amusement park and I became extremely afraid on one of the rides. So much so that they had to stop the ride so I would stop screaming. He took me off the ride and we sat on a bench and he took me to the arcade and we played a football video game of some kind. Now the fact that I remember it, is that enough?"

I pause the video the moment the HealthLine is cut off.

"This is the moment that he dies." I shake my pointed finger behind me. "We need to live inside that moment. Not in a moment of someone dying, but of something that simply can't be repeated. Anyone can put on a beige jacket and walk down a beach. Real work should radiate. It should destroy people. It should be in that one moment."

I leave the stage, my father's death flickering in the dark, in the stunned silence.

13 ~ *livestream*

Holly Day, our HR person, sits quietly at her desk with a strange death rictus grin. I'm confident if I turned the monitor around, I would see nothing but gibberish. Her office is normally vacant, on the other side of the building. Human resources. What a strange term. Our hiring and firings are automatic, controlled by our main systems and calculated from our stats, so I'm not even sure what she even does. I don't think I've ever even had a conversation with her, just seen her face on our office screens. Maybe they see her as a mascot, the cheerful human face to a vast, impersonal mechanism.

Her door makes an unsettling baby's laugh when I enter. Holly's office is a pink puffy nightmare of candy-colored striping and girlish fluff. White, happy clouds dot a baby blue sky on her walls, sprinkled with rabbits and singing birds. Her desk is a giant pink plastic blob and she sits on a beanbag cushion. This is a woman who seems always on the verge of frenzy, clawing desperately with ruffles and charm bracelets like ancient magical amulets to stave off something terrifying about to consume her. There's a silence here only broken by the rhythmic hum of sickly fluorescent lighting.

"Hi Holly, I need a moment of your time."

Her head swivels like a security camera. Her face only slightly flutters, like she was hoping not to see me, yet she soldiers on.

"Mister Scaggs, hello! I received the news from the board. Congratulations! Would you like a RealWater or a Koffee?"

"No thank you."

"What about a Premium? Or a-"

"I said no thank you. Show me the new work contract."

She shrinks a little and acquiesces. The contract looks real, 100% legitimate. I feel tingly. To be sure, I call an independent contract hotline in the middle of Holly's office and examine the contract. I'm charged $149.99 but it was worth every beautiful cent.

"There's some blank space here under pay and benefits and such."

Holly perks up. "The board has yet to negotiate those."

The number Holly quotes me as their initial offer is almost blasphemous. I agree almost instantly. To settle my nerves, I take a quick hit off of a calmer, a single use relaxant. A cool pulse flows through me.

"I'm sorry, Mr. Scaggs, but we don't allow those in here."

"Yes, you do. When do I formally start?"

"Well, Mr. Pierce needs to be appropriately resolved." She shifts in her chair. Her eyes dart. "We like to let these things just resolve themselves. We don't like to confront an associate with, uh, unfortunate news like this whenever we can. Eventually Security will just show him out."

"So let me get this straight, as of now, I am the head of this company?"

She nods. "According to the contract, that's correct!"

"And that piece of shit right now has no idea?"

She nods again. I lean back, as much as you can in a beanbag chair.

"Keep it that way."

~~~~

At my cube, I log in with my newly reactivated account and continue to push units like nothing happened. The Koffee still tastes the same though; that watery, sour flavor. Blake hasn't seen me yet, and the people around me are too busy to acknowledge me sitting there.

There's a sick thrill watching Blake trying to figure out why he can't access his marketing grids. That precarious little world where he used to be on top and everyone else was an ant. Where he was the smart one, the winner, the king. Smug and entitled that the entire world was his and he could do with what he willed. Jerry in IT has no answers for him. He storms off eventually and returns even angrier. Then he simply gets quiet, stares at the wall, his hands. I drink his confusion like a top shelf wine: smooth and warming. There are men like him all over the Dome, infecting others with their worthlessness.
~~~~

I know I've won. Against all odds and predictions, I won. But it's not enough. He must lose and know that he's lost. When he figures it out, he's going to drive himself mad wondering how I got the better of him. Fine with me. I want this feeling to last forever. He's trying to "coach" a nearby employee about her copy turnaround times. Her hands sometimes shake so badly.

"Now Angela, you need to ask yourself, do you have in you to do this?" He's right beside her face, hovering over her. That waxy skin, the cigarette breath.

"I don't know…"

"I think that if you look deep inside you, that you can really rise above this."

"Don't fuck with me, Blake. Not today. Do not fuck with me."

He takes a step backward.

"FUCK OFF!" Her voice drips hot liquid metal. The enormity of her pain in her voice is frightening. After Blake walks away confused, she tucks her arms around her stomach, her head turned down to her plain flats.

Every person in the Dome has some secret tragedy that only they feel they can bear. And then there's Blake, smiling and chuckling at what he feels is inevitable success. Well, not today.

I stand, go to Angela, and touch her shoulder. I whisper in her ear that everything's going to be alright. She grabs my hand, and at the volume of a ghost, says "Thank you."

I pick up my phone, dial my outside access code, and make the call. Coyote picks up on the other end.

"Hello, Corwin. Congratulations."

"Thank you. We're good to go."

~~~~

Blake's retirement party is coming along quickly. Product placements are good, and most of the brands are hot to the idea. "It's very meta" and "I love how energetic it is". Empty phrases like that.

To complete the illusion, to seal it like a present, I make Jerry go and apologize for the computer issues, groveling to him, practically prostrate in his office. He says he'll fix the issue ASAP. Make him feel like a precious, sacred object. He's the one the prophets have been foretelling in the sacred scriptures. Just give him anything he wants. He screams at them for a good hour and then Jerry claims he needs to check on a server issue down at the datacenter.

"You owe me," Jerry says.

Raylene still doesn't know. Until the show is over, I don't want her to know. I want to surprise her, but first I need to make sure Blake is getting his own surprise.

Several days later, on an anonymous Friday night, Blake Pierce, former Creative Director of Infinite Solutions, a soulless shell of a man, takes a sip of Koffee from a special blend made in his personal machine in his office. Except now it has a new special ingredient. He's huddled in his office, that cubical sanctum where he coldly crushes a person's heart because he enjoys it, cruelty being the only feeling he appears capable of. He feels drowsy, like a warm hand is pushing him to the ground. He closes his eyes, maybe it's just the late nights, all the dancing and singing he must do to make the
~~~~

board happy. They've been extremely disappointed with him lately. "A distinct lack of vision" they've told him, words that reverberate.

He then falls into a deep slumber, his head cocked back in his chair, the monitors and stations all around him feeding useless rivers of information to an unconscious man dreaming of nothing.

I'm at the door to his office, phone in hand. I walk in, grab his chubby face right in my hand. I give him a long, long look.

"Showtime."

~~~~

A colorless gas that smells like almonds is released into Blake's office. The door, however, is shut and if he tries to open it, it doesn't lead into the Infinite Solutions office anymore. Blake stirs, rubs his eyes, and looks at his watch. He thinks he's only been asleep for about twenty minutes, but in reality it's actually been six hours.

I'm below the stage, standing on my soon-to-be-elevated platform, listening to the crew chatter. Two faceless voices in my ear.

"Star is awake."

"Copy."

"Prep opening. Go hot when the door is active."

"Copy."

On the monitor, Blake staggers to his feet. He stumbles, his face turns a bright pink color, and then he violently vomits into his trash can. I laugh and applaud his commitment to Infinite
~~~~

Solutions. To make the show the best it can be, regardless of what it costs.

"Well done, Blake! Well done!"

The voice again. "Ten seconds to scene."

The voice counts down to showtime.

His office rumbles, walls falling away to reveal an enormous open soundstage, black as midnight. It's not much from a distance, but it's impressive when you're a terrified, confused former creative director who just got finished puking up Chik-N-Lil Cordon Blu. The original idea was to simply shove him along with tasers from scene to scene, but that was too unpredictable. Too many ways he couldn't play along.

The "office" is encased in shatterproof glass, moving on a track. Our opening score is a bombastic musical number, complete with a chorus line of women dressed in regular office attire, who at the crescendo, rip them off to reveal skintight blue bikinis. There are digital fireworks on the ceiling. Blake bangs on the glass walls, throwing his chair, his monitor, screaming in a mute howl. I'm happy to say I can't hear a thing, except the chatter that comes over the radio.

Blake Pierce is about to go on a trip through his own personal Memory Lane. His cage slides silently across the ground towards each compartment, a wonderfully detailed reproduction of his sins. Art department did a pretty amazing job considering how little time they had. The soothing voiceover, provided by Max Vox, recants the history of Blake's sins.

Three former employees, Tyrese Manger, Cyrill Hamm, and Draco Phillips were all mid-ranked account managers, all good at their jobs. Not ones to make trouble or complain. Skilled, effective. The three of them earned over 45% of our current business. These are decent men, ridiculously decent to a fault. Cyrill is 56 years old and enjoys model ship building, even though he's never been on a boat. Tyrese is married to an overly polite man named Alex and has three licensed daughters whom he loves "more than life". He used to annoyingly show me pictures of his daughters on his phone, post countless statuses about what they were up to, birthdays and such. Draco is an aspiring art director, someone who paints by hand, and prefers watercolors over acrylics for their "sensuality" as he put it.

Blake Pierce thought it would be cute to lie that there was a single executive account management position that may become available in the next fiscal quarter, and that all they had to do was beat out each other in terms of revenue raised.

At first, the competition was friendly, may the best account manager win. No hard feelings, they agreed. It was part of the job. We're all fighting against everyone else, that's the truth of it. Blake got bored with their civility, and decided to toss in a dash of drama to their lives. He planted evidence that Tyrese was about to betray the others by intentionally clusterfucking a dual presentation Draco and Cyrill were making to MetaCortex by delaying their art. When the two of them angrily confront Tyrese, he in turn presented them with a series of faked messages about how Tyrese grew his daughter in Chik-N-Lil vats and recanted a complete fake story that Tyrese had given a prospective client a rimjob in the pay stall of the second floor bathroom.

Ugly is not the word I would use to describe that situation. Their feud was the stuff of legends, playfully prodded and stoked by Blake's cold glee. Draco almost poisoned Cyrill thinking he had hired an industrial agent to clear his desk, so to speak. Tyrese's marriage soon dissolved after Blake had an escort prank-called the man's husband pretending to be a collections agency asking about "executive massage" charges that had not been paid.

And then, descending like a dropping nuclear bomb, Pierce fires all three of them. Tyrese and Cyrill got summary ones. Draco was, for some reason, fired by a video chat, so distraught by the news he couldn't stop from crying. Blake recorded it and passed it along the intranet for all the other managers, who all had a big laugh. In the end, Blake hired an "outside consultant" to fill the position. Some child barely out of Training and paid him a sacrilegious amount to essentially attend meetings, speak little, and shake hands.

All three of those wrecked men, standing together like war monuments, in a set decorated to look like a battlefield had taken place in the middle of their former office. Two of Tyrese's daughters join them. One of Tyrese's daughters, Shalia, had accidentally killed herself during his messy divorce. She threw herself on his car so he wouldn't leave and she slid off the hood when he stopped too suddenly, then was run over by a self-driving delivery truck.

Blake in his glass cube is no longer laughing. The show moves on.

Next: a junior associate copywriter named Hart Breaker, some brand name kid barely old enough to shave, was hired to run basic errands for us, restock the Koffee machine, clean out desks of transferring employees, simple stuff. He wasn't smart or clever, or even particularly good at his job. He was actually kind of a prick at first, and I genuinely hated his smug little smirk and the trendy tattoos. The whole package stunk of someone who'd never lost anything in his life or had to do anything more complicated than look at a phone.

What's more ironic is that Hart wanted the entire Dome in his greasy, status-updating, narcissistic hand and after one fateful afternoon that literally became impossible.

That's mankind's factory default setting, burned into our brains by eons of evolution and staring at advertising that Infinite Solutions creates. It's like the weather, controlled and perfected to just the right temperature: a boiling hot fog of anger and disappointment that you're not good enough for anyone's love, that you will never be loved if not for our product. You are worthless, but you are the most important being alive.

Hart was just terrible about it. He didn't know how to sell himself, wrapping his exterior in whatever was trending for the day, slithering out of his own clothes and identity like a chameleon. He was faceless, nameless, a cypher. Like I said, he wanted the Dome in his hands. That may have happened. Who knows. That is, until an afternoon when he was asked to replace color toner in a fast-speed printing press spool, which grabbed the right sleeve of his casual denim jacket, one of those pieces intentionally worn down by machines to look "lived in." The whirling mouth of the printer spool chewed the top part of his arm and its expensive tattoos into a pain-soaked stump of crushed bone and meat. The kid's fingers were like an optical illusion.

Pierce demanded the investigation into the accident was deemed to be worker-caused. He failed to exercise caution around a machine he had no training on and frankly no business going anywhere near. Investigators also insinuated that he may have done it intentionally to garner sympathy in the next round of promotional lotteries, or even to get a reality series based on himself.

They had to amputate, by the way. He couldn't afford to have a replacement grown, so he became a lefty. After that Hart became Blake's pet object of ridicule. The asshole put up a whiteboard that stated "Hart Has Gone This Many Days Without Fucking Up" and announced the results over the intercom almost every day.

Hart is fine now. He works in Food Reclamation.

We set him up in a tableau of shattered hands and arms like a forest. His missing arm has a temporary replacement, one made of brittle plastic that Hart violently throws against the glass.

Blake jumps back like a scared child. He is beginning to realize the totality of what is happening to him.

Angela. She was a graduate from the Training Master Class about 3 fiscal years ago. A confident, smart lady who entered our office on her first day with her head held high, cutting through us like soft cheese. She wasn't naive or power-hungry, never went for office power-plays. She simply wanted to do a good job, settle down, start a family maybe. Pretty but not beautiful, dressed modestly. Angela always had a helpful word of encouragement and she never complained. She was eager to help others learn, even at the expense of her own unit counts, earning the begrudging respect of her co-workers one at a time.

She kept track of birthdays. Smiled with the rare ability to make it feel genuine. If you were in a conversation with her, she listened to you, and didn't just wait for her turn to talk. When she married Fred and got pregnant, I was maybe too secretly happy for her. Maybe she could make it. Axel had just turned 10 at that point, and she would nervously ask me about his infancy and basic parenting stuff. At first, I was incredibly annoyed by her questions. Just look it up, I thought. I relented and told her I had just muddled through it, and that there were no set rules. Try your best or whatever. Watch out for behavioral issues early, such as continual crying, fidgeting, annoying habits.

Angela is a good person. She played by the rules, or at least the way she understood the rules. I would catch her every now and then looking into space, her hand absentmindedly resting on her stomach. When the first pains shot through her abdomen, she followed policy and bought two hours off to see a medical technician the next week. Approved. There was a problem at the health franchise and she ended up missing the rest of the day.

Pierce very calmly sat her down and explained the rules of Business 101, like she was 5 and it was her first day of Training. If associates aren't here, units don't get made, we lose business, we lose jobs, blah blah blah. On and on. She sat very quietly, her hands in her lap, nodding along and promising that it wouldn't happen again.

The second time the pains came back more intensely. She never complained but did ask for another appointment with a technician. Denied.

She even went and talked to him again. Denied again. Maybe if it's really bad, he said. He openly said she might be exaggerating, that she might be faking it.

She kept her head up, ignored the agony, and worked through the stabbing in her gut. An older woman sold her some pain meds for practically nothing. The third time she was almost doubled over, and pushed people away, including me, when they came to help her. She kept working, kept adding clouds and happy smiles to all these fake faces and met her quota for the day. When she stood up finally and hobbled out, we could see the blood stain on her chair.

She had miscarried.

When she came back on Workday, her chair was not even cleaned or replaced. Our work equipment is rented by us, and Blake was trying to save money. I should have paid for a replacement, or for it to be cleaned, but I just didn't want to get involved. There was no crying or anger from her, she had buried it all the way down in that special place that women have for suffering at the hands of men like Blake.

"You know what she was working on that was so important? A toilet paper ad with the slogan 'A Pillow For Your Throne'," Max Vox says in the voice-over. My words in his smooth, darkly seductive voice.

The grand finale. Blake is silent as a statue, head down, arms flat at his sides.

I had planned to have Dad, or since I couldn't move him, an actor that looks like him in a hospital room slowly coughing and dying. Very dramatic. Poignant even. I decided against it, considering I committed one of the largest, most complicated wire frauds in HealthLine history.

Also, I need to remind myself that this is Blake Pierce's show, not mine. He earned this monumental humiliation in front of the entire Dome so many different ways, both big and small. He's a symbol, I told Coyote. A symbol that needs to be erased.

I remember endless conversations with him ending with "We're done here, Corwin," he had said.

Oh no, we are not done.

My radio squawks. "Mr. Director, ten seconds."

"Thank you."

"Let's see some blood," I hear Coyote hiss into my earpiece.

I begin to rise up, bathed in a bright column of white stardom. Blake has taken off his shirt, that enormous, comically spherical gut shining under the hot stage lights, slumped against the replica of his desk as the music swells around us like the rising tide. I'm dressed like I'm about to announce a new top-of-the-line smartphone, my teeth whitened, my eyebrows plucked, covered in a light dusting of tanner. I'm wearing a slick, styled hairpiece. I'm wearing a stark black suit, cufflinks, and a gold tie pin.

I look like a god.

Blake, on the other hand, looks like a panicky caged animal knowing the end is near. I didn't know someone could sweat that much. It must be sweltering in there. Let him roast. I march towards him with the solemnity of an executive funeral, a military conference. Our finest moment together.

The music dims. All cameras are on me and Blake Pierce.

Time for your closeup.

"Are you a happy man? Are you fulfilled? Have you achieved all of your goals in life? Are you blissfully triumphant in your success? By the way, have you met your unit counts today?"

I press the transmit button on his cage.

"Blake, you can speak now. Everyone can hear you."

He stands up. "I WILL FUCKING END YOU, CORWIN. DO YOU HEAR ME. YOU ARE DEAD. YOU ARE FUCKING DE-"

I mute him. "That's enough of that." He yells blank words against the glass, pounding his fists. Sweat pours off him in rivers. I smile like a blade, my joy is boundless.

"You know in movies or TV shows there's this moment where the bad guy, which you think is me probably, turns to the good guy in the cage, which you think is you most definitely, and say 'This isn't personal, it's business.' It's a cliche, but it's a good one. Well, this is personal. This is what you do, Blake. This is what everyone like you does. It's not that you're shitty, selfish or cruel. Lot of people are like that."

I pace. My breathing is heavy, deep gasps.

"And for what?! It wasn't even that profitable."

Blake doesn't shout or scream or curse. He leans against the desk, sweating, and just stares right at me. Good, I want him to see me. He needs to hear this coming out of my mouth.

"The worst part is, you didn't have to. I've had a lot of dumb moron bosses in my life, but they were playing the game. You made these people suffer because you liked it. Because it made you feel good. Let me ask you something, do you feel good now? This is what it feels like to be on the other side. Smile for the cameras, Blake. It's your big moment."

The same techno Blake used on the day before Black Friday plays. The cameras swirl around me like a tornado of ego. I kneel down to his level.

"We're done here."

He is mute and still. Not a glimmer of recognition. I imagine someone who was just royally humiliated on a live streaming broadcast would still be furious, that same fury he had moments ago. The polar opposite. His mask is serene, an ocean of waveless flesh peering into a distant horizon. I wanted him to beg forgiveness, throw himself at my mercy. I wanted to crush him under my polished shoe.

Instead I feel cold and ugly. Nothing released, nothing solved.

His cage slowly descends down and he'll be escorted off the premises by Security. Initially, I was going to have them put their boots to him and sell that footage as an extra, but I radio for them to call it off.

"Just let him go. He's Bargainville's problem now, and that's good enough for me."

As he vanishes below the stage, his eyes never leave mine.

~~~~
~~~~

The livestream after party at the Infinite Solutions office has a small but specific client list. All of the various people Blake Pierce has used up and discarded over the years. Some people have a terrifying dream that they go to a party where everyone that hates them is there. For Blake, this would be accurate. Revenge brings people together.

Most of the attendees are former blacklisted copywriters, women he slept with and ghosted, clients who were burned by his contract doubletalk, even industry enemies. A few of his enemies even wanted an industrial hit, but I said it didn't make good streaming.

"There's no narrative. Plus you can get snuff anywhere. It only has one moment, when he dies. Everything else is a distraction. It's fluff. With this approach, every step, every scene was one more brick in his tomb. It's more fascinating if you never see him again."

I chose to stop that man from being beaten within an inch of his life. From being outright killed. Blake probably felt this power when he drew up his random list of people to be fired, or decided to announce how much weight one of the ladies had put on over the loudspeaker in the guise of a "healthy workplace".

The walls feel too tight, everyone is too drunk with agony and misery to be happy drunks. Lots of yelling and crying, but not that sweet cosmic orgasm we all needed. I've been drunk on hating Blake Pierce for too long and now I feel hungover. Only a handful of people talk to me.

Partygoers are circled around Blake's old office, betting each other to piss in his trash can or shit on his desktop. I tell them not to and send the party to Club Inferno.

Already two sheets to the wind, I fall on the couch, ready to just sleep and figure out what I'm going to do tomorrow. A blurry figure stirs at the giant desk. A pad stylus is flicked at me and I scramble to my feet.

"Sorry. I didn't know you were in here. Go to Inferno, I'll meet you there." All I see are dark shapes and window blinds.

"I'm very proud of you, Corwin. My special little guy."

"Coyote, you scared the shit out of me."

"You really are a prize, aren't you?" Coyote says. She uncoils herself from the remnants of Blake's life and stalks me across the room. The whites of her eyes are bright and sharp, following me as I try to make for the door. With a swift limberness, she stretches her left knee up to my mid-chest, and tightly pins me against the wall. I can smell vanilla body wash and the afterglow of expensive perfume. I grab her calf, almost slipping on the sheer nylon of her stockings, trying to move.

"Coyote, please stop.."

"Please stop what? Let you go? Go where? Back home?"

Her shoeless foot caresses my crotch.

"I'm married."

"Sure you are."

"Stop it, Coyote."

She flexes her knee against my ribs, spreading herself more. "Hello there, been working here long?"

She leans into me, her teeth inches from my neck. I can't quite see, but I imagine they're as sharp as daggers. She tastes me. She tastes more of me. There's no words anymore, just boiling air and the television sky showing us the lie of a cloud and so much more.

"You're mine now," she whispers. She says it over and over.

We're twined together like those snakes on hospitals and now we're on the couch and I can't speak because her hand's on my mouth. Her breath is fire and she laughs in the blackness around us like naked ice. If I could shout I would call out all the names of oh god we're not supposed to be here because it's my office and it's not ready. A river and an ocean and a beach from some shore I put in an ad for arthritis pills. No I'm not here, I'm in my garden with my plastic plants and everything's on fire and melted and there's faces in the burning acrid stench of her perfume and that laugh she keeps laughing and when she's done I lay on my back and fall for a long time until I am in the dark.

~~~~

Workday morning and I'm in the fog again. The entire building is white fire and choking me with thick plumes of milky blankness and I'm lost in it, hovering above the ground like a Security drone until I get into the office.

I am greeted by a crowd of cheering faces, like a conquering hero. I don't even know what they're applauding for. And there was Coyote, pushing me along like a shopping cart, filling me with her poison. There's a blank space after the party. I slept at the office, went home to a slightly frightened Raylene, and spent Saturday hiding from the world. A staggering shame blossoms in me like a virus. I tried telling her what happened. I tried. I did but I couldn't. The words didn't materialize.
~~~~

At Infinite Solutions, I'm not sure what these people expect. These strangers. I certainly don't feel like a savior. I'm small and frightened, dwarfed by their applause and cheers. I play along.

All work stops. All clients are informed of the restructuring, and a half dozen drop immediately. It cuts our revenue by 17% in one day. Blake had given many of these clients ridiculous sweetheart deals, costs so low that they must have been something under the table. He was greedy and dumb and did whatever suited him best. It was just the quantity that mattered, we learned he cooked stats to appear more productive that we actually were. I stay focused to stop my mind from thinking about other things.

Three of the clients that canceled their contracts didn't even have contracts to begin with. A clerical error, they say. Sure.

Everyone is gathered in the main conference room, seated in rows like they're back in Training. Ready to take their Placement Tests. Wondering who will get the axe. Who will suffer my petty, childish wrath. Gathering allies and listing their enemies. But I refuse to play this game. When I enter, all is quiet, like the TV being turned off.

I probably would have said something insightful or reassuring, but I don't. I don't have time.

When I first hear the sharp pops, they sound like cheap fireworks or someone snapping a piece of plastic in half. Six or seven of them, loud enough to hear inside the conference room. I haven't said anything yet and I peek my head outside the door. Richard, the head of the Printing Department, stumbles out into the hall, holding what looks like magenta printer toner to his head.

"Everything okay?"

He says nothing, but keeps stumbling forward. Then the screaming comes up the halls like a wave of sound. The next few minutes are a splintered tornado of screams, blood, and flashes of motion as hundreds of people scramble over each other in a raw tide of panic. Every few seconds, another sharp pop like a crack of lightning, louder now as the firing gun draws closer. Someone will get hit and have the identical look of confusion and agony, watching the red bloom on their shirt or pants like a flower. This kind of thing doesn't happen to me, their faces say. This happens to other people. This happens online.

Movie gunshots sound like a cannon being fired, not the sad, anticlimactic snap of gunpowder. More gunshots now and they feel like they're everywhere. I feel like I should be in control of an evacuation of some kind, but I'm frozen behind the break room table, upturned to block the door. I can't see what's happening. What's happening. What is going on. Where is Security. Where.

I hear Jerry shouting for people to get out through the stairs and he runs into the break room. I peek over the table to see Jerry standing in the doorway, shirt ripped at the color, pale as the walls, sweating cold and breathing huge gulps of air.

"Corwin, come on! We gotta-"

The right side of his head explodes, painting the break room sign in a red spray. I don't hear the shot. He falls straight down, cracking his bifurcated head on the freshly mopped tile with a sickly crunch. His eyes are still open, blood pours from his nose like a waterfall. I am not seeing this. I'm not. Jerry is alive and this is some hilarious first day, new boss prank that they came up with. I told them to think outside the box. Yeah, get your head blown off, Jerry. Right in front of him. It'll be hilarious. I laugh robotically.

My head swoons and bright static fills my vision. A hand rests on the door. Around the corner, Blake Pierce enters the break room. It's him, but it's not really him. A hollow man. His face and hands are painted bright red, like with spray-paint. That shiny, plastic look you see on children's toys. For effect, he's shirtless and has drawn large red circles around his nipples. He's also holding a rifle with an extended drum magazine. His eyes are dead tombs, corpse-grey and devoid of awareness. Screams waft in from outside, breaking glass, moaning.

I duck behind the break table, hoping he doesn't see me. How could he not see me. He saw me. It takes him an eternity to cross the room. As I curl up, expecting the gun in my face, he sits on the couch, the gun laid across in his lap, but still pointed at me. The gun barrel is the center of all known existence. It is all that has ever been. He slowly turns towards me.

"I want to pitch you on something, Mr. Scaggs. An advertising campaign for Joob." His voice is like he's reciting something poorly. Every word is emphasized, as if he's never spoken out loud before.

"Okay. Let's hear it," I croak. I look over at Jerry, his remaining blank eye staring right at me. There's so much blood.

Blake licks his lips, bares and grits his teeth at me. His breath is small, hurried. Then comes the mask again. Calm, in control.

"Joob is a family friendly product so we should accentuate its fun factor for young children who have never felt agony picture it if you will, a young boy locked away in a cold windowless room he is bone-thin, starving even there is no love in this room then there is another room where there is love and light and hope and Joob what do you think."

My chest heaves and my voice is cracking like ice.

"It's good, Blake. It's really good," I say, barely getting the words out.

He sits back, his head turned up towards the ceiling.

"Do you have any other notes?"

"No. Let's move forward," I realize those are my last words in this world. I'm going to die in this stupid breakroom that stinks like lemon vomit, killed by an asshole with giant red nipples. Raylene. Axel. I love you so much and I am so stupid. I'm so sorry.

"Thank you. Your feedback is very important to me. I also appreciate you having this review discussion in an open environment of inclusiveness and understanding. Fuck the world," Blake says.

He stares down, starts breathing in and out, heavy and fast. It's getting faster. He's building up pressure to explode. His nostrils flare like pulsing dark lights. He's heaving up and down on the couch.

I am going to die.

I'm sorry.

Jerking his arm up, he shoves the gun in his mouth and pulls the trigger. A wet, gagging sound erupts from him like he's choking as he slides off the couch, his sweaty leg brushing my hand. I jump at the clammy touch. Face down on the tile, his last breath gurgles blood and his limbs twitch. There's a hissing sound from the back of the pink mass that used to be his head. A warm patch spreads on my pants.

I reach my hand out and shake his calf. Nothing.

Frosty air pumps from the air conditioner. The vendi-fridge plays a small jingle. After my heart grows quieter, I clumsily kick the gun out of his hand. Outside in the hall, I can hear someone crying.

Security shows up in full regalia, helmets and boots and such, storming the building. At this point, a workplace incident like this is tragically normal. We're all statistics now. 17 positions were terminated and 26 more were remaindered. The news doesn't even bother to ask for names. We'll lose around 1200 work hours, totaling $650,000 in lost potential earnings. In an outreach coup, our logo is splashed over the news feeds for the entire Dome for almost an entire day, mainly from how closely it followed our successful livestream. There's the rubbing of hands and meaningless gestures of sympathy. The lobby is filled with plastic flowers. There are a dozen funerals.

The producer for the now famous "We're Done Here" livestream shows up at the Infinite Solutions office. In an annoyed tone, he asks if there's footage and when he suggests a re-enactment, I almost choke him to death. Three security officers have to pull me off and I almost find out what pepper spray tastes like. That gets on camera.

The narrative is crafted without us, molding us into stock characters for the camera. Most of the employees are just shaking wrecks like me, but a few are eager to start building their brands. Blake purchased the gun from a vending machine out near the

Rim, in that grungy fringe before the industrial shipping yards and the Dome's exterior wall. I ask if I'm the villain in the story. Rubbing his neck, the producer tells me not to worry about that.

"Consumers like a bad guy. They need someone to hate. Your takeover of the company, the livestream, his revenge. It's such good content."

They already have a preview image of the primetime special ready to air at the end of the week. I'm confident they'll neglect to add in that awful gagging sound he made when he shot himself. The bullets will be thunderous like they should be. Slow motion. Lots of lens flares. A quiet, grinding electronic score.

I don't see them take Jerry away. I don't want to. Oh God.

I'm cleared by EMT's, who take my treatment payment on the spot. They give me an injection that makes me float. I stumble outside to the bright afternoon light, when the sun is right inside your eyes and everything sparkles. Raylene and Axel are escorted through the Security line and I grab them and hold them.

The cameras and phones and questions are everywhere, and they capture this reuniting moment, but I ignore them. The producer must be beaming. Everyone is watching.

14 ~ *shrine*

At Jerry's funeral, I look in the casket at his LikeLife and I feel nothing. I want to cry, but I can't and wander away from it. I choose to not think about it.

The next week is a blur of work and fielding media inquiries. No one really knows what to do and I don't have answers for them, so they just kept doing what they used to. These thoughts keep coming on like a rerun marathon, over and over, and when I can get quiet, stop thinking: all I see is Jerry slumped staring at me, Dad in his bed. 17 bodies covered with black plastic. Dad's hand raised in the air. Reaching for something I'll never understand.

A party happens on our mutual day off. I never see any planning, it just appears in our living room. Phantom people float in and out, I catch names and faces but they blur together. They're financial analysts and consultants and brand managers and couture foodies and viral video stars. A one-of-a-kind, limited run collection of people with vacant expressions. I try to be polite, hand clamped around my drink like someone's throat. A coiled and lethal feeling sinks in my gut, but in an impotent, directionless way. It's maddening. I sign the rights for the re-enactment without really paying attention.

Angela is here, in her slightly rounded, soft affect, as out of place as I am. She doesn't have my hollow agony, though. She's just adorably awkward, shaking hands with people. She dressed up in her best clothes: a bright teal dress and giant pearl-style earrings, a light purple purse clinging to her like a refugee. She obviously doesn't want to be here and I don't blame her. This is a vending machine for sickness, stocked with junk food. She doesn't deserve this. I put on my host face and walk to her. She sees me coming, locks eyes with me, and matches my mask.

"You seem miserable," I say. I take a swig from my drink.

"Um... what?"

"I said you seem miserable. Everything here seems like something else. You seem like you're not having a good time."

"I'm sorry, Corwin. I'll try harder."

I wasn't expecting something so truthful, so raw. Her absolute honesty knocks the wind out of me. I expected a hidden snarky response, like something I could say. She excuses herself and goes to the bathroom, and I follow, waiting outside the door.

She's on the phone with someone. I think she's crying.

When Angela exits, I try to apologize but she just smiles, nods, and leaves soon after.

After the party, I sit on the couch staring at the floor. An empty bottle lies on its side. I stare at it intensely.

"What's wrong?" Raylene says, cleaning up in the living room. The "living room": where the dead go to rot.

"I don't know."

"I'm just happy you're alive. Can we just, I don't know, get on with everything? I mean, we're okay. You're okay."

"I honestly don't think I'm okay."

"Then please talk to me. With all that's happened, you can't keep this all bottled up. The new job, the shooting."

"I'm fine, I'm just tired," I say, lying. She knows I'm lying but pretends not to.

She sighs, indicating that she's not mad at me. She's put up with me for long enough that anger doesn't register for her, just a slouching acceptance. In her patient disappointment, she rubs her forehead with her manicured hands, those smooth palms buffed and scoured. Somewhere in the room, automatic dust vents are consuming flakes of our skin.

~~~~

When you have such a close handshake with death, you have a cloak of awful, naked guilt draped over your shoulders. They died and I didn't and I just watched it happen. I was there in the same space where their life was extinguished and mine was not. At first, there was just regular guilt, now it feels gnawing and eternal. I am cursed with survival. I make it through just fine and everyone around me suffers. I have no answers, no greater truth to fall back on.
~~~~

Kids are working on their personal brand younger and younger, and Axel talks my ear off pitching me personal slogans after Jerry's wake. I was shuffling around some debt numbers to put us somewhat in the green for the month. Thankfully, I had been able to break us even, as opposed to how it normally went, which was just adding to the pile. Another good commission and I can start paying our Number down. It's a small but welcome turn of good fortune. The cost is so high.

Looking at the Number, it didn't give me any absolution. The Number is on the surface a collection of smaller numbers that flow into each other and produce your Brand value. Mine has risen substantially and bewilderingly. Money is simply not something I am used to having.

Axel pitches me, I listen the best I can. The ones I had heard were not very good and I tried giving him pointers about emotional connection and accessibility, showed him our marketing grids, but I think it went over his head.

~~~~

After the cleanup at Infinite Solutions was finished, Pierce's house became surrounded by cameras and onlookers. An entire media network was created to analyze and dissect every moment of his life, and the morbid fascination with the shooting played out in horrifying detail 24 hours a day, 7 days a week. He became a Main Character. A procession of psychoanalysts and armchair theorists drawing diagrams of his converging mental illnesses fighting it out, and that the inevitable conclusion was murder. 3D animated
~~~~

images of my friend's faces being blown apart in gory detail by realistically modeled ballistics, made from the exclusive purchase from Security's internal files. There's not a channel for Dad. He went quietly, tucked out of the way, pathetically like a dying goldfish choking his last breath on the carpet.

I am grieving in reverse.

Viewers forgot about Pierce. And Jerry. And the sixteen other names they never even bothered to learn.

And that bloody spot in the break room? Where Blake signed his resignation? I had it framed.

I thought that would let me conquer that moment, just like how I taped Dad. It's in my office now, but the framing doesn't conquer it. You don't own it. It owns you. You can't even bring yourself to discard it. The pain just latches onto you like a bloated parasite, feeding off your inability to move away. I don't think about the couch, I had it removed, Coyote falling back into the background. Maybe that was just a dream. It had to have been. I make it a dream, something unreal and far away.

In front of me, Blake's house is an empty box, abandoned. Flaccid security tape is draped across the door frame. The sun is about to set and the house looks especially dark, like the sun was setting on it alone. All the cameras have been packed up, the makeup chairs and transponder dishes removed. The phones have vanished as well, their attention floating elsewhere. The leering eyes got bored when the network ran out of secret documents to have exclusive exposes. I absolutely refused to be interviewed at all. Jerry's girlfriend got her own show out of it, a competitive goth-themed cupcake bake-off, and I feel no ill will towards her. I miscalculated. I should have thrown myself into the network with all my soul, then everyone would have forgotten about me. Instead, my reclusiveness about the event made business pour into the agency. They felt my presence lent an air of danger to their fruit juices and children's toys. We doubled our client list and I hate every moment of it.

I step in the road, 6 lanes of heavy traffic zipping by on their own ways home. The electric columns of cars automatically change lanes and shift silently around me as I pass through them. Like they're afraid to be around me. I half-heartedly want one to crush my legs so I'll stop walking towards the house. But they don't. I am still a blessed person, it seems. I am a survivor.

The lawn needs a refresher coat for color and vibrancy. It's a luxurious front yard with rows of Plastik Pine and Falsetto hiding the detached house from the road. He doesn't live in a stacked unit like I do, but he doesn't live in the Sprawl. Some midway place.

A death house. A murder mansion, even though not a single body was found there. All the fun happened at Infinite Solutions. The Pierce House is just a carnival ride, a spooky slideshow for the exhausting interviews and specials. There was talk of turning the house into an actual attraction: the Blake Pierce Murder House Spectacular. Nothing came of it, there's so many shootings, it's hard to monetize them all.

The locked door, made of cheap particle board and flimsy hinges, nearly comes off the frame. A quick kick right below the doorknob sends it rocketing aside. I must look like a demented scavenger, eager for a gruesome trophy or souvenir. A pair of his underwear, some hair from a pillow, a toothpick that cleaned his gums. The brush he used to paint his face and nipples red.

Unimpressive green patterned wallpaper, brown shag carpet, overhead light in the living room. Empty Chik-N-Lil takeout containers everywhere. A stale, acrid smell like the inside of a well-worn golfing shoe. I step across the threshold.

Every picture on the walls is of him from different moments in his life. Young to old in no particular order. There are even pictures cropped to exclude other people, leaving just him smiling in the frame. And there are dozens of them on every wall, all framed on the mantle over the electric telescreen used for a fireplace, the kitchen, the hallways. On the wall over the couch, there is an enormous painting of Old Blake standing in front of another painting of Young Blake, like a portal through time.

The bathroom is bright pink. I piss in his toilet, not bothering to pay for a flush. And of course, atop the tank is another little picture of Blake Pierce in a white business suit, staring at me with a smile as I urinate.

I'd hoped to find a shrine to me upstairs, some sort of ritual altar dedicated to my death. A temple bathed in oppressive shadows and red light, beams overhead like ribs. Twenty or so jars filled with urine. My name scrawled all over the walls in huge, jagged letters. A picture of me sounded by bones, a posed dead rodent and symbols he probably made up. A shrine to my death that could be a wonderful cherry on top of a pile of bodies, the arcane mysticism of death and ritual murder, mixed with that dark underbelly of the soul splayed open like a bloody carcass and so forth.

But no, it's just a sparse bedroom, almost like a hotel room. I head downstairs to leave. There's nothing for me here.

"Why did you kick the door in?"

I spin, my heart racing. In the doorway, there's a young woman in a wheelchair, examining the broken frame. She's an ashy brunette, with dark colored eyes, and a face worn down smooth like a sanded table.

"It was locked," I say, shrugging. I put my hands out, showing her I'm not a threat.

A glimmer of recognition flashes over her face, then she settles into confusion.

"What do you want?"

"I don't know. Answers, I guess?"

"They had a whole bunch of answers on TV. You didn't watch?"

"God, no." I spin my head around, looking for other surprise guests.

She folds her hands in her lap. "You wanted the real thing. Some sort of sick thrill?"

"Like I said, I don't know. If it makes you feel better, this is disappointing. Who are you?"

"I'm Veronica. I used to be Blake's wife."

"Huh."

"What?"

"Nothing."

She doesn't say anything for a long time.

"Well, did you have a good gander? Get a souvenir for yourself?" she says. Her glare is hateful.

"What about you? A note? Did he leave you with a little something to remember him by?"

"Yeah, a little something." She lifts up her shirt and shows me a fingertip-sized hole in her abdomen, right above her belly button. Her colostomy tube runs down to a yellow pouch on her chair. She lets me get a good look.

"Being so close to something like that. Turns the world a different color."

"You're not wrong," I say, remembering the red spray on the wall, the black of the gun barrel.

"So was this little expedition worth it? Did you find what you were looking for?"

"No."

"Good. You owe me a new door. Now get the fuck out."

15 ~ zero

In the beginning, there was nothing.

And then there was the Company. The U Corporation. Ultimart. And then the Dome. A holy trinity of all things.

And then there was Infinite Solutions and its small carpeted cubes packed with meat trying to sell plastic items to other meat. And then there was me. I. That walking fleshy pile of neurons and amino acids digesting meat grown in another vat so I can grow in my own vat. If there's a picture of life, it's things in vats helping other things in vats grow. All these vats pouring into each other. We are born, grow to capacity, die. We're fed to the Dome in piles. I imagine the Dome lifting up, its eyes those yellow U's, chewing millions upon millions in its giant handfuls. Swallowing us down its gullet, its hunger never satiated. A person is made of flesh and other complicated things like families and horrors.

Infinite Solutions doesn't close shop, not in the way you think after some calamitous drama of apocalyptic doom. There weren't any sweaty backroom meetings where the executive board and I hammered out some Hail Mary brand plan to save the company by landing a huge client, like TekCore or Drain Age. Employees just stopped showing up a few at a time. Emails and missed phone calls piled up. Unit counts crater. I fired a client just to know what it felt like. Then I fired them all. The executive board wasn't even upset. They looked at me with curious intent.

The floor is empty and dark. I'm drinking a thick blue liquor. The glass jug is from a twitchy, exotic smelling street vendor in a torn maintenance smock who took paper cash only and disappeared into an alleyway. I told him I was famous.

The idea never became a spoken thing. It just sort of happened like childbirth. I don't know how else to describe it. There were only about a dozen other people left in the office when the first ones started. We had the building until the end of the month and I wasn't quite sure what I would do. I briefly shopped around the idea of a reality show or a livestream of the office, but no one took to it.

I don't have an agenda or memos or action items. No leaderboards. The survivors just started talking about how we felt about how things were for us. The overall sensation was that there was nothing we could do about it, and the angrier we got, the more powerless we all felt. The five people from the livestream stayed. Hart Breaker got a brand deal and then left. Tyrese, Cyrill, Draco, and Angela form a core of people most interested in just talking to each other.

I walk in with my jug of blue liquor and pass it to Tyrese.

"Drink," I command.

He takes a swig and immediately coughs hot fire.

"They use it to burn warts off your feet. It's good. Anyone else want some?"

Angela immediately grabs it, drinks. Her face ripples and she does her best not to vomit and fails.

I sit against the wall and we burn things in trash barrels. Angela burns her chair and her face is terrifying in the flames. Tyrese and Draco start to paint on the walls. Skulls and veins and organs in piles. Shapes of things they saw in their dreams. Worlds within worlds. They paint over the ads we plastered over the walls. Three tits on the ladies. Penises for eyes. Draco does a scrawled hand with the Ultimart logo smack in the palm. It's gnarled and horrifying. I love it.

There's no revenue really, just some legacy contracts on autopilot.

We're hovering around a flaming barrel. I start talking without thinking.

"It's advertising, but not for clients. For ourselves. And not for some personal brand. We put it anywhere we want. Paint over other ads. Make them our own. No one can afford to turn off ads, even in their own houses. So let's make life a bit more interesting for them. Spread the joy. It'll be in their minds. It'll just live there."

No product, no targeted campaign. There isn't a language for what I'm asking them to do, and they don't need one. We call the thing "Zero" as in zero accountability, zero purpose, zero restraint. We don't even draw a logo, just a single, ugly smiley face drawn in black marker. The seed had been planted, now it grows.

I see a dark shape, a man, eyes alight in the shadows as if he owned their dark and space.

I drop some more plastic into the barrel, sending out stinking fumes. I'd set fire to everything if I could. Dump gallon after gallon of fuel over all the department stores and broken promises filled with bulbous shoppers and their horrible spawn screaming for colorful garbage and drop a single match. I'd stare into the flame with cold deadness. They'd scream for help, for someone to come along and save them, and I'd press my expensive shoe down on their face until they stopped. They make their choice everyday to be who they are, to be a part of this. Everyday, when they wake up and shit and put on their disposable clothes, they choose. When they squirt out unwanted babies into a dumpster, they choose. When they vote for their favorite soda flavor every four years, they choose. Every second of every day when they breathe recycled air, drink bottled water, stare at a television sky, they choose. When they eat trash and watch trash and vomit words and consume and consume and consume, they choose.

Coyote hugs me from behind and I tense.

"Pretend I'm not even here."

I'll show them something else. Their own mutilated face in the mirror, the blackened eyes and cracked lips, their wet cow eyes and wavering voice that might just be all their own fault. That all of it is a great, festering lie. There is just an ocean of chaos and we are all drowning in it. There are no rules, or at least any rules that make sense. The gun is always pointed in our mouth and we think it tastes great, less filling.

I call it "The Big Lie". Coyote's crooked smile tells me all I need to know.

The residents of the Dome live in the lie. Live is the wrong word. They are born, grow up, earn and spend money, grow old, and die in this lie. They exist in it, breathe it in with every recycled gasp. The lie that is written into every conversation, billboard, TV ad, house, and car. In the face of someone about to spend their last cent on a bag of white powder, or have their flesh sliced open and plastic inserted. When they laugh and chat at parties. When they put their children to sleep with pills. When they look at the sky or their TV set, the lie is there in every breath.

The lie is pure and raw and hot, like a twisted, exposed wire arcing a blue flame into a room pumped with methane. I see a sad man hunched over a trash fire, pockmarked and tired in the bone-white lighting talking to a small group of people. I walk into the dark, leaving him behind with his grief and tragedy.

"One last thing, Corwin."

~~~~

The Fight begins so small, so innocuous, like most world-ending events often start out as. Raylene is clicking through the channels and she won't pick anything to watch for more than five seconds. Coyote said to start it over something pointless and watch it spiral helplessly out of control. She says Raylene is a D45 personality, prone to irrational bursts of self-importance and indignant anger, and she is a fan of procedural security shows. The
~~~~

kind where the person won't bother to ask for an arbiter and everyone wears sunglasses.

"Would you just pick something and stay on it?"

"I'm bored. This keeps me from staying bored."

"Then let's just pick a show already. This…" I gesture to the constantly shifting TV, "Is giving me a migraine."

"Don't yell at me. If you don't want to watch, then don't."

"I wanted to spend some time with you watching a show. So let's do that."

"Alright." She turns to one of the ten or so financial channels. Lots of angry red arrows pointing down and tired faces. It's gibberish to me. I can take about a minute of it.

"Please change it to something else."

"Change it or don't change it. Now my pretty little girl brain is all confused." She grabs the side of her head, rocking from side to side.

"Stop being so dramatic."

"What is wrong with you?"

"Nothing, I'm fine."

"You are NOT fine. I have been trying to be there for you and-"

I laugh. Coyote and I decided I should laugh right at the moment that would hurt her.

"Be there for me? Be there for me?! You don't have the slightest idea what I've been going through." That last bit was unrehearsed, but I felt the need to improvise.

She stops. "Then talk to me. Stop shutting me out!"

"Why? So you can have fun ignoring me? Make an excuse for me to buy you something?"

The gold-digger accusation cuts her just as it should. "That's so unfair. I never ask you to buy me anything. You are becoming so ugly."

"No, you just make me guilty enough to drive up our Number. It's so skillful, I'm actually really impressed. 'Corwin, we could sure use a new carpet because this one is so last season. Corwin, what about a new living room set? It's all dated.' Why don't you just drug me and steal a kidney?"

"I have clients here! This house is where I get new business. You know the business that keeps us from going under. Your new job is helping, but it's not enough all the time." She puts her hand up, palm to me. "It was hard enough when your dad was here."

"So sorry that my dad fucking dying was too much for you." I'm actually impressed she went there that quickly.

She sinks into the couch, realizing what she said. "That's not what I meant. I'm sorry."

"You're never sorry. You're incapable of ever being sorry for anything. You're just so wrapped up in this ridiculous look you have going on. What are you supposed to be, a leather popsicle?"

"Because it feels nice for people to look at me and want me. Something you haven't done for a long time."

And she goes right for the jugular. An apex predator.

The Fight explodes for about twenty minutes or so, critical mass for us to be shouting all our past sins at each other. Out of the corner of my eye, Axel clings to his bedroom door. Raylene's back is to him, and I make sure he sees everything.

"I can't do this anymore, Corwin. I can't. I won't."

"What are you saying?"

"I don't know."

Yes, you do.

~~~~

After the Fight, I leave, make sure to slam the door nice and loud. I head back to the office. That night in the darkened conference rooms and upturned offices, Coyote and I play House. She's the dutiful, dependable breadwinner and I'm the homemaker. The rest of the team claps and awws when we smooch and tell flat, colorless jokes.

Raylene calls me and leaves a message. During a commercial break, I see the notification on my phone. Heart pounding, I press play.

"Corwin... I don't... Please call me. Just call me back. I don't know where you are and I don't care but please call me. I'll do anything you want, just call me back. I can't do this on my own. I can't I can't I can't I can't. Please." Sobs interrupt her. Those thick, choking cries that suck all the air out of you. That sound like a dying animal.

Aww, the crowd says.

If there is a great lie, I am telling it with every breath from my mouth. I am in the TV now. The way I walk, my clothes, the way I shake your hand firmly and warmly, when I grasp my son's shoulder and tell him to be a good boy. When I buy a new fun product and then spread the word to my friends. The status update I click "Like" on. My informed and eloquent political opinions on
~~~~

Red's policy of being fizzier and supporting the traditional franchise.

Here comes the crying again. It's a good thing this means nothing. This nothing is warm, like a hot relaxing bath. It feels good to feel nothing. The numbness is a welcome guest.

Coyote laughs along with me at some unspoken joke. She speaks and it's funny how her words and mine now mix and merge. I honestly don't know how long I've been at the Infinite Solutions office now, the beard growth on my face says at least a few days. I smell my pits and pull my face back. I decide to go back home and clean up.

I sneak in and Axel suddenly appears, scaring the shit out of me. I haven't seen him for a while. Normally, when I get home, he's plugged in online, playing a game, swearing at the TV, or in a druggy haze. He looks stockier, more frazzled around the edges. Red bags hang underneath his eyes, and his skin is more pale than normal. This weird little stranger stares me down without really looking at me. His eyes float elsewhere, his mouth slightly open. I used to be like this. I remember the foggy, weightless feeling of behaviorals my own parents gave me. In the living room, out of sight, I hear Raylene hosting a client party or something. Cackling laughter, drinks clinking.

Raylene must have dressed him. He's wearing a shiny, silver shirt, adorned with the words BAD AZZ, with green and yellow camo shorts, an enormous skull and crossbones belt buckle, topped off with cheap plastic orange shoes.

"Hey buddy, how's it going?" I say in my happiest, fakest chirp.

No response. Doesn't look like anyone's home.

"How's, uh, how's Training going? You learning a lot?"

Nothing. I snap my fingers in front of his face and he gently follows them. He blinks several times and is lifted out of his fog. He actually speaks.

"Hey Dad."

"Hi."

"Yeah, I'm doing okay."

I nod. "I'm sure you are."

"Are you guys still having that party?"

"What party? Yes. The party. I'm hoping they all die of mercury poisoning."

He chuckles unexpectedly. I'm not kidding.

"What?" he asks.

"It's called hydrargyria. You see, mercury poisoning makes you unable to sleep and then your skin peels off."

"That's dumb."

I straighten up. The little brat has some steel in him.

"That's stupid," he says, wavering on his feet. He pauses. "Why are you being such a dumb jerk? You're never home and Mom is acting weird all the time. She's all sad."

I glance around to make sure no one else is around.

"You want to see something cool?"

"Sure."

I pull the 9mm Calcetta pistol I started carrying after Infinite Solutions shut down. After Blake blew apart my best friend's guts, I decided not to be put in that position ever again. Let me tell you something, I wasn't once necessarily afraid of guns, but I had an aversion to them. They just made me feel uncomfortable. A flat, ugly hunk of composite. The first time I held it, I understood. I got it. The power of life and death. The power to "defend yourself". They're surprisingly heavy, too. And anyone can buy one. So simple a child can use it, and they do. You don't even need to use your ID at most places. It's optional. The Calcetta holds 14 rounds, which means 14 lives if you think about it.

Axel's eyes grow enormous. His mouth is wide open, a slight squeal starting to seep out. He could put his entire fist in there.

"Keep it down," I mutter. I glance back again to double-check. I slide out the magazine, pull the action back and catch the chambered bullet in mid-air. I slide the pistol around and hand it to Axel, grip first. He takes it slowly.

"Is this real?"

"And yes, it's real. I said keep it down. If we get busted, fun's over." I hold up the bullet. "That look real to you?"

He has an idea. "Can we shoot it in the house?"

I laugh. "No. What is wrong with you?"

He can barely hold it up with both hands. "It's heavy."

He lifts it up in defiance and aims down the sight. Shockingly, he's got good form. His right arm is straight, his left elbow crooked, with his feet shoulder width apart. I nod in approval. Probably from all those VR games he plays.

I snap my fingers for him to give it back, and after some reluctance, he does.

"It'll be our little secret."

"Take me shooting... or I tell Mom."

"Fine."

I walk him to the Training pickup station. He doesn't talk the entire way. I wave goodbye and he flips me off with a big smile. I flip him off back.

They grow up so fast.

I check my phone for the view count on Dad's video. 50 million hits. 50 million. That means everyone in the Dome has seen my Dad die twice right in front of their eyes. I smile with pride. I go to the sleep dealer, get freshened up, and head back into the world.

~~~~

Our first order of business is to create the Dump, an anonymous drop box where anyone can submit documents, videos, and we will publish them without prejudice or edit. It's relatively untraceable. Zero hosts its own server farm now, and we bounce our information through several proxy nodes, which keeps us under the line. Not completely untraceable, but hidden enough that we can operate.

Our first corporate client is real cornball cloak-and-dagger type stuff. He wants to meet face to face in a fucking parking garage. I laugh and immediately say no and tell him to grow up. We don't meet face to face. There is no such thing anymore. The best thing we'll do is a VOIP call with my voice masked.

The guy wheezes on the call. Stress headaches and burritos make him not long for this world. He lays out what he wants: financial info for a competing toilet cleanser. His company wants to buy their company and it bores the shit out of me.
~~~~

I tell Mr. Wheezing that we will be in touch to discuss payment. Half up front, half after, all in crypto.

On the surface, all is calm and drab. I'm a middle manager at a new company called Financial Product Innovation, or FPI. The group gets a drab office and hires several bodies to fill seats everyday. They enter numbers from one website onto another website, and it looks official and important, but those numbers don't go anywhere. An enormous database maintains these worthless numbers. Everyone from Infinite Solutions is here in some respect. Angela wanted to be a receptionist to ironically play up the stereotype. Draco is a financial data analyst, whatever that means. Tyrese is one of our database engineers, and Cyrill is constantly on the phone, too busy to actually describe what he does for a living to nosey outsiders.

The goal is to look as dull and uninteresting as possible, so boring that even if anyone starts sniffing about, they'd get so annoyed they'd just leave us alone. We're just moving on with our lives. Deeper and deeper someone went into FPI, the more they would feel they were tumbling off a cliff into a bottomless abyss. Endlessly looping and rebounding financial algorithms, dense verbal language in contracts, incomplete records, confusing instructions on risk mitigation, an ocean of grey mush you've have to power through and at the end, collapse from exhaustion right before you open the door. FPI is a smirking monument to the insanity of the Dome, of UCorp. No one can even tell what we do, except for one brightly clear example, we sell financial product patents, our flagship product being the mortgage-based CDO.

Zero doesn't have any business cards or mission statements. It acts almost as its own organism, pushing us to make decisions almost by its own sheer will. Zero is a concept, something said with and without words.

Before we can begin any serious operations, we have to perform a sacred ritual: to delete our digital selves. The Dump is slowly amassing documents, some critical, some not, and Zero needs the infrastructure to ensure anonymity for those who deposit and those who remove. Zero sets up an independent private network with no outside connections, off the main grid, sealed and contained. You need to know exactly where to go to leave something. Tyrese has a blast setting this up, it's a playground for him, a wonderland of cool new toys.

Over the next month, Zero makes its mark. We steal financial data, reverse engineer software patents, sabotage investment deals with misinformation, manipulate small-scale penny stocks, destroy billboards, deface websites with shit porn, and socially engineer company contract defaults (my personal favorite). Zero is a wholly unique entity: an economic hit squad for hire with no center or allegiance. There are other industrial espionage groups, obviously, but none with our connections. We thrive in the dark: no brand names, no networks, no media. I wear a suit and tie, shake hands, and wait for the client to drop an email address or a network IP and then we're in.

You remember Mr. Wheezing? After we did his job, we did another little job. He was dumb and gave us a limited admin account to his financial databases so we could directly upload the information we stole from his competitor. Mistake #1. That limited admin account in the FBPR system has a fatal bug. Install certain photo manipulation software and the limited admin account will accidentally give you access to that computer's registry. You can then install an add-on to that software which will (incorrectly) rewrite certain keys in the computer's registry and all of a sudden, you have backdoor admin access to the entire virtual machine mirrored on FBPR. You can change anything you want. We then delivered the computer to Mr. Wheezing, who forgets to wipe it afterwards and then we have our own little mole. One fifteen minute connection to it and we basically ransacked all their R&D and sold it to the very same competitor we stole from. He didn't even know what happened.

"You're a goddamn artist, Tyrese." I say as the download finishes. I hand Tyrese a cup of Koffee.

"I am, aren't I?" he says, smiling. He drinks and laughs. He's a mountain of a man, and when he laughs, his whole body shakes.

Although this type of work pays the bills, and brokerage commissions from FPI are good but not great, the real fun comes from the Dump. Most of the stuff from there is vengeance burns, veterans of companies who get ceremoniously laid off and then want to righteously torch their previous employers.

Then there was Zee Brite.

~~~~

We contacted a man named Palmer Jacobs after his rant was posted to UNet complaining that he had been unjustly fired for speaking about the fact their product can potentially cause birth
~~~~

defects. We had him pull the video and provide us with all the docs he had. When I initially saw it, I was originally bored by it, taking it for conspiracy theory. Practically every chemical in the Dome can cause those, but Angela, she wouldn't take no for an answer. Adamant is not the word I would use. When Angela found out I was passing on the job, she quietly walked up to me and punched me so hard in the chest I practically spun around. The woman worked out, took care of herself, and her fist was like a hammer.

"Thanks," I said, rubbing my jaw. The pain was refreshing, eye-opening. I was really listening to her now.

"We are going to take this job and burn that company to the fucking foundations."

"That's not what we do."

"It's exactly what we do. I want this."

I got to my feet. "Okay, you're in charge of the op. Three days. I want it to be public and brutal."

"Consider it done," she said. Her face was tight, her attention focused. There wasn't a hint of anger or hysteria. Calm, focused, exactly where she needed to be. She spoke with Coyote at length about what they should do, just the two of them. They had a girl's night out.

Palmer provided several internal case studies done with women who had terminated their pregnancies after accidental exposure to Zee Brite. Things don't come with warning labels, and most cases like this are settled in arbitration. As if a modest check could ever pay you back for something like that. Angela didn't even get that.

Zee Brite was all too happy to move on. They successfully suppressed the arbitration hearings, no real news emerged because of it, but a small internet rumor began to circulate. We didn't propagate it, but instead let it grow organically. Zero latches onto an idea just before it breaks into the mainstream, molds it to suit our message, and then lets it run wild. In the end, Zee Brite got its ad.

~~~~

Marilyn Dietrich lost her son on May 31st of this year due to contamination from Zee Brite accidentally touching her skin. The fetus had an adverse reaction to heavy metals in the powder and soon went into shock. Later that afternoon, she lost the baby in the toilet. Zee Brite LLC paid her off, but never admitted guilt. An ironclad NDA silenced her, but not us.

The ad starts on her face, folding laundry in a baby's gender-neutral nursery. The walls were painted a pleasant yellow, adorned with baby ducks and sailboats. Outside, the sun is shining brightly, partly cloudy, a perfect day. Green trees softly wafting in the summer breeze. All is well in this little storybook universe. We made sure of that, shooting her against a greenscreen and filling everything else in later. Draco greatly enjoyed making the room as close to what you would see in a real ad. The baby ducks, the sun, everything.

The shoot happened at a rented office space with Angela and Coyote in masks. Marilyn arrived with a black hood over her head, which they removed and apologized for the secrecy. Marilyn said she understood. She was remarkably composed, eager, and even had ideas for how to do the shoot.
~~~~

This is how most ads are made. About 9 times out of 10 the actors themselves are digital, so photo-realistic you can barely tell the difference. Sometimes, you can see it in the eyes, they're just off. What was not computer generated was the tiny malformed fetus being wrapped in a comfy-soft white blanket. Marilyn raises the small wrinkled body into frame. At the bottom, text describing the effects of Zee Brite on pregnant women were displayed, using the same round cartoon font as Zee Brite's claims to get rid of stains fast.

Angela originally didn't want to use that, opting for a doll or computer effect, but Marilyn insisted. It was the cornerstone of the entire statement. To fake it would be like faking their evidence, regardless of how real their claims were.

Coyote and Angela reported they were impressed with Marilyn, they expected some trodden down victim practically bawling on the floor. After the shoot was over, Angela and Marilyn talked for a long time about what Marilyn went through. They confided in each other. Angela was careful not to reveal anything specific about her own experience, considering her personal tragedy had been broadcast to the entire Dome during the Livestream event. I imagine it must have been a surreal sight, Angela in a black balaclava, sipping hot tea with Marilyn, talking about motherhood and their own private pain together.

The ad had all the markings of a laundry detergent: bright colors, a clean home filled with the fresh scent of lemon chemical purity, the joy of motherhood permeating every frame, and how a fresh start for your baby is paramount. The image of the mother and child, safe and warm in the product's glow is the centerpiece.

We simply replaced their fake image of life and love with the reality of it.

A premature fetus looks plastic, bright red and bug-eyed like a deep sea fish. At first, I thought it was fake until Angela told me it wasn't. Watching the ad made me feel ill, sick to my stomach. We released it to an unsuspecting world the next week and it soon burned through the trending topics like wildfire. It left a bitter saccharine taste in people's mouths.

This was a new language of advertising, using the syntax against itself. It was cannibalistic, primal, and the juxtaposition of these two things turned on people's brains in ways they were not used to. It made most viewers confused and angry, yelling that the makers, us, had exploited this young woman's pain, that it was in bad taste. This coming from assholes who enjoyed watching X Fighters tore each other apart live on TV, or through their own apathy, let other families be destroyed, children tossed to wolves, all just because they couldn't pay their bills they were never designed to pay back in the first place. The gears and wheels of the Machine were starting to show and I want to throw them into the thresher they helped create.

Zee Brite wanted blood. Fair enough, considering Zee Brite was all anyone could talk about for days. The elusive and enigmatic filmmakers never came forward, never claimed credit, and even after the original video was taken down due to Zee Brite's trademark complaint, hundreds of copies sprung up soon after. It wasn't going anywhere. Zee Brite soon began a futile case of whack-a-mole, shutting down one video upload after another so aggressively, it was more fun to post it just to fuck with them.

Their stock took an enormous, painful hit, and they soon announced, due to internal testing, that they would be changing their formula to a new scent, and this decision obviously had no relation to their recent PR nightmare.

Angela and I are watching a video about the story together, some random outlet making some pointless point.

"I saw you and Marilyn talking after the shoot. You whispered to her. What did you say?"

"Nothing you'd understand."

~~~~

I open the front door to my house. I've been in and out these days, Raylene and I barely talking to each other. I think we're okay now, I feel guilty for leaving her so alone. Coyote has been trying to convince me to split up with her, but I just can't. I look around. Quiet as a store after closing hours.

I check every room, except for the storage closet. I avoid it like a disease. As I'm passing the door, it creaks open and my chest nearly implodes from the sound. It's Axel and he smells like a dumpster.

"Wow, buddy. When was the last time you took a shower?"

He shrugs. He's not embarrassed, he just doesn't remember. His Slurora is peaking, so his eyes are glassy marbles. His hands twitch.

"I'm hungry. What's to eat?" The words come out like long breaths.

"Where's your mom? She didn't feed you."

He slowly shrugs again. No one's home it seems.
~~~~

"Sorry I haven't been around much. Everything okay?"

He nods very slowly. This is getting annoying so I get a Funtime Boost-X and crack it under his nose. He sniffs in deep and snaps out of his little fog.

"Hey Dad."

"Mom. Where is she?"

"I haven't seen her for a while. I've just been walking myself to Training. What day is it?"

~~~~

We head out and hit up a few toy stores. Axel has always loved shopping, like any kid, and he's incredibly adept at buying something the Son would buy from him for a profit.

The Son's birthday is coming up soon, as well as Axel's. We get the Son a Destrux, some sort of neon robot thing with jagged, angry edges. They are the defenders of the Dome and fight the dreaded Sovietz who want to steal the gold bricks of the Destrux. The Sovietz want to give it to their shifty foreign lazy whatevers. Children's toys are not exactly subtle on the narrative, you see. The Sovietz have distinctly non-Dome features: lots of black hair, enlarged facial features, claws, and vaguely Asian writing for their packages.

At home, Axel and I play video games and stuff our faces with fancy-sounding ice cream. I give him half of my adult sleeping pill and he drops right off and he should be asleep for most of tomorrow. I pick him up and lay him in bed, my lower back
~~~~

groaning from the effort. Using the climbing harness tomorrow is not going to be enjoyable. We haven't even had time to practice.

I go into our bedroom. Raylene's phone is there. It's locked but I have a small cracking device that I wave over the screen. 10 seconds later and I'm in. I quickly realize it wasn't even locked. It was just left here, waiting for me.

A sudden surge of adrenaline pumps through me.

There's a single icon on the home screen. A video file. I tap it.

It's a crudely animated short from a popular app called Filmix about a "Supreme Princess" who lives in a magical kingdom outside the Dome in outer space. She dreams of the stars. She marries her one true love, a simple carpenter who makes her laugh and tells her he loves her every day. "Carpenter" is a rare word, it's someone who works with wood from actual living trees. Trees are disgusting and dirty and I can't imagine touching one covered in bugs and germs. There are no carpenters in the Dome. The pair build a wooden spaceship and travel to their own star, and live on the warm, loving surface forever. There is a child, a baby, nameless and faceless.

The story continues. The carpenter leaves her alone and shackles her ankle to a giant molten rock. She then chews off her foot, which magically grows back, and then leaps into space after the carpenter. She realizes she can't breathe in outer space, but keeps trying to follow her carpenter, who grows smaller and smaller. The last thing she sees is the stars applauding her, admiring her courage, and then the celestial audience letting her finally become one of them. A billion years in the future, her light finally reaches the carpenter. She has exploded and gone supernova, expelling all her innards across the cosmos. The carpenter cries, alone and destroyed in his failures. The story ends.

I throw the phone on the bed, confused. All of Raylene's clothes are still here. The bedroom is remarkably clean. I check the bathroom. None of her toiletries are gone either. I open the door to the storage room, connected to the master bath, and glance around. Nothing but dust motes and ghosts. It's like she evaporated through the walls.

The emptiness of the room hurts. It throbs. I suddenly get the enormity of what may have happened.

Raylene's brush is on her nightstand, wrapped in her stringy bleached hair. I leave it there. I leave everything just the way it is. In our closet are all of her things. Those objects that populated her life. I sift through them. Her dresses and yoga pants, shoes, bras, panties, negligees, socks, pantsuits, wigs, false nails, false eyelashes. All the colorful plastics she used to spackle her existence together.

Axel was not planned. We tried to relive our drunken Training days, sneaking off to the backroom to screw and then we ended up with a tiny human being to take care of. We changed when he was born. The world shrank to the size of our inability to cope with the concept of Axel. All those mistakes. All those pills and toys. All that regret just crashing down on top of me. I knew we were never going to make it, I just didn't know it would end like this. Part of me wanting to cling to hope. But no, it ends in a quiet little room filled with the debris of a human life like so many other regrets. Who leaves without packing?

I have a thought and back away slowly.

Someone not looking to come back, that's who.

There's a loud thump from Axel's room, and I run to see what happened. Axel fell out of bed and I gently pick him. Boys his age are invincible, long before their bodies betray them like mine, and turn soggy and flabby around the middle. What would Axel look like as a middle aged man, an old man, a grandfather? I can see the line of his life heading straight towards the emptiness of mine, that enormous black hole that swallowed me so slowly I didn't even realize it.

No. Not for him. Problem is I don't know how to be a father, even after a decade of trying. I don't know how to teach him anything. I don't even know how to be a particularly functioning person and now I'm all alone with him.

His body is so small, his chest rising and falling as he slightly snores. He was once a pink blob. His small little life that we built for him. This tiny cage, his own little Dome trapped in a haze of behaviorals and when to sleep and go to Training and it's suddenly all too much for me. I can't breathe and I leave the room.

I'm curled up in the hall, my knees biting into my chin. My pants are soaked with tears and the spit from my grinding teeth. I imagine my breath, my skin, and the weight of the air pressing down on it. Counting backwards from ten, my skin slowly disappears, until the voice disappears into that void, and I connect with the air in the quiet flowing blue nothingness of my breath going in and out and then everywhere. There is nothing between me and the cool air now.

16 ~ *house*

The model home I arrive at is set up for an open house. Model homes broadcast a flavor of hostile tranquility, a mocking example of life in the Dream. Something you can never reach but always see just outside your grasp. Their perfection and sterility create a naked and alien landscape. Immaculate white carpets, spotless windows, color coordinated blue glass dishes, light green drapes hanging in all the rooms. The dining room, where you do your dining. The living room, where you do your living. There is no dying room. Any of them could suffice. For Jerry, it was a boring break room. For Dad, a storage area. One loud, one quiet. I imagine what Raylene would joke about with this place.

Coyote opens the door, dressed as a pre-Dome housewife, a yellow cheerful sundress, tight white apron, holding a cocktail and a cigar for me. I wordlessly pass right by her without accepting either. I tug Axel behind me.

"Well hello there. I don't believe we've met, young man!" Coyote exclaims.

"Don't talk to him. We have work to do." It's been set for dinner, looks like fried chicken. I push the plates aside to make room, then eventually grab the tablecloth in my fist and dump everything on the floor. I drop my bag on the polished dining room table.

"Daddy's grumpy. He might have to be put in a time out if he's not more thankful!"

Coyote offers me a bucket of chicken from the kitchen, and I take out a fried hunk. I look her right in the eyes and drop it on the floor. She half-smiles, but I can see the rage building.

Axel noshes on his Kiddie Meal, his mouth smeared with grease and crumbs. This isn't love. I don't forget what she did to me, not for a second. I said no. It doesn't have the acrid desperation that normally accompanies love, that hot breathy anxiety when you realize this person is whom you are now paired with. This is bitter, acrid. But she's useful and I can stomach a lot. She teaches Axel about the emulsification process of Chik-N-Lil. They carve off still-warm chunks of the things, throw them into a thresher, combine them with starches and recombination agents, deep-fried, and then pressure-molded into these globular shapes.

Coyote eats heartily and tosses a greasy napkin over her shoulder. "You need to understand something, Corwin. Zero is a fun hobby, but it's not going to get you what you want."

"I know. That's partially why I wanted to pitch something to you. It's boring, but I know you'll appreciate the subtlety of it. It's a financial product."

"Oh so you're done being a sad sack of shit. And you're right. It is boring."

I swipe my tablet and send her the compressed file. She opens it and scans the docs.

"Okay, it's mortgages?" she says after a moment. She belches.

"I know, let me explain."

"If this is brute force market manipulation, it's not exactly our style. We don't do that. There's only so much artificial demand you can manufacture."

"This is not manipulation. No insider trading, no short buys, no penny stocks. It's subtle and totally above board. That's the best part." I pop a piece of breading into my mouth.

"This is a three part system. Consumers, investors on opposite ends, with financial firms right in the middle. Our three players. Before I go into this, define the Dream."

"Being stupid rich for no effort," she says.

"No, what specifically is involved? How do you know you made it? What's required?"

"Expensive house, car, trophy spouse, brats like yours."

"The house. The home. The physical embodiment of your success. You live inside of your success, quite literally. Every moron wants a house, but not everyone can have one. That's the lie we bank on. Let's take a look at the typical Domer. Can't read more than a few words, obsessed with pointless things, consuming constantly. Dumb, violent, paranoid, and terrified of everything. Anything longer than a commercial break or a status update is lost on them. This is our client. The best part is, they think they live in the greatest society humanity has ever produced. That's the Dream."

Coyote takes a sip of her drink. "Continue."

"Normally, you have to leverage an enormous amount of debt to buy a house, even a long-term lease like mine. The Sprawl might as well be on another planet. That puts you in a near-constant state of anxiety about going into the red. You won't quit your job. Training fees keep you locked into your first job for what, like a decade or more?! The main way to stave off this anxiety is to be continually reminded that the enormous, crushing debt you took on will pay off at some point in the future. It has to, or else you basically put the barrel of a gun in your mouth. Housing prices have been going up fairly steadily for the last couple years. You flip your house or get stupendously lucky."

"I'm not seeing a project here. Get. To. The. Point."

"Okay, person buys a lease or a house, gets a mortgage. Right now, these are just a mortgage, a single financial product. People buy and sell mortgages all the time, but they've never done the way I'm suggesting. Package garbage mortgages into groups and mix them with other financial products that are more quote unquote stable. Normally, mortgages are not ranked are particularly safe investments; regularly they get C or B's if they have unaggressive interest rates. Right now, Finance has dropped interest rates to nearly zero percent. That means their regular investments, like UCorp stock and bonds, are less attractive. Houses are continually going up in price, and everyone wants a house. These have a sell rate that's almost four hundred percent of a UCorp stock."

"Why hasn't someone already done this?" Coyote asks.

"Lease and mortgage financial rules are particularly rigid right now. Money stores, since they can't drop rates anymore on their own investments, are set to loosen the rules for mortgages. Next month."

"How did you find out about this?"

"I thought it up. Strike of inspiration from some doc we got from the Dump. That's how I learned about the rate drop."

Her eyes are locked on me. She looks coiled, ready to strike. "What about the investment side?"

"Investors will be convinced that these new products are the next big thing. They're still reeling from the UCorp restructuring and net leveraging changes from before Axel was born."

"I mean, why would they consider these safe if they're filled with trash?" Coyote asks.

"Because they're fucking idiots. After we sell off the product with all the stuff mixed together, it's someone else's problem. So if the dumbass defaults on the mortgage and goes off-contract, I don't care what happens to that mortgage. Plus we're under no obligation to buy it back. They're stuck with this toxic bullshit and we're..."

"Stinking rich..." she says, trailing off.

"It's a cycle. Mortgage, product, sale, mortgage, product, sale."

Coyote picks up her tablet and types. "I just checked the market rates for packaged financial products. Even a modestly-sized company..." She stops, flicking towards me. "How many people have you told about this?"

"Just you."

She looks impressed for the first time I've known her. "Keep it that way. Fuck doing it ourselves. We're actually going to patent this and license it."

"Why a patent? Why not just do this at FPI like the IS takeover?"

Coyote pushes the rest of the crap off the table, setting it clattering to the ground. "If you license it, that's one more step between you and the sucker. They need to buy our product license in order to sell one of these packages. You make a license fee on every sale. You're not selling it, they are. This is…"

"Big money," I say, "Sprawl money. Dream money. I need MA to seed it like the Healthline thing, but a thousand times as much."

She's mid-pulling out her phone but a thought crosses her.

"How far forward have you extrapolated this? How many cycles?" Coyote looks off into the distance, out the window, into the model neighborhood.

"Pretty far."

"You know then that has a tipping point?"

"Yes."

"What then?"

"We buy stocks in the companies, knowing they'll fail in advance, we sell them for a fat profit, then buy them back for a discount when they fail. If it succeeds, we're on easy street. If it fails, we're still rich."

She points to the horizon, the skyscraper and glittering buildings jutting into the sky. "What if they catch on?"

"They'll be blinded by the returns. They can't see five minutes in front of their face."

"Okay. What'll happen to the poor poor widdle investors stuck with all this debt in the end? They'll be howling for your blood."

I shrug. "Tough shit."

"Done. You beautiful idiot."

Axel and I play video games in the living room while Coyote makes some calls. He's focused on the game, his tongue stuck in the corner of his mouth. We're playing some sort of sports game. I don't even know the controls.

We leave the house filled with our refuse, our trail of the discarded and disposable.

~~~~

An incredibly large file appeared in the Dump drop box at 3:23 am Workday morning. The file was approximately 160 GB compressed, containing documents rated "Sensitive" to "Confidential". Included in the file were financial statements, HR records, internal emails, network traffic statistics, architecture of botnets, administrative account credentials. It was like Xmas morning and the enormous present in the corner was just opened. It had nothing to do with my mortgage idea, which made its appearance all the more confusing.

In the introductory analysis of the more confidential files, I keep noticing a reference to something called "EVM" and "EVM ratings". I carefully scan for the term elsewhere, but there's no real hits. Some random acronyms for manufacturing processes, some product codes. Nothing. There's a few bland companies with that acronym, but they stand for Environmental Validation
~~~~

Management, a consultancy group for air quality, and Earnie Villiard Media, a porno company. There's a subgenre of dance pop called electrovolt music enjoyed by putting electrodes on your temples.

There are thousands of documents in the Big Dump. Text documents, too. Meant for serious management and infrastructure usage. After a very long time of painstaking research, the computer endlessly combing and cross-referencing, a clear picture begins to develop. An image that is utterly horrifying, unbelievable in scope and size. Impossible. Unthinkable. Like staring at an enormous undead leviathan rising from the ocean.

We're having a party to celebrate nothing in particular.

I stare at the results, dumbfounded. Coyote has been snorting something blue all night, and now she dances with Angela and the rest of the gang. I'm glued to my laptop. I swipe up and down, scrolling the page, trying desperately to understand the results I'm reading. It can't be correct. I don't want it to be. Tyrese and his husband Alex cuddle with their drinks, exchanging drunken smooches. Draco passed out hours ago, his face now covered in drawn penises and vaginas.

I get up from the couch and cross the room, avoiding Coyote and Angela. I turn the music off and everyone gives me an annoyed blank stare.

"Someone wake up Draco."

Tyrese and Alex applaud and cheer. Coyote and Angela stare at me.

"So, what is all this shit?" Tyrese says, Alex nibbling at his neck. "Stop that."

I don't quite know how to start. "I'm still trying to wrap my head around this exactly... EVM doesn't stand for a company name or a department or anything like that."

"Then what is it?" Angela asks, buttoning up her shirt.

"It's... it's an algorithm. It stands for 'Economic Viability Model'."

"What, like a credit check program? Big deal," Tyrese says.

"Yes and no. From what I'm seeing, the EVM is part of the main Dome system architecture. It's firmware and software combined. It controls... everything."

"Like a giant system-wide monitor," Coyote muses.

"Correct, but it's more than that. EVM is the foundational architecture of the Dome's economy. According to this, it's the main operational and control structure of the Machine, installed right after the Dome's founding. We have this idea that the economy of the Dome is a completely free market. Companies sink or swim, ruthless efficiency wins, the strong survive and the weak die. That's half true. The EVM is an extremely complex algorithm that is applied to every single resident of the Dome regardless of who they are. Even the CEO."

"Well, what the fuck does it do?" Coyote asks.

"It takes in information, much like Memetic Analysis does, but it's not doing targeted marketing or trend predictions. That'd be duplication of effort. The EVM takes into account every single piece of information about you, your personal life, job, franchise, health, house, car, purchase history, licensing, physical movement around the Dome, what you buy out of a vendi-fridge, even your fucking bowel movements. It takes all of this information and pushes it through the EVM's calculations..."

I can't bring myself to say it. The idea is too insane, too unbelievable.

"And decides if you're worth keeping alive."

There's dead silence. Tyrese laughs incredulously. My face tells another story.

"I mean, the market does that already. Number go down, you go down," Coyote proclaims, like what I'm saying is perfectly obvious.

"No no no. That's an indirect effect of a market, Winners and losers. This is intentionally choosing. The Dome is a limited ecosystem. We import from China, we recycle, but only so many people can live inside. There's a real physical limit. I know they like to pretend the economy can grow forever, but it just can't. At some point, the EVM decides."

"Bullshit," Angela says.

"I know, I said the same thing."

"How?"

"It's extremely complex, but here's an example. A guy works his entire life, has a family, grows too old to work, then takes a second career as say, a celebrity impersonator at an executive retirement village. EVM tracks this. One day, he has a stroke which leads to liver and kidney failure. Maybe he was given a stroke. Someone rotting away in a hospital bed only makes them so much. They have to depend on an additional party to maintain that cost/benefit ratio. Cost of his care is suddenly too high. EVM decides to automatically alter the cost of his Healthline to make it completely unaffordable. We think it's market forces, but it's not. There's no reason why Healthline should be rationed. No reason!"

"I don't know, Corwin…" Tyrese says. "That seems like a stretch."

"Okay, here's another example. Something more concrete. This document directly tracks an autolayoff to cost-benefit analysis. It's then laid over off-contract rates." I put it up on the big screen.

"Yeah, people who lose their jobs tend to go off-contract. There's no conspiracy there. It's just the brutal math of it," Coyote says.

"Do you see a fucking tinfoil hat on me? This isn't conspiracy, it's design. It's the system. It's the Machine. Okay, here's the final piece. This is what's called a 999X Order." I put it up on the screen as well. It's a bland digital form with vague, meaningless numbers on it. There's not even a name on it. I click through the forms, pointing out the elements as I speak.

"Big Dump has most of a person's entire EVM profile. There's basic information, like the person's ID number, age, weight, address in positional coordinates in the Dome. Then some other consumer factors the EVM takes in, like potential for job viability based on skills and activity, expected lifespan in months, air consumption, food consumption, how many D-clothes they'll use, how much electricity they'll consume, online bandwidth usage."

"Corwin, slow down," Angela says.

I don't. "Then there's political volatility, associations with undesirable elements, negative comments they left online about management, painstakingly cross-referenced with recordings made of their voice, emails, phone calls, texts, status updates, biometric data from security scanners. Every single piece of information possible to gather and analyze, EVM does. It swallows it up and then spits out an answer."

"Alright, I'll bite. Say someone's hit by a car, how did 'they' kill you?" Coyote asks.

"Hundreds of different ways. My example before was just one. They can slowly raise the cost of your food, your water, your air, lower your paycheck. Your example, you may have a 'run in' with an automated truck, or Security, or maybe even a subliminal message through your TV to kill yourself. They have unstable people happen to bump into each other at a nightclub, a fight escalates, someone dies. You're off contract in the Machine and an air vent sucks you into a fan blade. Maybe you just got humiliated on the internet and they make it very easy for you to buy a gun, or don't try and stop you when you do. They run the numbers and 'Oh, looks like maybe seventeen of your coworkers can go, too. Bonus!' An infinite number of solutions, some subtle, some not so. The EVM is invisible, right behind everything that's happening, all the time. A television sky, pretending to be real."

"People say stuff like this all the time, Corwin," Tyrese says. His voice is small, quiet. Everyone is looking at me like I'm crazy.

"They didn't have this," I point to the screen, "Hard proof, evidence, documents straight from the source. The entire picture put together. Put the pieces in the right order and you see it. You see it. You all see it, and you all know it's true. You've seen it work everyday of your lives without even realizing it. Now it has a name."

~~~~

The ceiling of the cramped, noisy basement isn't stars, but grey concrete. I groggily rise. My head pounds, weighing a thousand kilograms. Thick wires run the length of the room to naked bulbs, and as I come to, I'm not alone. Banks of monitors and haphazardly assembled equipment are piled in electronic hills. Somehow it all ties together as a half dozen pale techs type and click away at screens with incomprehensible graphs and data. Coyote hovers, her fist under her lip, her attention fixed on the monitors. I realize I'm watching her do something I've never seen her do: work.

She paces, pointing to a screen. "How are we on BBCA penetration?"

A woman with a shaved head clicks open some windows, "We're good. We need to build a few more portfolios and then we can bundle and submit about ten thousand."

"How soon till investor evaluation?"

"Instant. We're predicting triple-A ratings for all."

"All?"

"Mmm-hmm."

"RE packages and applications have been building at sixteen percent, correct?"

A bulging young man with one leg turns to her. "Yes. Nice and steady. Clockwork. Mortgage creditors were... insistent, and they went above and beyond what we suggested and even expected."

"How far?"
~~~~

"Some of the sub-primes are predicted to jump to one hundred and sixty eight percent after only one hundred and twenty days. It's almost funny how badly they'll get fucked."

"I know, it's hilarious." I could see her teeth in the light of the screen. Sharp and hungry.

"No one reads," he says, almost sad. I've been spotted. "Your guest is awake."

A wave of caution ripples through the techs one by one. They stop chatting, some even close their screens. I'm an interloper and I don't even know how.

"Morning, sunshine. It's alright, everyone."

"What's going on? What are you doing with all this?"

She leans against the woman with the shaved head, running her finger along the scalp, making little figure 8's.

The woman smiles, giggled. "Stop it. That tickles."

"I know." Coyote's hand is gently moved away.

"What's going on?"

She smiles, laughs to herself. "We're planning a party." Everyone else gets the joke, and I feel like I'm the punchline somehow.

"Uh huh. Can I get some meds or something? My head is killing me. What time is it?"

"Almost sunrise. It's a new day."

"Who are these people? MA?"

"The Party Planning Committee."

"Like a Dome Day party or something?"

"Yup. Just like a Dome Day party."

"We're ready as we're ever going to be," the one-legged man says.

Coyote paces. The only empty chair sits before the biggest wall of monitors, some on the financial news, several just abstract graphs, colors and shapes, one on cartoons. She leans back in the chair now, stretching.

"How soon till party time?"

Another woman, older than time, licks a fleck of something from her gums. She brushed a shock of grey hair around her ear.

"We're looking at disruption almost immediately. It's a fast injection of new portfolios, but not unheard of. Sub-primes will go toxic first, probably at the end of the quarter, and since they're packaged with other markets, those will get infected soon after," she says, her voice the color of silver.

Coyote nods. "What are our most up to date projections right now, at this moment?"

"We'll have a zero by the end of the fiscal year. We can get an actual date and time after the shockwaves hit and we can calc some reactions."

"Good."

Shaved Head interjects. "Ready for incep, Voyd."

"Final checks," Coyote announces, "Media?"

"Green."

One by one, she calls them out, words with no meaning to me. Calc, Securities, Fire, RE, and Ops. Every tech responds with the same terse approval, "All Green."

Coyote touches the side of my face. It's surprisingly tender coming from her. I don't know how to take it. "Corwin, what you told us all last night, do you believe it?"

"Yeah, I do. Look for yourself, don't take my word for it."

"This operation right here will set into motion your mortgage idea. Remember that? Do you still want to go through with it?"

I take a breath and think for a long time. Faces stare at me from the overhead chairs.

"Do it," I whisper.

On the monitor displaying the cartoon, a robot is frying a human being alive and it's supposed to be funny. His skin melts and his muscles ripple in the burning heat, his mouth locked in silent terror. After a moment, she waves her hand forward, like she is commanding an advancing army to charge, confident and sure of its eventual bloody victory. The screens erupt with the throbbing pulse of finance, that secret language of numbers and power.

My head is the weight of a concrete block and filled with broken thoughts. I need to get home, make up a story, an apology to Axel, and eventually mold this night into a shape I could recognize. I was cold and nuclear at the same time, like a massively small star made of ice. As I drink some day-old black Koffee, I'm hypnotized by the bouncing bar graphs and the churning output of the printers. The music of finance. Coyote ignores me. The universe ignores me. At that moment, I am watching the birth and beginning of the end of the world, my end, and I find it oddly beautiful.

~~~~
~~~~

A pile of naked human bodies are piled and dropped into a vat by a mechanical arm. Engineers operate the machines, and dart back and forth with their peculiar quick step. There's no audio. Large tubes pump green and blue liquids into the vat containing the bodies. We have three angles on the whole process, which takes a total of 22 minutes per load. At the end, Engineers remove twelve vats of various chemicals from the machine. Only the dry bones are left, which are then crushed and powdered into a fine white particulate, whose use is unknown.

The process is drably called "Special Chemical Reclamation", and it's as brutal and mechanical as it sounds, resembling the deconstruction of a malfunctioning microwave or an impounded car. I was right to run from Dad's memorial, from that plastic body pretending to be his.

I don't know what to do with this video. I try to show it to Angela and she can't watch it.

We're contacted by the same source that sent us the recycling video, asking what we're going to do with it. We can't just post it, it won't have the same impact. People will get so turned off by it, they won't want to imagine their loved ones being pulped like old magazines and turned into floor polish and toilet cleaner. Plus it's long, almost a half hour of three static camera shots. Plus you need context to what's being shown. The bodies going into the vats sort of look fake, rubbery. That's the nature of a dead body, more fake than fake. The video needs an angle no one's expecting.

Tyrese Manger turns it into a Chik-N-Lil ad.

17 ~ *birth day*

The night before.

On my couch, LIFE on mute in the background, I'm pouring over the final plans and schedule. Raylene's absence feels even larger. Our place is smaller, colder. Angles look wrong. I tried calling around, looking for her. No one's seen her. I don't blame her, not really. I know who I am and what I can give. I just miss her. I open her closet, her drawers. When I do sleep, I don't sleep in our bed anymore. I find single long brown hairs and I wonder how old they are. Did she brush them out? Did they escape, like she escaped? She hasn't called, no note, nothing. If she did something to herself, it was her secret to keep.

There are ads everywhere for the Son's birthday tomorrow, his big 11, almost the same age as Axel, and the security grid, catering, and outfit pickups need to be finalized before tomorrow. My offline laptop sits next to me. I log into our VPN and check the test feed. All looks good. I close shop for the night.

The next day at the party, I appear calm, collected, pleasantly so, the host of this shindig. My mind is elsewhere constantly. The second count down slowly. I'm a trap about to close, waiting for the prey to enter oblivious to danger.

The Son's birthday parties are a glorious monument to distraction. I decided our cover would be Axel's birthday party as well. They're very close together and no one pays that much attention anyway. Food is barely eaten and thrown away, toys gather dust in a box, children whose names I can barely remember, parents with blank faces droning on about their Numbers and their tiny, little lives. I smile, sip my drink, and keep my eye on the Tower, showing the Son's own birthday party on a live feed.

I was able to outbid some rando and rent a backyard. Axel's party will be well-attended, considering I had to hire almost all of his Training friends to attend. MA and our clients pay Zero very well for what we do, and the new financial product sales are excellent, shockingly so. It's infesting the housing market like a parasitic outbreak. The Big Present for Axel, wrapped and ready to be torn open, is actually for everyone in the Dome, and especially for UCorp. We're stirring the pot, making their underlings scramble for control amongst themselves.

Angry techno music blasts in the background. Kids beat each other with bats. It's some sort of game. Axel can handle his own, he's a tough kid, stronger than he looks. Everyone looks at him and constantly underestimates him. He's a winner.

The Son will be having the opposite of Axel's party. A small, intimate affair with a homemade cake, streamers above the doors, a few modest presents, and the Husband putting the finishing touches on a fire-red bicycle, one of those weird foot-pedaled things you see in Sprawl videos. Axel raises his arms in victory, a child doubled up, crying underneath his feet. I watch with pride.

The Wife is slowly applying white icing to a delicious-looking chocolate cake in preparation. She stops and licks a dab of icing off her finger, smiling at the sweetness.

I make a few calls to other operatives who have spent the entire night probing the Tower video feed.

The Son's previous birthday plays in a montage. The Wife brings the cake out, candles lit, and sings "Happy Birthday". We'll have to mouth along for the real thing tomorrow, or we'd be in copyright violation to even sing it out loud. I couldn't afford that song. The venue's sound system would pick up on unauthorized performances of copyrighted material and charge us a small usage fee. I should disable that on the way out. Axel is entranced to the sight as well. LIFE streams will be blowing up about the cake and the candles, what's it made of, who are the other kids at the party, etc. Lots of hashtags, pictures of people watching the event.

It's almost time for the test.

My heart slows. Time stretches.

I place my hand on Axel's shoulder, and he moves it away.

10 seconds.

Happy Birthday is almost over on the replay. The Son leans over to blow out the candles. The screen cuts to black. Showtime.

The black screen shudders, shakes, and lets out a violent series of electronic chirps and squawks, like the signal itself is in its death throes.

All 4 sides of the Tower mirror the same distorted static. If you were watching on TV or your phone, you would hear the shrieking sounds of Chik-N-Lil growths dying in agony, a shrill, orgiastic scream. A single image appears, an opened eye, its iris a keyhole. Above and below, the words read "Everything is not going to be OK."

I hold back my laughter. We did it.

Axel cocks his head. "What happened to the TV?"

Overjoyed, I pick up my phone. There's work to do.

~~~~

The petite, redheaded girl in a NuBorn work uniform runs across the parking lot past me and jumps into the arms of a slightly disoriented and shoeless man. I'd like to think they were long-lost lovers, or he just spilled out of a Security drunk tank and wandered to meet his girl at work. She hugs him close, almost like she's afraid he's actually an illusion and may disappear at any moment. For almost ten minutes, the entirety of her lunch break, she grips him and they say nothing to each other. I want to run to them and scream that it's all going to end someday, so why bother. That pit opens up in my stomach, like the moment you're about to jump, and brick by brick, breath by breath, I seal it back up.

Coyote's leaning against a wall outside Birth Silo #2, her arms crossed. Bluish vapor pours from her. She's checking her phone and doesn't look up when I approach. The Dome has given us a spectacular sunset, a bluish-orange mix of flowing clouds that
~~~~

stream across in ribbed bands. Cracks of digital sunlight beam through like rivers of liquid gold. Beautiful.

We go inside and she unexpectedly takes my arm, me trying not to jump, her face changing from glum, stern iron to a cheerful glow. She tugs me towards a customer service rep, the same petite girl I saw jumping into the arms of the shoeless man. Outside, NuBorn is a sparkling mirrored cube, reflecting your happiness. Inside, it's a dingy off-white with ripped carpeting and shifty-eyed hopefuls furiously bidding on NuBorns. Numbers and pictures flow across the screens. The hopeful viewers angrily tap on their phones, placing bids.

This is where your life can start, in one of these places. Your birth mother signs a franchise contract with NuBorn, shows up when she's leaking and screaming, and either you make good on the contract, or the NuBorn is auctioned off depending on your Brand profile. Axel has a genetic predisposition for depression and anxiety, just like I do. That's why Raylene and I were able to pay off his contract. It's the modern world, you get to know what's wrong with your down to the molecular level, and you're just as powerless to fix it.

The redhead, whose name I see is Lorelai, greets us with a cheerful face, welcoming us to NuBorn. I weakly return it. She instinctively knows I'm not into it and turns her attention to Coyote, who pats my arm, mock-understandingly.

Lorelai points to Coyote's stomach. "So when do you break ground?"

Coyote blushes, "We're just trying at this point."

"Funnest part, isn't it?! Practice makes perfect."

"I know, right?!" She laughs. I laugh. We're all laughing.

"So what can I do for you two?"

"We're here for a tour," Coyote says.

"Oh, right this way!"

We're taken around the facility. The first stop is a video wall of various stages of the baby's development in cartoon form. The real thing is too intense. Cartoon pictures of our ghost baby. The next stops are the showroom for our robotic midwife assistant, the "brand name" generator if we get a platinum birth package, and the clothing store. Some of them look extremely small, like doll clothes. I take a tiny red and blue princess dress off a miniature hanger.

"Why is this one so small?" I hold up the doll's dress.

"Um, those are for what we called 'pillow angels'," she says, trying to change the topic as quickly as possible. "Do you know what those are?"

"Yes, yes I do," I say.

"I don't," Coyote says, her finger to her chin. I'm not amused.

"Those are, uh, babies that don't get to market, so to speak. Some parents like to pose their attempts for photographs before they go to, well..."

"You mean these are for stillborns?" I say defiantly.

Her face scrunches up like a fist. After a moment, she relaxes. "We don't use those terms around here. Please do not repeat them, especially to any other hopefuls."

"Are they available for boys?" Coyote asks.

"Yes, they are. We have several options. Shall we continue?"

We're escorted through a dazzling series of options for painkillers and top-of-the-line medical treatments few can afford, like a cold laser bath or 3D placenta printing. There's an implant you can get that turns your embryonic fluid a bright blue color, and they can replace part of your abdominal wall with a clear plastic bubble. Actresses like them, it's like their pregnancy is the role of a lifetime, and their uterus is its own little TV. We're shown the gene scrubbers, artificial insemination chambers, and the stem cell incubators.

Welcome to the business of being born. I wonder how many children are born in alleyways and filthy Ultimart bathrooms.

The grand finale, the last curtain being pulled back, the moment we've been pitched and marketed to has arrived: the maternity ward. Rows of screaming babies all wailing out in cutesy confusion and adorable terror.

"This is my favorite part of the tour," Lorelai says. "Just imagine. One of these could be yours."

"Imagine that," I say. Axel's birth happened in the back of a UCar.

Some of the cribs have branding on them already. They're being adopted by the company adorning their beds. I don't know if they're lucky or not.

Coyote puts her hand up to the glass, her head slightly bowed, shoulder slumped. She says nothing and walks away.

"Did you want to discuss possible sponsorship or maybe-"

Coyote heads for the nearest outside door. I follow. Lorelai chases up but soon we're outside. Coyote heads to the nearest ladder and climbs up. I glance around to make sure Security isn't and head up after here.

The sun is just dipping down for the four hour night. Coyote holds her arms close to her chest, like it's cold outside. But it's never cold outside.

After a solid minute of silence, I speak up.

"What is this about? We don't have a lot of time and-"

"Hold on." She taps a few buttons on her phone and waves it around herself and me. She presses another button and there's an audible buzz in the air. She disappears around the corner to a hidden alcove strewn with cigarette butts and beer cans: the local make-out spot for hopeful parents.

"Maybe I should get a tapeworm or a parasite colony in my intestines." She taps her lower stomach.

"We really don't have time for this."

"That way instead of one boring baby, I could have an entire civilization depending on me for food, shelter, love. The infinite traffic jam. Mmm... An entire civilization just stuck in traffic. Movement forward, even by inches is an earth-shattering event. A new economy emerges out of the stalled cars and trucks. Luxury limousines become vacation destinations."

"Children grow up thinking the TV in their car is some kind of god. People die having only gone half a kilometer. Old soda cans and chewing gum become precious commodities," I say.

"They forgot where they were going in the first place. They forgot. Everyone is still thinking they're stuck in traffic, when in fact, they are traffic."

"I can't imagine you with an actual child," I say.

She stares at me with cold, small eyes.

"Maybe it would be fun to destroy yourself, your body, creating something else. Intentionally grow a deformed baby. I don't know, maybe you got me pregnant. Maybe I already had your abortion and you don't even know it."

I don't laugh. Not because it's not funny, but because she may be right.

"You realize I know almost nothing about you. I don't even know where you live," I say. Maybe she'll tell me, that might be good information to know just in case.

"You know me enough, sugar."

"What I know, I don't like."

"You're here, aren't you? This is boring. What is really bothering you? Get to the point."

I pause. "Tomorrow is no small thing. A million things could go wrong."

She grabs my hand and pushes it against her breast. "Just think of these, big boy."

I recoil. "Do you think we can do this?"

"Of course I do."

"I'm not sure. Maybe we should abort."

"Ha ha," Coyote says dripping with sarcasm, "Funny joke is funny."

"I'm serious. This is getting out of control. What we're about to do is beyond unsanctioned ads or corporate espionage."

She stands, towering over me. "Nothing stops us. Nothing. You are doing this tomorrow."

"Or what?"

"Or you'll see a side of me you definitely won't like," she says. Her voice is utterly vacant of life.

"I find that hard to believe."

Out of her stylish handbag, a small silver gun appears. Not the one-clips you get out of vending machines, like the one Blake Pierce used to redecorate our office. Something special ordered. Something loved.

"A gun? Seriously?" I almost laugh, holding my hands up in fake surrender. "Oooooh. You got me."

She moves closer with the gun and it grows enormous until it's right under my left eye. She might actually kill me. That familiar fear, the rising acidic panic is all I feel. She laughs. I don't. She pulls the trigger and there's a sharp metallic snap.

"Got you," she says.

I'm shaking. She gives me a long, wet kiss and I have to let her.

~~~~

The harness tugs at my crotch and makes my shoulders ache. I rappel a little further down on the dark side of the retaining wall. Pipes and tubes and cables spread everywhere; an electric odor permeates. Unbearably hot.

LIFE is set on a huge soundstage that encompasses the neighborhood, called the Town, that the show takes place in. It's a cordoned-off community all to itself: the House, the Office, the School. Hundreds of actors simply live out their lives in their own little dome inside of a larger dome. Domes within domes. Lives within lives.
~~~~

Today there's a rare but important opportunity: a gap in coverage while they set up for the birthday. Yesterday's penetration test is also keeping them on edge; it happens more often than you would expect. Every few months there's a disruption, someone hijacks the feed to sell crypto or whatever. It's a maintenance window. The blackout takes place all across the Town. During the day, a special marathon plays, showing highlights from the wedding, the conception of the Son, his first tooth, first day of school, the Wife's dinner party, the Dad's new management job, the argument about the car. All the hits. You've seen them.

I contacted and paid off a very sensitive technician whom we were blackmailing for selling pictures of the Wife's used underwear. She's just a woman trying to raise her son, decent and hardworking, loving. She deserves better.

The radio earpiece squawks new instructions and I check my pad's map as it refreshes. I'm actually not supposed to go near the set like this. Too many cameras, pressure detectors, invisible infrared laser nets. The whole shebang. The broadcast is full of holes, but the Town itself is a fortress. The only place more secure than this set is the Executive Suites in the Tower. I'm up in the dark, hidden from all that, rooting around in the boring ducts and wires strung up around the set. Just outside, a bright and sunny day, a cool breeze.

I check the map and see someone on the crew fucked up big time. All the cameras and ghost nets along the ceiling of the Town have been put in standby. There's not an ounce of heat coming off them, no signals. I find one of the black boxes for the show (which is actually orange striped) and I plug in. Tyrese pings me the code to enter into base files, overwrite some stuff. The black box lights dim, then restarts. Instead of a pleasant green, they're all sickly yellow. We are officially tapped into the LIFE livestream and with a few modifications can override at any point. Now is the part in the plan where I climb back up. I have decided not to.

Beneath me, inside the retaining wall about thirty meters down, two Security officers trade tips on Legend of Heroes min-maxing for the new raid. I'm hidden above in the ductwork, but I can barely make out the black helmets below. I freeze. I drop a spanner, grabbing it in mid-air by the very tip of the handle. Dangling from my grip. I carefully draw it back up and gently place it in my kit. Had it fallen, the clamoring racket would have sunk me.

Climbing down the retaining wall to this junction has been one of the most physically arduous things I've ever done. My arms are jelly and I know I will be plastered with bruises. The two guards wander off, bored and aimless.

There is weird air here. I'm supposed to just plant the broadcast device and leave, but I don't.

I turn off my radio and location, officially in the dark now. The people back at the hub must be losing their minds, thinking I've been discovered, scrambling to break everything down as planned. Burning files, hard drives, disappearing. Even if every single one of us were arrested, the plan would still execute now. No way to stop it. I travel further down and the jagged angles of metal look like teeth ready to chew me up. I can hear it growing around me like living circuitry and pipes that twine and grasp the girders, sinking their fingers into its lustrous flesh. The Town bleeds pixels and I cut in like a surgeon.

Across from me, a pair of yellowed eyes meets mine. A feral child, no more than six or seven, dirty and grizzly-haired, holds a rat in his mouth, locks gazes with me. Hundreds, maybe thousands of them live in the ductworks and pipes of the Machine. Sometimes they emerge on the surface, steal a bit of food or colorful plastic, and sneak down below. I don't move an inch. He is wearing a silver-tin crown, beat to shit, cocked on one side of his head. I briefly consider stopping this whole thing, taking this grease-caked face home to something better.

"Hey there."

He doesn't speak, maybe can't speak. He picks at his hair, flinging a louse, blinks at me, then disappears into a square duct back to his lair.

We should hire you. The Wild Child's Playhouse, where filthy meat is a currency and fire is God. All technology is sorcery, and the world exists in the flickering images of a TV screen.

I continue down, towards the House. Towards an answer.

The next junction I pass through is more confusing, as if the set vomited cables and I have to swim through them downwards, pushing aside fleshy ducts and snapping cords pumping with information.

Electricity hums around me, an invisible blood flowing through plastic veins to power televisions, internet streams, images of Home as they should be. Clean surfaces, fresh carpets, photogenic foods being shoved into mouths. Problems that have tangible solutions. What should the Son do about his math final?

Should the Wife cook stew or pot roast for supper? Should the Dad go to that work meeting across Town, or watch the Son play baseball?

There's never a question about what to do when Dad shits the bed and there's no one willing to help. Or when your child's eyes are glazed and dead when they look at you. Or when your loving life partner vanishes and you don't have the guts to face the truth. When you're trapped and entwined with a demonic psychopath.

My support ropes plink against aluminum tubes and steel girders, roping down the darkened shafts. The television sky of the Town, much nicer than ours outside, breathes in and out just outside my reach.

I travel deeper like an elevator, or maybe the ground travels up and I'm standing still. On the next level down, the next channel, a hanging stage light creates a dim circle of purple light on a flat supporting horizontal platform. A creaking, groaning sound of wheels emerges from the black, followed by a soft, repeating ping of a HealthLine monitor. Dad's bed, the one I salvaged, is wheeled into the light by unseen hands. He is alive, sitting up in bed, flipping through a magazine.

"You should just scream then," he says, not looking at me. I'm not sure he has eyes.

"But everyone will hear me."

"So?"

"I'll be embarrassed." My skin feels hot, flushed with blood.

"So?"

"I don't want to feel that way."

"I don't want to feel that way," he says, slightly mockingly. "Your son is screaming for you."

"No, he's not. He's with people."

"He is screaming for you. Like I screamed."

"No," I whisper.

He angrily flips a page in the magazine to a new video. I can hear it, a brief on Cherry Poppers auctioning her old child-sized breast implants.

"Why did you save me?"

"I didn't save you. You died."

"Fine," He throws it down. He used to do this all the time. My persistence would finally break him down until he was so annoyed he would acknowledge me. This was talking to my dad. "Why did you try?" He finally looks at me. His glasses are delicately perched on the end of his nose.

"I don't know."

"Yes. You. Do."

"No, I don't."

"I know why."

I loosen my grip on the support line and rappel slowly downwards, leaving my father's ghost and other lost things in the between spaces of this place.

<div align="center">~~~~</div>

That permeable membrane between that perfect life and me. I just want to see it with my own eyes. Unedited. Live and in the flesh. I know the Town better than my son's face; the layout of the streets, the Family's neighborhood filled with colorful, wacky characters, Main Street lined with shops packed with the finest products, driveways pregnant with shining vehicles, a world filled with plenty. Always clean, beaming with the shimmer of sparkling pool water. Barbeques. Tanned skin smeared with lotion. Laughter.

Ultimart appears clean and shining from a distance, and the Dome looks well taken care of until you get close and see the grime and mildew, the herds of dull-eyed people shuffling through lines, burning alive under bone fluorescent lights. Dying in small, dimly lit rooms while their sons watch helplessly. Decaying teeth biting into processed meat grown in vats.

No one dies in the Town. There's no suffering. No choking. No pink brain matter sprayed over white tile. No emptiness.

The panel to the wall comes away easier than it should. I reach my hand out and touch damp coolness of their grass. Real, living grass. A carpet of things that are alive, real, soft, desired. The smell is intoxicating. I penetrate the Town, wriggling my way through the dense mesh of cables and wires creating the hi def sky for the Townspeople. The digital warmth that falls on her face when she hangs laundry outside. I wriggled out, birthed onto the cold green vegetation, dampening the right side of me. The owner must have just watered it. People in the Town turn on the tap over something called a "kitchen sink" to get water. At home, I punch buttons on a machine and a bottle is delivered to me, my account conveniently deducted automatically.

It's only 12:24. The party won't start for another few hours or so. Some of the Townspeople are walking their mechanical dogs who lay mechanical turds, and even though the cameras are off, they still go through the motion of picking up the plastic shit, putting it in a plastic bag, and discarding it. I hide behind a shrub and unzip my black jumpsuit to reveal Ultimart blue, the company's color. The color of fresh water and open sky. I'm a lowly maintenance tech with no face or name. If I look busy and pissed enough, I'll be ignored. The cameras are not off, but no one's paying attention.

I briskly, but not too briskly, jog down Elm and then make a left onto Birch, company issued backpack and tablet in my hand. A Security Officer, a chubby and thoroughly disinterested woman about my age, glances in my direction. I give her an annoyed look and she dismisses me just as fast.

The houses are asleep in the midday sun, and the streets slumber with them. It's like the Town was put on pause. The Town is a memory of some kind, but it's a memory of a place none of us have ever lived in. A memory that's part of our DNA, but there's no actual substance to it, just the haunted skeleton of something you never experienced.

What's actually most surprising is the complete lack of serious security. I'm not a secret agent or anything like that, and yet I was able to infiltrate the Town with basic equipment. I just crawled in the back door. The black box for a livestream control junction wasn't even locked.

The houses are so unique and important they are not stacked on top of each other like ours. There are no towering buildings or crisscrossing highways piled with cars. There is no crazed droning noise of traffic. They are castles. I am a camera drinking it all in. At Birch, I take a right, walk three streets down, and end up on Poplar.

Like a giant circuit, Poplar is plugged directly into the House at the end of the lane.

At the end of Poplar Street, there are several trucks plugged into hidden panels propped open in the sidewalk. Bunches of engineers and technicians huddle around monitors, drinking cans of something called Green, their tiny eyes illuminated like electronic stars. They do not even acknowledge me as I pass by a few meters away with my backpack. I walk along the left side of the lawn until I pass the invisible boundary of their lawn from the Henderson's yard. Their house is a tomb, no lights, no movement. I draw closer.

In the shadows past the mulberry shrubs, I touch the House's outer wall, a building I've seen from every angle in countless hours, in hundreds of photos, in color, black and white, inside and out. And I am touching it with my bare hand. I shiver. My breath is small and shallow. The enormity of what I am doing makes me lightheaded.

The vinyl siding is slick and cool to my fingertips and I run them across the beige plastic pattern, which I know is called "woodgrain". This House looks made of wood, something that was once alive, grown specifically in the Dome for this one function, to remind us of the past.

The backyard is empty and the pool glistens with the underwater lights, and I remember the parent's pool party a few weeks ago. The Son did a cannonball and his parents watched. I can smell the sweet odor of freshly cut grass everywhere, charcoal from the barbeque, probably used earlier today. They take water and raise a non-edible crop, then use a machine to cut it down. I don't always understand the show, but the ritual of watching the Husband take the lawnmowing machine out of the garage, gas it up, and yank on the starter cord, I find it all very relaxing. He walks in straight rows up and down the yard until all the plant life is the correct height. His battle with weeds and quality of the grass makes for excellent story arcs, especially when he and Mr. Miller had a gentleman's competition for best hedges. The loser had to wear a chicken suit and get dunked at the Town Fair. The Husband lost, but not by much, and took his dunking like a champ. I keep thinking about the grass: an organism so large it touches everyone.

Inside the first floor, the Husband opens the fridge door and I freeze in my tracks like a man-shaped lawn ornament. I duck behind his second-place hedges, the ones that got him dunked, and pull out my phone.

I film him. I only film Dads, it seems.

I'm not sure what the Husband is looking at, because he stands there for an extraordinary amount of time, his arms slack by his sides, his slight pudge poking out from underneath his shirt. The most famous man in the Dome looks bored, defeated by his choices of food. He takes out a 2 liter jug of Smilk and removes the cap, dropping it on the counter, and chugs straight from the container. I almost gag. The amount of germs on that lid must be extraordinary. He replaces the jug and leans against the kitchen island counter, rubbing his hands through his hair. Next, he gets an apple from the tree out back, takes out a knife and slices it in two. He does it too fast, because he nicks his finger.

"FUCK!" he yells.

They never swear. They never nick themselves with knives. The only blood I've seen on the show is when the Son skinned his knee, and that was a small and tastefully modest patch of dark red soaking through a flesh-colored bandage.

I've also never seen what he does next.

He's fascinated by the blood, letting the red droplet run down his hand, then his arm. He takes the knife and cuts a line across his palm, and a small slit appears. Blood soon follows and he plays with it. He closes his fist.

I wait. The novelty leaves him, he goes into the den, shutting the door behind him. I put my phone away and tighten the straps on my backpack. After checking for Security one more time, I climb the ivy trellis on the side to the second floor roof. I check around the corner of the House and see the techs in the street, doing whatever they're doing. Lots of computer screens and cables and hurried movement.

Inside the house, the air is cool and dry, like the inside of an empty can. The familiar beige walls, the simulated wood flooring covered with tasteful throw rugs. My heart races, practically pounding out of my chest, so loud the thumping blasts in my ears. Little white dots flow in front of my eyes and I grab the side of the window to avoid falling. Cold sweat coats my back and I may puke.

There's something about the camera that infuses this place with magic and mystery. There's none here, just recycled air and the slight chemical smell of lemon floor polish. The upstairs hallway connects all the bedrooms, and I know the Husband is still downstairs. The Son's bedroom door opens and I quickly duck down. If I'm caught, my story is checking cables. Sure. But he doesn't see me, and makes a straight line for the bathroom down the hall at the top of the main stairs.

He's a real kid. Almost the same age as Axel, who thinks the commotion outside has little to do with him. I wonder how much he knows about his LIFE and the show itself. Does he perform the same as his parents? I suddenly have a thought: are they even his parents? Did she birth him?

He talks to the Wife, who is in the bathroom. After a few hushed words, she says some reassuring words and sends him back to his room. A nap maybe to rest up? I inch towards the master bedroom and slip in, and head towards the walk-in closet, which connects to the bathroom. I tuck myself behind a row of her sundresses, their clean scent, things that have touched her. I forget where I am for a moment and almost cry out.

My phone films the bathroom. A length of her bare leg and her auburn hair dangling down in her lap. The door to the bathroom is cracked just enough so I can zoom and see inside. She has the overhead light on, creating a dagger of orange in the closet. I try and stay out of it, watching through the phone, which records her silently.

She's softly weeping on the shut toilet. She pushes her hair back and I see her red-rimmed eyes in the light, bloodshot and exhausted. She looks at something above her, single lines of tears streaming down her face. She slaps her hands together quickly, mashing her palms. Smacks them again with a wet slap. She looks like she's praying.

The three of them are the Father, the Son, and the Holy Ghost. A woman who now seems barely there, haunting her own life. Dad yells from downstairs that he needs a bandage, that he cut himself. She sighs, rubs her temples to stop what is most likely an unimaginable migraine, and starts to wash her hands. I think she is going to head out into the hall, maybe downstairs, so I half-extend myself out into the dark closet, ready to leave.

The closet door opens behind me.

I'm as still as a statue. For a ridiculous second, I imagine that if I stay perfectly still, maybe she won't see me. I'll be confused for a schlubby coat.

"Who are you?" she commands.

I say nothing at first. I swallow hard and without turning around, I say "I'm sorry, ma'am. I got turned around and I didn't want to disturb you."

"What did you see?"

"I'm sorry. I'll just be-"

"Shut up. What did you see? Answer me," she says again, this time with a curt clip.

"I'm just a video tech. I'll be out of here in a second."

"You're lying."

I turn around and look at her. She is wearing a thin t-shirt and white capris. Her arms are crossed and her face is steel.

"Wait. Come into the light."

I don't.

"Step into the light or I scream."

I slide the blue maintenance ballcap off my head and walk into the light of the bathroom. She can see my bald spot.

"I know you," she says, squinting with recognition, "I know you."

"I doubt it."

"Corwin... something. Right?"

What.

"This job seems a bit low for someone as notable as you."

"What do you mean 'notable'?" I ask, confused.

"That video of your dad. It's the third most watched video of all time online. It's more popular than Hobo Cat Tales or Dome Boys."

"I didn't think you watched that kind of thing."

Her eyes narrow. "What are you doing here?"

"I have a job to do."

After what feels like a century, she looks hard at me and says, "Don't move."

She reaches out her hand to me, not like she's going to hit me, but like I'm a robotic dog toy, and I'm going to lick her palm.

"Don't move or I will scream."

I obey. She brushes the side of my face with the back of her hand, and I nearly implode. Her skin is dry and rough but slightly warm, smelling of lavender hand soap and cherry blossom cream, and my cheek trembles. She's touching me. She is actually touching me. She moves her hand down and violently grabs my chin in her small hand.

"You see, there is no me, Corwin. There is no you. There's nothing between us, not even the air. We live in a dream. Sometimes it's a lovely dream. Sometimes it's a nightmare. We're all air in a dream. And that dream will end."

I'm trembling so hard I can barely stand. A raw, hot tear falls down my hand and hits her forefinger. She takes her hand away, brings her finger up to her mouth, and tastes my tear.

"You should go home."

My body is a giant, man-shaped balloon that is about to burst. I float away from her and somehow I am outside the house. From the backyard, I look up to the bedroom window and see her silhouetted in the darkened room. She raises her hand, a single unmoving wave. Saying goodbye.

As I look up from my phone, I see the Husband glaring at me. He and I locked eyes and he knows. He sees that I know that he knows. I bolt into the brush. My veins pulse acid as I pump my arms and legs at full throttle through the placid backyards.

A klaxon screams through the streets. I scramble through backyards and over a fence to see Dr. Schultz and his husband ready to take an afternoon dip in their pool. Their barbeque goes flying into the drink as I shove it aside, launching over the next fence towards my exfil point.

Almost there, almost there. Go. Run.

The trip back up through the Town's interior wall is a blur of pulling myself through cables and avoiding heat sinks. Sweat slicks my face as I pull myself out of the Town's dome and slide down to the ground below. I turn my radio back on to hear an incoherent screaming voice in my ear. Beneath me and all around I hear shouting, boots trampling, radios squelching robotic words.

I take alleys and service tunnels to get close to the meetup point, keeping my maintenance blues on to stay incognito. I hide scrunched over in pipes for most of the day. The sky is turning an ugly bruise purple, the sun setting just behind Evergreen Pines, an empty mall structure that went under after Sofo Enterprises spent millions to renovate, build stores, and then nobody cared. This mall is the bleaching corpse of some enormous animal, its bones wrapped around a steel toothed trap. Hallways filled with the dead eyes of stores, naked mannequins piled in corners, broken neon veins cracking underfoot, faded ghost faces on posters, matted fast food pelts carpeting. I jog to the main atrium, hugging the wall, broken glass crunching under my boots. It's empty, no one in sight, so I make my way to the corpse of the food court.

A few people are supposed to meet me at the EZ Freeze, between Jack Rabbit and GuNom, but they're nowhere to be found. A black gloved hand clicks the trigger of a taser, and the two prongs fly out in a smooth, violent arc. Red hot searing. My teeth crack together. I immediately seize and fall flat on my face.

And that's our show for tonight, folks. End credits. A blinding flash of white as the outro song starts: the melodic warbling of Security sirens.

18 ~ dream

An army of black-suited Security in mirrored helmets, armed with batons and shields, swarm into the food court like a crashing tide. A baton cracks me in the side of my head, my vision immediately filling with stars. 6 seconds later and I'm zip-tied, belly down on the floor.

"Now what?" An officer says to another, to no answer.

A security drone hovers above, emitting a loud whirring noise. After a few seconds, the drone peels off. These Security are not the slack-jawed children you see mulling around grocery stores or gyms, sneering at pretty girls and busting shoplifters with tasers for clicks. Regular Security lean against their cars smoking or dicking around on their phones. They're for show, these people are the genuine article.

I'm lifted again, moved, and deposited on the floor outside the abandoned electronics store like an overflowing garbage bag. They eyescan me, and the bright flash leaves a yellow fading circle, even when I squint my eyes shut.

One of the pair speaks into their radio, checking in. The other leaves. The remaining helmeted face turns to me.

"We're very sorry about the face. How does it feel?" she says, genuinely apologizing. The maternal female voice, deep and honest, surprises me. Just a woman doing her job. A vicious, highly trained cog in the Machine.

"What?"

She smells like tangerine body wash. She probably has a boyfriend or girlfriend, a favorite show, annoyances about how clothes fit, pictures from vacation.

"Okay, up we go!" She hauls me up to my feet and pushes me to the food court railing, the brass bar knocking the wind out of me. I let out a barking yell and struggle for breath.

"Whoopsie."

Down in the food court, dozens of ferals and houseless are being rounded up, tranq darted, put in nets. A small APC sprays powerful jets of blue water, breaking up the packs. Parents scream, kick, and scratch for their filthy children hauled away. An old woman kneels with her head in her hands, weeping, her back rising up and down, clutching a child's dirty blanket in her small hand.

"Just letting you know, I have to hit you in the stomach."

"Wait, what-"

She clubs me sharply in the solar plexus, and I'm totally unprepared for it. A hot fire burns in my abdomen, and I crumple into a pile of limbs and pain on the tile. She places her left knee right against my neck. I'm pinned and I panic, I can't move, breathing is a chore and for some reason I'm slightly thirsty.

I imagine a trio of security officers are pulling Axel out of the bed, giving him a series of injections, checking his pupils, and handing him over to a specialist.

Happy Birthday, Axel.

Someone in charge, a prudish little twerp tells something to a group of Security and they jog off. Blond hair, dark grey suit, wearing a pair of decorative glasses which he pretended to adjust. He's a few years younger than me, someone who's climbed the ladder faster than he expected.

"You are Corwin Scaggs?" he says, scanning a tablet.

"Yes. How can I help you?" Once I respond, he checks an item off his list with the flick of his hand.

"My name is Simon Finch, I'm an Executive Liaison."

"Fancy. I guess that makes me the Executive Detainee."

There's not a drop of sarcasm in him. "Good to see you have a sense of humor. All this hullabaloo can be scary for some folks. So if I understand from the ladies and gentlemen here: you somehow broke into the Town set and took photos, is that correct?"

I say nothing. He looks me up and down, tapping out something on his pad.

"There's been some weird disruption of the feed. Care to shed a little light on that?" Once again, he's not playing Bad Cop. He simply wants to know, his finger poised over the tablet.

"I don't know what you're talking about."

"That's a pickle for me, Mister Scaggs. You see, we need to know, and I prefer to ask politely first."

"I appreciate that."

He waits, not saying anything. He motions to the Security officer and she picks me up and dusts me off, like I'm a toddler who fell off a jungle gym. She even smoothes out my shirt.

"Mister Scaggs, what were you trying to do?"

A high pitched squelch comes from the LIFE feed. The screens on every channel displaying the show, including the huge TV towers supporting the Dome from floor to digital sky, glitch out to static. For 10 seconds, the sound is grinding electric screaming.

Finch, bewildered, looks around at the dozens of helmets fixated on the static, then at me.

'What's going on?" Finch says.

I smile at him, a mouth full of bloody teeth.

~~~~

Zero, the most exciting venue for hot new content, is proud to present a very special episode of LIFE. And also the basics of the EVM for all to see. Bring the whole family. We created several lifelike CGI replicas of the Family, fake enough to be convincing, and we set them on a little journey through what we could extrapolate from the Big Dump.

We still don't have a complete picture of all the machinery, but the large strokes are there. How UCorp coldly determines whether or not to throw you into the thresher. How EVM rates are calculated, and most importantly by whom. That this is a known system with tangible culpability.
~~~~

Names and addresses of the people responsible. 11 vitamins and minerals, everything a growing revolt needs.

Our narrative show how the Husband loses his job based on a computer algorithm, desperately tries to keep up with his Number payments until his credit is so destroyed employment is impossible. He donates plasma, even one of his kidneys, but it's not enough. Due to his low viability, we show a faceless bank of monitors that slowly tick his EVM rate downwards. The Wife tries to get a job herself, but is rejected at every turn. Eventually the day comes where there's no more options. The Son is sold to the head of a hedge fund as a new boy toy, never to be seen again. They simply drown.

The Husband and Wife are forced into a Security corral, hooded to hide their fear, and tearfully pushed into the elevator. The final shot of them is the carriage descending down into the darkness of the Machine, to Bargainville, where we see them torn to pieces by crushing, grinding poverty. It's very dramatic. Grim lighting, sharp, quick cuts, the works. Dad overdoses in a half-filled bathtub after he is forced to test a bad batch of Trips, and the Wife is last seen crying over a toilet, vomiting in sheer grief and agony.

We end with the real video of the bodies being slowly dumped into the recycler, ground up into floor polish and bleach, careful to remind people this is not fictional. It is all real. There is no set, no commercials, no sponsors. We tried to identify as many of the dead as possible, give them names and faces, give them back their real selves even if just for a moment in time. They were people who had memories and lived with others who cared about them. They felt pain and joy and shame and sadness and love. Each one of them was deeply important to another person. They were born on a day and time. They were flesh and blood. We couldn't help them, but in the end, they helped us.

Roll credits.

And the whole Dome saw this nightmare play out on every screen, every tablet, every streaming device capable of showing LIFE. Towers stretching into the sky showed it. They eventually had to hard kill the entire feed by physically cutting cables and shut down all broadcast mirrors to stop the transmission, but not after 23 million pairs of eyes saw everything.

~~~~

Detainment at Security is a blur of grey rooms and corridors, endless digital forms I sign with my fingerprint, whether I want to or not. Hands grabbing and pulling me in one direction or another. They string you up on this conveyor belt, strap you into this coffin-like contraption in the same restraint jacket, and you slide down a metal rail to the various departments for processing. They take hair and blood samples, fingerprint you, eyescans, stool samples, the works. They insert a catheter into my penis so I can piss to my heart's content. There's so much noise, mostly screaming, which would scare the shit out of me, but I'm weirdly serene. I sign everything they put in front of me, I hide nothing, and never once lie. They scream and point at me trying to decide what to do. No one's ever done this before. Flush me down the toilet, they shout. Down into the machine. The blonde guy, Finch, is there, too, following me along, watching me. There's 2 factions
~~~~

arguing, one for the chopping block and the other faction quietly, calmly presenting a defense, I guess? I can't really hear or see very well, but I know courtroom drama when I see it. Maybe this is all just for show.

No idea how long I've been here. Days, maybe? Without clocks or windows, time loses much of its meaning. The food is mostly beige, tasteless matter. Bottled water in sippy cups. A chemical toilet, reeking of blue gel, to shit in. The bare minimum to keep me alive.

I lay back, I breathe.

Millions saw the broadcast. Word spread inside the holding pens, and while I was strung up on a rail, arms locked inside of a restraint jacket, it was music to my ears.

Soon I am floating in a deep, dreamless sleep. I awake to see a man sitting on the edge of my bed. It's Finch. I tried to sit up, but realized I have been shackled to the hard slab while I was knocked out. My head swims.

"That was... quite a show," he says, crossing his legs. He has a tablet he taps on with a single index finger.

"I don't watch TV." I smile at him, a little groggy.

"I'm sorry, but this isn't a social visit. I regret to inform you that you have formally been charged with over one hundred and eighteen violations of company policy." He shrugs his shoulders, genuinely apologetic.

"Sounds about right. Can you read them off to me, please? I have a contractual right to know what they are."

He points at me, as if to punctuate the rightness of what I've just said. "That is correct, Mister Scaggs," he says, smiling.

Patiently, he reads them off one at a time. It takes almost a half hour. When he is done, he swipes along the tablet.

"Do you understand the charges that I've just read to you?"

"No, I'm sorry. I wasn't listening."

He doesn't budge. "A copy of them has been emailed to your account. Unfortunately, due to maintenance work being done right now, they are unavailable for viewing. Do you have any questions for me right now?"

"Yeah, what's for lunch?"

"You're actually very fortunate. Initially, the original order was to shoot on sight."

"I'm so lucky, aren't I?"

"You disseminated false information that has led to a momentary widespread panic. Certain stocks are not doing well and they want to pin this on you personally. You're gonna take all the heat."

"You're right, it is a little warm in here. Can you turn up the AC?"

"Initial metrics say forgotten after the next commercial break, so they say. A minor one-hit wonder. Maybe some merch, but nothing more."

"I don't think so. Not this time."

"I'm sorry, Mister Scaggs, not here to argue the modesty of your fame. I'm here to discuss the terms of your arbitration and assessment of penalties."

"No big speech about the errors of my ways? Trying to shame me into confessing? Maybe even a mild threat against my son. I'm probably off contract as we speak."

"Technically no, you're not. Penalties have not been assessed, repayment plans haven't been discussed. This is just…" He struggles for the words, "An informal chat. By the way, your son is actually missing right now. He wasn't at your house. Doesn't that bother you?"

"He plays a lot of first person shooters. He can handle himself."

"Okay." He adjusts his glasses, scans the tablet. "Your arbitration fines that were automatically leveled are… substantial, let's put it politely. Approximately three hundred million dollars. Based upon your current account balance, which is nothing to sneeze at by the way, you will be looking at going off-contract almost immediately once they're applied. Payment plans are pretty much nonexistent at this level. I'm here to help you through this process, and answer any questions you may have about your relocation to-"

That's enough of that. "Here's what's going to happen. Maybe in the next few hours, if it hasn't happened already, you're going to get a call or a text or whatever from PTS Financial authorizing the payment of any fines that I currently have. You see, I've been busy. A little side gig called mortgage-backed collateralized debt obligations. Heard of them?"

"Yes, I have." His face screws up, he realizes what's going on.

"They're licensed from Financial Product Innovations. FPI. Very popular. Very profitable. Some of the largest, most powerful financial institutions license this technology from FPI. From, well, me. I've put in a little clause that states as long as I am indisposed for twenty four hours for any reason, those licenses are frozen unless I'm cashed out, so to speak. We can sell that license patent for quite a nice profit. Much more than that any fines. Here's another fun fact, without that patent running smoothly, billions are at risk. Seriously, it's a little hot in here."

He adjusts the cell's temperature on his tablet.

"You picking up what I'm putting down?"

"Yes."

"I'd also like this thing removed and some cream from my wrists. For the chaffing. And a soda would be nice. A Blu."

He checks on his tablet, makes a quick call to Financial. He sounds exasperated on the phone, but I can't hear him exactly. Just muffled complaints.

He comes back, ending his call and stuffing his phone into his pocket. "This is... uh... not standard. Also also also, company policy overrides any private licensing contract, Mister Scaggs."

I give him a mocking, shocked look. "Maybe, but at this point you have another teensy problem: every single person in the Dome is affected by the product I just described. You wouldn't believe how many financial firms license this product, the hundreds of billions of dollars in assets. You're not dealing with me, you're dealing with all of them. Hundreds of billions."

I lick my lips, stare him right in his small, smug face.

"You see, I'm my own brand now, Simon. I'm ready to pay my tab. Say thank you."

He gathers his things and leaves. About an hour later, my restraints are removed and I'm rubbing a peach-scented salve on the red marks across my wrists and ankles.

"You're welcome."

I demand my clothes. I'm handed my things and a soda, a Blu, just like I asked. Wiring over that much money isn't just pressing a button on a screen. Several layers of approvals have to take place. Simon is all cheerfulness and diplomacy, but still tries to get me to waive my right to arbitration. He even hints at dismissing the charges. He must've gotten some scary calls. I take a sip of my soda. It's nice and cold.

"Clean slate."

"Yes."

I laugh. "Why the golly gosh would you do that?"

"We'd just think it's best to put this all behind us. The charges are extensive, but ultimately we'll see this as a childish prank. Falsifying information that the company is running some sort of... uh... nefarious scheme is going to require a public apology and statement refuting that claim. These are requirements of your release."

"What in the whole wide world is going on out there?" I give it my full ah-shucks attitude. "Did you folks get yourselves into a big ol' bucket of syrup?"

Finch says nothing. Something changes in Simon. A seriousness I haven't seen. His face hardens. "How do you think this is going to end, Corwin? Do you think it's going to end well for you? Let's say you walk out that door. What then?"

"Now that we're on a first name basis, Simon, I honestly don't know. But better than you."

"I've looked at your proposal and here's ours." He gestures to the guard behind me.

Before I can retort, there's a sharp crack of a baton against my knee. I crumple to the ground. A Security Guard, a man the size of a vendifridge, takes out a taser and shoots me in the back with it. White hot pain. The room turns into the inside of a furnace. Simon doesn't look in my direction as I scream in agony.

"I know, it seems horribly unfair. But it really doesn't matter if your fine was one dollar or a hundred trillion."

I make various guttural noises.

"I've been tasked by Corporate to offer you a very unique opportunity here. Let me ask you a question, do you like adventure? Travel? Excitement?"

My hands are violently shaking and there's a warm stain on my pants.

"Technically, that was three questions," I say, laughing and crying at the same time.

He lets out a small, sick giggle. "Well, do you?"

"What, Simon?"

"We're all very excited about this partnership. It's a new, innovative way of bringing your fresh ideas to the consumer." This guy has a lighthearted ruthlessness to him, someone who would politely kick every tooth of your head, but offer to pay the bill to clean up the bloodstain.

"Am we negotiating?" I say, breathing hot gasps.

"No, that's all done." He glances at the tablet. "Breaking into the Town was rude. Spreading lies about the company like that, you're really just hurting yourself. This puts your son in a desperate situation."

"I'm listening!" I cry out.

"I can tell you're a straight shooter, so I'll just get right to the point."

Simon Finch is beginning to terrify me worse than the nice man with the taser. A practiced, easy-going malevolence. He's a predator and worse, he knows it.

"Maybe we need to try another method."

"I'll tell you everything. Just say please."

"Please. Go ahead."

"Santa Claus made me do it."

The taser strikes me again. A black hood flies over my head. All goes black.

~~~~

I'm shoved into a car that smells clean and new. I breathe heavily through the hood. It's hot and itchy and my hands are zip-tied again.

"Can we stop and get Chik-N-Lil? I am ravenous."

"Shut the fuck up." A gravely male voice.

"No, I think that's a good idea. I could go for a bite," I hear Finch say. We stop and order in the drive-thru. My hood is lifted up over my mouth. A meaty hand feeds me a Grilled sandwich with algae lettuce and tomato, my favorite, and a straw to drink out of in regular intervals. He even dabs my chin with a napkin.

About an hour later, the car door opens and a blast of fresh, clean air smashes into me. I'm shoved out, stumble onto pavement, and forced to kneel. The hood is ripped off in a single tug.
~~~~

Blinding sunlight everywhere. I shrink away and wait for my eyes to adjust. I expect a gun in my face, but instead the world goes from a blown-out photograph to a blue sky. A handful of puffy clouds wander by. The sound of children and a light breeze. A strange plant-like smell, tart and bitter, strangely soothing. Fresh-cut grass is what it is, I remember it from scents you can buy for your turf yards and it's nothing like the rich, immaculate version in the town. I smell smoke, an early afternoon barbeque is happening a few doors down. I have no idea what is going on.

The car has stopped in front of a single level ranch-style house with a brown tile roof, outside vinyl siding a pleasant earth-tone color. Standing by itself. An enormous front yard is filled with lush imitation grass and a tree, surrounded by a blob of gnarled ivy. A dark green animal statue peeks out at us from the front holly bushes. I think the shelled animal was called a "turtle".

"If this was your house, you'd be home already," Simon says. He claps me on the back and chuckles.

"What the fuck," I whisper.

"There are the most lifelike plants we could find. You can't even tell the difference. Plus you never have to mow. But if you want, for a small fee, we could put in the kind that grows in case you like to mow as an activity."

"Is it like live grass?"

"No, of course not. You can't afford that." He laughs as if it's the most ridiculous thing in the world.

The street of the house is set in a square, with this particular house being on the far end of the square, pointing towards the center of the Dome. There's so much space, so much sunlight. It's so quiet.

"Go inside. There's a surprise for you."

"What, a bullet in the back of my head? Doing this to torture me?"

"No, quite the opposite. Officer, please remove his restraints. Corwin, do me a favor and be polite, please."

I nod, too dazed to think straight. The officer flicks out a knife and cuts the black plastic band in a single swipe. It falls to the ground and the officer dutifully picks his litter.

Simon motions for me to follow him. This is all a scam, another layer on the cake. I'm being tricked, I know it. Simon uses a red bird-shaped knocker by holding up a little swinging hammer, which playfully chimes when he drops it.

"What's the catch? What's going on here?"

"There's no catch here."

"There's always a catch. There's always fine print, Finch." I say, stepping towards him. The officer starts to move towards me, but Simon holds up his hand, and he stops.

"Where's my son?"

"Let's take a tour, shall we?"

He opens the door. I smell warm baked bread, new paint inside. Fresh carpet chemical stink. How a hotel room or a new car smells. That strange tangy waft of fresh particle board.

This dollhouse or whatever it is, complete with its pristine furniture, sparkling walls, clean floors, windows showing the pleasant view of flowing trees outside. It looks like a set.

The click-clack of plastic hitting plastic comes from the family room near the back of the house. I nearly run towards the sound and there Axel is, playing with car toys and military men on the floor. The TV is on but mute, playing some cartoon war, mustached men shooting lasers at each other. Coyote is there as well, casually flipping through a tablet on the couch. It's like they were always meant to be here, just as they are, purely existing like this on lazy afternoons.

"Hey, buddy."

"Hey, Dad!"

Axel runs to me and shoves his hand up for a high five. I run towards him and snatch him up, hugging him so close I practically strangle him.

"Dad, you're hurting me."

"I'm sorry, I'm sorry. I just..." I start scanning the room for exits. "I haven't seen you for a bit and I missed you."

"I missed you, too. Where were you?"

"Trip for work. Last minute. Who's been taking care of you?"

"Your lady friend."

"What lady friend are you talking about, buddy? I don't have a lady friend."

"That hurts my feelings, Corwin," Coyote says, looking up from her magazine. "Simon, thank you for dropping him off. Did you want a drink or something?"

"No, Miss Voyd."

"Best to the family."

"Will do. You two have a bit to talk about, Mister Scaggs. Join me out back when you can? Thanks," he says this with a slight whiff of sarcasm.

I watch Simon leave from the window, hiding behind the blinds. The house feels strange, empty, immersed in an old silence, save Axel's conquering of the galaxy in the other room. I sit cross legged with Axel on the ground.

"Unbelievable, isn't it?" Coyote says, gesturing around her, "What's waiting here. What's outside."

"How do you get here?" I ask.

"I'm fine, hero. I can handle myself."

"Explain. Right now."

"Go talk to that dipshit outside." She lets out a little laugh. "The old adage is money doesn't buy happiness, but it can certainly rent it from time to time. Do these people here look unhappy to you?"

"No, they don't."

"It's because they're not pretending. Everyone outside the Sprawl pretends to be happy because they have no choice. Either that or succumb to whatever is eating you alive."

On the sidewalk in front of the house, a mother and her unleashed son, who looks about 6 years old, walk past the yard hand in hand.

"The best part is, they don't even know it. They're just going about their lives. They're probably decent people, or at least they think they are. I'm sure they feel for you in some abstract way, understand that times are tough if you're off the island, but it really doesn't interfere with their lives any. Food is still in their fridges.

Something's on TV. The sun comes up, goes down. Babies are born. So what do you think of the house?"

"Is this yours?"

"It could be ours. I'll be out back. Tell me how your talk with Finch goes. Don't fuck this up." She puts her gardening gloves back on and heads out the sliding glass door, shutting it behind her. On the way out, she says something to Finch, her hand on his shoulder. He nods and goes back to his pad.

Everything about this is wrong.

"Hey Dad, you wanna play games?" Axel says, holding out two action figures.

"Sure! That sounds good. How do you play?"

"Like this." He quickly explains a complicated mythology of the Murder Squad, 3 seasons of the cartoon, and assembles a defensive army for a frontal attack. I pick up one of the figures, a bug man with evil written all over him.

"Can I be this guy?" I hold out the figure to him.

"No," Axel says, shaking his head.

"Why not?"

"Because he's a bad guy. And you're not the bad guy." He doesn't look up at me, but stays fixated on arranging the figures. I'm struck by the sight, I've never seen him sitting still and admiring something. Normally, he's a wild animal, barely contained. His new, quiet demeanor strikes me as ominous, a little creepy.

"What's new in the world, champ?"

Axel thinks. "I like this place. The trees are pretty. Can we stay here?"

"Maybe."

I wonder if he knows they're textured plastic, manufactured down in the belly of the Machine. Their branches are molded to resemble an actual tree right down to the veins of the leaves.

"Did you want to go outside? It's nice out," I ask.

"It's always nice out, Dad."

"Go for a walk, then?"

"What for? Where're we going?"

"No place. Just to check out the neighborhood."

"I don't get it."

"You're not supposed to 'get it.'" I make little quote marks with my fingers. "Sometimes it's just nice to go for a walk."

"You never say stuff like that."

"Come on. Let's meet the neighbors. Have an adventure."

"You always told me to never talk to strangers. Why can't we stay here? I like that lady."

"I don't know, Axel, I don't even know where here is."

"Why not?"

"Because I just don't."

"Why not?! It doesn't make any sense, Dad!"

"Because I said so. Enough. How about we go for a walk, just you and me, buddy?"

He smirks at me. He weighs what I say, and after a short nod, gets up and heads to the front of the house. He's rustling through the closet, and I have no idea what he's looking for. I leave him be and he comes back to the living room. He's wearing his kid leash, a little embarrassed now. The people setting up the house must've anticipated this to help me out. Old habits die hard. Coyote takes my arm.

Axel looks years older and it's only been a week. Years older, like I'm watching him rapidly evolve into some other creature. I can feel his shame.

"You don't need to wear that anymore," I say, holding the limp strap in my hand.

"Why? Because you say so?"

1 point to Team Axel. "Do you want to wear it?"

"No."

"Why not?"

"Because it makes me feel stupid. Like a baby."

"And it didn't before?"

"I don't know. I feel different. They gave me a shot or something."

"A shot. Did it hurt? You're pretty brave to get a shot."

"No, I think I was asleep. I just feel different. Like things are clearer. I dunno."

Simon agrees the three of us can go for a walk around the block. Simon agrees, but we have to take the Security officer with us. I take a second to sponge clean myself, comb my hair. There's a fresh shirt that almost fits me in one of the closets.

~~~~

The houses are all quiet outside, and the street is, for all appearances, abandoned. As if everyone was simultaneously
~~~~

abducted. Here the houses feel like they've been assembled by robots and left as a warning.

Two doors down, a man a little older than me, stands in his front yard, staring intensely at a notepad, pressing a button every second or so. He's dressed in a fresh pair of slacks, a clean polo shirt, and a new watch. As we pass, I give him a small wave. He looks up, smiles politely, then dips back down. His head immediately comes back up when he recognizes me somehow.

"Did you three just move into 3006?"

"Yeah."

"Newlyweds?"

"Yes," Coyote says.

"Congratulations!" he says. "What line of work are you in?"

"Finance," I say.

He goes back to his little pad. "Uh huh." One more click, and he puts it away, tucking it under his armpit. He approaches us, and sticks out his hand. I'm suddenly wary.

"Let me guess, first time in the neighborhood like this?"

"Uh, yeah." I shake his hand. My palm is a little sweaty, which he discreetly wipes off.

"Name's Alan Jefferton." He points behind him. "That's my place."

"Corwin Scaggs, and this is my son Axel."

"Nice to meet you, Axel."

"Hi," Axel whispers. He hangs back, as cautious as me.

"Who's your big friend back there?" The security officer is about 5 meters behind us, scanning the yards with his eyes.

"Uncle. He's shy," Coyote says.

Alan nods, understanding. "Where are you folks from?"

"Around," I spit out. I spoke before I could think of a lie.

Coyote rubs my shoulder, I try not to jerk away. "We hit it big in finance," she proudly says.

"Good for the both of you." He slaps me on the shoulder. "Welcome to the neighborhood!"

"Thanks. You married? Kids? Franchise?"

"I am. Little lady is off teaching something called 'yoga'. And, uh, we call them 'families' around here. Just a heads up."

I nod. "I'm still getting used to all the changes here."

"Yeah, like we don't have vending machines in our kitchens!" He laughs. Or guns. Or death just right around the corner.

The three of us continue on our walk.

"Engaged? You don't have a ring," I say. Two young girls, one around Axel's age, the other a teenager, help their mom unload paper bags of stuff from their car. I see food inside them.

"Only women ask to see the ring."

"What makes you think I want to get married to you?"

"Is she going to be my new mommy?" Axel says. I'm still getting used to him talking so much.

I say no, Coyote says yes. We walk home in silence.

A proud father washes a car with his son, also around 10, laughing and spraying him with the hose. Axel waves, the boy waves back. An old couple, married for decades, floats in neon inner tubes in a crystal-clear pool, staring at the sky through dark sunglasses. They tell jokes only they know the punchlines too.

This feels like another planet.

The terror of everyday life, the life I had, the one I carry with me like an anchor, is so far away. No one is staring mindlessly at the ground, muttering to themselves. There's no slow death in the same room as you. Ghosts follow close behind, in my shadow, stepping where I step.

~~~~

Sitting at a backyard picnic table, Simon is tapping away on his tablet with a new vigor.

"Corwin, I'm sorry if we got off on the wrong foot. This is a very delicate situation, and we're just trying to have everybody come out a winner."

I start laughing and I don't know why.

"We're thinking that since you'll be a brand name now, that you'd be happier with no attachments. Axel would be a great match with a speculative commodities broker as a new franchisee. Axel's disinterest in everyday life would suit a career person's needs very well. Very pliable. Also, physically he's not very aggressive. That makes the new franchisee... more comfortable. Listen, we've been going about this completely backwards. It's like you won the Lottery here. This is the Dream. And it's yours. I'm here to deliver a full franchise employment contract to you and your biological son, eradicating any past indiscretions. This will provide you and your son, and your former franchise partner and franchisee if you wish, a new life in an explosive market."

"What's the job?"
~~~~

"Special Financial Advisor," he says the words like a holy mantra, as if they contained magic, power. He waves his hand, like it's put up in lights. "Pretty fancy, huh? All you have to do is sign your thumbprint at the bottom of the contract here, and you get a new life. And a shower, you could certainly use one."

"Do I have a choice?"

He shakes his head incredulously. "Of course?! Why would we ever make you do something you didn't want to do?!"

"I got tasered twice." I gesture to the Security officer, whose name I still don't know.

"Like I said, we got off on the wrong foot. I'm sorry we had to give you the hard sell. We'll get you some sort of massage chair or something."

He didn't answer my question.

"Axel stays with me. No negotiation." My left arm is starting to feel numb.

"No problem!" Simon's face scrunches up like a fist. He smiles. "Sounds good. If it's not too much trouble, if you could provide me with a list of all your 'professional references', we could get you set up almost immediately."

"What do you mean, professional references?"

"Folks you've worked with in the past." His meaning is clear. "We'll need all of them, and once we contact them and get some feedback, you'll be all good. If you refuse this offer, eventually we'll locate and contact your references, and... you know. But if you give us that list now, they'll be given brand new opportunities in an exciting fast-paced environment. And you can stay here. In this house. Safe."

He means the people that helped me. The people from Zero. If I give them up now, they'll be sent down into the Machine, to Bargainville. If I don't, they're dead. I see their faces. Angela's laugh, Draco and Cyrill bickering about a TV show they like, Hart showing me the stump of his arm.

Simon waits patiently. The sun flashes off the glossy surface of the tablet.

The air suddenly feels close and tight. The moment stretches out in front of me like a silver, infinite ocean. I'm staring into a series of mirrors, reflected a thousand times back in on itself. I think of Axel, Dad, Jerry, Raylene and the wind simply drains out of me. There were so many bodies in that video. The enormity of this bears down and crushes me.

I can't breathe.

"Take your time," Finch says in his paternal, sing-songy voice.

I feel faint, stars in my eyes, and I push back from the table, trying to stand. I fail and my limp body flop-sweats on the floor, damp and cold. That dropping, sick feeling you get from falling from a great height. Nothing left to do but land. I puke a thin white stream of bile.

I just can't do this anymore.

I just can't. Axel knocks on the back door glass, waving at me. His eyes are dark. Dad's hand reaches out of the dumpster they piled him into, into a single shaft of sunlight, dust floating in the air. Jerry's head explodes in slow motion, the red mist coating a powdered donut in the break room. All of their faces, all of their voices growing louder in my mind, roaring in violent smoke. Fog envelops me. I'm lost.

"Stop," I whisper.

"This is a once-in-a-lifetime offer. Your popularity and brand appeal give you certain privileges right now, but honestly, that can fade fast. You should act quickly and decisively."

The tablet slides into my view. Coyote clips a flower and looks at it with love.

"Make a smart choice, Corwin. Be a winner." he says.

I smash my thumb to the tablet. A green light and a happy face blips on and off. I start talking, giving names, addresses, locations of our blackbox servers, everything. Even all the information on the Dump, how we set it up, how we gathered information. I'm shedding a shadow talking about it so openly; like my skin is pink and new, fresh out of the womb. Raw and screaming. I'm just so tired, so exhausted and depleted. There's nothing left. I am a dead channel tuned to nothing.

19 ~ sprawl

Artificial trees sway, powered by motors and animatronic branches. The air smells faintly of citrus. Aliens walk among us, dressed in bizarre clothing most likely the result of a designer's bet for the most ridiculous. Everyone looks like they're posing for a magazine cover, including Simon, who seems always aware of being scrutinized.

On the outside, I'm peaceful, sipping my drink, chatting with Simon about the training process. Inside, needles and sharp broken glass.

"First thing we're going to have to do is get you cleaned up. I don't know if you can smell yourself, but it's not terribly appealing. Our first stop: get you hosed down, shaved, and then some new clothes. Should take most of the day."

I realize I'm a prisoner of war, a trophy for them. Look, everyone, a previously faulty product, recalled to the factory, now being retrofitted with all the latest and greatest.

At the spa, several Sprawlers give me disgusted looks. I haven't slept in I don't know how long, unshaved, and there's a dribble of puke on my shirt. I smell like a toilet. I don't have shoes anymore and I hobble up the curb.

The sterile chrome and brushed metal make it look more like a morgue or an abattoir. I'm ushered in and carved up. The meat needs to be prepared first. Four technicians, clothed in yellow plastic suits surround me and start talking to each other, describing my weight and height, using code to name my many future improvements. Meat inspectors. I'm skinned as they remove my clothes with scissors, leaving me buck naked in the cold air. I'm given a paper gown.

My old clothes go into an incinerator chute.

The chefs pump about a hundred gallons of warm, deodorized saltwater into a tub and force me to soak in it up to my neck. Soften the meat. Tenderize it. The water turns a dull yellow color almost immediately as I step in, then after about ten minutes, the shade of bottled iced tea. The water is comfortably warm, like a loving hug all over my body. When I step out of the tub, there's a sharp grime line around my head, like a mannequin dummy with the wrong model attached.

The chefs move me to a barber's chair and strip my face clean, scrubbing harshly like a caked stovetop. I have to slap one of the more zealous hands away, which surprised the group. They're not used to the meat ordering the cook around.

"Sorry," I whisper.

The sink has a brownish-rusty ring around the drain when done. My beard is clipped, then trimmed shorter, and finally shaved. My beard was growing into something unshapely, my chin is the texture of an alien planet. Getting that meat ready to be seasoned, seared, cooked, and eaten.

Colored contacts are the first touchup for my eyes, then a slight corneal touchups with some shine. My dull brown eyes are not good enough. "Too generic" they say. I get a brighter brown, almost amber, since my originals don't "pop" enough. They look larger than normal. Big eyes mean sympathy, kindness, altruism even if I'm staring at a bus explosion with mild indifference. Wiping off the blood, the residue of that previous life.

"The eyes are everything."

My eyebrows are tweezed. My teeth are whitened so they're almost blinded. One, growing a nasty cavity, is yanked and replaced with a plastic replica. I tongue the slick texture.

I become an ad for myself. A pampered doll dressed in a grown-up's suit, a flesh-colored disguise made of putty. I look into the mirror and see a stranger.

~~~~

A lot of people think they know what the Sprawl is. They like to dream about it, fantasize about what could be. Driving their cars, eating their food, watching TV, minds wander to the shapeless half-truth of glistening pools, leisurely afternoons, and golden moments everywhere. The Dream, the concept of it, so permeates the Dome, it's like the weather, but just as human-made as the breeze I feel on this porch right now, the electronic sun projected from the inside of the Dome. Being here means that I crossed over
~~~~

the invisible threshold into a new world, that secret universe I knew existed but was always unable to touch or taste.

The actual location of the Sprawl is crucial to its success: the center of the Dome. All roads lead to the Sprawl. All eyes turned towards it. The digital sun crosses over its exact equinox, slicing the island in two. The idea that it's an island is also integral: surrounded on all sides by the masses wanting in, a citadel of money and pleasure and comfort. Almost unreachable except by a few controlled bridges crossed only by the fortunate few.

Size-wise, it's only a tiny fraction of the area and population of the Dome. Since they don't publish or brag about numbers, leaked estimates place the population at a paltry two hundred and fifty thousand. Structurally, the island is a mixture of low density, single family housing with a smattering of office buildings and upscale businesses.

The houses, squatting on the ground level, are expansive mansions that, in other sectors, would house 10-15 families per unit. The homes are brick textured, with angular roofs, with big windows like friendly eyes. They have enormous front yards with sculpted topiaries and colorful flowers. Roads lazily slope and loop through neighborhoods. Their asphalt is smooth black or beige concrete, free of trash and graffiti. A fresh, clean scent is everywhere. Life here is calm, slow-paced, with the most dramatic interruption is a child wandering into your yard, politely reminded to respect the borders of our lives. Adult pedestrians, smiling at their fortune, wander out to chat with their neighbors, pick up deliveries, or stand in their yards and marvel at their good fortune. They are happy because they know they are the lucky ones, the apex predators in a violent jungle, and they emerged bloody and beaten, but victorious. That, or they never had to fight at all; you're either born here or get to the Sprawl on a sacrificial pile of bodies.

Beauty, wealth, freedom, and immortality await you. Just over there. Look, you can see it now, glowing on the horizon. The pretty ones come from there. We all want to be like them, resemble their graceful movements, their confidence, their power over the world. Our own pitiful inadequacy reflected against their shine. Glamour is an elusive thing, hard to describe the individual features, but the total package is easy to admire. Hold us up, the golden gods say, hold us up for everyone to see.

When you're young, you're presented with a pantheon of saints of the Sprawl: the holy prophets who came back to tell us of its glories. Those who crossed over into the light, and came back transformed. In proper dramatic fashion, of course. Remember, you're selling an idea, a concept of a place. But not the real place itself. That's almost always a letdown, an anti-climax. Showmanship is everything. The Sprawl is a product, just like a copier or a dildo, it's about what the Sprawl promises. The Sprawl is a Dome within a Dome, a hermetically sealed world removed from the horrors of suffering, poverty, debt, and cruelty.

What's not said is that despite all the glamor, the power, the prettiness, and cleanliness of this place, the Sprawl can never really deliver what it promises. When you're a child, a teenager, an adult, the promise is that if you work hard, play by the rules, stay clean, and go with the program, that you can be here by the sheer will of your being.

Behold the power of the Dream. Voices on screens tell you to give up a part of yourself in service to them. All that we ask is your silent consent and obedience. All that we ask is blood sacrifice. And maybe, someone will show up with a contract, a new life on a platter for you. All for you, the sole inheritor of the earth. The favored son. The golden child. The chosen one.

I think about old faces, my weakness, betrayals. All my rationalizing and intellectualizing of what this place is fades as is replaced by my memories of them. I can say "it was for my son" and live with my grief. I can lie with the best of them. I have arrived.

~~~~

The fridge simply keeps food you've already bought cold, there's no charge to open and browse. I marvel at it. Ice cubes, edible ice cubes are made for free in a compartment in the freezer section. I turn on the tap and watch it run for several minutes, curious to see how much it costs. No automatic charge, it seems. The sink and fridge lack any sort of emotive advertising, no waiting periods before I can take something out. Coyote tells me that we have to go to a place called a "grocery store" and buy the food we want, and we can store it in the fridge. Take it out whenever you want and eat as much as you want.

The house doesn't come with a Number or the terror that proceeds it. My old house had the familiar readout device that tallied all your hourly expenditures, and if you looked hard enough, you could see your future. The axe hanging over your
~~~~

neck, ready to lop off everything you cared about in the white-hot flick of its blade. Not here. That sense of sheer relief is addictive.

My new car is parked in the garage. I run my hand slowly down its curved hip.

I change channels on the TV. Slowly, one by one, I click through them.

The blinds go up and down. Doorknobs open and close doors.

I check in every room in the house. Not one microbox on any of the appliances. Not one.

After a quick piss, I have to fight the urge to not flush. It doesn't cost anything anymore. I flush once, twice, and then a third.

The carpet is smooth and soft, and feels amazing against my face. I lay on my stomach, with my hands outstretched. Axel drives a little toy car over my back, making little vroom vroom noises and then the car pitches into the abyss, exploding.

~~~~

Tonight, the first night in the house, Coyote sleeps next to me in a light blue nightie. Axel is asleep in his new room, in a race car bed. She wanted to "make love", but I politely refused, citing the excitement of the day.

At some point I fall asleep. I dream.

It's dark now, darker than before, dark as it gets. I'm in a tunnel of some kind, following a strange sound. There are thick rubber cables running through the middle of the tube, winding and twisting around each other, disappearing into the walls. The
~~~~

tunnel curves, the soft glow of television sets lighting the way. The TV's populate the walls like luminescent flowers, all showing snow.

They look like eyes. Blinking.

I come to a pile of broken gadgets, like phones and laptops and tablets piled almost two meters high. There's children's toys strewn as well. The bones and skulls of modern technology, piled like a mass grave. I have seen a mass grave for real. I can see light and I shove a dozen vending microwaves and 3D printers forward, and they tumble out like a chunk of cholesterol. I see half-people, living bodies, screens for faces drawn with ghoulish blue scanlines. A gigantic mouth, a nostril, a bloodshot eye.

The entire house is built with love, security, strength. A fresh coat of paint over the rust, bloody stains, broken teeth. Outside, in the dusk, a dog howls at the moon. Space is infinite. No, everything is okay. We can do this. We can make it through this. This is not happening. I shrink the world back down to the size of the dining room, where we're having spaghetti. Coyote bought groceries today before picking Axel up from school, where they learn about the world. And we eat. Piles and piles of it, bowl after bowl of white, salty pasta slathered in sauce. We fill our guts with it. Stuff our faces, as if eating more makes us more normal. More invisible. More part of the backdrop, a tableau of people all doing exactly what they're supposed to. Coyote's changed. Her jet-black hair is chestnut brown. We are the Family. This is LIFE and we are the stars of the world. People will model their entire existence of the smallest choices we make. What shirts we wear. What words we choose. Gestures, body language. How long we sleep. What soap we use to clean our genitals (tastefully blurred out). Every action and conversation we have will be scrutinized, examined, ripped apart and reassembled.

Dad is here, alive, decades younger, slurping spaghetti strands, the ones hanging from his mouth. They're plastic tubes leading to his nose and mouth. Giant metallic machines pump air in him, circulate his blood, void his bowels, transport mashed food into his intestines, rotate him to prevent bedsores, spray sanitary mist over his skin to clean him. Keeping him perfectly alive, in stasis.

Axel has found the howling dog. He beats it with a pipe.

Dad is dying. His tubes grow like vines and consume the perfect room with their plastic. Miles of tubes and fluids pumping and we raft down it like an amusement park ride. White walls grow into cubes, and we're inside of them now. Robotic men wheel decaying bodies from room to room. Dad is strapped to a bed, slowly dying again. He admires my vigil with huge, wet eyes. He's TV dying, that special type of death that makes the person more glamorous. He's dying of some vaguely defined illness, a suitably dramatic death where you can have meaningful monologues and final conversations with key cast members. He doesn't shit his pants or ramble about stars.

Dad lifts his head, and in a mahogany baritone, says "Son, I just want you to know that I don't blame you for this. You did everything you could."

"I could have done more. I could've done more."

"Everyone's taking real good care of me. I just don't know how much time I have left. Just stay with me, okay? There's a chance. There's always a chance."

"I love you, Dad."

"You're my son. That's all I need." He holds my hand in his, those rough, blue-collar hands, indicating he's a humble, yet proud man.

Dad says his final farewell, dies in my arms after providing me with a valuable life lesson, but falls away from my arms into an abyss like a fading memory. His body grows small as he sinks into a metal vat. There were thousands of them, each with a human being slowly being broken down into base chemicals.

I walk down the endless aisles of green-colored tanks, pipes and tubes flowing into the ceiling, pumping away little bits of my Dad to become industrial solvent, laundry detergent, pod paint, drain cleaner, vitamin pills, and a galaxy of other helpful household products. I go berserk.

Jerry appears, applauding softly, the gunshot still oozing from his head and lung in thick, floaty trails, like he's underwater. His eyes are black from the head-wound, his skin a pallid cold color. He laughs and cheers as I destroy computers. Faces and smiles. He pumps his fist in the air as I sever pipes and open valves, dumping the half-decayed bodies onto the pristine, private beaches littered with overpaid sunbathers. An avalanche of death to brighten their day. The sun doesn't tan, but beachgoers spray sticky chemicals on their skin. Chemicals possibly made of people. I make the sun bleed red. I stain the beaches black. I hate everything. I love you all.

Rewind. Change the channel. Dad lies in his bed in a grey, featureless room. Piles of boxes stretch to the ceiling. They're filled with old, broken things. The whole room sways back and forth, like a drunkard. The house again, dark and cold, filled with ghosts and naked wind. Plastic tarps cover the furniture like murder victims. A chandelier swings slightly back and forth like a clock's tongue.

Outside, a shambling pile of metal and concrete, fashioned into the shape of a man, carries the house on its back. Neon signs tempt with endless sales, fine print, curved breasts, broken promises, and hot deals that won't last long. We're on the back of the Dome, and it's carrying us over the water to an island in the middle of a blue, undrinkable lake.

Dad reaches his hand up to the light. The world is a dead, cold place, filled with the trash of people's lives, their undead bodies lying in the piles waiting to be pushed into the metal trench. I'm laying with them now, too exhausted to move, too tired to keep trying. It's so much better to just lay here until I rot, and am swept up by janitors, and sealed in a convenient, recyclable box for processing.

I take hot showers, buy some new, fresh clothes, splash on some cologne. The new me: reborn, remade. Back to work. My arms and legs move the way they're supposed to. My stomach digests breakfasts. I defecate on a predictable schedule. I am concerned about how others view me. I have sex appeal. I brand appropriately. I am a mover and a shaker. I call Coyote and offer a mutually beneficial agreement that suits our dual lives of excitement and adventure. Everything has lens flares to make the image pop. I pose like I know everyone's watching. Coyote and I accept the inevitability of our mutually beneficial disgust.

Eventually I will die in a hospital while Coyote flips through a magazine. Axel is too successful to attend. Axel's face is blurry, indistinct, like someone is smearing his colors around. The boys will be notified by text message. After processing, my body is recycled. Parts of me become industrial polisher for fake brass table lamps. I am one with the universe now. I am the Dome. I am sold on the shelves of Ultimart everywhere and regarded as a quality product. I have a mascot, an ear of corn waving his hand to magically clean a kitchen.

My face slowly fades away. My suit is very sharp, neatly pressed, jet black like a dead pixel. Ruined drapes and ragged carpet stained with blood and garbage. It's been abandoned for a long time and I'm just realizing it. The television sun, bright as a knife, stops on me and me alone. I put my hand up to block it, and it burns me away.

~~~~

Morning comes and I carefully wake up Axel with a small gas injection on the back of his neck. We've been at the new house for several weeks, but the dream won't go away. I keep having reruns, reposts of the same bizarre game show. I don't know how to make it stop.

Axel slowly rises from his deep sleep, different than from before. His eyes don't shoot open, they're not bloodshot and raw. His new behaviorals keep him more level and stable. Coyote is making breakfast in the kitchen and the hot, spicy odor of sausage and sizzling bacon fills the first floor of our house. It's artificially flavored with a slightly gummy texture. Our new situation doesn't allow for the luxury of fully grown specialized meats. Normally, you see a person smiling while they cook, yet Coyote scowls, her
~~~~

face hard like concrete. Her metal whisk violently slaps against the side of a shiny bowl.

I sit at the breakfast bar with Axel. Coyote serves us both a healthy, balanced breakfast on white plates.

20 ~ *the machine*

I can't sleep so I walk through the quiet rooms, marveling at the lack of ads and neon screens, and just enjoy the silence. I think about Bertrand, he was ahead of the curve, driven to a breaking point that seemed inevitable to him. The weight of the Machine bore down and eventually crushed him to fine powder. We are part of the same production cycle, him and I, with me being the raw materials, filled with potential and a glimmering future. Bertrand couldn't hack it. He failed Quality Assurance like a malfunctioning toaster, now a cautionary tale for new initiates like myself. It is effective. I am never going back. I gave up too much.

I watch TV to not think.

The TV doesn't have as many channels as my old one, but that's fine. Everything's fine. I can live with that. My time is no longer a precious resource, and I can spend it as I wish. It's the financial news, and a plain-faced but cheerful anchor recites the daily mantra.

"A startling report of growing subprime mortgage defaults emerged from official sources. UCorp is advising additional credit lines for cash-strapped families to avoid default."

Cut to commercial.

"Get yourself a Doober, man. You deserve it!"

Back to news.

"Today, Maintenance welcomed over one thousand new applicants for its Adventure Pack employment opportunities today. Engineers set them to work on the new air circulation turbines, dubbed Silver Flow, which previously has had a high turnover rate. Average contract termination is still holding steady at thirteen percent in the first fiscal year."

I click to another channel.

"I don't know what to do about Bobby. I'm in love with Steve. They both love me. It's so confusing!"

Back to news.

"UCorp is lowering security interest rates to an all-time low of point five percent in an attempt to stem the rising flood of securities runoff in later day markets. One trader reluctantly described the situation as an 'market implosion'."

Another channel, another crisis.

"We need to stop these socialists, Captain. At any cost. They're bleeding the system dry. We need that nuclear launch platform online NOW."

News again. Another anchor, more cheerful than the last. It's financial pornography, titillating and raw.

"CEO Victor Winn spoke today before the Board in order to calm fears of a junk securities scare, calling it 'alarmist bullshit' to assert that previously triple-A rated securities, which are typically as safe an investment as Ultimart stock, were anything but secure. He then went on to describe how much he likes a particular game show and how if we all just won money, we'd be fine."

The broadcast cuts to a previously recorded video of Winn, who appears in front of a blue background, proudly showing the UCorp logo. A bank of photographers flash and click at him, like a pack of wild ferals hungry for his words. I can't see the faces of the crowd, but I know they are practically in a frenzy. I know I am.

He smiles, holds his hand up until the ravenous murmur subsides.

"Can we turn the teleprompter off? I don't need it. Just get rid of it. Get rid of it."

A smart move. Look casual, off the cuff. Speak from your heart.

"Listen folks. A lot of bad news lately. Lots of problems. Bad news is never good! But hear it from me. I can assure you this is just a few bad deals from people too stupid to know the difference. Hey, we're okay. We're doing fine. We're optimists. We're winners. The future is always brighter, we are always growing stronger, and I CHOOSE for that future to happen. Let's make this place the best it can be. All I ask is that we all support our brands, support your company, and enjoy what you've earned. That present to yourself that you've always wanted? Buy it. You've earned it. That new house? You've earned it. Heck, even buy a Doober." The crowd laughs in anticipation. "You've earned it. The point is this small downtick that we're seeing is just another opportunity for smart people with big brains to step up and show us why my faith in them is earned. Don't be a loser. Win big or go home. Thank you."

Back to the anchor. "Today, the Number took a sharp decline to end at just under thirty eight thousand. Now, nude sports with Makayla Winters."

I turn off the TV and go out to our porch. Even the idea of having a porch to myself startles me. We don't rent, we own. This is our house. Home. Even if it's lame and plastic, at least it's ours. All that shit on the TV is a million miles away. I haven't looked at my phone in days. I start work at this new job the day after tomorrow.

Maybe this is all it's cracked up to be. Maybe it's worth it. Maybe not, I don't know, but I'm going to enjoy it while it lasts. Even if I end up like Dad or a destroyed wreck like Bertrand or Herb Allen, I don't care. I don't. I'm tired of caring. I did all my caring once. I'm done.

~~~~

Inside our garage is a new car. A Z-Series Grandia, fireball red with a pearlescent cherry finish. It seats four, and I have suspicions Coyote wants a baby with me. I'm certain of that. She wants one, like it's some way to fully own a part of me, and that conversation is about to crest like a wave.

She handles like a powerful speedboat, slicing through the curving rivers of Greenwich Park and Outridge Hollow. A blue car follows us the entire way, which I think is from the Company watching over its investment. I don't know. Making sure we're not
~~~~

getting into trouble anymore? What the hell would I do? I got all I wanted.

I allow myself to miss Raylene for a moment. Just briefly enough to be a flash of pain.

After the details of my release went public, I was briefly but intensely underneath a white-hot media spotlight. Several large interviews. A film adaptation. Even a show starring us, which Coyote and I severely rejected. The smarmy VP who showed up at our door and suggested it ended up with a burst eardrum as his answer. I think about carrying a gun all the time now, a small robbery piece tucked underneath my armpit. Coyote absolutely refuses to let me get one. Eventually, like all outrage, the attention surrounding us evaporated and we became background in our neighborhood.

~~~~

My new job is "Special Economic Advisor" for Ultimart. I'm not sure exactly what it entails but it involves me sitting in on a lot of meetings and providing vague but optimistic sounding statements. My first day is a blur of forms and phone calls and handshakes. The office is stark white and blue, large rectangular windows, jet black furniture, no sounds or smells, no music, no leaderboards. No one seems to do much of anything except chat with each other, create presentations, strategize about priorities. I simply float along, like a dust mote.

There's a "welcome to the team" party tonight specifically for me. It's a family thing, so the three of us attend. Coyote wears a
~~~~

nice (but not too nice) cocktail dress and I let Axel pick whatever he wanted. He wears a shiny silver shirt, basketball shorts, and flip flops. I awkwardly sip my drink and shake whoever's hand is extended, forgetting names instantly. Coyote pops a meat-flavored appetizer into my mouth.

"Stop fidgeting, you look like you just got cancer," she says, trying to smile.

"I'm not doing well."

She stops and turns to me and the noise of the party slips away.

"If you mess this up for me... I will end you. I will burn you down." Her tone is bone-dry, hard as steel. She looks at me with eyes like gun barrels. "Good good good. Good stuff. Come with me, I want to introduce you to someone!"

She grabs my shoulder like a proud father, gently pushes me towards another room. It's a small alcove, an atrium with a reflecting pool in the center. Against the railing, there's a hunch of a man staring at the floor. Next to him, his small boy, around Axel's age, stares at a phone, robotically tapping. The boy gets no enjoyment out of what he's looking at: an angry, lonely child absorbing information from a plastic screen. The man, whom I assume is his dad, has the same characteristic slump mine did, like the weight of everything slowly squeezing him flat.

"This is Bertrand Strauss. He's a former associate of ours. We invited him here to celebrate his retirement. I'll leave you two to get friendly. I'm so excited, Corwin!"

Coyote kisses me on the cheek and squeezes my bicep, vanishing. Something strikes me like an arrow in the heart. We uncovered a disgusting, awful, horrible secret about the Dome, and she realized the true ugliness about it: no one really cares. The most powerful secret the Dome could hide: the intentional and systematic destruction of lives and it barely mussed anyone's hair. It's invisible like the recycled oxygen. The lights are still on, food is still in vending machines. The comfortable sleep peacefully in the Sprawl, with me now to join them.

Bertrand sighs, rubs his forehead, but lights up when I outstretch my hand. He pumps the shake up and down. We get a trio of fresh drinks. Bertrand and I have Oak Barrel-style whiskey with blue ice. Tueford is having a Hazy Laser. He takes one sip, his face puckers, and he hands the drink back to Bertrand.

"There's no sugar in this."

"Oh, sorry. I'll get you a new one."

The kid rolls his eyes.

"Do you think he should be having one of these?" I say, motioning to the drink.

"I used to say no, but you know how kids are. If they're not happy, I'm not happy."

We wait for a moment. The music changes from a thumping techno beat to another thumping techno beat. I finally break the agonizing silence.

"So, um, retirement huh?"

"I was a Special Economic Advisor. For the company."

"Oh, that's what I'm doing."

He clears his throat.

The picture suddenly becomes a little clearer. "Am I your replacement? Is that what's happening?"

"Yes!" He exclaims this rather happily, like he's won the lottery.

"Okay. Is that a good thing to you?"

"Here's the thing: I like change. I like a new opportunity! It's fun! This is just another episode that's ending. It's not the end of the series, it's not syndication, but another adventure."

"Bert, where are you going to go?"

No answer. He smiles at no one.

"My wife said this job, this place was bad for us, for our son. You know she tried to buy his license? But if I'm sure of anything, he looks happy to me! Look!"

Tueford taps, his face lit up by the phone. Bertrand leans back on the railing, his arms locked tight, his face down on the ground. His face shifts from polite civility to pained grimace every few seconds.

"We'll be okay. We'll be fine. Just fine. Everything's going to be okay."

I nod, say nothing.

"But you know, you gotta be safe out there. Lotta crazies. Freeloaders, you know? I got a little something. From one of the vending machines. For protection. To keep us safe. From robbers and things like that. It's downstairs in my car."

I keep nodding, almost robotically. "Yeah, I know what you mean. There's some crazies out there." I drink.

"You want to see it?"

"No thank you." I play it nice and relaxed. "I was thinking. I don't need this job, Bert. I'm not really qualified for it. It's all yours. Keep it. I'll just get my son, who's here with my date, and you and... uh..." I blank on the kid's name. I snap my fingers.

"Tueford. Like the car."

"Little Tueford. You two can keep on going on and whatnot. Sounds good? No hard feelings?"

I don't see Security anywhere, but I feel the weight of my phone in my pocket.

"I appreciate that. I really do. You are a standup kind of guy. You know that?" He pokes my chest with his index finger. "A standup kind of guy. But this is your opportunity, and I wouldn't want to muck up your mojo. I have other... opportunities. Ways to make my mark. One day, you may even see me on the news with some big stuff happening. And today was the day that made that happen." He beams at me. "So no worries!"

"Dad, are you done?" Tueford yells from behind us.

"One second, champ!"

"For fuck's sake," Tueford mumbles.

"Kids. Can't live with 'em, can't kill 'em."

"No, you can't, Bert. You can't kill them. You definitely can't do that. That's wrong."

"Yeah yeah yeah yeah. Uh huh. Uh huh. Okay. Yup. Sure thing. Good luck to you, Corwin." He sticks his hand out and I shake it. He glares at me, but I maintain my default pasted happy face.

"You, too," I say.

"Good luck."

"Thanks, Bert. I appreciate it."

"Please, good luck. Good luck. Good. Luck." he says, a giant grin on his face. He's starting to cry.

"Thanks, Bert. I should get back." I have to wrestle my hand away.

I spin 180* on my heels and blaze a path directly for the exit. Bert starts laughing to himself, his son telling him to shut up, which only makes him laugh louder. I navigate through the crowd like a homing missile and find Coyote and Axel chatting with two ladies, both of which are painted blue. Axel is fascinated by them, and one of them lets him touch her arm.

"We need to leave right now. Laugh like I told you a joke," I whisper in Coyote's ear, and she lets out a vapid laugh. I grab Axel's shoulder.

"Hey buddy, I hate to break up you and your girlfriend here, but we gotta get going."

"Gross, Dad. She's not my girlfriend."

The blue lady waves goodbye to Axel, who returns with a sad shake of his hand. Her aqua-colored friend says something scandalous, and she playfully slaps her partner's arm. We go down to the ground floor parking garage in the stale dark. I say nothing on the ride. Axel snoozes in the back seat and Coyote chooses photos from the party to post. I keep watching the rear view mirror.

The car's battery is low on the way home, so we stop at a charging station. Coyote gets out and stands with me. Axel squishes his face against the window, smearing his open mouth along in giant arcs. Coyote ignores him and squeezes my arm, rubs my chest. She gives me a kiss on the cheek and Axel responds with a grossed out smirk on his face.

"What did you and Bertrand talk about?" she asks.

"I'm not sure, actually."

We drive home, I need a break so I set it to self-drive, and Axel plays a game on his phone, his mixture of joy and rage equally so. Coyote watches the world go bye, a little drunk, I think. Maybe she falls asleep or pretends to, I'm not sure. I watch Axel play his game, cheer his successes, revel in his victories, and comfort him when he loses, which to a boy, can be devastating. He can't beat a certain level and he shuts off the game in frustration.

"It's okay, buddy. You did your best."

"It's just a game, Dad. That party was fun. Did you see that weird hairdo on that guy?"

I have no idea what he's talking about, but I pretend to.

~~~~

I decide that our new family needs to engage in the most basic of rituals here, one we haven't done yet as a trio: shopping. Keep up appearances, figure out your next move, how things will land. I feel like a gambler watching a pair of dice land but not stopping at their destined result. I announce we're going shopping to the pair of them in the living room. Coyote nods in agreement. Axel jumps into the backseat, plugged into another game, Coyote is taking her time in the bathroom applying eyeliner. I politely shout that we're about ready to go and she appears in the hallway, purse draped over her shoulder, smiling. She's taking to this role rather well, maybe because, unlike me, she always saw herself here and was just waiting to arrive. I was a key to this door. She pats my chest with her hand as she passes and gets in the car. I run my hand along the sensual curve of the hood, drinking in the newness of this model. A V-Volt
~~~~

electric engine hides underneath the surface, pulsating energy that makes me ache. I swallow the dryness in my mouth.

I stop the car outside of the Ultimart parking garage, and a helpful valet gives me a ticket and extends his hand. Coyote takes my keys and hands them to the man, who drives off in our car to park it in the underground garage. There's no place for something so ugly and utilitarian above ground. This space is meant for the most realistic trees, grass, sounds. The air is clean as the three of us approach the Ultimart. Stores outside the Sprawl are crowded, loud concrete tombs, but that also has no place here. The Sprawl Ultimart is more like a neighborhood market, made of pleasant brick and cloth awnings, with carts filled with fresh 3D printed fruit arranged in small pyramids. I pick up a pomegranate, squeeze the bumpy surface, and smell the fragrant skin.

We don't have to pass through any metal detectors or eyescans. No fingerprinted entry. There's not even a queue for Security of any kind. Shockingly, there's no admission charge. You just walk in and shop, as if this was always the way it was supposed to be. I expect blaring music and subharmonic neutralizers inside. Instead, we are greeted by soft, almost inaudible, classical; tinkling piano and warbling strings melt into each other. You can't tell which composer it is, and you're not supposed to. It's meant to fill the silence with a warm background radiation. The interior is inviting, with products carefully arranged in attractive tableaus and dioramas as if to say "This is how all things are now." If we are being monitored other than the store security cameras, I can't tell. I think the man in the blue jacket is following us. I can tell he has electronics in him. The white fog creeps in my vision, but recedes.

These shoppers at Ultimart look fit and healthy, far from the mole people in stained shirts and ripped jeans clawing at each other for discount television sets. No faded tattoos stretched across their buttocks. No seedy, skinny tweakers clawing at their skin. All the deranged alcoholics must be in their shacks, being done stumbling through the aisles muttering about how z-rays are shrinking their penises.

Axel asks if he can go to the toy section, and I oblige him. "Just to look," he says. I know that trick, I pulled it on my own dad.

"We'll meet you there in about a half hour," Coyote says, tapping her smartwatch.

"Okay, Mom," he says, dashing away.

Mom. The word hits me like a speeding train and my chest collapses in on itself. Molten mercury pours into my veins. Names and faces and moments rush out at me from the dark and I have to violently shove down the feeling, lock it away tightly before it explodes. There's no death allowed here, no regret permitted. It's too colorful and bright to think of these things now. Coyote sees my distress and touches my hand with hers.

"Did you hear that?" she says, touched.

"Yeah, I did. Did you tell him to call you that?"

"You know what we should do? Let's redecorate the bathroom. It's so dated."

We pick out some new hand towels, a bath mat, a silverware organizer, some measuring cups, a new bathrobe for me, some house shoes for Coyote, and flameless candles.

"Have you thought about brand names for us yet?" she says, turning a coffee mug in her hand.

"Honestly, no."

"Hmm. I mean, it's a big opportunity, and I know why we turned down all those offers. Because they weren't us. I mean, I have my own brand name, but I could go for a change. You should, too."

"We can talk about it later."

"We just did." She places the mug back on the shelf.

We walk over to the toy section and Axel is looking at some action figures. He begs and pleads with us, and when I initially refuse him, his face turns a bright red and he starts to violently shake. I acquiesce and let him pick one out. Coyote says nothing.

Out of the corner of my eye, I see a green and orange can. Joob, marked down from $29.99 to $9.99 on clearance. Just last year, these ran up to the thousands for the red/blue kind online. Now they are forgotten, passed over, desperately wanting to be chosen. Like orphans holding out their dirty palms to passersby. I pick up the can like a holy artifact.

Down in the bowels of the Machine, the vast automated manufacturing facilities receive an electronic schematic for a jiggly gel toy product. Maybe this comes from some overly complicated marketing algorithm. Maybe the Machine just makes it in a gush of creative inspiration. Like a frustrated god, it simply needs to create. The valves and pumps shudder to life, like the stiff limbs of a sleeping giant. Complex chemical compounds are synthesized and recombined from raw materials, deep down in boiling metal vats in the dark, probably containing the atomized flesh of those deemed not valuable enough. Chemical reclamation, like alchemy, makes wonders from the ordinary. Something is changed miraculously into another, the alkahest as the blood of the engines. The heart of the Machine is the crucible of creation, the beginning of the universe. All things flow from it.

The lonely grey blobs are birthed from the womb of the chemical vat, squirted onto a conveyor belt, carefully molded by mechanical hands, then injected with a fluorescent orange dye. They are given form and purpose. Soon after, the blobs are lovingly birthed into the trademark orange cans, each stamped with their own serial number. They are given names. They are loved. The lids are attached, sealing their sacred freshness in. Colorful stickers are applied, images of safe round shapes and letters, and in this ritual, they are made whole. Their logo, their sacred namesake, is laser-etched into the lids. Now they are Joob. Now they have meaning. The proud parent then gently packs its young into cardboard boxes, seals their fate, and sends them out into the world. They make the ascent through the freight elevators, automated distribution sees their value, sorts them according to their role. The can meant for me travels on computer-driven trucks, unloaded and displayed by robot stockers. All without a single pair of human hands intervening. That is, until I pick the can from the shelf. Most likely the first time it has felt the touch of a person. Until I choose to buy it and give it a home again. I have fulfilled its purpose: to be used.

Cash is exchanged, or a card is swiped. The object is mine. I own it. I could put it on my mantle or destroy it with a shotgun. It belongs to me and all it represents does as well. The object complements my life, shows my personal choices, advertises to the world what kind of man and father I am. I have no idea who that is.

Millions suffer outside, being smashed down under boot heels and endless debt in the crushing cycle, all the meanwhile the EVM coldly deciding their fate, and I save pennies on toilet paper. Their agony is far away across the water, unwelcome as death here. I also put the toilet paper in our shopping cart.

~~~~

The car drives down the quiet streets. Our shopping in the trunk. The sun shining. The radio playing soft pop music. Coyote on her phone, tapping away. Every now and then, she'll giggle and show me a funny post. I repeat my phrases:

"Oh, that's nuts."

"No way."

"I don't believe that."

"That's pretty good."

And so forth. It feels good, so good it's hard to put into words I could speak out loud. I can breathe and an enormous weight has evaporated. We're moving in slow motion and I can see every second as it happens in its totality. Coyote's peach body wash, her hair lit against the window. Her white teeth smiling, like this was how it always was and always will be. Nowhere to run because you don't have to anymore.

Axel starts a new Training class tomorrow and he'll be put into a special class for new transfers from outside the Sprawl to help him adjust better. I can already tell he's different: more controlled and stable. He sleeps better, no bad dreams or night terrors. I would prefer not to dream anymore.
~~~~

Our car suddenly skids to a stop, jolting forward. We're only half pulled into the driveway and the car is warning us that there's an obstruction ahead. There most certainly is.

A filthy figure stands in our driveway, naked and covered in a sticky black goo. His hair is matted down to his scalp and two tiny white eyes pierce outwards. Arms flat at his sides, stiff as a plank, he's swaying from side to side. It's the middle of the day, and most are either inside watching TV or doing whatever people here do on lazy afternoons. I immediately recognize the stooped shoulders and the messed combover. It's Bertrand Strauss.

"Is that...? That is. What the-?"

"Stay in the car," I mutter.

"I'm calling Security," Coyote says and dials.

"Axel, stay in the car," I repeat. Axel hasn't even looked up from the tablet. Coyote is speaking with Security, but I don't hear her words, just see her mouth moving up and down. I look forward to see Bertrand is gone.

A black hand swats against the window, his palmprint smearing down the glass. Coyote is screaming silent words, Axel not even paying attention still. The radio has changed songs to another chirpy electronic beat.

The feral creature who used to be Bertrand Strauss gnashes his perfectly clean teeth at me like a caged animal eager to devour his captor. Black droplets and spit fleck the window. He stops. My eyes are pinpricks. There's a fizzing sound. Suddenly, a gush of white and orange light, burning heat even through the window, screams, and flames burst against the side of the car. I see his white capped teeth in the orange and red slashes, his tiny pink tongue flailing as he howls like a beast, engulfed in his fire.

Security responds to the scene and subdue Bertrand by shocking his blackened corpse on the ground. He left no note. They cart the remaining chunk of him away and we file a report with the friendly and unassuming Security Officer, a baby-faced young man with perfectly combed hair. He attentively takes down our information and what happened, providing us with a heavily discounted invoice since it was our first call.

~~~~

We have to sedate Axel. Coyote seems shaken but contained. The day passes wordlessly as we fill out forms and avoid windows for gawkers. Our phones ring constantly.

The night is cool and calm. Coyote joins me outside on the porch and hands me a drink. I'm still getting used to being on the ground floor of a building, having a yard and a patio to relax on. Coyote's wearing a light blue nightgown with a matching housecoat, which gives her a modest sensuality that's very much unlike her. I take the perspiring glass from her and she sits with me, gives me a tiny kiss on the cheek. My arm is pulled over her shoulder as she rests against me. Her skin smells like vanilla and lavender, most likely a skin cream she will be applying before bedtime from now on. I sip cold lemonade, which tastes mostly sour, but with a pinch of sweetness. We enjoy the night together, the first of many quiet nights I hope. I wonder where little Tueford is.
~~~~

"Do you like that Ultimart? We can always go somewhere else. I hate ordering online, I like to see something before I own it," she asks, taking a drink herself. "Mmm. Good lemonade."

"He was here at our house. Do you think this used to be his?"

"No. Play the game, Corwin." I hear the old steeliness of her voice return for a moment.

"Yes, honey. That store is fine for now."

"That was certainly a traumatic event we saw. I hope we can heal and move on from this terrible time."

"He lasted longer than you would think."

"They always do. Flame resistant clothing, I assume" she says, shifting her weight under my arm. "I hear his wife and son are recovering. They'll pull through."

"That's good. I feel bad for them."

"It's like he doesn't exist anymore, like we made him up as a scary story. He's just gone."

"Did you want to watch some TV before bed?" I ask, wanting to change the subject.

"Sure."

"Let's stay out here for a bit," I whisper.

"Okay."

Our neighborhood plays a pleasant audio track during the night. Crickets chirp, frogs belch in a gentle soundscape of our nighttime. Every now and then, a car passes by the house, enters a driveway. Someone down the street is having a small get-together, their joyous, muffled voices float in the yard. There are lights and music from behind their fence. The playset in our backyard is a gallant ship slowly sinking into the grass, sunk by pirates.

The stars tonight look so real; tiny crystals gleaming against the curved black surface of the Dome. Random smatterings of dark-blue clouds pepper the night sky, every now and then slipping in front of the bright off-white moon. Even if the stars only glow for a few hours, they do so beautifully. Everything is so fragile and ghostly, as if you could poke your finger right through the thin skin of it.

It's too much, too fast, like I stepped off the roof of my old garden outside the Sprawl and plummeted. Like I had wanted to at one point. A thick lump wells up in my throat. I choke on it, trying to keep my composure, but I can't. Coyote takes my face in her hands, staring me straight on, not letting me escape. My face is stinging, red, and hot. I am shaking, but she doesn't let go. She'll never let me go. Her eyes are sharp and impossibly blue. I try to hide. My face rolls in her hands, and she holds me close like a baby.

This broken, stupid man that I am, if there is anything left in my worthless self to give, I give to her. I let myself fall into her dark gravity. I will wrap myself in this home, this life, this woman. She is like a dangerous but calmed predator in her den and I am the object of her pleasure.

We are alive.

We beat them.

I keep saying and saying it over and over in my head, and maybe if I repeat it enough, that lie would come true. There is no escape now. I allow myself the lie that we are all just waiting to get here and will arrive as soon as we do that one simple trick and you can't believe how easy it is. That enormous, pulsating, sickening lie that lives at the heart of me. The lie that I exposed for everyone to see and no one cared. You can't destroy it though, not without tearing it all down and rebuilding into something else. What else is there, though? But this place, you can't reform it. You can't just put a new coat of paint on rot. You can't teach it tricks. I thought if I just told people the truth, they would just wake up and change. Maybe I could change. Make something real and true. I was so wrong. The Machine just keeps going.

So let everything else simply drop away and vanish, but let the dead stay dead. They have no more lessons to teach me. Tomorrow, a new sun will rise in the television sky and our new future will begin together. This wonderful lie, more real than real. There will be moments of sadness, like any other life, but also could be moments of joy. A new baby, perhaps. New friends. New life after so much death and nothingness. True, maybe it's a life of dullness, but dullness thankfully without pain. That's fine. I have earned the right to no longer suffer. That's the promise that this place makes to me: eternal freedom from pain, but not without the cost of living. I accepted and signed the contract. I curl up on the porch swing, my chest rising and falling with each ragged breath. Hot, ugly tears. I implode. Stroking my new hair, Coyote softly shushes me.

"Everything is going to be okay."

Acknowledgments

First and foremost, thank you to my wife Rachel, whose love and support and wonderful laugh has sustained me through the tough job of not only drafting this novel, but revising, finalizing, and publishing. I love you more than you know. And yes, I found your phone.

Thanks to John for the incredible cover. Your stuff is insane. You're insane. A true American Weirdo, a mad genius, one of the funniest people I've ever known. In death, we shall cruise the highways of Valhalla in the Bōsōzoku Weinermobile.

Also thank you to the following for their invaluable lessons and friendship over the years. This book exists because of you all.

Lawrence Coates
Michael Czyzniejewski
Seth Fried
Dr. Sarah Hagelin
Evan Lavender-Smith
Dr. Harriet Kramer Linkin
Mark Medoff
Mike Meginnis
Candice Morrow
Joseph Scapellato
Ryan Orr
Joshua Wheeler